WILDCAT
FIREFLIES

Also by Amber Kizer

MERIDIAN

WILDCAT FIREFLIES

AMBER KIZER

Delacorte Press

Text copyright © 2011 by Amber Kizer
Jacket art copyright © 2011 by Chad Michael Ward

All rights reserved. Published in the United States by Delacorte Press, an imprint of Random House Children's Books, a division of Random House, Inc., New York.

Delacorte Press is a registered trademark and the colophon is a trademark of Random House, Inc.

Visit us on the Web! www.randomhouse.com/teens

Educators and librarians, for a variety of teaching tools, visit us at www.randomhouse.com/teachers

Library of Congress Cataloging-in-Publication Data
Kizer, Amber.
Wildcat fireflies / by Amber Kizer. — 1st ed.
p. cm.
Sequel to: Meridian.
Summary: Teenaged Meridian Sozu, a half-human, half-angel link between the living and the dead known as a Fenestra, hits the road with Tens, her love and sworn protector, in hopes of finding another person with Meridian's ability to help souls transition safely into the afterlife.
ISBN 978-0-385-73971-9 (trade) — ISBN 978-0-385-90803-0 (lib. bdg.) —
ISBN 978-0-375-89824-2 (ebook)
[1. Angels—Fiction. 2. Supernatural—Fiction. 3. Death—Fiction.
4. Good and evil—Fiction] I. Title.
PZ7.K6745Wi 2011
[Fic]—dc22
2010030405

The text of this book is set in 12.5-point Apollo MT.

Book design by Angela Carlino

Printed in the United States of America

10 9 8 7 6 5 4 3 2 1

First Edition

To our dearest, Kathy Kraft:

A WOMAN WHOSE HEART IS BIGGER THAN THE SKY ABOVE US—
WHOSE SMILE ALWAYS WELCOMES AND WARMS—
WHOSE EYES TWINKLE WITH THE MISCHIEF OF FAIRY LIGHTS—
AND WHOSE DETERMINATION IS IMMEASURABLE.

WHOSE HUG BRINGS TO MIND CREAMY HOT CHOCOLATE, WITH THE
BONUS OF LITTLE MARSHMALLOWS—

WHO TAKES CARE OF OUR STOMACHS WITH SOUP AND PIE,
OUR HEARTS WITH BOWS AND GIRLIE FRILLS,
OUR SMILES WITH SILLY CARDS AND SILLIER JOKES—
AND WHO HELPS RETAIL THERAPISTS PRESCRIBE A SPELL AT HELIOS
FOR HEALING.

THE WORLD IS BRIGHTER AND MORE BEAUTIFUL WITH YOU IN IT.
MY WISH FOR YOU IS ENDLESS LAKE-LOUNGING WITH GREAT BOOKS,
A WARM SUN WITH A COOL BREEZE—
AND THE SATISFACTION OF KNOWING YOURS IS A LIFE WELL LIVED.

You filled my world with JOY. You are missed.
Thank you, Kathy.

Nothing is dead: men feign themselves dead, and endure mock funerals and mournful obituaries, and there they stand looking out of the window, sound and well, in some new and strange disguise . . .

—Ralph Waldo Emerson,
"Nominalist and Realist"

WILDCAT
FIREFLIES

PROLOGUE

Dunklebarger Rehabilitation Center was not a center by modern definition; more an old drafty mansion converted over generations from family home to funeral home, to sanatorium, and finally an iteration where the old and unwanted were dumped to die. "Guests" transferred there shared the same profile: elderly, no living family, friends awaiting them on the other side, critical-life-taking conditions. Their hourglasses dribbled grains of sand into abundant piles below, coughing up the last bits in spits and spurts. Medicare paid guests' bills. When possible, the invoices reflected state-of-the-art care, top-of-the-line medication and therapies, even weeks of life beyond when bodies let souls pass. Miraculous or fictitious. Fraudulent, most definitely.

Life and living were never confused at Dunklebarger. Guests didn't leave alive. Of course, patients arrived there as a last resort, by design and with fanatical deliberation. Human neglect and greed at work? Perhaps. Or maybe the reality was something else entirely? Maybe the elderly deaths served a purpose, beyond the money, below the surface? Perhaps there was a greater plan that turned the headmistress and the elderly guests into victims of the light-sucking darkness.

To truly speculate, it must be mentioned that the re-habilitation center also served unfortunates at the other end of the timeline. Children who found themselves un-wanted, abandoned, removed for their own good from homes and streets. Children ages six to fifteen from the foster care system were placed at Dunklebarger, which pretended to be a group home. But the children quickly learned to call themselves inmates. To call the center DG, tagged so because Dunklebarger was a mouthful for the smallest kids, though no one remembered the child who stuck it with DG instead of DB. The eldest inmates knew the initials truly stood for Doom and Gloom. Disgusting and Gross. Death and Grief.

Dunklebarger was a prison for old and young alike. The old were prisoners at the whim of bodies drowning in deterioration, crushing the souls within. The young were prisoners of those in power, battered and tossed about by a system not suited for anything but killing time. Of course, the child welfare system was taxed beyond its budget, time, and human ability. Even in the best of circumstances, it was appallingly easy for kids to get lost in the piles of paperwork. These weren't the best of circumstances.

The kids served two purposes for those who profited from the establishment. They brought in income from the state, and they cared for the infirm. Which was why children under six weren't accepted as residents. Six-year-olds can do a lot of work, and they don't eat as much as twelve-year-olds. Child or adult, resident or staffer, anyone who questioned, who spoke up, who complained, disappeared quietly. And ignorance doesn't know to ask certain questions, to notice certain unusual things. Like all the children had one single, solitary social worker. One woman, of indeterminate age, was the sole connection for these kids to a system intended to protect them from the very existence they experienced at DG.

Someone, *something,* else manipulated the greed and careless ambition of the headmistress to put handpicked children into the presence of death.

Juliet Ambrose was approaching the end of her time at Dunklebarger. She remembered nothing from before her arrival there around her sixth birthday. Told by the headmistress that she was unwanted, neglected, and unloved, Juliet accepted abuse while trying to save those around her. She knew sixteen-year-olds left Dunklebarger for boarding schools and job training, but she had not yet heard what was planned for her. Now, nearing her supposed sixteenth birthday, even with new companions, Juliet had never felt more alone than she did counting down to February tenth. She dared not ask the headmistress directly about her future.

Juliet dreamed of city lights and the noises of bustling traffic. The smell of a bakery in the wee hours of the morning, the aroma of Christmas goose, and the texture of sea urchin straight from the ocean. She dreamed of people she felt she'd known since the beginning of time but had never met. She saw faces, and sights, in her sleep that she couldn't name upon waking. She knew recipes, secret ingredients, and how to make almost anything ever eaten by a guest who died at DG. There were moments when she felt utterly insane, incomplete—as if a crowd lived inside her head. As if she were a chef puppet desperately trying to cook up a tender future full of sweetness and spice and abundance.

Awake, she dreamed that at sixteen she could take the little ones with her to a safe, warm, free place and burn down DG. Preferably with the headmistress inside. But in the end, she simply hoped to survive the storms waged on the fields and farms of Indiana when late winter collided with early spring. The tornadoes that ripped and gutted, and turned the sky to pea-green mash. The lightning that cracked silos, stirred stampeding cattle, and started fires. The hail that pounded the corn shoots flat and flooded the creeks and rivers.

With a measly ten minutes to herself, while Mistress ran errands and Nicole minded the other children, Juliet poked her toes into the rushing, laughing waters of the Wildcat Creek gurgling behind DG, tucked her head into her knees, and sobbed.

Juliet was sure she was in this world alone, but the cavalry was on its way. Everything she knew about her life was about to change.

From the shadows, side by side, allies beyond time and space and earthly knowing scrutinized and watched her. These unseen eyes belonged one pair to *Felis catus,* and one pair to *Canis lupus.*

There are four kinds of people on this planet, a seasonal four types of souls. Those who die in the summer, when the land is parched and the soul thirsts for slaking. Those deaths that herald bright flashes of autumnal color, transitions like leaves falling toward a winter sleep. The winter deaths belong to those who are contemplative and introspective, the souls that prefer crisp, bare, unfettered change. And those who die in spring are singular in hope; my personal favorite, as spring is the optimistic death. The promise of birth and life resurrected, of faith and belief in tomorrow. This is the outlook of the spring dead. This is my favorite time of year.

Meridian Laine
March 21, 1929

CHAPTER I

"Pulloverpulloverpullover!" I screeched as we approached the outskirts of another small town.

One more bump, one more pothole sitting in this beater truck, and I was going to lose my mind. Tens and I were just past three weeks from leaving the wreckage of Revelation, Colorado, on our Divine-tasked quest to find other Fenestra. More people, girls, like me. More Protectors like Tens. Supposedly, there was one, somewhere in the state of Indiana, who needed our help.

"Pleasepleaseplease!" Now at the tail end of January, it had been nearly a month since Jasper's granddaughter brought us the newspaper article about a cat who predicted deaths and a girl called the Grim Reaper.

It was impossible to think in the bouncing, flouncing truck. I refused to inhale any more hay dust, mud particles, and springs of decades past, not for another second. I heard my brain rolling in circles around the inside of my skull like a Super Ball. "We've been driving for lifetimes, Tens. Pull over!" I shouted.

Unflappable as always, Tens didn't take his eyes off the road. "Meridian, we're almost there. It hasn't been that long today. You're exagger—"

I cut him off. "Long enough. I need to stretch. Just for a minute. Here's good." I reached for the door handle as we passed a sign proclaiming WELCOME TO CARMEL, INDIANA.

"Here?" He slowed, but didn't stop the truck.

I needed *out*.

Right.

Now.

"Here." I leapt out. As Tens parked the truck along the curb, I breathed in warm pre-spring air, huffing and puffing like I'd been running instead of sitting.

Custos sprang out of the truck bed, disappearing into the shadows. If I glanced around, I knew I'd see her. But knowing she was watching from the periphery was enough for the moment. I hadn't truly figured out whether she was more than dog, more than wolf. But I suspected.

Tens unfolded and walked around to the front of the cab, waiting for me like one of the Queen's guards. I knew that expression. All patience, calm, and deliberation. He used it with wild animals in traps.

I closed my eyes against the irritation with him I felt bubbling up. "I have a feeling about this place." I knew it as truth, as soon as the words left my mouth.

Tens brushed the area with his glance, taking in every detail, assessing our safety in a blink. "Good or bad?"

Frustrated, I blew out a snort and rubbed my palms on my thighs. Our third day on the road, the newspaper article had mysteriously gone blank, the ink disappearing. Now all we had left was flimsy newsprint and our memories to guide us. I kept expecting another sign. Something I recognized, something that told me we were on the right path. Only nothing presented itself. Each day flowed into the next and failure frayed my edges.

Where was she? This mysterious girl like me, hunted by the Nocti, needed by the good, by everything that was light, clean and pure. What was she thinking? Was she wishing someone would fall from the sky and tell her she wasn't a freak? Or did she understand her destiny and feel confident in herself?

"Meridian? Good or bad feeling?" Tens loped toward me, carefully keeping his distance. I didn't bite, but I'd been cranky enough lately that I understood his reticence.

"I don't know yet." I turned away, trying to puzzle out the gut feeling twisting me up. "Why don't you sense it, too? Why can't you sense her? What good is your gift if we

can't count on it? What if we don't find her? Are we supposed to drive every road in the state, and the next state,
and then . . . what? Canada? Mexico? I can't believe we're
supposed to drive around for the rest of our lives eating
burgers and sleeping in crappy motels." We had plenty of
money, thanks to Auntie. What we didn't want to do was
grab the interest of authorities—the last thing we needed
was a Good Samaritan wanting to rescue a minor from life
on the road. Although sixteen and old enough to drop out
of high school, I still resembled a barely pubescent girl. I
didn't look a day over fourteen, and Tens's intimidating
nature screamed criminal. Not a good combination for
keeping a low profile.

"You're tired." He said this like it explained everything, including my volatile attitude.

Pissed, I hissed up at him, "Don't patronize me." Of
course I was tired. We never ceased driving, not for more
than a few hours at a time. We'd been to every retirement
and nursing home from the southern Indiana border to the
middle of the state. I walked in circles, kicking the truck's
tires.

I craved a bit of balance, stillness for my soul. Direction wasn't enough on this quest; I wanted a clear purpose. What was the point of sending us out in blind
ignorance? Not for the first time I wished for a conversation with the Creators—the rule makers. I wanted one of
those comment cards. Fenestras shouldn't have to operate
alone and vastly outmatched by the community of Nocti,
who had each other and leaders and clear mandates to de-
stroy and bring suffering. Me—my team? We simply had

journeys and lessons and growth. *Yee-haw for the good guys.*

Tens sighed and leaned over the hood of the truck. "Fine, you're not tired. You're thinking clearly and you're not wailing like a toddler who didn't get the lollipop. Tantrum much?" He rested his face in his hand, huffed a breath, and straightened toward me.

My mouth gaped. Then I choked back an utterly bitchy retort. He was right. He was always right. "Wow. Harsh."

"Yeah, sorry. No excuse." He softly brushed hair off my neck and kneaded the muscles knotted in my shoulders, successfully turning my claws into purrs. "I'm hungry. You have to be hungry. Let's go in there." He kissed the top of my head and turned me gently toward the restaurant behind us. He patted my butt flirtatiously, shocking a giggle from my throat.

A golden sun unfurled its rays on a sign that beckoned us to come inside Helios Tea Room. It seemed like the shop was a once-working farmhouse, now swallowed by the town around it. It sat back from the road and up a set of lopsided concrete steps, with a sloping green lawn dotted with winterized flower beds, metal benches, every type of garden art imaginable. The friendly banana-yellow paint, with glossy white trim, was accented with wind chimes and floral and holiday flags. Garden statuary guarded each step, and ribbons wound around the columns and trees flickered in the breeze.

I grinned and my irritation vanished. I thought of Auntie; she would have adored this place. I fell in love with the kitschy, easy delight that radiated life. "Auntie loved tea." My smile grew as I teased Tens. "I bet you'll enjoy scones. A little cucumber sandwich, perhaps?" I did my best worst British accent and the remaining tension between us melted away like a sugar cube in hot tea.

Tens tugged my hand. "Come on."

I pointed at the calligraphed sign in the window. "Look, they're hiring. You'd be a cute waiter."

Tens snorted and held the door for me. "You know I'd drop stuff."

That was me, not him. He had the grace of a leaf floating on a warm breeze. *I* was the klutz. Unfortunately, my newfound powers to shepherd souls to their happy place didn't extend to coordination. Alas, any dreams I had of being a prima ballerina were done for. The Swan in *Swan Lake* would probably stay dead with me in the production.

Bells of all sizes, from tiny jingle to massive cow, chimed our entrance from hooks on the back of the door. The first thing that enveloped me was the combination of scents: vanilla and cinnamon and warm chocolate with hints of lemon and cherry. As we moved from the front door down a hallway, I walked through pockets of aroma, each one a comforting embrace of all that was good in this upside-down world.

My eyes couldn't take in all the details, and the foyer became a blur of color and textures. Dried hydrangea-and-rose arrangements sat next to tiny teasets, and candles of all sizes teetered on antique hatboxes draped with cotton hobo bags and pearl necklaces. Flour-sack towels hung over the arms of concrete garden statuary. Stuffed rabbits, the size of small children and anthropomorphized in bonnets and frills, sat at their own little tea tables of plastic delicacies and toys. All of that was artfully crammed between the main door and what I think might once have been a living room but which now served as the cashier's station.

Tens clutched my hand like he was afraid men weren't only unwelcome here but were served up on the chintzware with parsley garnish.

"Welcome, welcome to Helios. Is this your first time?" A bubbly sixtysomething not much taller than me smiled warmly. She had deep grooves beside her eyes that acted as exclamation points to her welcome. Her face was darkly tanned, as if she spent more time outside than in, and her chestnut hair, naturally highlighted, curled under at the chin. She didn't falter at seeing Tens tower over us. *Maybe men of all ages are conscripted into coming frequently?*

"Are you here for lunch, or tea, or both?" She led us into and through a second heavily merchandised room, to a covered porch full of light, with floor-to-ceiling windows.

"Lunch. Lots of lunch," I answered with a grin of my own as I sat down, my back to the entry. Tens insisted on having his back to a wall and his face to the door. Not like he was armed. *I think.*

The hallway and converted porch were decorated with artwork: prints and canvases, gilt-framed photographs, raffia bows, and candle sconces. Piles of skillfully arranged candlesticks with tapers, lacy guest-bathroom fingertip towels, metallic gift bags, and fussy wrap were organized by color or occasion. Strangely overgrown, and overfull, the place looked like a dessert buffet of rich delights. For the first time in days, I felt myself easing into a charmed relaxation. *Nothing evil lurks in a place so full of joy.*

Hanging from the porch's ceiling were round glass ornaments in every color and combination. Deep ambers, butterscotch-pie yellows, fresh grass greens and cherry-blossom pinks, ocean blues and teals. All of the balls were about the size of a softball or a cantaloupe. Each cradled a pattern—a bare tree in winter—that seemed captured in the middle of the globe.

We both sat for a moment trying to piece together the details of this enchanted world around us. I knew Tens well enough to know he'd want to get a shovel and start clearing space—he couldn't think in a place he considered cluttered. He'd told me that one of the hardest parts of living with Auntie was being among all the generations' leavings, lovingly collected and kept. But this felt like a vacation spot to me. Foreign and exquisitely exotic, in a homey, lacy way.

Tens rolled his eyes at me discreetly.

"It reminds me of Auntie's," I said, goading him.

"Why do you think I spent so much time in those caves?" he asked me in a whisper, and winked. He'd prefer a diner, or the Steak & Shake we'd eaten at last night. In that moment, I decided we'd spend hours exploring this place because I didn't believe him. He was fully and utterly devoted to Auntie; he'd kept her house exactly like she wanted it. Even at the end. Of course, time spent here also meant we weren't back on the road feeding his incessant need to drive for hours without stopping.

"Wow, look at that. They're glowing." Our college-age server pointed above our heads, drawing our gazes back to the glass globes. Sure enough, it seemed as if the ornaments were giving off an internal light. "Must be the sun hitting them just right." She shrugged dismissively and placed our menus on the table. "What can I get you?"

Tens and I purposely didn't glance at each other. I tried not to stare up, instead flattening my gaze to the menu. The sky was gray and overcast, with snow clouds; there was no way sun was causing that light. But what was? *Me? Him? Someone—or some*thing*—else entirely?*

Tens cleared his throat, tapped the menu with one finger, and asked, "Do you have any recommendations?"

I smiled, letting myself get distracted. I knew what was happening. I'd witnessed it often enough over the past month.

She contemplated his question with the utmost care, answering as if she came to work every day wishing someone would actually ask for her recommendation. "Sure. The salad combo is a hit among the heartier appetites; the Italian wedding soup is great. Hmm . . . so is the bisque on special today, but definitely save room for Derby Pie, or one of the special desserts like the cream éclairs. And the shortbread is delish. I'll give you a few minutes to decide." She moved a step away.

"Actually"—Tens stopped her—"I'll take one of each."

"Everything?" She looked like he'd asked politely to

rob the place, but she covered quickly, turning to me. "And you?"

I grinned. "The wedding soup and Derby Pie, please?" I'd never heard of either, but could I go wrong with anything wedding or pie? I didn't think so.

"Spiced iced tea to drink?" When we nodded, she moved toward the swinging kitchen door, scribbling madly. "Coming right up."

I choked back a laugh. "You're impossible."

Tens shrugged. "Hungry." As if that answered everything.

"You're always hungry." I giggled. In the short time since I'd known him, he'd grown another inch or two, and his ropy, lanky form had a bit more punch to the muscles. He was still crazy skinny, but the angles had smoothed and the dips shallowed, his edges more rounded.

"What's with the—?" He pointed up.

I shrugged, baffled. "Should we try to figure it out?"

"You browse. Let's see if they dim?"

"Shop?" God, something so mundane and normal sounded alien. And utterly delightful. "With pleasure."

My glee must have snapped Tens back to reality, because he warned, "We don't have much room in the truck."

"Pooper." I stuck my tongue out at him.

He leaned back against the wall and turned his attention out the window with calculated nonchalance, but I knew he studied every person in the room checking for clues, answers, unspoken things that might be useful to us.

I saw Custos lying at the edge of the trees. Even at close to two hundred pounds, she was oh-so-good at disappearing in the middle of spaces. People didn't see her unless they wanted to see, and no one knew to look. Her butterscotch coat was tinged with amber and gold. Her face was masked black, and a stripe of black ran down her spine, from her head to the tip of her tail. She was frosted with black guard hairs and her eyes were like gold glitter.

My current theory was that Custos wasn't simply a wolf or a dog, but a creature sent by the Creators to help us. Just like my mom promised in the letter she had given me. My heart cramped at the thought of my parents and my younger brother, Sammy. This had all started on my sixteenth birthday, when I came into my Fenestra destiny. I blinked onto the radar of the Nocti and my mom had to finally tell my dad the truth. I was shipped from Portland, Oregon, to Revelation, Colorado, to save my life and learn what I most needed to know about helping souls transition to the afterlife. My parents were forced to go on the run with my little brother because the Nocti might, and did, try to use them against me. I didn't know when I'd be able to see Sammy again. But I was angry at my mother for lying. It wasn't as if the omissions were harmless. Because the dead and dying were naturally drawn to me, my father spent years thinking I was a serial killer; I thought *freak* was too nice a word. That part of my life had been such a mess, I pushed it to the back of my mind. All I could do lately when I thought about my family was hope that someday Sammy would understand why I had abandoned him.

I wandered, sniffing fruity candles containing the whole rainbow of a produce stand. I shook cellophane bags of potpourri, bundled-up pine needles, and cinnamon sticks. I tried on sunglasses covered in sparkling crusts of bling, pictured them on Custos's snout. They were more her than me.

I wrapped an embossed velvet scarf around my neck and reveled in the luxurious texture. I ran my hands over soft flannel pillowcases printed with bright spring flowers, butterflies, and yellowish-bottomed insects I didn't recognize. I closed my eyes, wishing for a bed—a *real* bed, not a motel bed—with real sheets, and a couple of days without riding in the truck. My ass was flattened like a pita.

"Your soup is ready," called a soft voice behind me.

I thanked the server and unwound the scarf, then wandered back to our table. A couple of granny types dressed up in embroidered sweatshirts and velour pants and a few ladies who lunch decked out in Ralph Lauren country chic, complete with Louis Vuitton bags, had joined the crowded dining room while I browsed.

Tens had already polished off one bowl of soup. "I told her to let you do whatever so I could get a head start."

"I only saw two rooms, didn't even get upstairs. Carrot?" I pointed at the empty bowl as it was whisked away with a smile and a tea refill.

"Yeah, bisque or something." Tens paused. He pointed up at the glowing glass globes. "That's all you. Most definitely you."

My stomach clenched. Another mystery. Another blindside by Fenestra questions.

I'd been afraid of that.

A young girl, pregnant and seeking sanctuary in a town unknown and far from home, makes my story vaguely reminiscent of another one. —R.

CHAPTER 2
Juliet

"Psst. Juliet? Come quick." Bodie's face peeked around the corner of the antique buffet, into my peripheral vision. Intent on staying out of sight of the kitchen itself, he was hiding from Dunklebarger Rehabilitation Center's headmistress, who was dictating my daily list of duties. A list that would take most people three days to complete. Bodie didn't want the Mistress's notice any more than I did; it never ended well for any of us.

When she finished her endless critique, I wiped my hands clean on my apron and turned down the heat on the soup pot. Industrial packaged tomato soup and grilled cheese was our lunch menu every other day.

Her nasal Northeastern twang spat at me. "Where are you going?"

"I heard a patient's bell." *Who was in the Jungle Room right now?* I'd learned ten years ago a calm voice and a steady answer solicited the safest, least painful reaction from her. She was predictably unpredictable. I gave any answer she wanted so I could break away and find out what Bodie needed.

"I didn't. If I didn't hear it, how could you?" She continued to question. Always with questions. If only she'd listen to the answers.

I didn't respond, simply moved out of the kitchen, down the drafty hallway, far enough away so that Bodie was in no danger from Mistress. Moving targets were much less likely to be hit. Literally and figuratively.

Bodie's stubby legs ran through the warren of damp hallways at the back of the house and up the murky side stairs even servants must have avoided generations ago. "Come on," he hissed in an urgent whisper, one we'd all perfected. "Hurry." We minced around these walls like ghosts, ghosts who didn't want attention. "She's sitting with Mrs. Mahoney."

She in this case, the cat, Mini. Fellow inmate and newer arrival Nicole had researched cats on the Internet and pronounced Mini an oversized Maine coon. With fluffy long hair that looked teased like the hair of an eighties rock star and an expansive, demanding personality, Mini gave the impression that good-sized dogs were no match for her.

When did Mini arrive at Dunklebarger? At my side? When did I first notice her sitting beside the dying, before we even knew they were actively dying? Those barely alive bodies that gave the impression their souls had more than one foot in the next world. *I don't know.* There's a definite glitch in the time line that divides my life between before Mini and after her, but when was that? Blurred in my memory. It must have been somewhere around fourteen months or so ago she'd appeared at the bedsides of the dying.

My world is brighter with her here.

I bounced up the stairs two at a time, overtaking Bodie's running steps. His six-year-old legs were chubby and short, in that transition period from baby to child.

"When did you notice?" I asked.

"Just now. I came to get you like you said." He stopped at the doorway of Mrs. Mahoney's bedroom. His chin quivered. "I did good, right, Juliet?"

I paused with my back to him, shutting my eyes against the tears his tone evoked, so he wouldn't see how his pain and uncertainty wounded me. I turned to him and knelt, bending farther at my waist, my eyes level with his. "You did exactly right. Exactly. You're perfect, Bodie, and I thank you. I think there might be cookies later." I tasted snickerdoodles in the back of my throat, knew I wouldn't be able to rest until I made them. I hoped Mistress went out tonight.

His furrowed brow smoothed and his smile beamed; it seemed as though the forty-watt bulbs lining the hallway intensified their light.

I tucked his hair off his face, mentally noting he needed a trim. "Now go play, and let me check on her, okay?"

"I have to clean the bathrooms." His face dropped and he stuck out his tongue. "As punishment. I swore."

I sighed. It wouldn't have mattered if he'd sworn or not. Mistress was in the process of toughening Bodie's skin, so although the bathrooms were stained with years of use, that didn't stop her from making him think they could be cleaned with enough painful effort. He'd been here for only six months and he fought the dampening with everything in him.

I remembered trying to resist her discipline when I was his age. "I'll try to come help you, okay? Or see if Nicole can." I worried that the bruises on his knees from kneeling on the cold cereal he'd spilled yesterday morning would bother him.

I did my best to protect them all, the young and the old, but I couldn't be everyplace, every minute. No matter how hard I tried to do exactly that, it was never enough.

He shook his head, trying to convince me not to worry. "Mini needs you." He gave me a matter-of-fact look and ran.

I pushed open the door and Mini's eyes shot gold at me while her tail coiled and struck at the sheets. I almost saw the air around her head dance and pull at the curtains, but that was sleep deprivation catching up to my imagination. She was clearly upset it had taken me so long. Ten minutes maybe. If she could talk, I knew I'd receive a lecture about keeping elders waiting. I'd learned to pick up on her body language; mainly so she didn't resort to claws and teeth like in the beginning. She was fickle and demanding, but possibly the best friend I'd ever had. Quite pathetic to think of *friend* and *claws* together.

"Sorry." I briefly touched her head, scratched behind her

ears. Her hair felt like the delicate fluff of a dandelion, but her body was sturdy and muscular under all that pillowy down.

"Hello, Mrs. Mahoney, it's Juliet here. And Mini." I gently took Mrs. Mahoney's hand in mine. Her breathing was labored, her palm and lower arm chilly, her lips blueing, and her jaw slack. *Any time.*

I settled myself next to her on the mattress, knowing from experience that at this point there was nothing I could do to disturb her. I hoped my presence provided comfort. *Maybe.*

Her gasps were jagged, and silence lengthened between them. I smoothed her thin white curls off her forehead with my other hand.

Mini leaned against my chest and stomach, sitting herself firmly in my lap, her front paws perched across Mrs. Mahoney's heart. The first few times Mini had done this, I'd put her down on the floor gently, then with more force. But each time, she came back and took up the same position. I gave up. No one ever complained. How could vigil be anything but good?

"It's all right, Mrs. Mahoney, you can let go. I'm sure your family is waiting for you." As a small child, before coming here, my vision of death was like a light switch, or someone hitting the stop button on a song in midphrase. *So wrong.* I'd learned quickly, like Bodie was learning now, that it's hard work, labor. Between the dying there are always similarities—that was the second lesson. One I passed on to the other inmates, the newbies, the unwanted kids like me sentenced here until, or before, their sixteenth birthday. It was a lesson about knowing, seeing, making it less formidable a thing to be a kid around so much death. *There are signs.* Signs telling those who were willing to see, that the body's curtain was falling.

I always felt so inadequate in this moment. I never knew the right thing to say or do, how to help. So I sat and spoke quietly of nothing and everything. I wet their lips and washed their faces. I rubbed lotion that Nicole smuggled into the house for me into their dry skin. If I were dying, I think I'd miss casual touch the most. I dreamed about casual, affectionate touch. Touch in DG always felt like it had an agenda attached. Except for once, a brief time three years ago, when I felt valued.

I snapped myself back to the present. Dwelling wouldn't help.

The long days and short nights inevitably caught up with me if I sat still too long. My eyes drifted shut. I jerked awake. Mini never moved and her heat against me relaxed my core. Every time. I shook myself, trying to think of other things to say. When I sat like this, my mind wandered to my early years, to a featureless woman I thought of at the oddest moments. *My mother? Why couldn't I remember her clearly?*

I held no respect nor love for my mother. She named me for the most romantic heroine ever—Juliet. The idiocy is that Juliet killed herself; I fail to see how that is romantic. Live for me, don't die. *Live.* But then, that's what I've been told by Mistress: I'm named after the dead idiot in *Romeo and Juliet*.

Abandoned at a hospital, a note left in my pocket. One of those safe havens set up so young girls will stop flushing their babies down the toilet or throwing them away in Dumpsters behind a McDonald's. The law didn't say how old, or how young, a child had to be to receive haven. At least, it didn't back then. Or so I was informed.

Even undernourished, most six-year-olds aren't babies by any standard.

Mini yowled and purred. My eyes flew open, but already the empty silence descended and filled the space. Mrs. Mahoney had died while I'd . . . what? *Daydreamed? How disrespectful.* Yet no matter how hard I tried to stay present, awake, and with them in the moment, I forever missed the actual blink of their passing. I didn't know why, but I couldn't help it. I tried. *Maybe trying is all I can do?*

Mini jumped off my lap and hid under the bed.

"Goodbye, Mrs. Mahoney. Pleasant sleep to you." I stood, my legs buckling as a wave of dizziness flooded me. I shook back burning, twirling fatigue. I had to get to sleep earlier.

"Here's grape juice." Nicole moved out of the shadows of the doorway. "Bodie mentioned Mini's vigil. Have you eaten anything today yourself?"

I shook my head and gulped down the sweet slick of generic purple.

She clucked and frowned. "You need food too, you know? Not just cooking for the rest of us." Nicole turned her face toward Mrs. Mahoney. "She gone?"

I nodded, finishing the juice and then smoothing the blankets. My hands didn't stay quiet. Not for long.

"What's for dinner tonight?" Nicole asked with a half smile as she pushed a chair under my quivering knees.

It was a running joke, macabre though it might be, among the inmates. When a guest passed away, I cooked like a madwoman—something new, something old, just something—before I could rest. The other kids stopped questioning me and simply accepted the pattern. "Snickerdoodles. Beef Stroganoff." Of course, I did it covertly, when we were left alone, so Mistress was none the wiser. She'd been gone more often than not recently, which made everything much easier. But when Mistress was around, her wrath seemed amplified and edgy these days. I shuddered.

"At least we can help with those dishes. I live in fear you're going to say something with a French name and exotic ingredients." Nicole helped me acquire foodstuffs that Mistress didn't ordinarily stock. I never asked how she got them.

"Bodie doing okay?" I asked.

"He's cleaning those bathrooms. I have Sema posted as lookout and left a coloring book under the radiator." We tried to sneak play in where we could. I didn't feel the least bit bad about lying. I knew no other way to survive.

"Don't let Mistress see you, or she'll just make it worse," I cautioned.

"I know. I know." Nicole lifted her hands away from her body in surrender. "Why don't you disappear for a little while? Catch your breath? I'll call the funeral home."

She didn't stay long enough to see me shake my head. The list was too long for me to sit. Besides, I tasted cream coating my throat and felt slick egg noodles sliding down to a pleasant fullness. I needed the kitchen.

Dearest Sister,

I watched the sculptor deliver & install your head & footstone this morning. I know I shall see you again, & know you, but until then, this granite window will give me a place to sit in your company.

Jocelyn Wynn
July 2, 1842

CHAPTER 3

The closer I moved toward the glass globes dangling above us, the more intense the light became. "What's it mean?"

"Don't know. Book?" Tens asked, referring to the heirloom journal Auntie had entrusted to us. To me. "Another unknown?"

"Hate 'em."

"I know you do. But maybe the journal has something?" He genuinely seemed like he wished he could get rid of all the unknowns for me.

We'd learned shorthand speak, benefitting Tens's delight in abbreviated replies and my need to receive complete answers. Strong and silent was seriously frustrating when I couldn't read his mind. The fact that he sometimes empathically knew what I felt seemed to come and go, but his ability didn't extend to reading my thoughts exactly. Nor did he have the ability to transfer his thoughts into my head. We weren't telepathic. We needed real words most of the time, and those were increasingly hard for me to find.

I bit my lip, searching my brain for pieces of Auntie's Fenestra journal that mentioned glowing glass balls. "I don't think so. I haven't seen anything."

Of course, there were plenty of pages in Auntie's journal that I hadn't scoured yet. Onionskin parchment, fading spidery script, and pages completely covered with no rhyme or reason made reading entries a long, tedious chore. That and the fact I had motion sickness, so reading in the truck was out. Tens might understand the need to stay still for a little while if I explained we needed time to study the journal more. Maybe.

Tens tossed his head at the elderly ladies behind him. "They call 'em Witch Balls." He quoted what he'd overheard in a daring falsetto whisper. " 'Perfect new-home gifts. Made by a local glassblower. Good energy, blessings. A steal, too. Some New York place would charge five times this price.' "

"How's the soup?" Our greeter had been wandering over to each table in turn, like they were all old friends dropping in for a visit. Her silk daisy lapel pin glinted with pink and orange crystals. She'd added a big floppy pink crown to model for diners. "Got room for the pie?" she asked, as if she actually cared what our answer was.

Tens smiled back, astonishing me because he so rarely shared his beautiful smile. "Always."

"I'm Joi. I own this place." She held out a hand to me.

"Meridian." I shook her hand; she held mine a little too long as I nodded across the table. "He's Tens."

"That scarf was a perfect green on you." She turned to Tens. "Girlfriend or sister?" She hooked her thumb in my direction.

He blushed, but answered. "Love of my life."

She didn't laugh as most people might have. "Admirable." She cocked her head in my direction. "You?"

"Same."

"Good to know. Enjoy your lunch." She moved on to other tables, chatting up the diners like they came here every day, asking about grandbabies, weddings, and funerals.

I glanced at Tens. I couldn't keep the love out of my eyes and I didn't even try. I never expected to hear Tens refer to me so casually as his soul mate. Being in love still felt very fresh and clean to me, not lived in yet. Not on a level where I relaxed into it, safe and cushioned. A huge part of my problem was that I'd spent so many years virtually alone and shunned, even within my own family. From my birth, dying insects came to my cradle to die, and as I got older, the animals got bigger. Until by my sixteenth birthday, when human souls recognized me as their window to the beyond. My mom knew, since this Fenestra destiny was passed down, and kicks in if the baby was born on the stroke of midnight on the winter solstice. I was. But she didn't tell my dad; she went into the world's deepest denial, trying to ignore away my destiny. This made Dad think I was a sociopath, and made me think that the kids who called me horrible names were probably right. *Talk about baggage. This is what Tens is tied to.* It was hard for me to trust that Tens genuinely wanted to be with me, regardless of that fate thing. I didn't want an arranged marriage; I wanted a love match. And I wasn't sure I deserved that.

"What?" he asked around a mouthful of seafood salad.

Under the table, I brushed his knee with my hand. I hoped he felt me in that moment. I occasionally chafed at the invasion of my privacy that his gift allowed, but sometimes words weren't enough. I pinched myself daily, wondering how I'd gone from being so utterly lonely to being in love with my soul mate, my Protector. Auntie called it waiting for the other shoe to drop, which made no sense, but had me seriously questioning what else the Creators had in mind for me.

The moment fleeting, Tens stood, oblivious. "Do you think this place even has a boys' bathroom?"

I raised my eyebrows. "The woods out back."

"Ha-ha." He wandered off and I eavesdropped on the conversations around me.

I'd forgotten what inane small talk sounded like and

the passion with which people exchanged it. Poor Lizzie. Her husband was cheating on her, and everyone knew but her. George's bowels were acting up. John had lost his job to a younger, less qualified, and much cheaper man. The new glass artist was odd—his work was either genius or garbage, but the ladies weren't sure which.

I closed my eyes for a moment, enjoying the sensation of fullness. I wished I could indulge in a nap.

Tens wandered back. "Unisex should not be pink and floral. The TP is covered in cabbage roses and cherubs."

"The horror!" I snorted. We spoiled ourselves with dessert. My piece of Derby Pie looked puny compared to his various flavored slices that in combination made up nearly a complete pie. The dining room emptied with the lateness of the afternoon, but even as the sun slid lower, the glass balls above our heads didn't dim. I waited for someone to notice.

Our server brought the check, three pages of illegible scrawl, with a *Come back soon* next to a reasonable total. Carmel was a hell of a lot cheaper than Portland.

I tucked a generous tip under my iced tea glass and we meandered back to the cash register. Part of me hated to leave this cocoon of goodness.

"Where are you off to now?" Joi asked as she rang up our bill.

"Do you know of a motel or anything? I think we may hang around for a few days," I said.

Tens quirked one eyebrow at my question, but didn't argue.

She hummed. "You looking for work, too?"

"Maybe," Tens answered, handing her cash in fives and ones. We weren't running out of money, thanks to Auntie's generous planning, but it might have appeared that way.

Joi tipped her head up to Tens. "I need a handyman, yard-work help, and someone to work in the kitchen. You interested?" She made eye contact with me, too.

"Um . . . ," I hedged, knowing Tens would want to stay anonymous and moving forward.

She pressed. "Comes with board in the guest cottage out back, and all the day-olds you can eat. Just give me twenty-four hours' notice if you decide to move on, so we can settle up."

"Why are you offering this? You just met us." Curiosity battled my cautiousness, but my instincts told me this was okay: neither fear nor insecurity bubbled up.

She smiled, her face wrinkling into the lines of one used to joy and gentleness. "I have a feeling about you, both of you, that's all."

"A feeling?" Tens asked.

"Intuition. Don't you ever follow your heart?"

"Sometimes." I nodded and glanced up at Tens, trying to gauge his reaction.

"My husband says I also have a propensity for taking in strays." She winked at Tens. "Besides, your wolf has been lying in the shade along the cottage the whole time you've been inside. I think she likes it."

Not good at covering my shock, I gasped. I'd make a terrible poker player. "You saw her?"

"Kinda hard to miss. Follow me and I'll show you the

cottage. Then you can decide." Joi motioned us around the counter and through a kitchen that was clean but cluttered, the sink was piled with dirty dishes from the lunch rush. She sighed. "Washing dishes is part of the kitchen job. And if one of you can fix the dishwasher itself, so much the better."

I didn't feel comfortable walking out and leaving the tearoom deserted. "Can you leave?" The front door lay in a straight line to the cash register. That kind of trust felt completely foreign to me.

"I'll be right back." Joi waved her hand, dismissing my worry, and didn't even glance back.

We followed. Tens's fingers found the skin at the base of my spine, under my T-shirt, and rested there lightly. They heated my skin and made it itch as if my clothes were too heavy, too much, as if I could feel every individual thread and seam.

Lips smiling, Custos wagged her tail at our approach, and I felt Tens relax through his fingertips. If Custos liked Joi, and this cottage, there had to be a reason.

The cottage itself was a large single room, with a sofa area, kitchen, and bed. An entire garden of dried flowers covered the walls and hung from the ceiling. Photographs of laughing children and playful dogs, and watercolors and acrylics of Indiana scene-scapes, of red barns and covered bridges blanketed the rest of the wall space.

"I use the walls in here for inventory," Joi said. "But don't worry, I don't walk in unexpected. The bathroom is through there, with the washer and dryer."

A double bed covered with lacy pillows and teddy

bears butted up against the far wall. The kitchen had sunny yellow cabinets and counters. The color alone would do a better job of waking a person than coffee.

"Cute," I said.

"Good. Why don't you spend the night and make your decision in the morning? I'll send over coffee and pastries so you can fuel up. Carmel doesn't get started early." Joi closed the door behind her.

"She handed you the keys, didn't she?" I asked Tens without turning around.

"Mmm-hmm." Tens collapsed on the couch, his feet dangling off the opposite end. His boots were cracked at the ankles and deeply grooved in the soles; he'd retied the laces together.

"You need new boots." I studied him.

"Uh-huh." His eyes closed and a sigh settled him deeper into the cushions.

"Are we staying here?" I asked, knowing the answer I wanted to hear. *Yes.*

He didn't even crack an eyelid. "For the moment. Nap now."

I lay down on the bed, staring up at the ceiling. I was exhausted, but energy thrummed under my skin like I was nearing an electrical storm. I forced my eyes closed and practiced deep breathing.

"You're not going to sleep, are you?" Tens rumbled from across the room.

"I'm trying." Frustrated, I crinkled my eyelids tighter until spots and rainbows danced.

He shook the couch with his unapologetic laughter. "Right. Let's go for a walk. Explore the town a little."

I rolled to my feet. "Really?" I didn't wait for him to change his mind and launched myself onto his stomach. I started tickling him. On the list of things I'd learned about Tens since December 22 of last year . . . his ribs were mad ticklish.

He grunted and flipped me over, his hands wrapping around my wrists easily, then pinned my arms over my head.

"Not fair!" I screamed, laughing, trying to escape only halfheartedly as he returned the favor, my breath running ahead without me catching up to it.

"All's fair." He bent and caught my mouth with his in a kiss that promised. Always promised.

A rush of heat swept across my body. I enjoyed the nip and play of his tongue against mine. His fingers skipped down my arms and settled at the underside of my breasts, along my stomach.

He pulled away before I was ready to let him go. "Come on. Let's walk."

I let him distance himself, trying to hide my frustration. He loved me. I loved him. He felt good, great, even. I didn't know why he insisted we live like roommates or siblings, rather than as lovers. What was he waiting for? I battled myself in silence, not wanting to fight.

The cottage and Helios graced the edge of the town proper. The main street of Carmel was an adorable mix of shops, banks, restaurants, buildings that seemed to date from the early 1900s, and new construction, with plenty in between. Victorian-era gingerbreads and brick saltboxes stood beside Frank Lloyd Wright–inspired angles and utilitarian concrete blocks from the sixties. The people inside the shops chatted and laughed and seemed content. There were plenty of minivans and luxury sedans on the streets. Two steepled churches sat on street corners across from each other.

I felt watched; a niggle on the back of my neck sent up a warning.

"Do you see that? Her?" I pointed at a bench where a woman sat with her back to us. The dusk of early evening threw indigo shadows, but she wore a large floppy sun hat better suited to July beaches, along with a vintage Mary Poppins–esque overcoat. Something didn't feel right. My gut rang the itty-bitty panic bell.

"Yep." Tens slowed, glancing at me, puzzled and concerned.

"Is she moving?" I didn't sense a soul.

Tens stalked closer as I stood back. "Statue," he said, knocking it on the head. Painted in vivid details, the statue appeared ready to come to life at any moment.

"Them?" I pointed to a couple of top-hatted, suited men leaning against a building farther down the street.

Tens marched five full lengths ahead of me. "Uh-huh. Same."

Every street we meandered down had a bench, a couple, a stroller with a mother. All statues, and all in various period costume. "Is this odd, or is it me?" Knowing they were art didn't make them feel any less threatening.

"Odd maybe, but not evil." Tens linked his fingers with mine. "I don't think."

"There's the glassblower's studio." We approached a brick building with more of the colored balls hanging in the windows and from the eaves. As we got closer the balls began to light from within. I hoped the studio was bright enough that the artist wouldn't notice.

"Maybe I should go in without you?" Tens asked.

"Maybe." I shook my head. I had that peculiar, particular tingling feeling. I felt myself being drawn to the special death window. When a soul needed me, my soul became a portal to the afterlife. I'd be towed as though caught in a riptide, to a different plane where I stood side by side with the dying until they crossed over. I didn't know what that place was called and I didn't yet know how to go about my physical life while my spirit was otherwise occupied. It was possible, but it took more skill than I'd developed. Which meant Tens was given the duty to protect and care for my body in situations just like this. I felt the soul heading straight for me. "Tens?" I heard ambulance sirens nearing.

I felt him catch and steady me. I'd gotten much better at this part, but if I wasn't prepared for a soul to seek me, then it was a bit like riding waves and having a spectacularly large one pick me up and carry me.

Immediately, I was on a balcony overlooking a busy cityscape. I recognized it as Paris, from the Eiffel Tower and the Champs-Elysées in the distance. I went from a crisp January night to a spring afternoon on another continent.

"H-hello," I stuttered, remembering to breathe. What I did here I tended to do in the real world, and breathing was one thing I wasn't yet ready to let go of.

"What's happening? Why am I in Paris?" A gray-bearded man of indeterminate middle age rocked back and forth next to me. "I'm supposed to be cleaning the gutters."

"Does anyone look familiar?" I asked, evading his questions.

"I haven't been here in years. Who are you? Oh my God, that's my mother, my grandfather; they're waving at me. But they can't be—"

"Meridian!"

I heard my name and flinched, turning toward the source.

The first time I saw a relative outside my window I thought I was hallucinating; grieving so deeply my mind concocted his image. After that I began studying the souls who greet my charges. And there in the crowds I might spot my father, but I never heard him speak again, nor could he seem to hear me. I live in hope that someday I will be strong enough to will it so. . . .

Linea M. Wynn

April 1, 1963

CHAPTER 4

I leaned down through the window, almost falling onto the balcony next to the man. Auntie called up to me from the streets below, her arm slung around a woman barely older than me. She might once have been pretty—in a modern Scandinavian-princess way—but it was hard to tell under the pocked, ridged scars covering most of her face and disappearing down her neck. Wounds like that made the flesh look like melted wax. While Auntie appeared fully vital, the woman flickered from solid to milky transparent. Entreating, Auntie continued mouthing words up at me, but if she was yelling I couldn't hear her now over the traffic rushing in the streets below.

I pushed myself farther into the window, disobeying all of Auntie's rules about staying grounded on my side. I had to get to her. I had to hear her and talk to her and hug her. I didn't know if I'd ever see her again. I strained, feeling the casing gouge my sides, getting closer, ever closer, but heard the man instead: "My mother—there's my mother—I'm going to see my mother."

Immediately, I was back in Tens's arms, holding on to his shoulders with a white-knuckled grip. My side throbbed and I grabbed for my skin because it felt as if I'd been stabbed. No blood. I'd see a nasty bruise later, though. I had to remember that wounds I received on that side came into my body on this one. That was part of the danger of turning sixteen without guidance; souls inadvertently killed Fenestras who didn't know what to do.

The ambulance raced away, through a night already quieting around us.

"Auntie—she was there," I gasped, wanting Tens to know, to help me make sense of the unknowable. I folded into him, letting him support my weight completely. *What was she doing there? How was that possible? Who was the woman?*

Tens carried me to a bench and set me down, cradling me against him. I blinked my eyes until they focused. When would I get used to this process?

"Breathe, Merry, deep breaths," he reminded me, forceful yet gentle.

I tucked my head farther under Tens's chin, inhaling the spicy clean scent of his soap. If only I could stay in his arms forever like this. Seconds became minutes, until my equilibrium returned.

"Better?" he asked. Anyone else might think he sounded lazy, but I knew this was his way of trying to not pressure me. The tension in his thighs and jaw belied any laissez-faire.

I made eye contact and held it. "She was right there."

"Auntie? Really? I thought you were mumbling nonsense."

I rushed my words together. "Uh-huh. Right there. I haven't seen her. Not since—" Tears choked off my words. I hadn't seen her since before Perimo's melting, before the fires, the caves. "Before" seemed so long ago.

"Easy. Steady." He threaded his fingers through my lengthening locks to rub light circles on my scalp and pulled me closer. "This one seemed harder than the others."

"Maybe."

"Do you think it was because of Auntie being there?"

I shook my head negligibly. *If only I knew.*

"Did she say anything? A 'Hi, how are you' or something else?"

"I couldn't hear her. I tried to read her lips, but it felt like a different language." I broke out of his hold. Suddenly his arms were too tight, making me claustrophobic. From perfection to cage, in a matter of breaths.

He simply waited and watched, letting me move.

The pain in my side subsided to a dull ache. "There was a woman with her. Youngish. Deformed or hurt."

"How?" He rubbed his mouth, leaning forward with his elbows on his knees.

I frowned and tapped my fingers against my cheeks. "No one's ever been hurt. That's so weird."

"What is? Auntie being there, or the woman?"

"Both. People on the other side are usually themselves, only more so. Better, perfected versions of them. No matter what their bodies look like when they die, they're always perfectly formed on that side of the window."

"What do you mean by 'more so'?"

We hadn't talked about this before. I hadn't realized it, paid attention to it. My trips to the window were blinks of time, mere seconds in this world. Fuzzy when I came back, like a dream on the edge of my consciousness.

"Meridian? What do you mean by they're more so?" Repeating his question, Tens dragged me back.

"Like they're timeless. Recognizable, but not the same. They're the age my people recognize them as, but I get the sense that they're not really that age."

"Okay." He clearly didn't understand.

I pretended not to notice because I ran with a thought. "No one's ever been hurt there."

"And the woman was hurt?"

"She flickered in and out like candle shadow. And she leaned against Auntie. A lot. Like Auntie was holding her up completely."

He nodded. "I see what you mean. Auntie couldn't have held up a gnat at the end."

"Right. She was herself in those streets, old, and

exactly how I remember her, but she was also not like I had ever seen her. She was brighter. Stronger. Bolder."

"If everyone looks better and not hurt, then why show you someone who isn't?"

"Maybe she was trying to tell me something? I need to go to the hospital."

Tens leapt up. "Are you sick? I thought that was getting better? What do you need? Medicine? Ginger ale?" Tens was used to seeing me near death after an episode of delivering a soul to the window. I knew it would take time for him to understand that the critical danger had passed when I successfully transitioned Auntie with no ill effects to me. *I think.*

"No, no, no. I need to find someone ready. I need to get back to Auntie."

Tens huffed. "Merry, that's dangerous. You can't go seeking out dead people."

"Dying, not dead. Besides, that's my cosmic duty. Get with the program." I flashed him a smile. His worry was cute and baffling when it came to this. *Protect me from the Nocti, not my job.* Neither of us knew much about his destiny as a Protector. It was tricky to know where to place my boundaries or when to let him step in. I didn't want to be the damsel forever. I wanted to return the Protection as an equal.

"Right. But—"

I cradled his face in my hands, trying to impart confidence and understanding. "Stop worrying. I won't do anything stupid."

"Where have I heard that before?" He finally chuckled and wagged his head. He gestured at the studio behind us. "Glass balls or hospital first?"

I felt like saying "eeny, meeny, miny, mo." Both places felt necessary and fundamentally important. But we were already here and the balls glowed above me like street-lights. "Balls."

Why did they light up around me? And how did we get them to stop before anyone noticed?

"Meridian, look up." Tens pointed above our heads at the green street sign.

"Meridian Street?"

"As signs go, that's a good one."

"The right choice in the scheme of things?" Knowing that they—whatever name given to the Divine—existed and communicated unnerved me. I wished they'd simply learn English and text me instructions.

As we opened the glass door and entered the studio, the B-52s pulsed out at us, their voices inviting us enthusiastically to the "Love Shack." The space was all industrial pipes and brick, but somehow calming and warm.

"Greetings and salutations! May I help you?" A rotund giant of a man perched on a ladder, his back to us. He tied ribbons through what appeared to be an orange glass octopus dangling from the ceiling.

I shrugged at Tens and said, "Good evening, we're here to find out more about the—"

"The Spirit Stones, yes?" His voice was a rumble of an earthquake, powerful and commanding.

"Uh—no, um, the, um, Witch Balls." *Spirit Stones? Same thing, or yet another freaky thing I knew nothing about?*

He clambered down the ladder like a chimpanzee. His teeth flashed in a smile lost somewhere under more hair on his face than ever might have been on his head. If the ceilings of the studio were the regulation eight feet instead of industrial height, he wouldn't have needed a ladder. He dwarfed Tens by a foot, and several hundred pounds. "Same, same. Oh, look at you." He studied me and walked around us in a circle. "Wondrous. Simply prodigious. I've been a-calling for you. Never believed the lore. Not really. A story. Only a bloody *brilliant* story."

Initially, I grabbed my hands to steady them against his intense scrutiny. I wasn't scared, no—but uncomfortable, definitely. His enormous biceps framed a chest the size of a compact car, so his study intimidated, yet didn't scare. He was almost like a huge, goofy Great Dane that had no sense of its size and impact on people.

"What are you doing?" Tens asked, trying to put himself between the giant and me.

"You're a Window Light, the Good Death, aren't you?" he asked, squinting at and staring past me at the same time. I think he would have touched me if he could have moved Tens, but instead he merely invaded my personal space.

"Um?" I backed up a step involuntarily.

Oblivious, he turned to Tens. "And you, you're her Guardsman, correct? Am I right? You both are the reification, the tangible manifestation of the Spirit Stone idea."

What are these terms? Window Light? Good Death? Guardsman? And do our answers matter or not?

He continued squinting at me like he needed glasses. "I am gifted to meet you. I have traveled the world and heard pieces, but it seemed incompossible. I should have known better. Then, *wham,* this morning I woke feeling a dog lick my face and I knew you'd appear today. I knew it deep in here." He thumped his stomach.

Curiouser and curiouser. "A dog?" I squeaked, as Tens pushed me behind him.

The man reached out a hand as if to pet me, but answered my question instead. "I don't have a canine. I've never owned a pet; they never travel well. This wasn't only a furry intruder, it was a wolf—a huge wolf with these golden eyes. Huge tongue. Capacious. May I serve you coffee? Juice? Grape, perhaps?"

How does he know that? I wasn't sure he needed any more caffeine and I wasn't about to swallow anything until I knew more. *Color me a pessimist.* "Um, no thanks." I didn't feel like running, or hiding, or standing and fighting. There was no threat—not if I stopped and only listened to my heart. Fenestras love the flavor of grapes; I'd drunk grape soda or juice my whole life. When I met Auntie, she, too, chose grape, and she told me of our preference. She couldn't explain why, but it ran in the family. That and broccoli. Yes, broccoli.

"Oh, my Lord in heaven, my apologies! Where are my manners? My name is Rumi. Like the poet? I'm a glass artist, see? I blow glass and lampwork." He waved his hands at the warehouse around us. "I'm a historian, mystics scholar, rugby man, chef du jour to my friends, a reformed world traveler. A Renaissance man of elder times." He acted as though we'd been invited to a party, old friends merely getting reacquainted.

Rumi shook his head as if he were his own Magic 8 Ball. "You do have that glin about you. Peripherally. Fascinating. Sit, please. Sit down. Soda? Beer? Are you of age for alcohol? Does that affect your abilities? I can't imagine it matters, but is your gift temperamental? I wonder if it says anything in my Nain's papers about that. I'll check, shall I? How long have you known this? What brings you to town? Unless, do the Spirit Stones work that well? Can they beckon out of town? Are there more of you coming? Should I go to the market? How about accommodations? Do you take care of that, or shall I?" He went on with his questions, clearly not needing, or waiting for, a response from either of us, his childlike enthusiasm irresistible.

With each question, Tens melted a degree. I picked a chair of wrought iron made to resemble ivy leaves and vines. This place felt magical, but not in a weird, fictional sense, more in the inexplicable.

"Who is Nain?" Tens stood behind me, his legs spread and his weight balanced for anything, arms uncrossed but ready. His face had shuttered to blank.

Rumi sat on floor cushions and crossed his legs in an unnaturally limber configuration. "My apologies. You're a starlet for me. Well, not in the current pop-culture sense because they're people, not even terribly glamorous anymore. I've created glasswork for their homes. This and that. But you? You're amazing. A gift to all that is beautiful and right in the world. Honestly, I never thought it would come to fruition." He started squinting again, drawing shapes in the air with his fingers like he was trying to capture a fly and outline my form at the same time.

"What would work?" Tens asked.

I kept my mouth shut. I didn't feel threatened, like I might end up as a person-suit Rumi wore on special occasions. It felt more like I was watching a badly subtitled movie where I caught every other phrase but couldn't manage to put them in any order. *What the hell does he keep rambling about?*

"Sorry, sorry. I keep apologizing, don't I? Please bear with me. You sure you don't want anything?" He gracefully unbent, poured himself a huge mug of coffee, added more than half milk and what seemed like enough sugar cubes to build Giza's pyramids. He sipped it and sat again. Mumbled to himself.

Finally, he nodded as if he'd figured out where to begin. "My grandparents, on Da's side, came to this country from Wales. They came as children; their families were lifelong friends. They grew up together, married young, began having children. Thirteen." He paused and smiled at my expression. "Only six survived to adulthood, my father being one of them."

He shifted, sipped, continued. "My ma's family came over from Ireland during the potato famine. Her mother lost siblings, parents, and a husband. Started over here in the land of opportunity, in Chicago. My parents married at the turn of the last century." He drank, and gazed past both of us for a moment, but when I opened my mouth to question he ignored me and continued. "We come from a people who knew story as an intangible power, a way of manipulating energy and reality. My ancestors measured time over generations, not in years. My people are intimate with death, not fearful of it, but accepting. My nain and taid, my grandparents, both loved a marvelous story."

I seeped deeper into the chair, letting his words roll over me. He didn't look nearly old enough for the dates he threw around, but my gut said he was friend, not foe. I felt Tens exhale tension behind me, not enough for anyone else to notice, but enough I knew he felt it too.

Rumi's eyes teared up. "My da worked the mines; Ma raised us kids. Da died in his fifties from black lung, but Ma, she lived to be in her nineties. She told us stories as kids of the fey folk and mermaids and selkies, of battles of good and evil. She would have made a wonderful baird of the elden days. The doctors told us it was Alzheimer's at the end."

He shook his head. "I'm not so sure. She had what the medical establishment called hallucinations, delusions. She was never agitated or upset; her visions brought her joy and comfort. I started to act as a scribe; her words were something to hang on to in the years ahead without her. One day she woke up lucid, the common sense back in her eyes. She was grounded in this world for a brief time, but she grabbed my hand and hung on with the strength of a young man and told me, 'Open the windows, I need to let the light in.'"

Open windows? A shiver quivered up my spine and made goose bumps rise.

He continued. "When I raised the sash she began singing a lullaby I'd never heard before. For a week, the only words I could understand were requests to open the window. I did. I finally did and she settled.

"When she died I found scrolls, scraps of drawings and paintings, tucked into a box that must have come from Wales, and a little book written in ink, from Ireland. She must have put them together when Da passed. None of my brothers or sisters are what you'd call inclined toward difficult explanation. They like neat and tidy, technologically sound explanations for the world. I've always seen beyond; I've traveled and lived on every continent, experienced other realms with shamans and Buddhist monks. I'm an omnist. We don't see much eye to eye. Ma said I was of the 'home kind.'" He stopped, lost in thought.

After a few minutes of silence Tens asked, "What does this have to do with us?"

Rumi smiled but scolded, "Patience, my friend. I'm distilling generations into five minutes."

I reached behind me for Tens's hand, expecting him to react badly to the chastisement. Instead, he chuckled around an exhalation and pulled a second ivy chair next to mine. "Sorry." He gave the word ungrudgingly.

Rumi shook off the apology and continued. "The sketches were of human beings entwined in windows, windows with scenery and watercolor miniatures of these balls. I'd heard of the English Witch Ball, of course."

Or not. "Which is what?" I asked.

"The lore says the bright colors attract mischievous evil spirits and then trap them within the sphere. Other stories say the colors and light refraction are repellent to the darkness, and evil can't enter an establishment with these hanging as protection. Either way, they're good to have around. Those who could afford them brought them when they came to the New World, or went on any significant journey."

"Okay." I nodded.

"But the fascinating part in Ma's box happened when I started to find these bits of other traditions that said these balls weren't about evil spirits at all, but signals to angels, and their kindred, that they were welcome to rest and find solace within the walls. My family's writings said the Witch Balls attracted the angels of 'Good Death'; they signaled to the light that darkness was repelled there. That the window between life and death was always open. And served as a warning of Bad Death by darkening before the demons arrived."

He leapt and picked up a ball, and brought it over to me. He held it out, but I was almost afraid to touch it. Tens took it.

"See the bare winter tree in there?" Rumi traced the pattern along the outside of another ball.

"Sure," Tens grunted. I nodded.

"That design is the Tree of Life. It's an important differential. This is what gives it the power to signal." He paused, staring into the ball. "I think. I'm making that part up, but it's my best hypothesis. And mayhap something to do with the intent, the incantation said while creating the Stone."

"Like calling Batman?" I snorted.

"Maybe. You tell me?" His expression was reverent.

I hated to disappoint him, but I said, "I don't think so."

His expression went from excited to crestfallen. "Well, I started trying it. Figuring out how to get exactly that design in each one. They don't all take. And people love them. More so than any plain, ordinary glass ball I've ever made. Take fishing floats—I thought people liked those until I started blowing these. They gravitate to them. But you, you reflect the light, refract and radiate it; you glow. These balls luster in your presence."

"It's warm," Tens whispered to me.

I reached out and cradled the ball in my palms. "Like a heartbeat."

Tens nodded.

"Did you notice? It was like strings of Christmas lights being plugged in when you arrived outside the shop," Rumi added.

"Is that how you knew?" I asked.

"Like an early warning system. That's the first time. But I've been collecting anecdotes from other artists. There are multitudes of bits and pieces going back to Rome,

China, and further, to the beginning of the art form itself. So are you?"

"Are we what?"

"A Window Light? An angel? Good Death? And a Guardsman?"

As she grows inside me, I wonder if I'll see her grown to adulthood. Can we hide here indefinitely? Am I far enough away to be safe? Or will they come?   —R.

CHAPTER 5
Juliet

My favorite bedroom at DG faced east, so it filled each dawn with early-morning sunlight. The walls, swathed in a pale green wallpaper, reminded me of a cross between photographs of the Caribbean Sea and mint chocolate chip ice cream. We called it the Green Room. All the rooms had names.

When I first arrived, before I knew any better, I thought the Green Room would be my bedroom. Then I learned the

truth. Kids slept in the old servants' quarters in the attic, under the eaves. It was all very Grimm.

The bedroom furniture was slick glossy white, distressed shabby chic at first glance, simply shabby upon further inspection. Yellowing lace curtains hung on the floor-to-ceiling windows, and faded Degas ballerina prints, their edges curling, adorned the walls. The bed was a lovely double with four posts curved like balustrades. I slept in that bed for three nights years ago; Mr. Draper slept there for the moment. At least until he died.

A little desk for schoolwork and an enormous antique dollhouse were both pushed into a back corner. I dusted them, but no one played or did homework there. It was all for show.

My clothes were not stored in the armoire, nor folded in any of the bureau drawers. My stuff lived in the secondhand suitcase I arrived with.

The Train Room was decorated for little boys, with a twelve-car train that used to run around the ceiling, but now languished, gathering dust. The Horse Room's wall mural of hilly pastures and colts frolicking with their mothers seemed particularly cruel to all of us without parents. The Blue Room was decked out in enchanted undersea decor. And the Woods Room was done up like a rain forest of flora and fauna.

All six of the "kid" bedrooms were technically assigned to an inmate, but we weren't allowed to settle into any of them. The decoration was purely for the sake of appearances: a stranger might think we were very well cared for and DG met all the requirements of the law. At night, though, the kids

piled on top of each other, in sleeping bags in the attic. In the winters, we used smuggled-in electric blankets and space heaters that broke house rule number four. Mistress never came up here, and freezing to death was appealing only to some of us. We'd learned long ago, and often the hard way, that appearances deceived.

When our social worker, Ms. Asura, came, we were not allowed to tell her about the rooms or much of anything. If we mentioned the sleeping situation, Mistress wove elaborate tales about an overflow of elderly patients, not lasting more than a day or so. Ms. Asura never asked to see the attic or the bedrooms. She might pull out an official-looking form and caution us to be certain we wanted to file a complaint. If anyone ever did, I didn't know. Fear was stagnating, paralyzing, and we were trapped here.

Sometimes, when I sat by the bedside of the elderly, I wondered if any of the guests thought they were back in their childhood bedrooms, staring up at trains and stuffed animals and trappings of innocence. Most of the elderly who came here weren't conscious; thanks to Mistress's prevalent use of medication most spent their final days in a drugged stupor.

Of the kids currently at DG, I was the eldest. Nicole was closest to my age, a few years younger, and she'd arrived over a year ago. Her heart-shaped face had a clear, porcelain complexion, a strong chin, straight brows, and peach-blushed cheeks. Her eyes were caramel and matched her hair perfectly. She was tiny and much shorter than me, with a delicate, fragile-looking bone structure. She could lift twice my body weight and worked harder than anyone to make my life

as easy as possible. I counted my blessings every day she was still here, that she'd been assigned to DG.

Bodie had arrived on Halloween; at barely seven, he was the youngest. He tugged at my emotions as if he were my little brother, if not by blood, then by heart. I did my best not to let my feeling show; Mistress would punish both of us for any visible attachment.

Sema behaved like a shadow of a girl. She rarely spoke, wrapped herself in the curtains, and stared out the windows with her cheeks mashed against the glass. She wore the same outfit every day, a tunic with Disney princesses on it and leggings; I snuck it out to wash it as often as I could. Nicole promised to find a replacement in a larger size because Sema's milk chocolate belly was beginning to ooze around the waistband. She was plump and sturdy and hated bathing. Just to get her wet daily, I'd finally taught her to swim in the creek last summer, which she actually enjoyed.

January usually brought a deluge of new kids and elderly. This year had been different, with a total of only ten inmates starting the New Year together. Mistress liked having all the beds full, all of the time, and the attic crammed with slave labor, so I wouldn't be surprised to see our numbers swell three to four times the current occupancy by Valentine's Day.

Kids might come for only a day or a week, maybe a few months, but if Mistress decided we were a good fit, then we stayed until our sixteenth birthday. Her decisions appeared arbitrary and illogical, designed to inflict the most upset and pain. She divided siblings and friends.

No one stayed until a legal age of eighteen. I couldn't see

a pattern, a rhyme or reason, to why some kids qualified for the misery here while others were adopted out by unseen but wholly perfect families. Ms. Asura reassured me the few times I'd asked about placement elsewhere that this was exactly where I should be. She hinted that my history made me unworthy of finding refuge. She refused to give me too many details about the other kids because it might upset me. When I asked about Kirian, a boy I'd loved with all my soul, she told me I'd see him again soon.

"Come on, Juliet, another story. Please!" Bodie rubbed at his eyes, fighting sleep, while the other littlies dropped off one at a time into slumber.

I told happy tales. I weaved golden threads of harmony and love and warmth. No evil. No darkness. The good guys always won. The endings always told of wonderful new beginnings, and a real family usually played a central role. My neck stiff and aching, I arched my back to try to relieve the pain. I felt like bits of me were breaking off and dying each day; I had to find a way to ease up. "Okay, one more, but then lights out." I racked my brain for more creativity, more imagination. I felt like I ran out of it too often, maybe because I had so little experience with the good and the happy.

Days and nights of deaths made it unusually hard for me to concentrate. I reached deep and spun a tale of candy lands and tooth fairies.

Sema had lost a baby molar yesterday; when she woke this morning, magic had made it into a quarter. If my name is magic, then magic did it. I didn't believe in the stuff of fairy tales. Not anymore. But I wanted these kids to have faith in the invisible good as long as possible. So I played tooth fairy, Easter bunny, Santa Claus, and birthday queen; I did all the things I had so desperately craved for myself years ago. When I was able to, I picked the brains of the elderly for stories of their families and traditions. I learned a lot by listening. I don't think most people listen well. At least not the kids I'd watched age and leave ahead of me.

Nicole slept in the attic of kids and took over most of the nighttime mothering duties from me: calming night terrors, changing bedding when wet, administering baths and cleaning teeth. I wouldn't—couldn't—manage without her.

The house rules were often handed down with ominous stories. *Never call 911.* Ever. Once, long ago, an inmate fell and broke his leg badly, with bone sticking through skin. The kids didn't know what to do, so someone called 911. The injured boy was taken away in an ambulance, along with the kid who called. Neither returned. Whispers in the night told that Mistress went to visit the kids and killed them. The broken boy because he'd been stupid and would need months of care, unable to work, and the caller because she'd dared tell strangers that DG was anything other than a loving environment. Kirian said all the kids had been taken to the funeral, to be present at the gravesides. A warning. He'd been here then, but I hadn't.

I sighed, flexing my hands because my fingers kept cramping up in spasms. "Good night, little ones. I'll see you in the morning. Remember . . ."

"We are loved," they mumbled against their thumbs or nubs of stuffed animals. I wanted them to grow up hoping, believing, there was a world of good out there. I'd never seen it, except in my vivid dreams, but I knew it had to exist. I tried to create it, make it here. I only had hope to give them. And food, covertly cooked and with shared flavors from all over the world. Flavors that sang of the histories and families of the people who died at DG. I didn't know if I was talented or obsessed, but I knew techniques and flavor combinations that seemed to belong to the elderly I was in contact with.

Nicole followed me out to the hallway. Her cinnamon-bark eyes and hair reminded me of good fairies, wood sprites. She worked undeniably hard to lighten my load, as if she knew, before I did, what was coming next. "Ingredients?"

"Lemongrass, Thai basil, coconut milk." I reeled off a list, already tasting the dish, but not sure which form it might ultimately take.

"Curry? Yummy." She smiled.

"Maybe." I wasn't sure. Yet.

I slunk off to find Mistress in her apartments for my nighttime deriding.

Mistress's bulk seemed to expand with each day. I wondered if a sharp corner might pop her like a balloon. She squinted a glare in my direction. "About time. Why can't you finish earlier? Do you think I have nothing better to do than wait on you?"

"No, ma'am." I bit my tongue as I watched her apply bleaching cream to her mustache and the beard along her third chin.

"Why didn't you leave Mrs. Mahoney to die in peace, and

finish your jobs? Do you think she noticed or cared that you were there? How much of today's work will you have to do tomorrow?"

I kept my mouth shut; she went right on without noticing. Mistress was a mishmash of features and shapes that made her weight the least of her appearance problems. I had nothing against fat. I loved food, and one tended to go hand in hand with the other. But the sadistic streak that melted Mistress's humanity into a boiling blob of acid was strikingly visible in her ugly outsides. If she were thin our lives would have been even more hellish because she might move faster or with more agility.

"Have you written all of this down? Do you understand how much I have to do? I can't help but think you're not taking your position here seriously. Do I need to ask Ms. Asura to find you a new place? Do I? *Do I?* I hear they just busted a child-trafficking ring in the city. Perhaps you'd like me to inquire into finding you a home that way? There must be upset buyers out there without girls. And your birthday so soon?" She paused to let me think about her threat. "Face it, Juliet, your mother didn't want you. No one wants you because you're useless and stupid and aggravating."

The voice in my head spoke in unison with her pronouncements. They never changed. *Useless. Stupid. Aggravating.* I must have blinked because I caught her attention.

"How many times do I have to tell you to use your words? Will I see you working an hour earlier in the morning to make this up to me?" She huffed out of the room without waiting to hear any answers. It was never about the answers

I gave, just the impenetrable questions and judgments that she yelled.

At least she hadn't hit me tonight. I usually knew to be up and toiling by five. Tomorrow, four. *As if she'd really get up that early and make sure I was working.* But I couldn't risk her punishing the other kids to make an example for me.

I glanced at the clock. Eleven p.m. *Crap. Another day almost over.*

I made my last rounds to check on all the guests, the kids too. There was a night nurse who never asked questions, never really spoke to any of us. The face changed, but for the past few years the "no see, no hear, no speak" attitude had been the same. One time, seven years ago, right before Fourth of July, the night nurse reported our sleeping arrangements to the state. She tried to get me to tell her what really happened here, but even at age eight I knew better than to answer truthfully. No one came to investigate.

There was no use in hoping for rescue. In real life, no one ever swooped in. In my life, no one ever noticed the need.

Finally, dragging every exhausted cell, I opened my little door under the main stairs. I had hidden a blow-up mattress behind the cleaning supplies and paper towels in the storage crawl space. A square foot or two all my own was a slice of paradise. It was quite comfortable, all things considered. My only complaint—I was rarely there and was never awake long enough to relish my few moments of solitude.

I snuck in and maneuvered between the stacks of toilet paper to the far corner.

Mini was already there, waiting for me, purring. I collapsed onto the deflating air mattress, making a mental note to check it for leaks. A few hours of compression and it was flat on the ground. Tonight, too tired to care, I rolled onto my side. Mini watched me with her steady blink. Her tail flicked like a metronome feather duster. When I finished squirming, trying to find a comfortable position for my throbbing joints, she minced her way over to me.

Mini appeared not only for the deaths. Each night for over a year she showed up to cuddle against my sleeping self. If I believed in magic she would be evidence to support its existence. The rest of the time I assumed she hunted in the fields and forests around DG. But when someone neared death, or I dragged myself to bed, it seemed as if she was summoned by an unseen force to my side.

At night, she wrapped herself in my arms as naturally as my own skin clung to the muscles beneath. Her heartbeat mirrored mine, as steady as a water drip. Her head tucked neatly under my chin and she draped her upper body along my inner arm.

On my side, I folded my legs up under her tail and laid my hand between her forelegs, my fingers curled right beneath her chin. I held on to her like a teddy bear.

I slept easier with her next to me. My dreams became softer, fuzzier, lighter than they were before she arrived. This was the only time when my fingers and toes didn't ache with piercing cold. By nightfall my knuckles were usually so swollen and stiff I didn't want to use my hands, but petting Mini helped the swelling decrease.

Sighing, I poured my breath, my aching loneliness into

her multihued fur. I inhaled the mushroomy earth and pine sap of the outdoors, the warm sunlight and the silvery moonlight, the licorice darkness and the sugary light that clung to her.

Once again, I fell toward sleep wondering what I'd done to deserve this life.

Karma? Was I a serial ax murderer or slave owner in a previous life? Did I drown my children and thus have to live a lifetime as one of those unwanted children? When does life even out injustice and bring fairness?

At twelve, I'd opened DG's front door to missionaries who told me to know God loved me and thought me perfect. *Did I believe in God? Where was he? How did he let this happen? How could he not intervene?* Mistress beat me until I'd bled for opening the door to those people. She made me repeat, over and over again, *There is no God. No prayers. No Santa Claus or Easter bunny. No rest for the wicked or stupid.*

I'd tried to hope, for so long I'd held out for a sign to believe. In something, someone who looked down and knew how my story ended and why it was written this way.

Tears wet the holey wool blanket I pushed into a pillow shape beneath my head. Purring, Mini licked my face, scratching my cheeks with her claws in her haste to comfort me.

There simply can't be a God. Or destiny. Or magic.

When I woke, Mini was gone, as she always was, until someone else labored toward death in one of the rooms above my head.

People have the most reasonable explanations for the most unreasonable experiences. Science explains away more phenomena than religion ever will.

Meridian Laine Fulbright
October 21, 1981

CHAPTER 6

"Are you Good Death? A Window Light?" Rumi repeated with shining eyes.

Tens and I glanced at each other while Rumi's question hung in the air between us, a tangible thing. This was new territory. *Do we tell him? Do we trust him? Could we let anyone in on this conspiracy of silence? Certainly not in the first few minutes of meeting a person. Right? If only the world were different.*

Rumi waved his hands, then folded them beseechingly, "Wait, forget I asked. Why would you tell me? Maybe someday you'll tell me, you'll trust me and the hope of that will sate. That's the *juste milieu*." He inhaled, paused, exhaled, and asked, "What can I do for you?"

"What do you mean?" Tens asked.

"I take these matters seriously. By making the Spirit Stones, these precious handles, and by hanging them, I signaled my willingness to help the unseen. The inexplicable. I opened myself to the knowable, the whispered, the Good with a capital *G*. I proclaimed my devotion to the gods and goddesses, to creators and enlightenment." He entreated both of us with his eyes, his expression. His entire being radiated sincerity. "So what can I do? What do you need?"

"Um, well—" I didn't know how to reply. *Maybe he knows more about the town than we did.* I believed I needed to find a ready soul to make contact with Auntie again. "Do you know where the closest hospital is? Trauma center? Cancer ward?"

"Are you sick? Shall I call nine-one-one? Where did I put the phone? I had it this morning. Didn't I?" He jumped up and started lifting cushions, opening drawers.

Tens joined him, lightly touching Rumi's shoulder to get his attention. "No, no, we're looking for someone."

He quieted, thoughtful. "Well, of course there's the big complex downtown, but there's also a smaller sufficient hospital here in Carmel. Let me write down directions. Where is that pad of paper? A pen?" He patted his pockets, until Tens handed him a pen and a napkin to write on. "Thank you."

I walked over to where he scribbled. Risking exposing more than I maybe should, I asked, "We're also looking for a girl and a cat in a nursing home? They seem to predict death? Does that ring any bells?"

He studied my face and finally announced dejectedly, "They foretell death? I don't think so. It sounds like something I'd remember." He dimmed like a cloud blowing across the sun, but soon brightened. "Let me put the word out and see if my circle of friends know anything."

Tens cautioned him, "We need to do it quietly."

"Got it. Discreetly, of course." Rumi nodded, handing Tens the napkin with directions on it.

"Thank you."

"Sure. I will find you at Helios with any information. Or you can come here anytime, day or night. My living quarters are back behind the studio. I'm up all hours. I'll help you. Whatever you need."

I stiffened. *How does he know about Helios?*

He must have read my panic. "Don't worry, Joi is a friend. She knows I keep an eye on the place at night and didn't want me to worry when I saw lights tonight. Nothing sinister. She takes in strays, and has a good heart. Most of this town has Lightened souls." He patted my hand without stopping.

"Do you think we could take a look at your family's papers sometime?" Tens asked, gliding toward the door, tugging me with him.

Delight splashed across Rumi's face. "I was hoping you'd ask. Absolutely. Let me know if you need me. Anything."

"Sure. Thanks." I extracted my hand from his with one final squeeze.

When we walked outside, the cool night air tickled my nose and a breeze played with my hair.

"He reminds me of Señora Portalso." I broke our silence as we walked back to Helios and the truck. Señora had called me "pretty light" and seemed to see my Fenestra form before I even knew it myself. She'd turned out to be a friend, someone who followed the signs and let the Divine guide her. *Maybe Rumi is too? Can there be a type of human who shelters our secrets and helps us with the mundane?* I shivered at the feeling of déjà vu. "Was that whole conversation surreal, or was it me?"

"Rumi's definitely not what I anticipated. I don't know how he stacks up against Señora because I wasn't conscious for much of Señora and her doctor daughter's visit." Tens's cruel bout with Rocky Mountain spotted fever and the attempt Nocti made on his life to get to me, to make me choose between doing the right thing and losing Tens forever, was seared into my brain. With every detail so fresh in my head, I often forget he barely remembered anything from that time.

"She believed in Fenestra, in the Creators' intervention. She was willing to—what did Rumi say?—'be open to the unknowable.' She helped us, me, Custos, when she didn't have to."

"And he reminds you of her?"

"I think he's sincere."

"I get that too. But it's so hard to believe."

"I don't know. I wouldn't have believed in us two

months ago. It makes sense this is more complicated and complex than we know." I linked my fingers with Tens's and stepped closer, my feet moving double time to keep up with his long-legged strides.

"Hmm. Maybe." Tens pulled out his keys and broke the physical connection with me to pet Custos's head.

Staring at the cottage, I climbed up into the truck, enjoying the knowledge that for tonight at least this was ours. *I love the cottage, this parcel of earth.* Potential sang through me. "Nice to have a friend, though, right?"

I rewound Rumi's family history through my head as we drove in traffic toward the trauma center. *Can it be that there are people who know about us, who will help us, who care about our well-being? Can there be a support system to help me find other Fenestras? Fenestras of Irish and Welsh heritage? Are there more of us around the world?* It felt almost too good to be true.

"Mm-hmm," Tens answered, lost in his own thoughts, giving nothing away.

* * *

A harried desk clerk blinked at us while shuffling papers. "You're not from here, are you? Can't be. Why would we name it I-you-poo-y? Really? Say the letters. I-U-P-U-I." Her tone implied I'd personally insulted her.

"Oh, sorry." Even begging might not be enough to receive forgiveness if her expression was anything to judge by.

She cleared her throat as if ready to begin a lecture.

"No problem. I'm here to teach tourists, not save lives. It stands for Indiana University and Purdue University at Indianapolis, just so you know."

"Thanks." I tried to not aggravate her more, but clearly my mere presence on the planet was enough to make her day a bad one.

Tens broke in, saving me from the gathering wrath. "We're looking for Mrs. Eleanor Reynolds. She's a friend of the family." He pushed me behind him, as if he might get her to forget we were connected in any way.

She sighed, aggrieved. "Let me check." She clicked through the computer screens, the furrow in her brow never smoothing. "She's not listed. Are you sure she's here? She could be at Methodist. Or maybe St. Vincent's?"

"This is where Grandma said, but her cell phone cut out. She never remembers to charge the battery." Tens turned on the charm and gave her his hundred-watt smile.

Why don't I get that smile? I tried to make myself shrink deeper because it seemed to be working.

Tens asked, "Which floor is oncology? We'll find Grandma; she'll tell us what's going on. We love Mrs. Reynolds. I'm going to feed her parakeets while she's here, but she'll be worried if I don't reassure her they're going to be fine." Words and lies rolled off his tongue like melted chocolate. I envied his ease.

I could feel ready souls all around me. *Maybe this is a bad idea?* I couldn't back down, though, because Tens would never let me try again. The little hairs on my arms reached skyward and the need to sneeze grew stronger as we waited.

The clerk smiled back at Tens, completely ignoring me. "You're not really allowed to walk around the eighth floor without having a specific patient to visit. It's policy."

"Don't worry, Dinah." Tens leaned in like they were the only two people on earth, as if he hadn't glanced at her name tag. "We won't tell anyone." He pushed me toward the bank of elevators, not giving her time to respond.

"Smooth," I said. There was already another person bugging her as the door closed behind us. "You're almost invincible when you're all charming."

Over the days of traveling from Colorado to here, and from reading Auntie's journal, we'd learned that short of a straight-up mass-casualty tragedy, cancer was the best opportunity to find a soul ready to go. That popular slogan about cancer not taking away dignity or hope or self-worth, or any number of other things, is bizarrely ridiculous. People who sling that around have never been on the far end of the cancer fight. It strips everything, save the desire for relief. It's like swimming in the Nile without a life vest and dressed in raw meat for the crocs to dine on.

"Can you teach me how to be that adept?" I poked a finger into his ribs.

He brushed off my sarcasm and grabbed my hand. "Have you eaten enough today for this?" His tone betrayed his concern.

"I'm doing fine. Don't worry." I hoped I sounded confident and prepared.

Tens laced his fingers with mine. I tightened mine around his as the hair on the back of my neck stood up.

Human beings might have evolved past thinking of themselves as predator or prey, but our nervous system had not. Those parts of me bristled every time I was around death and the dying. At least now I considered it an early warning system and it didn't scare me. *Not as much.*

As the doors to the elevator opened onto the oncology ward, I heard alarms and bells start to go off around us in a strange techno-symphony. Nurses and doctors scurried like hamsters in plastic balls. Going nowhere fast, but frantic.

My vision blurred and the edges darkened as Tens guided me toward an empty alcove with a bench. I grabbed the edge of the bench as the first soul hit me. I think Tens laid me across the cushion, then draped himself over me as I was towed under, to the window.

Auntie had started my Fenestra practice with a summerscape window, but since her death, for reasons unknown, I couldn't manage to secure the window itself. If I did my job correctly, according to Auntie, I was the conduit, the window to heaven, to good. The dying saw me not as a teenage girl, but as the bright light enveloping them and guiding them past the physical death into the spiritual energy of the After. I provided the window in a room of my choosing and stood back while the soul transitioned across like a kid sneaking out of the house through his bedroom window. I stayed on this side of the exchange, but what the soul, the dying person, saw, and who greeted them, was entirely up to them, or the

Creators. I didn't know how that worked; I simply knew the dying recognized the scenery and the people coming toward them. I didn't usually, until Auntie appeared.

One, two, three . . .

But it wasn't working the way she'd taught me. The windows changed, rapidly, as each soul used me. They changed with the souls, everything different each time. Auntie made me believe I picked the window and the soul picked the scenery and the people. It wasn't quite working that way. *Maybe it's a learned skill.*

Like I was watching a travelogue slide show on fast-forward, my brain couldn't keep up with the changing frames and scenes and people. Modern architecture with lots of glass and light and chrome gave way to stone arches, then bamboo with rice paper. Each soul threw me into its own tableau. *Four, five . . .*

I knew enough, barely, to simply breathe through the changes. Not to try to make sense of the flashes. It was disorienting if I tried to follow it like a movie, so instead I let it flow around me like a busy avenue full of sights and sounds, without focusing on any of the details. Since these were souls whose bodies were in the hospital they blinked from injured in hospital gowns and bandages to whole and strong like hitting the refresh button on an Internet browser window.

Six . . .

A seventh window, the one Auntie had practiced with me, segued into my vision. Its billowing white lace curtains and sunny weather felt like coming home. The scent of fresh-mown grass and apple blossoms drifted over the breeze and stirred my hair. "Meridian." *Auntie!*

I ran closer to the window, and Chrystal Stans, breast cancer victim, crawled through, oblivious to me. I braced against the sill and leaned in, over, toward my name. "Auntie!" I called.

There in the meadow below was Auntie with the injured woman from before lying at her feet. "Look for Father Anthony . . . help . . . Custos . . . knows . . . four . . . three . . ." The static between her words was like a bad cell-phone connection with other conversations breaking through.

The injured woman lay on the ground, almost in a trance, her waxy melted skin flickering from solid to a milky, transparent shadow. She appealed to me with her eyes. For what, I wasn't sure. Auntie continued to gesticulate and mouth words, but I couldn't hear her.

Back on the hospital bench, in Tens's arms, I must have lost consciousness. When my eyes blinked open, we were in the truck. I groaned.

"Damn it, Merry, I knew this was a bad idea." Tens drove like he was being chased. "You never listen to me." Frustration and anger vibrated through his words.

I licked my lips and tried to swallow around the metallic taste in my mouth. I leaned against the passenger-side door, praying for my strength to return. I waited. I let him rant because I deserved it. Being a Fenestra was a destiny, a genetic predisposition toward being part human and part angel. But it was also a skill set that took time and practice to master. I'd learned reading from Auntie's journal that centuries ago there were more of us, as well as special convents that started teaching little girls how to do God's work. I had a crash course over two weeks with Auntie while she died. I was still a novice, and without a Master, like Auntie, to teach me what my limits were, too often I forced my fledging abilities off the ledge to fly.

Back from Indianapolis, we once again passed the sign welcoming us to Carmel and pulled into the parking lot behind Helios. A lamp burned from inside the tearoom, and the cottage blinked with twinkling fairy lights outlining the eaves, windows, and door.

Tens carried me from the truck and plopped me onto the bed most gracelessly. Gently, but not happily.

Custos raised her head from her relaxed position on the couch and whined a little at us in question. *When did she go from the truck to the couch? How'd she beat us inside?*

It wasn't that I was ill any longer, in pain on a daily basis. All of my childhood I'd been racked by mysterious illness, injuries, bruises, and headaches. Because I didn't know that I was a Fenestra—much less how to be one—the souls of animals who used me tangled my energy in theirs when they went through. My physical self was adversely affected on the tangible plane. If I hadn't been with Auntie, a human soul who used me could have entwined so completely in my energy that they dragged me through. They could have killed me without meaning to. Now that I knew how to operate the window I was no longer in danger of being twisted up in the dying, but I didn't quite have a handle on large numbers of souls using me concurrently. It was like running a marathon without proper training. "I need to do that more often." *Training. Why not?*

Tens shot me the dirtiest, angriest glance. "Over my dead body."

"Funny." I didn't have the energy to laugh at his serious, if odd, declaration. "The only way it'll get easier is to do it more." *Right? It makes sense to me.*

He shook his head, ripping at the laces on his boots. "You didn't see yourself. You paled to chalky paste. And . . . your hair." His voice grew gravelly and lowered an octave.

"What about it?" I pushed myself up on my elbows to watch him.

"The curl left. It was like a drooping plant."

"Seriously?" I put my hand to my head and felt the curls limp beneath my fingers. I joked to lighten the mood. "Do you know how many hours I've spent trying to straighten it? And that's all it takes?"

Cool. But *cool* wasn't the word Tens needed to hear right now.

My hair hack job had grown out to the point it brushed my shoulders even in the curliest moments, but I preferred it straight. *I guess we always like what we aren't born with better than what we are.*

"This is not a styling tip."

"I know." I sighed. I wanted him to smile again. Worry made him loud.

Stamping in his sock feet, Tens marched over to the

kitchen area and picked up a note card. "Joi left us soup, rolls, dessert, and a coffee cake in the fridge."

"Wow. Nice." I toed my sneakers off onto the floor by the bed.

"You think it's safe?" Tens sniffed at the containers.

"I'll take my chances." *If she is Nocti, I deserve whatever I get. TSTL. Too stupid to live.*

"I know, it's just that—"

I straightened at the self-doubt in his voice. "I get it. You want to protect me, but you can't necessarily protect me from doing my thing." *The food isn't the problem, my talent is.*

"You take too many chances." Dishes rattled and cupboards slammed. He wouldn't look over at me. Not even for a second.

"I'm doing my job."

"It's not the transitioning, Merry. It's searching out the dying to do so many all at once. You could hurt yourself."

"We're past that."

"We are? Are you sure?" He turned around.

"What do you mean?"

"If you really had everything under control, then you wouldn't faint, you wouldn't be tired, you wouldn't turn pale. You're pushing your limits."

"Like Auntie didn't—"

"She didn't."

"Oh, come on."

"No, listen. She could transition a soul like she crossed a street, on the crosswalk, on green."

"And what, I'm jaywalking?"

"Kinda. You need to work up to large numbers of souls. You need to be careful."

"Auntie doesn't appear at any other time. Only when a bunch of people use me." I held my hands out toward him in surrender.

He stilled. "Did she?"

I stood and walked toward him. "Yeah, but the words were jumbled, broken. Like before. I got a few of them. We have to find Father somebody? Ask Custos?"

"I still say it's too risky."

"I'm careful."

"No, you're not."

His words slapped.

"I—" I sank down into a chair, the fight flying out of me. "I'm a wuss."

"What?" Bafflement paused his hands and he leaned against the counter.

"I want to go to Siberia or Antarctica and hide."

"What are you talking about?"

"Nocti hunting us. Me supposed to find other Fenestra and save them. Helping the dying reach the highest plane. I don't want it." I laid my head in my arms. "They picked the wrong girl."

"No, they didn't."

"They did." I raised my head and my voice. "They should have picked a brave, confident girl, instead they got me. What if that's what Auntie's trying to say?"

Tens came closer, knelt at my side, wiped my tearing eyes with his thumbs. "Auntie believed in you."

"You're just saying that."

"No, I'm not. Why do you think she asked your parents to name you after her? Why do you think she sent you quilts with Fenestra mojo and prayers for strength in every stitch?"

"She did?"

"She wanted you to come live with her immediately. She asked your parents to bring you so she could teach you, but your mom wouldn't."

"She'd have to have been honest with my dad." I shook my head.

"Auntie used to talk about you. Your mom wrote her and sent her photos."

"Photos?" Fenestras don't show up on film until we figure out how to operate the window. The light overexposes it, I think.

"They weren't good—you were mostly just a blob of light—but she kept sending them. Auntie knew, and still knows, that you are exactly who you need to be to do this job."

"Really?"

"Really. And so do I. I'm sorry I gave you a hard time. But you need to understand how helpless I feel when you're gone and I'm watching your body. When you do so many souls, it's like the energy drains out of you. I can see it happening. First your skin pales and your hair loses its curl, then your heartbeat slows. And all I can do is sit there with you and hope you don't go through." His voice roughened and his eyes swam with tears. "I can't lose you. I wouldn't survive, Supergirl."

"I'm not going anywhere." I leaned my forehead in the curve of his neck and held on to him as tightly as he gripped me. "I'm sorry I scared you."

He nodded against my head. "I want you safe."

"Me too."

"You'd get bored talking to penguins in Antarctica."

I giggled. "I'd teach 'em poker."

"With fish and chips?" He laughed.

"Ha-ha." I snorted snot bubbles, which made me laugh harder and break away for a Kleenex.

"We're supposed to ask Custos? Seriously?" He turned to me, then glanced over at the couch. "In English?"

I nodded. "I guess."

Custos rolled over on her back, spread her legs wide, and wagged her tail.

"So, in the morning, we ask her to help us find Father *somebody*?"

"Anthony." I snapped my fingers. "That's it, Anthony."

Tens nodded, but didn't say anything else. He poured soup into bowls and nuked them until they were piping hot. I rubbed the headache pounding at my temples.

"Head hurt?" he asked.

"Yeah, just a normal human headache."

"You sure?" He sounded skeptical.

"Yes, positive." *Like we are going to have the I-get-a-headache-and-cramps-with-my-period conversation. I don't think so.* Before—before Revelation and all this—I rarely had a period. The doctors said it was because I was too thin, too anxious, too something indefinable. But for the past two months, every twenty-eight days I counted on needing tampons, Midol, and chocolate ice cream. I tried my best to keep this to myself. There wasn't anything romantic about sharing this part of my life with my boyfriend.

"Do you want this in bed or . . . ?"

"No, I'm fine." I forced myself to move to the table. I found myself famished. I wasn't used to being hungry and having food taste good. It continued to be a new experience, feeling satiated.

I ate almost as much as Tens. *Almost.*

I liked watching him eat. I enjoyed studying him, period. His eyes went from dark chocolate to solid black when he worried or grew angry, but lightened to brown-sugar syrup with love and laughter.

His blue-black hair grew much faster than mine, so he was forever tucking it behind his ears. His cheekbones were chiseled angles under his eyes, leading my gaze toward his full lips, every single time. His were the lips Hollywood starlets paid insane amounts of money to manufacture. But on him, the voluptuousness was completely masculine and unpretentious. I wondered, not for the first time, if he looked more like his dad or his mom. He didn't talk about them, not enough to slake my thirst. I knew from photos at Auntie's house of Tyee, Tens's grandfather.

He caught me staring at him and grinned. "Like what you see, Supergirl?"

Relieved he'd forgiven me, I laughed as I carried my dishes to the kitchen. "Maybe."

He snorted and joined me at the sink. "Your color is better."

"And my curl is coming back too, right?"

"Maybe." He smiled and kissed the top of my head. "I'm going to get our stuff out of the truck."

I gazed out the kitchen window, into the shadows. *What's waiting out there? What's watching? What, or who, is baiting a trap?* "Tens?"

He stopped at the open door, Custos by his side.

"I wish——" I broke off, unsure how to articulate myself.

He paused another beat. "What?"

"I— Never mind." Words failed me.

His brow furrowed, but he believed me. Or at least he dropped it, and walked out into the night. Custos wagged her tail at me and whined.

Why is it I feel she knows exactly what I think before I think it?

Our bag opened and our clothes roughly organized, I changed into flannels that a month ago were too long and baggy, but were now snug and shorter by the night, and scrubbed squeaky clean. I crawled into bed. "My pajamas are smaller." *Did they shrink in the wash, or am I really growing?*

"Yeah, I'd noticed." Tens sat on the couch and whittled his wood blocks into animals and magical creatures. *Will he come to bed tonight before I fall asleep or wait until after? Is he avoiding being near me?*

"Why didn't you say anything? Am I growing too?"

"You're eating now. You're healthier. So, yeah, you're growing. What do you mean by 'too'?" He paused.

"You're taller." I sat up and stared at him.

"So are you." He raised a single eyebrow.

"And broader."

"You too." With a slight nod.

"I guess food agrees with us?" I smiled. Other girls might be upset by their boyfriend noticing their weight, but I was glad.

"Auntie said you'd catch up to where you should be as soon as your body wasn't having to fight so hard to stay alive." His voice trailed off, troubled.

I tried to lighten us back up. "What's your excuse, then?"

"I'm a late bloomer?" he replied with a grin.

Sitting up and grabbing the nearest fancy, I threw a lacy pillow across the room at him.

"Thanks. How'd you know I needed that?" He snatched the pillow out of the air and tucked it behind his neck, like I'd been thoughtful.

I flounced back onto the mattress with a smile and barely suppressed giggles. I heard Tens's chuckle as he stayed firmly on the couch. "Why don't you come to bed?" I asked.

"I'm good. You go ahead and sleep."

I lost the happy feeling. *Am I repulsive?* "Are you sure?" *Do I bring up sex? Should we have a conversation? Don't all men want sex all the time?*

"You know we have different sleep patterns." He wasn't convincing. He insisted on sleeping in shorts and a T-shirt. I was sure he'd prefer sleeping without anything on. Certainly that's what he'd wanted in the caves. It wouldn't bother me. I'd rather be skin-to-skin honest than properly chaste and frustrated.

Why is he avoiding being in bed with an awake me?

I turned onto my side with a sigh. The silence grew thick, and the lump in my throat settled into my stomach. I usually liked the way the world quieted and sighed at night. It was the time when I let a day's events wash over me, when I assimilated any new soul-info, when I focused on breathing life into my deepest places. *We have all the time in the world. Right? I should concentrate on the mission, finding the girl, not my lack of intimacy with Tens. Stop thinking about sex, damn it!* I knew I'd feel better if he made advances and I spurned them. But he conducted himself like he'd read the *1604 Gentlemen's Guide to Relationships and Courting. He should throw himself at me and I should be the one saving no. Dysfunctional much?* I was a teeny bit twisted. I knew it. Owned it. Moved on.

Without the boundary of consciousness nighttime added a vulnerability that brought me nightmares. Terrible contortions of Perimo and his mighty band of followers ran on an unending loop in my mind. Panic made my heart race and my palms sweat. Simply thinking Perimo's name brought dry heaves of anxiety. I tried repeating it to myself, over and over again, until I didn't physically react to it. I'd kept trying. *Perimo, Nocti, Perimo, Nocti, Perimo, Nocti . . .*

The sound of friction from Tens's whittling created a rhythm, a slide and stop, a rough and smooth background track grounding me. I kept my eyes closed, but deep sleep eluded me. Nights also ripped open the wounds of grief I carried. They were no longer the raging hot coal of acute pain, because scar tissue had begun building up around my heart. But I found myself searching for Auntie in those breaths between sleep and waking, in that twilight glow of utter relaxation.

In truth, I was searching for her all the time. In the daytime, I sought among the shadows for anything to remind me. I smelled her as I entered a room sometimes, though what it was that made the scent so utterly Auntie, I didn't know.

The gritty sound of sandpaper meant Tens had finished a piece. *Didn't he just start that one?*

In the death times, I hoped for Auntie's spirit among the windows. But at night, the times I dreamed of her, she was moving. I helped pack her bags and boxes with belongings I knew, and others that didn't quite fit my memories. The house I dreamed of was different than the one in Revelation—it wasn't her house at all—and she never spoke to me. She merely handed me things: books, scarves, figurines. Or I ran out of boxes or time, or the house began to crumble around us. But she never spoke. Even in the midst of these dreams, I knew it wasn't really her, this dream Auntie of my imagination. But until I saw her in the afterlife, I'd assumed that was the only one I'd ever see.

But now, I knew she had tried to speak to me, yelling up at me in that window. Not simply when a soul needed me, but deliberately, with my own agenda, I felt compelled to go there again.

To hear more, to ask more.

To beg her to come back and take charge.

"Stop it, Meridian." Tens leaned over me, wiped tears off my cheeks. "She wouldn't want you tearing yourself up like this."

My exhalation tore out of me like a child crying so hard, so long, she worked consciously for breath.

"You're okay. You're okay." Tens kept repeating reassurances. Petting my hair and rubbing warmth into my arms.

"Don't leave?" My demand sounded more like a question, a request.

"I'm not going anywhere. Sleep." He scooted under the covers.

I snuggled tighter against his side as he tucked us together. We were like a baby spoon and a chef's serving spoon trying to cradle each other. And yet it worked. It felt perfectly imperfect.

He smelled clean, of minty toothpaste and Dove soap. I drifted away, toward the oblivion of rest. One minute warm and safe, the next jarred awake by his shouting. "No! Wait! Talk to me! Tell me! No, no!"

My legs tangled in the blankets, I fell out of bed.

Thump!

The hard landing shocked the dregs of sleep from my mind.

Tens screamed.

I scrambled back onto the bed. "Tens, Tens, wake up. Wake up!" I yelled, trying to make him hear me over his fear.

Be especially careful near hospitals or refugee centers—any location where people regularly die will present souls queued and impatient with their body's slow deterioration. With the added presence of a Fenestra, the soul can force its body to release it.

Melynda Laine
February 14, 1918

CHAPTER 7

Tens threw his head around and thrashed his legs as if wrestling with an imaginary assassin. An all-or-nothing battle. *For what?* I didn't know.

I grabbed his forearm to rouse him. I was afraid he'd hurt himself. Instead, his strength merely jerked me into the action and I flew, with the motion of his arm, across the bed.

"Tens!" My *umph!* as my head hit the pillow broke through his nightmare.

"Merry?" Sleep and fear roughened his voice. With every labored breath, his sweat-drenched shirt heaved.

I crawled back over to him. "Are you awake now?"

"Yeah." He sat up, rubbing his face. He tucked his legs under him to sit, back against the headboard. "Hurt you?"

"No, I'm fine." I scrambled to turn on the light. He reached for me, his touch surging with energy. With me straddling his hips, he embraced me like a teddy bear. He hung on, tight, like I was a life raft in the middle of a stormy ocean. "What was that?" I whispered.

"Mom." Anguish colored his tone a deep indigo.

His mom? He never talks about her. Never. I waited. I'd learned not to push too hard. He needed to open up at his own pace. In his own time. Even if it killed me.

Tens exhaled words with his breath. "And my grandfather and a man—a boy, maybe, more like a boy. Your age, younger than me." He shivered as the sweat cooled and his heart rate normalized.

My skin stuck against his. I'd waited for weeks to learn more about his family. "You seemed scared? Angry?"

His arms flexed around me. "Yeah, the dream morphed into Perimo and more Nocti, but it started out with my mom by my side. We watched this young couple in a diner share an ice cream sundae. Happy. So much joy. They were entranced, in love with each other." He smiled down at me, his eyes intense. "This huge bowl." He chuckled. "Enough ice cream for an entire state, with sprinkles and sauces and huge amounts of whipped cream. And two spoons. They were so into each other, they radiated. They didn't need words. No words and all smiles."

"And your mom was there too?" Tens didn't talk about

his family. I never knew if it was because it hurt too much or because he didn't want me to know. More likely he didn't think any of it was applicable to today and tomorrow. To us.

He shifted against me. "Yeah, watching with me. She held my hand. I'd forgotten what her hands felt like. So fragile I felt each bone. But strong. So completely capable. And she smelled like jasmine in the late afternoon."

I warmed with the love in his voice. I nodded, hoping he'd continue.

"Then Grandfather arrived at the diner and the whole scene changed. He limped into the building with his walking stick and everything grew dark. The spoon clattered to the table, the ice cream melted instantly. The couple stilled, frightened, and Mom's hand tightened in mine. Grandfather didn't say a word, simply grabbed the girl, and then Perimo was there and the Nocti swarmed in."

He rushed his words together, with pain and anguish. I gripped his waist for support, leaning more fully against him. "But no one else noticed the Nocti tearing down the building. Someone grabbed Mom and pulled her hand from my grasp. I couldn't hold on." He thrust me away to stand. His breathing grew ragged and hurried. Again. Sweat plastered his hair to his head in odd angles.

"Just a dream. It was just a dream." Tens let go of me completely and staggered over to the kitchen sink, gulping down water from the running tap. He drank like a man who needed more than water.

I shivered. Bad dream or not, the mention of Perimo's

name made my stomach twist into knots. The Nocti, short for Aternocti, were the balance to the Fenestra. While we helped souls achieve peace and find an afterlife of joy, they caused chaos and destruction to suck souls to the lightless place. *Hell,* to use a popular term, but it was more than a Heaven-versus-Hell thing, more than just Light versus Dark, or Good versus Evil.

I glanced at the clock and saw that dawn was not far away.

Tens came back to bed and brushed my hair from my face. "I'm sorry I scared you."

"I'm okay. Are you?" I didn't mind the role reversal, I just wished I knew what to say or do to make him feel better.

He tugged on ragged running shoes from his army surplus duffel bag. No socks. "Go back to sleep. I'm going to go for a run, get rid of this adrenaline." He kissed me, preoccupied as he tugged a clean shirt over his head, then a sweatshirt. "It was only a dream."

I lay back and stared at the ceiling. I hoped he was right, but what if my seeing Auntie and him seeing his mom and grandfather were connected? *What if we need to find out more about his past before we have a future? What if these aren't dreams, but visions?*

I threw on dry clothes, turned on the laptop, and started Googling local churches, looking for any Father Anthonys in the state of Indiana.

Hours later, when I stepped out onto the path heading toward Helios's kitchen door, Tens was clearing ivy from the trees and the stepping stones. He'd come back from the run, showered, and headed out to work on the grounds without speaking. He waved to me, frowning absently. I'd learned not to take his frowns personally. *Not always.* He shuttered his face, and his emotions, like he was forever prepared to ride out level-five emotional hurricanes alone. He let me behind his walls chink by chink. It wasn't that I had to earn his love or his protection—those were given—but we were still working on friendship and communication. He wanted me to be vulnerable and open to him, but didn't understand I needed the same thing in return.

The scent of ginger and lemon billowed off fluffy scones cooling on the counter. "Good morning. Are you hungry?" Joi turned from the oven with a smile and friendly eyes.

In the not-so-big-but-notable-changes column, I'd been eating breakfast and enjoying it for several weeks. *Surprise, surprise.* "No, the coffee cake was wonderful. Thank you for—"

She cut me off. "McClamroch family recipe. Best there is with a cup of strong black tea. Are you ready to work, or do you need another day to get your bearings?"

I fairly buzzed with pent-up energy. "I'm ready." *Ready to do something, anything to keep my hands busy while my mind wanders through the maze that is my life.*

"Good, that's what I like to hear. We do a lot of the baking now, but I've got that covered. The servers arrive at ten-thirty to help prep the dining room. I know it's not glamorous, but I need you to dust all the shelves—that means moving the inventory off them and putting it back exactly so. And clean the mirrors, the glass cases. Can you do all that?"

I nodded. "Seems like a good way to get familiar with the products too, right?"

She beamed like I'd passed a crucial test. "Exactly. That way you'll be able to help customers find things. The upstairs rooms need it the worst—they're where we store the out-of-season holiday merchandise. Right now they're more storage than anything else, but customers insist on going up there even if it's a mess. We'll need to bring down all the Valentine's Day goodies and display those later today, plus add the inventory arriving this week. Start with the dusting. When we begin serving, I'll need you in the kitchen trying to stay on top of the dishes. But best to start—"

"With the dusting?" I said. Clearly, she was blessed with a battery that never lost juice. I envied her multitasking. The entire time she instructed and trained me, she flew around the kitchen, both hands blurring in busyness.

"And if you see anything you'd like, we'll run a tab and take it off your paycheck later." She smiled.

I headed up the stairs armed with feather dusters, paper towels, and Windex. The rote work gave me time to consider our next steps. Father Anthony, Custos, a girl and a cat. My suspicion that Custos was more than a wolf was worth exploring. *Is she Divine? Part of the Creators' help Mom wrote about?*

Seeing the chaos, I huffed out a breath and surveyed the disaster around me. Strewn together in piles like they'd been brought up and deposited hurriedly were stockings jumbled among gift wrap, stuffed bears wearing quintessential holiday sweaters, and artificial trees full of sparkling ornaments crammed under the eaves. The rest was stacked on shelves and rocking chairs and piled into decorative baskets of red and green. Overwhelmed for a second, I found the irony in getting exactly what I wished for. *Busy hands. Busy mind.*

I cleared off a tiny section of the floor and began the cleaning in small increments. I couldn't imagine shoppers pawing through for long. I turned inside myself, toward the big questions that weighed so heavily on my heart. *Why did Auntie have the woman with her each time I saw her? Could Father Anthony tell us who she was or where to find the girl? Why couldn't Auntie be like OnStar and give us step-by-step directions to the goal? Why all the subterfuge?*

Joi called me down to meet the servers when they arrived, showed me the reservation book, and taught me how to answer the phone. Once the sign was turned to Open, the door had barely banged shut after the first customer before other regulars glided through. Friends and families came to browse, to eat, to catch up.

"Joi, can I organize the scrapbook section, too?" I pointed up at the ceiling.

"It needs it, doesn't it?" She sighed.

I nodded, not wanting to overstep.

"Of course—make pages too if you'd like. It's addictive!"

"Thanks." I got back to work, careful to clean first, arrange second.

As I put the scrapbooking room in order, I found myself picking out stickers and doodads, brads and paper cutouts. I arranged them on a page of parchment, paying no attention, until I heard footsteps on the stairs. Then I folded the paper and stuffed it into my waistband for later. Customers browsed, chattering like finches as they shuffled around my newly arranged area. I got out of their way as quickly as I could. With the dining room full, the kitchen needed me more than the dust bunnies did.

When Tens bustled into the kitchen to eat lunch, I showed him the page I'd made. "I think maybe I've found my thing." I knew the excitement in my voice might be difficult for him to understand, but these feelings were hard to articulate.

I have heard of musicians, painters and sculptors, gardeners and bakers who excel at their craft because of the Fenestras' collection of soul dust. Each Fenestra must learn how to clean that dust off her own soul.

Linea M. Wynn
February 28, 1968

CHAPTER 8

"Your thing? Could you be more specific?" He glanced down at the page, back at me, then turned to concentrate on his Irish stew in a dismissal that stung.

"My quilting *thing*," I snapped. *So it isn't rocket science, but still.*

He put his spoon down and raised his eyebrows. "I thought you didn't like to quilt."

I sat, shaking my head. "I like to quilt, but I'm more a pincushion than a fabric maestro. Bloody cotton isn't warm and cozy to me." Nor were the holes upon holes I put into my fingers trying to sew by hand. Machines scared me. I'd be the first self-amputee, of my whole hand, if I tried that.

"Okay, so?" He didn't get it. He stuffed a cheddar biscuit in his mouth.

"Scrapbooking." I tapped the page.

He swallowed, then spoke around the remaining crumbs. "Scrapbooking?"

"Look." I pushed my page closer to him, as if proximity would bring understanding.

"Um, wow?" His tone said he knew he wasn't giving me what I wanted, but that didn't mean he could. He picked the page up, then set it down again.

I smacked him lightly with it.

"Ow!" He pretended I'd really hurt him.

"Paper cut?" I sneered playfully, teasing him while tracing the Eiffel Tower's black shadow with my finger.

He peered at me, then the paper. "What is it? Paris?"

I sighed. "That guy from the other night—this was his window scene."

"The ambulance?" He stretched, his legs bumping mine.

"Yes, that one."

Comprehension filled his eyes. "So, now you're going to scrapbook your window scenes? Or the souls' memories?"

I shrugged it off. "Maybe. I don't know. I just went with it." But suddenly it didn't feel like quite the right fit. I'd give another couple of souls their own pages before I searched for another thing. I sighed. Until I started to tell him about it, I really thought this might be it. Now doubt crept in and camped.

"No, I get it."

"Reading the journal, it's clear Fenestras each have a way to remember and let go at the same time. A way to . . . I don't know . . . to—"

"To cope with the souls?"

"Yeah, with all the pieces we see and feel and hold on to even after the soul has made it through. I'm searching for my own. Did Auntie talk about it with you? Her quilting? Should I be doing that even if it doesn't feel right?" A sliver of jealousy wiggled in my heart. Tens knew more and had spent more time with Auntie than I had the chance to, and that felt odd.

"About her quilts and whatever your coping type might be?"

I nodded.

"Not really. I know she worried, hoped maybe you'd have the knack for the quilts too. It seems like it's something you have to find on your own, in your own way. I don't think she obsessed about it. Not that part." The implication was he had much bigger things to worry about when it came to me. *Thanks.*

He finished eating in silence and I played with my serving of stew. Then he went back out to the yard without a kiss or a bye. *Clingy much?* I berated myself; it felt like weakness to need him. I had times where I needed almost constant reassurance from him. I hated being that girl. Would that get better the longer we were together?

When the lunch crowd descended on the tearoom, I made my way to the sink and tried to keep up with the porcelain, crystal, and china. Then at my ebb another tide of late-afternoon tea ladies brought dainty teacups, fragile saucers, and tiny plates to the counters around me. I broke only three.

I stared out the window as Tens manically cleaned the gardens of winter debris, then tackled the curls of kudzu and ivy creeping up the trunks of leafless maple and tulip trees. He scrubbed stone statuary and peeled moss from the outdoor furniture. While I watched, my hands pruned up, reddened, and chapped in the dishwater.

Hours flew by as the ache in my feet crawled up my legs and into my back, sending piercing arrows through my hips. I wasn't used to working this hard. I needed more stamina.

"All done." Joi breezed through the kitchen. "Last check. We may have a few shoppers for the final hour, but probably no more dishes."

I almost cheered, but I was too tired.

"How many did you break?"

I flinched and said apologetically, "Three? I will totally pay for them."

"Nah, that's not bad for a beginner. Are you okay? You don't look well." Joi crowded me against the sink and felt my forehead like a television mom might. My own would have kept her distance.

"I'm okay." I tried to reassure her, but fell short of convincing.

"Are you sure you should be working? Aren't you recovering from something? Suffering?" She wouldn't drop it and her sincerity felt genuine.

It didn't feel right to lie, so I evaded. "I was ill last fall; I'm just getting back on my feet. It's nothing. I'll be fine. I don't have a lot of stamina. Not yet."

"Hmm." She accepted my half answer without continued pressure, but clearly she would have appreciated, maybe even enjoyed, more details. "Well, Tens has done the work of *ten* men today. So you both take tomorrow off. If you need a place to stay without working, let me know and we'll talk it out, okay? I like having someone I trust in the cottage to keep an eye on the business at night."

"I don't need tomorrow off," I protested halfheartedly.

"I say you do. And I'm always right." She smiled at me. "Wrap up the leftovers and take them with you, then get out of here. And tell Tens to lazy up a bit—he gets paid by the hour." She smiled and petted my hair, much like Sammy used to.

Before she moved away, I asked, "Have you heard of a Father Anthony?"

"Catholic? Episcopalian?"

"I don't know."

"Not off the top of my head, but his name sounds familiar. Let me think about it." She scuttled back to the cashier's counter for the ringing phone.

"No problem." Deflated, I headed to the cottage with Tupperware and foil filled with lots of food, all of it ladylike.

I didn't remember lying down or closing my eyes, but the next time I stretched and opened my eyes the windows framed dark night. A propane fire burned in the fireplace. Tens puttered in the kitchen, the air steaming with fragrant chili and corn bread.

With my waking sigh, Tens's head snapped around. "Hiya, Supergirl." He strode over and stretched out next to me on the bed. He curled toward me. "You slept forever. You feeling okay?"

"Sorry." I snuggled against him, tucking myself into his shoulder and side. "Tired."

He nodded across the top of my head. "You hungry?"

"Hmm . . . let's stay here like this for a minute, okay?" I reveled in the weight and feel of him pressed to me. *So different from me in his proportions and shapes. Safe. Secure.* Butterflies tickled my insides, not with anxiety but excitement. He smelled like sunlight and sap, a touch of wet dog, and loamy earth.

He ran his fingers through my hair, untangling my sleep from each strand. My curls had recovered fully from the latest batch of transitions. "Hmm." I sighed my pleasure, my breath moistening the cotton covering his chest. If I could have purred, I would have. *Don't stop, please, don't stop.* I enjoyed the tug and soothe on my scalp. His heat and strength drove my worry away.

He kissed my fingertips. "Dishpan hands."

"My one brush with the fifties. I'm a feminist. I hate doing dishes."

"Is that what 'feminist' means? I thought it was something else." He chuckled deep in his chest, but without the raucous abandon I longed to hear. Laughter for Tens was a small tremor. I still didn't know who, or what, had stolen his laugh machine. He settled silent again, quiet.

Intermittent traffic outside created soft white noise and people walking around the neighborhood occasionally yelled greetings to each other. Car doors slammed, crows called, and dogs barked. I felt like we were in a cocoon and the world outside was happening without us. This quiet was relative.

I missed Sammy's antics—his goofy faces and spontaneous giggles. The games of chase and tag. I hadn't known how much I'd relied on him to balance the burden of so much death until I no longer had him. I needed Tens to provide some of that for me. I needed goofy playing, flirting, and touching. I'd told him this while we were stuck in the caves; he'd made monumental strides in occasionally giving me lighter, airier moments. This wasn't one of them. I felt him waiting to have the serious conversation that stalked me. It hung there like the gallows. The reality of death being an integral part of our lives made the act of living oppressive. "Thanks for not telling me I overdid it today," I said, breaking our silence.

"You're welcome."

I wondered aloud, "How did she do it?"

"Who? What?"

"Auntie? How did she balance it all? She had Charles, a home, and quilting. A family. She did charity work and was a nurse. She had all these amazing dimensions to her life."

"And you don't?" He leaned over me to catch my gaze.

"I don't mean it that way. I'm blessed to have you, I know that."

"But you want the rest? Right this minute? You're comparing the life of a hundred and six years to your sixteen. Do you really think she had all of that in the beginning?"

Good point. Of course she didn't. I held my tongue.

Tens continued. "My grandfather was the epitome of a shaman, an elder, the person everyone turned to for advice. Lessons. Actions. He didn't just give empty words; when the talking was done he acted. Every day of my life, I will strive to be like him and I will never get there. Never."

I pushed myself up until mere inches separated our faces. "That's not true. You're special. You'll be him and then some, because you started with the foundation he set for you."

"Maybe. But what I'm trying to tell you is that you and I can only do the best we can in the moment. When we know more, we'll do more; when we *are* more, we'll make bigger choices and have bigger impacts. We're just starting, Merry."

"Why does it feel like I have to steal normal, though?"

His lips twitched. "Because you do."

I rolled my eyes, knowing he was right. Again. I kissed him lightly on his lips and chin and cheeks.

The kitchen timer dinged. Our dinner was ready. We shelved our conversation, but over bits and pieces of the tearoom leftovers, Tens paused to stare at me.

"What's going on in your head?" I asked. His expression

clouded. I pressed. "You worked so hard today, like you were driven."

"I felt like I needed to move. To sweat."

"How long was your run?" *Didn't he run for hours before even starting work on Helios's grounds? What drives him to push so hard?*

"Couple of hours. I don't know. But—" He stopped and ate a square of honey-drenched corn bread.

I knew to hold my peace and wait him out.

"I took the ravine path back there. It runs along Wildcat Creek. Bike path, maybe? Nice. Paved."

I nodded, licking my chili spoon. Shoving food in my mouth kept me from pestering him with what he'd consider annoying questions.

"I wasn't keeping track of the time or distance. Went from town development to rural farmland fairly quickly. Wide-open spaces or woods. No people. I found a rhythm and pounded it out." He ate a few more bites.

"Custos kept to my right, between me and the creek. She kept leaping over logs and chasing possums or rats or whatever. She crossed over into my path and tripped me." At her name, Custos stood, stretched, and wandered over to her bowl of chili and corn bread. She wouldn't touch dog food and she didn't much like people food, either. But I kept offering it to her, unsure whether she needed nourishment of this type.

"Then she tripped me again." Tens shook his head.

"Are you hurt?" I reached for him automatically, coming out of my chair. "She did it on purpose?"

He grabbed my hands and gently pushed me back, but he didn't let go. "Fine. I'm fine. I fell sideways, onto grass. Custos bumped me again. Hard. I tried to stand and she threw her paws into my stomach. Enough force to keep me down, but not hurt me." He paused, rubbing idly his thumbs across the backs of my hands.

Between Tens and me, Custos's loyalty was clear. She liked me. A lot. But she stuck to Tens like corn syrup.

"Weird." I'd never seen her behave with anything other than the utmost deference to Tens. It wasn't like I didn't know she was capable of being scary and physical— we hadn't met in the best of circumstances. I would forever chill thinking about her howl and growl in the Colorado snow.

"Her hackles rose and she barked at something behind me."

Nocti? Perimo? I hated that my first thoughts went to the big, bad evil rather than a squirrel or an unlatched window shutter.

Custos wandered over and licked my hand, carefully getting every corn bread crumb and speck of honey off my fingers.

"Go on," I prompted Tens. "What was it?"

He dished up seconds, continuing to eat between explanations. "In the low light, I saw a wrought iron fence and the shadow of an estate in the distance."

"What was she barking at? Was there a person?"

"I didn't see anything. No one. Not right away. And then"—he leaned forward like he was going to deliver a punch line—"she wagged her tail and what looked like a huge raccoon ran by, up a tree."

"A raccoon?" I snorted, grasping Custos's face and kissing her nose. "Custos is scared of a wittle, itty-bitty raccoon?"

Tens stopped me. "Worse. I thought it was a coon, but turned out it was a long-haired cat. Huge cat." He smiled.

I clucked my tongue. "She chased a cat like a regular dog?" If she had, that would be the only quasi-normal thing about her.

Tens scratched Custos's butt while I rubbed her ears. She moaned and whined in ecstasy. It was nice to be good for something. "That's the oddity, that's when she relaxed."

"Course she did." *I take it all back. Our Custos never does anything normal.*

Tens finished eating and carried our dishes to the sink. He ran new soapy water, grabbed a clean dishcloth, and stared out into the night. "I want to take you there, see what you think. I don't know what to make of the place." When he turned to me, the furrow was back between his eyes.

"You're worried."

"A little. But there's more." He said it as if he knew I wasn't going to like whatever came next.

"More?" I braced. *What earthquake is coming now?*

He paused, deliberating.

"Spit it out." I walked over and faced him. "Just say it."

"I had a conversation with Joi while you slept this evening."

"Okay?" *Not the worst thing I imagined.*

His expression turned apologetic, then defiant. "I know you hate it when I know things, but I can't help it. I can't turn it off. I wish I could. But even she noticed."

The rest of this conversation was not going to be pleasant. I agreed with everything I knew he'd say and it pissed me off. I hated my physical weakness. I'd gained so much strength since my birthday, but I wanted more.

He softened his tone. "You're not ready to work a full day. I can feel how torn you are about finding the other Fenestras, and at the same time wanting a life that's normal, or at least has the regular parts, but I don't think—"

"I've made a lot of progress." I felt like I needed to point out that I was better. Taller. Stronger. No longer in constant pain, no longer bruised unexpectedly, or too ill to eat.

He held my shoulders and gazed into my eyes with the sincerity of wisdom. "That's true, but it's not going to happen overnight, Merry."

I hated knowing he was right. My rebellion was directed firmly at the powers bigger than Tens and clearly more all-knowing than me. "I know—I took a vacation today into the ordinary and I liked it, but I know."

He stepped back, but didn't break his hold. "What do you mean, you know?"

I leaned my forehead against his heart. "We can't waste time playing at having jobs and making friends and forgetting."

He growled, "I'm not talking about forgetting."

"No, but I am. It's tempting. So tempting." Tears leaked from the corners of my eyes. "I thought as soon as I learned my powers, got my mojo, that I'd be healed and whole and ready for anything. That we could date, and have fun, and save the world while being teenagers." I envied the teenagers in movies who had friends, went to school, and worried about college, prom. I would never be that. Have that.

"But you're not ready to juggle all that." Tens held me.

"Not yet."

Tens smoothed my neck and traced circles along my spine. "Joi's going to rent us the cottage as long as we need it."

"No work?" I glanced up at him.

"We can work whatever hours we want to. She'll keep a list or we can come find her and she'll tell us what needs to be done at the moment. She also asked about your health."

"What'd you say?"

"I lied. I told her we were looking for your family for medical reasons. You were adopted and now you're on the hunt for your genetic match."

"That's a big lie." I blew out a breath of regret.

"I couldn't really tell her the truth, could I?" Sadness tightened his mouth.

"I hate having to lie." *Really, really, abysmally hate.*

"Me too. Maybe someday we won't have to." His tone was dubious.

"Tomorrow we hunt again for the cat, the girl?" *Will*

I feel something? Will an alarm go off in my head, or will I see flashing lights in the presence of another of me? Will there be an apparent kinship? I feared walking right by her and not knowing her until too late. I tried to remember if I'd recognized Auntie immediately and I simply couldn't untangle the threads of all of it. The whole trip to her, of learning the truth about myself, was so foreign I hadn't been looking. "Yeah, vacation over. I'll check in the journal and see if there's anything about how to spot another one of us," I said.

"Only you would consider working a vacation." Tens kissed me until my regret faded.

Last night I slept in a church. It was the first time I'd felt *safe* in forever. Dear baby, what will I do with you?   —R.

CHAPTER 9
Juliet

The social worker, Ms. Asura, was due to stop by DG today for her twice-a-month check-in. Recently, she'd been coming more frequently, but never unannounced.

Nicole grabbed my hand tightly and dragged me into the pantry. "I don't trust her. You shouldn't either." Tension pinched her cheeks and drove the color from her complexion.

I shook my head in confusion. "Why? She's nice. Just because there isn't anything she can do to help us—"

"She doesn't try to help, Juliet. She's never tried. She doesn't want to know."

"You don't know that; you haven't been here that long." I'd never seen Nicole so worked up.

"Long enough. But it's more than that. There's something really wrong going on."

I paused. "What do you mean?"

"We shouldn't all have the same social worker."

"I don't know that. How do you know that?" *Who says? Who cares? Whose rule?*

"It's not the way the system works. But if that isn't enough, we should be in school, being kids. This is slave labor. You're a prisoner. You should be thinking about what you want to be when you grow up, not how you're going to get Sema fully potty-trained before you turn sixteen."

I stopped being a kid a long time ago. "We're homeschooled." I wished I believed that. I'd started parroting too well.

"When exactly? Because I've never seen a textbook or done homework or taken a test."

I sighed. "I'm taking my GED later. That's the way it works."

"By choice?" Nicole shook her head at me. She gripped my fingers like a vise.

We both knew I hadn't gone to real school. School here was bookless. Kirian taught me to read. Another teen I couldn't picture taught me the birds and the bees and what to do when I got my period. The elderly guests who could talk, even briefly, gave me other lessons. History. Art. How to sew buttons. How to cure the stomach flu. Decades of life bestowed an expertise they shared gratefully, one that I would never get sitting in a high school classroom.

Nicole held eye contact with me. "Ms. Asura is not a good person. She turns a blind eye. She likes this place. She doesn't help."

"What do you want from me?" I asked, defeated in all the ways that counted. *When did I give up fighting for us, for myself?* I barely recognized my own soul.

Nicole didn't answer, simply stared at me with an expression that spoke for her. *What can anyone do? There is nothing anyone can do.*

"It could be worse. There are families that abuse the kids. We could be on the streets or we could—"

Nicole stopped me with the saddest smile I'd ever seen. "Just be careful. Please? How can she not know what's going on here? Think about it." Nicole hadn't been here long enough to begin the process of acceptance. First there was denial, and anger, and frantic attempts to escape, then resolve and acceptance. I was already past acceptance, to the void of oblivion.

Ms. Asura called and spoke with Mistress before bringing new kids. They removed kids at night. The one time I asked about that, Ms. Asura said nighttime was easier on the human psyche for change. *Really?* It made the rest of us cry rather than sleep. How easy was that?

I stopped trying to tell Ms. Asura about the kids, about the realities of DG, years ago. I'd long since understood I was on my own. I handled the retribution. But the littlies, the Bodies and Semas of this world, needed someone to stand up for them. *Maybe I can try again? To show Nicole the only evils in our world are Mistress and luck.*

We each received ten minutes with Ms. Asura, no first name. I knew nothing about her life. I tried to get to know her when I was younger, but she deflected questions deftly until I stopped asking them. She was the indeterminate age of adult. Her fingers were covered in blingy rings, and bracelets jangled with her every movement, echoing the intricate silver earrings touching her shoulders. Her clothes changed, but her jewelry remained static. Her hair, blackened by dye, was harsh against her pale skin, but gave her an authority I envied. Her cheekbones and nose were perfectly symmetrical, too perfect, and her makeup immaculately applied and maintained. I used to think she looked like a movie star playing at being a social worker. I didn't waste energy on wondering about that, about anything, anymore.

"Hi, honey. How are you?" She put her notebook down and embraced me like she'd missed me. *I want to believe she does.* A cloud of subtle perfume enveloped me with her arms and made the back of my throat close and itch. She held on to me past the moment when I wanted to break away, almost tightening her hold as if she knew to cinch me more.

"Sorry." She laughed off the hug. "I've just missed you so much. We should go shopping. Just us girls."

This wasn't the first time she'd promised me an outing. I didn't answer.

"Tell me everything. How *are* you?"

I perched on the edge of the sofa. "I'm fine."

"How are you really, Juliet? I'm on your side, remember?"

I nodded. "I'm . . ." I searched for the right word, the word I think she wanted to hear. "Good?"

She relaxed with a sigh of delight. As if any other answer was unacceptable. "And are you doing okay in your studies? With your duties here?"

"Um, those are good too, I guess." *Studies? What time do I have to study? What subjects? How to clean grout and old people's poop? How to cook for kids on a budget designed to slop one pig a couple of times a week? How to do laundry in a machine that's outdated and never quite spins all the water out of the clothes? How to survive on three hours of sleep, five if I'm lucky?* These were the lessons I'd learned. And learned well.

She tapped her pen, ever ready to take a note, though she never did. "Are you prepared for the GED? It'll be very important when you turn eighteen to be able to get a job. Your headmistress will write you a recommendation, I'm sure, although she did mention to me that you're resistant to do what she asks. I hate hearing that you're not living up to your end of the deal, Juliet. It disappoints me." She pouted.

I stuttered an apology without knowing why, or what I had to be sorry about.

"I simply need you to try your best, right? Like we've talked about before?"

I nodded.

"Now that the not-fun part is out of the way, is there anything you'd like to talk about?" She reached out and patted my leg, my arm. I imagined a mother looking at her child like this—interested, alert, hopeful.

I bit my lip and picked at my hands. *Do I try? Do I say*

something? Can she really help? "Well, Bodie is having a hard time adjusting. I'm worried about him."

She frowned, leaned in toward me. "What specifically should I know? Is he getting sick, or wetting the bed, or starting fires?"

I blanched. Starting fires wasn't what I was thinking about, though kids who did that came through here too.

"No, none of that." I never mentioned the bed-wetting of any kid. I laundered the sheets, so why did anyone else need to know? "But he's scared, alone . . . I think Mistress might be . . . too . . . hard on him."

She reached into her briefcase and extracted a wad of forms. "Let me dig out the correct form for a report."

I swallowed. Panic clawed at my throat.

She paused and considered my expression with a serious one of her own. "You need to know, I'm obligated to write down any concerns you have and share them with your foster care guardian. I also have to put a copy in both your and Bodie's files. The thicker the file, the more difficult to get placed in a family; people don't want children who create problems and controversy. They want malleable, dutiful, cute kids." She paused, letting her words sink deep. "So I want you to be very careful about what you say to me. Make sure it's the truth."

Her message was clear—continue with the report and life gets more challenging, or let it go and suck it up. I wasn't getting a family. But Bodie might. *Can Nicole and I shelter him more? Can we create a better buffer against Mistress?* We had to try. Reporting wasn't an option. "You'd have to tell Mistress?"

"If you're telling me he's abused, then yes, I do." She

appeared saddened but still primed to take my statement. The paperwork was more important to her than the abuse. "Of course even if you can prove it, investigations take time. When's your birthday?"

A tickle behind my ear made me look up, above Ms. Asura's head, to the back corner of the room. High upon a bookcase full of glass vases and porcelain figurines, Mini flicked her tail. She hissed at the back of Ms. Asura's head, but the social worker didn't hear her. Mini seemed to shake her head, warning me to be quiet. I needed more sleep.

"I didn't say abused." The room spun. Bodie would be belted, or worse, for crying to me. I wouldn't escape punishment either. I backpedaled. "There's nothing specific, I—"

She sighed, aggrieved. "I need to know exactly what is going on, if I'm going to protect you. Juliet, I need you to be brave and tell me. Bodie is a handful. Are you sure he's not just getting a little tough love?"

I nodded, taking the direction. "She made him clean the bathrooms."

"Oh, well." Ms. Asura put the forms back into her briefcase and shared a brief frowny smile with me. "Juliet, you know that discipline is completely up to the guardians. Even if we don't agree, cleaning the bathrooms is not abuse."

It is when he doesn't get to eat and is told to use a toothbrush and his own spit. I couldn't get the words out of my mouth. It wasn't worth it to argue.

"Juliet, have you noticed anything else? Last time I was here you mentioned finding dead rodents and lots of insects. Any more of those? Did the traps work?"

Rats, mice, butterflies, and moths floated and drifted

into corners like dust bunnies. The animals seemed to die in places I spent a lot of time, like the kitchen, laundry room, and attic. The bugs seemed to come into the house to die wherever they could.

After Mistress heard of my complaint to Ms. Asura, she had made me cook and serve a rat to the kids. Now Nicole swept the tailed and winged corpses up and away as quickly as they settled in.

Mini flicked her tail again, drawing my attention back to her.

"No, that's better," I lied. We'd found a beaver and a couple of stray cats by the back door last week.

"Oh, good!" Ms. Asura clapped her hands. "See, when you tell me things I can help change them. We're a good team. Juliet, I want you to be able to tell me anything. I'm on your side." Her smile didn't quite reach her eyes.

I nodded, forcing my lips up. I think she believed that she was helping. I hoped Nicole was wrong. "I know." I lifted my eyes to the bookcase.

"What do you keep looking at?" Ms. Asura turned around in her chair to follow my gaze.

My breath caught, but Mini had disappeared.

"Just a fly." *Lying. I hate lying.*

"And you're feeling all right? More headaches? Dizzy spells? Cramps or nausea?"

"Nope. I'm good."

"Great. I just think you're doing so well, sweetie. You'll do fine out in the world and that's all we can hope for. You call me anytime, though, if you need to talk to me, okay? Anytime."

I wouldn't call. I didn't have her phone number. I'd never had it. I would have had to ask Mistress for it.

"Okay, I'll see you in a few weeks. Why don't you send George and Matilda in, okay? I'm taking them and the twins with me today to place with a lovely family. Oh, before I forget, Kirian sent you a new postcard from Venice. Where did I put that?" She dug around in the pockets of her case and finally extracted a beat-up postcard showing a boat and the canals of Venice.

I took the card with my fingertips but didn't read it. Not yet. *I'll save it. I thought Kirian would take me with him. I thought he wouldn't leave me here.*

"You look so sad." Ms. Asura wrapped her arms around me again. "He's happy. We have to be happy for him. I'm sure you'll see him again, sooner than you think."

I nodded, stepping out of her hug to breathe. When had her embraces gone from comforting to smothering? They'd changed. Or I'd changed? Maybe they'd always been that way? Maybe Nicole opened my eyes to a dynamic already present.

I plodded out of the room, trying not to run. Nicole waited for me behind the grandfather clock.

We watched the next kids bounce into the parlor and shut the door behind them. Their delighted squeals flowed under the cracks, out to us.

I needed to pack their stuff. Quickly, or they'd leave without it. Fewer kids meant fewer targets for Mistress. Every instinct said to run out the front door and keep going.

As soon as she could, Nicole dragged me around the corner. "Are you okay?"

"Yeah, I didn't say anything."

"You didn't tell her about your sick stuff, the fainting, right?"

"No, I didn't tell her." My whole left thigh was mottled blue and green and my knee was swollen. I was forever injuring myself, but I rarely remembered how things happened.

Her relief was palpable. "Good. We'll figure it out ourselves. With Google."

"Google is your God." I tucked my arm through Nicole's and headed toward the kitchen.

"Nah, my God has many names, but Google isn't one of them." Nicole tugged my hasty French braid. It felt good to laugh. Even for only a moment.

Each of us is a piece in a puzzle greater than human understanding. When we're in the presence of another, our unity strengthens us.

Omnes sumus quasi aenigmatis partes quod intellectum humanum superat.

Luca Lenci

CHAPTER 10

The birds were barely singing their first hellos by the time Tens and I took up positions surveilling the estate Tens had seen on his run. I had wrapped one of his flannel shirts over my jeans and cotton sweater and tucked my hair up under a baseball cap. He wore all black, which made him seem even taller and leaner and more devastatingly handsome.

We'd parked the truck at a boat launch, along Wildcat Creek, a couple of miles back. It was not yet spring; fields lay muddy, ready for planting. Maybe corn? That was my sole image of Indiana from television and movies. That and basketball.

Tens crouched beside me in the shrubs. "This is it."

We'd snuck up as best we could, trying to appear like two people out for a morning stroll. We'd even brought a leash and put a collar on Custos to give strangers an authentic dog-walking impression. She'd probably eat me if I tried to attach the leash. It was bad enough coaxing her into the mesh collar. It had pink hearts and fake diamonds on it and came, of course, from Joi's Valentine pooch display, so maybe that had a little to do with Custos's reluctance. She was lucky I hadn't decided on the tutu and tiara that came in gigantic for the larger puppy princess.

Tens poked me. "What do you think?"

"It's creepy as hell." I couldn't help the quiver of fear in my knees.

He nodded. "It would make a great set for a horror movie." I think his eyes might have smiled behind his unnecessary shades. He hid his eyes often.

I tried to laugh past the fear. "That would make us, what? The stupid, snooping, soon-to-be zombified extras?"

"Nah, we'd be the ones to survive because of our wits and stealth." Tens's teeth flashed in the muted light of early morning.

"What is it?" I asked.

"I asked Joi, did a little online recon, too. It's a rehabilitation center. They don't have a website, but other sites list them as a place seniors over eighty can go to recover from a stroke, surgery, or broken hip. That kind of thing." Tens spoke in a low whisper while Custos whined with each breath. She added to the conversation, even as she poked her snout through mole holes in the earth around us. "Joi says she's never seen the inside, the staff rarely come into town, and she's never met any patients who recovered there. Sounds like they mainly take indigents and those living alone."

"I'm not surprised about the lack of a website. It doesn't even look like they have electricity." I crawled forward a little. "Are you sure it's not abandoned completely?"

"Psst."

We jumped. So startled to hear a third voice, we froze for a moment.

"Up here." A child's voice directed our gazes upward.

Custos wagged her tail, then pawed at the tree trunk as she gazed up among the boughs.

"You're big, doggie." A delighted giggle rustled down to us.

I peered into the branches above us. "Hello?" I asked, my voice scared and shaky. A little boy with fiery, burnished curls and dressed in a Colts sweatshirt three sizes too big and jeans too small clung like a monkey to spindly branches. His tongue slid through where his bottom teeth used to be and his grin was mischievous.

"I'm Bodie. Who are you?"

Tens leaned against the tree, pushing his sunglasses onto his forehead. "What are you doing up there?"

"Hiding. Mistress wants to switch me again. Did you

know there are starving children in China who'll get my breakfast if I don't clean my plate? Ick. It's glue when she cooks. I like when Juliet cooks, but that's it. I don't want the food; the starving kids can have it and not starve no more. I wish she'd give it to them without hitting me. That's not fair." He was so matter-of-fact that I felt at a loss, not sure what to say in response.

"I don't think she meant—" Tens glanced at me for help.

"Oh, she meant it. She always means it. Mean. Mean. Mean." The little boy shimmied down the tree and giggled while Custos cleaned his face, inside his nostrils, and behind his ears.

There's nothing in this world that sounds like the twinkly joy of a young child's laughter. My heart seized. He reminded me of Sammy, which made me ache for my little brother. *Where is he? Is he safe?*

"Why are you spying on us?" Bodie asked, with the directness of a child forced to grow up too fast.

"Oh, we're not." I tugged on Tens. We sat low on the bank of the lawn. No one could see us from the house.

"Yes, you are." Bodie shook his head sadly before mumbling, "No one tells me anything. Juliet won't tell me, you won't tell me. I'm not a baby." His pouting lower lip screamed a refute.

Tens patted the ground next to us in invitation. "Can you keep a secret?"

Custos bumped Bodie over toward us with her nose. He patted her head with absentminded affection. He picked a seat across from us and she leaned against him. "Uh-huh." His head bobbed like a fishing lure in rough water. "I keep the bestest secrets."

"We are spying. You're right. We're looking for a girl like us," Tens whispered.

"What's she look like? There's lots of girls in there. What do you want to do? Are you here to rescue us? Or are you mad at her?" Interest, fear, curiosity, and resolve flitted consecutively across his features.

I answered. "No. We want to be her friend. And maybe, I guess, rescue her, but—" It didn't seem to matter to him that I stumbled over the words.

"Will you be my friend? I don't have many friends." Bodie scooted over to me and plopped himself into my lap. Just like Sammy used to.

"Sure. We can be friends." I meant it. My stomach clenched at the memory of my brother. Would he talk to strangers this way? Be so trusting?

"Will you adopt me?" Bodie ping-ponged his gaze between Tens and me. "You're old enough, aren't you? I'll call you Mommy, or Daddy, or whatever you want." His expression was utterly sober. I felt his seriousness in the tension of his small frame.

"Uh—" Tens straightened, his expression a bit wild and frantic.

"Won't your parents miss you?" I asked into Bodie's curls.

"No, they left me here. I'm foster." His shoulders dipped and his eyes focused on the ground.

"Oh." I floundered. "I'm sure they had a good reason." Even as the words floated past my lips, I wanted to clamp them together and take them back. *There isn't a good enough reason for abandonment. Ever.* Anger for Bodie, for me, at my parents, battered my insides and I felt my heart pick up its tempo. I battled to temper my reaction and remain focused on Bodie and the now.

Tens caught my upset and took over the conversation. "How long have you been here?"

I blinked, trying to compose myself.

Bodie squirmed, picking grass blades and tearing them to pieces. "Not long. We get moved lots. Place is nasty. Mistress is a demon."

"Is she in charge? She's mean to you?" Tens questioned.

"Yeah, bad mean, but Juliet tries to make it better, and so does Nico."

"That's good, right? And maybe you won't be here long, right?" I interjected.

"Bodie! Bodie, where are you?" A girl's solemn voice called from the house.

"That's Nico. I have to go. Will you come back and see me? I hide in the trees a lot."

Tens answered, "Sure, we'll come back. But you gotta promise not to tell anyone you saw us."

"Not even Juliet or Nico?" He seemed sad to be reminded of the secrecy.

"Not even them." Tens shook his head with the utmost sincerity. Even to me it seemed like he was laying it on a little thick. I didn't underestimate kids—Sammy was smarter than most adults.

Bodie agreed carefully. "Okay, but you'd like 'em. They're like you." He trotted off, shimmying through the fence to face us one last time. "Watch for the mean ivy— it'll get you if you let it."

We peeked our heads up above the berm, and saw an umber-haired teen wearing a long-sleeved denim dress embrace Bodie. She wasn't much taller than he was. As she shuffled Bodie back toward the house, she seemed to touch him with care and love. To Bodie's credit, he didn't glance back over his shoulder or give any indication we were there.

"Interesting," Tens muttered.

"What did he mean about the ivy?" I asked, shivering. It had sounded like an ominous warning.

"No clue." This was a lightless place. Stagnant and airless. I wanted to scrub away the filth and despair that seemed to clog every pore. I couldn't imagine living in that building—a hundred feet outside was too close. It made me desperate to get away. "Foster kids live there? I thought it was old people? Gross. Auuhh—"

"That's why we're here. We'll figure it out." Tens glanced up at the sky as the pink fingers of dawn gave way to bright sun. "I think our new friend might be a help."

I turned back to stare at the monstrosity of a structure. "Do you think she's in there?"

"Something or someone is." Tens let me grab on to his hand, and squeezed back.

I concentrated. "Yeah, I feel that. Shouldn't we go knock on the door? See if she needs us? Now?" I wanted to sweep in—with an army and a plan.

"He said the headmistress is a demon. What if she's Nocti?" Tens rubbed his palms along his jeans.

"You can't think he meant it literally." *Can't be that easy.*

He shrugged. "Kids pick up on things. I'd hate to not believe him, then regret it later."

"True. A Nocti living in there, though? With a Fenestra?"

"What if she's no longer a—"

"Don't say that. I won't believe that we're too late."

**What will I tell you about your ancestry? How
will I explain when no one has ever explained
it to me?** —R.

CHAPTER 11

Juliet

Deep into the wee hours of the night Bodie called out.
"Juliet?" Soon he was crawling under the cleaning supplies to
get to my bed at the back of the stairs. "Can I sleep with you?"
His voice trembled.

"What time is it?" I blinked as his flashlight blinded
me. Mini stretched and moved out of my arms to make room
for him.

"I dunno. Please?" His expression punched me in the
gut. He expected rejection. *We all did.*

"Course," I quickly reassured him. I'd fallen onto the mattress hours after the kids were tucked in and accompanied by stories intended to nourish sweet dreams. I picked up my little travel alarm, once belonging to Edith German, and saw that only thirty minutes had passed since I'd crashed. I hadn't even had the energy left to brush my teeth or wash my face. I wore my nasty clothes from yesterday.

Bodie was oblivious. He squirmed, pushed, and kicked until he was comfortable, touching as much of me as possible.

"Did you have a bad dream?" I asked. Among the inmates, nightmares were as common as bed-wetting and dirty dishes. I'd yet to meet a kid who came here who didn't cower in the wee hours for some reason.

Bodie kept his flashlight tucked in his arms like I held Mini, so I angled my face exactly right to keep the light from searing my retinas. "Juliet?" he asked.

"Umm-hmm." I barely managed a few syllables around my irrepressible need for sleep.

Mini made her way across us to curve around my head like a furry crown. She purred, kneaded my scalp, and groomed my eyebrows with her sandpapery tongue.

I was almost asleep again when Bodie asked, "Why did your mommy not want you?"

Not a question I had anticipated. In my startle, I glanced right into the lightbulb. Tears washed my eyes as I blinked and replied, "What?"

"Why didn't your mommy keep you?" He stared up at the ceiling, but his legs squirmed, fidgeting.

Ah, the eternal abandoned-child question. I wanted to say that he was wrong, that my mother desperately wanted to keep me. Because the question really had nothing to do with me or my mother—it had everything to do with his.

"I don't know, Bodie." *Oh yes, you do know. You just don't want to believe it.*

"Didn't she love you?"

"I hope so. I think so." I had no idea. Only what I'd heard. What I hoped. *How could she have possibly loved me if she left me, let me end up here?*

"So why?"

"If I see her, I'll ask her." I tried to evade. "But I know something."

"What?"

"That I love you. And I'm blessed to have you in my life." I said the things to kids I most needed to hear when I was their age. I meant them, but it's not about me. Not anymore. It's about trying to mitigate the damage I knew happened daily.

"But why?"

"Because you're smart and kind and funny."

"Brave?"

"And brave," I added with a smile.

"Then why did she leave?"

"She had to. She didn't have a choice." This was my standby: telling a lie because it got them through the days and weeks until they were adults. *Until they're old enough to know that I lied to them and they hate me instead of themselves.*

We all hated someone, somewhere. It was better to hate

than to hurt. To wonder why my mother left me, why I didn't get adopted by a nice family, what in the world I'd done to deserve this hell? Those wonderings hurt. I preferred the hate.

"Mistress said they gave her money because she was a crack ho. What's a crack ho? Was she?"

I loathed Mistress. "No. Mistress is mean and ugly and hateful."

"Then why'd she say that?"

"Because saying mean things makes her feel better."

"Really?"

"Really." This I knew without doubt. Inside of our headmistress, horrid, wizened, blackened, smoking remains of what used to be a soul curled and writhed. If there was a hell, she had a prime table by the band.

"I made new friends today." Bodie's head relaxed onto the crook of my arm and his breathing evened out. "You'd like 'em."

"Really?"

"Wolf, too."

I had no idea what or who he mumbled about, but I didn't care. I let my own eyes close and dreamed of Kirian.

"Who are you?" A cute blond boy knelt in front of me.

I said nothing, huddling in the corner of the attic with my arms wrapped around my knees.

"Don't talk, huh?" He smiled. "I'm Kirian. I'm nine. I've been here three years. Want me to show you around?"

I shook my head. I didn't want to move.

"Come on, I'll show you a nest of robins. Have you

ever seen baby birds? They're kinda ugly, but they'll fly soon."

I shook my head again, but I was intrigued.

"They're down by the creek. Do you like to fish? I like to fish. And swim. Have you ever collected fireflies in a jar?"

I shook my head again. I loved fireflies, but I couldn't remember the last time I'd seen them.

"Do you like jelly beans? I have a stash. I'll share with you. I like grape ones and buttered popcorn together. What flavor do you like best?" He held out his hand. "You don't have to talk if you don't want to." He smiled. "I've got a worm to feed the robins. Wanna come watch?"

I heard running feet on the stairs and adults moaning in the rooms below. I wanted out of here. I nodded and took his hand, letting him pull me to my feet.

Nicole found me in the morning doing yet another set of sheets. They had to be washed, dried, creased, and pressed to perfection. It was a job I tried to delegate as much as possible, because letting the other kids do the simple, if time-consuming, tasks like this kept them away from the dying guests.

Kids at DG were "homeschooled." But when we turned sixteen we were sent to boarding schools or to job training. I supposedly studied for my GED in the five hours a day I devoted instead to beauty sleep. I couldn't think past the next meal or load of laundry or death. I couldn't picture a future for me. I got to my sixteenth birthday and then the world blackened and I couldn't see past it. I had to start thinking about it soon, because February tenth was coming at me with its arms open and teeth bared.

I used to daydream of a time beyond this place. Kirian and I talked about backpacking across Europe or going to Mexico to live on the beach and eat seafood and coconuts. I used to imagine a wedding and a baby, a home of our own. Those rainbows evaporated and turned to ash when Kirian turned sixteen and left me here.

I have kids to think about. And the old to comfort.

"Bodie sleep with you last night? He left the attic while I cleaned up Sema's vomit," Nicole said, grabbing a set of sheets from the dryer and wrestling them into folds.

"She okay today?"

"Fine."

"Yeah, he came to me." I nodded.

"How are you feeling?"

I blinked and licked my lips. I didn't want to worry her, but something was wrong with me.

"Where do you hurt?"

"Where don't I?"

"Give me your hand."

"Why?"

"Just do it."

I held out a hand, which she grasped. "Close your eyes."

"Nicole—"

"Just do it."

I closed my eyes and she rubbed my hand. The heat of the friction felt divine. I swayed.

When she stopped she asked, "Better?"

I swallowed and did a quick inventory. "Yeah, actually. What'd you do?"

She shrugged. "You get any sleep?"

Sleep? Not in this lifetime. Bodie was a kicker. And he liked to sleep sideways across the tiny mattress. "Some. He asked about my mother."

"Not again." Nicole moaned in sympathy. "What did you tell him?"

"The usual." *I pretended.*

"Do you know anything about it, your history? What's the truth?"

I shook my head. "Not really. I asked in the beginning." But stopped asking when I heard a different story each time. "Do you know yours?"

Sadness filled her eyes. "Drugs. My parents couldn't keep me. But my uncle and aunt wanted me. Then we were separated too."

"I'm glad you know they wanted you, loved you. That has to help." Better than knowing no one cared. I flicked the yellowing cotton sheets to straighten the folds.

Nicole paused, fingering her necklace in an absent gesture. "Maybe yours loved you—"

I didn't want platitudes or empty reassurance, so I cut her off. "What's on your necklace?"

The heart-shaped silver pendant never left Nicole's neck. She kept it tucked under her clothes. I worried if Mistress saw it, she'd take it from Nicole for safekeeping, which meant it would end up on eBay. But fortunately, she never seemed to notice it.

"It's a verse from the book of Exodus." Nicole walked closer so I could read it.

All I saw was *Ex. 23:20* in tiny cursive script. "What's it mean?"

"The verse says, 'I am sending an angel ahead of you, to guard you along the way.' My family gave it to me, before we were separated."

"That's sweet." Sweeter still that with everything Nicole had been through she continued to believe in guardian angels. *I don't. I can't.* There was no evidence. I needed to see to believe.

She frowned at me. "You don't believe in angels, do you?"

I shook my head, seeing no reason to lie. "No, I don't."

"I understand." She sagged.

I felt the need to assure her that I was glad she believed. Someone should carry hope. "It's not that I don't think it's possible. I've just never seen evidence of one." *Nothing miraculous or divine or otherworldly, just stinking, obscene piles of reality.* I shrugged. "Not here."

She beamed at me. "I think you'd be surprised, Juliet."

My voice raised, anger flaring. "If there were angels they'd get us the hell out of here. Not keep us here," I argued, knowing I was right.

"Maybe they can't do that type of thing? Maybe they're just trying to help you survive?" She tucked her pendant back under her blouse and picked up a stack of finished laundry.

"What good is that?" *Surviving?* That I do on my own. "No, we're on our own." I slammed the dryer door so hard it bounced open again.

"Maybe someday you'll believe me." She paused.

"Maybe." I shrugged, filling the washer again.

"The records are all kept in that gray filing cabinet, you know? In case you want to read your file."

"It's locked." I'd snuck into Mistress's office countless times early on, hoping to gain access to my file. Maybe it gave my parents' address and contained a bus ticket home.

Nicole cocked her head, staring through me. "There's a spare key taped behind the framed picture of the Mistress's son. Just saying."

I nodded, more to acknowledge Nicole than because I planned on doing anything with the information. "Is that her son? The blond guy who looks like a movie star?"

"I assume." Nicole shrugged. A buzzer on the intercom sounded. "That's the new guy in the Green Room. I'll go." Nicole squeezed my shoulder as she went by.

When she was gone, I whispered under my breath, "Where's my angel? Why don't I deserve one, too?"

Sema ran down the hallway toward me, her pigtail braids flapping like licorice wings. Her pudgy cheeks matched a stout frame. I needed to find her bigger clothes before Mistress took exception to Sema's belly showing between her shirts and pants. She frantically said, "Come quick. Green Room is having trouble breathing."

I raced up the stairs toward the room, fury fueling my footsteps. Rage at this place and this life ate at my calm. *This isn't normal.* Kids shouldn't panic because a stranger died every couple of days. It wasn't right. It would be one thing if this was their grandparent, or another loved one, but putting a child in charge of care was abuse. I couldn't spin it any other way. Trapped, there was nowhere to go but forward.

Mistress was bent over Mr. Taylor, performing torturous CPR. "Where have you been? He just got here two hours ago. It's too soon. The paperwork hasn't been filed. Do something!" she screamed at me while thumping on his chest. I didn't understand why she couldn't just lie on his paperwork, too. But instead she seemed to be escalating her mistreatment of us all.

A wave of dizziness knocked me sideways into the doorframe. A sharp pain in my chest felt like a steak knife and needles radiated down my left arm. Nicole was there instantly. She grabbed me and I caught my breath; the nausea settled immediately.

"Where are you going, old man? Come back here, you hear me?" Mistress continued to shout questions while pumping the man's chest and forcing air into his mouth. "You're supposed to stay alive until she gets here—"

Nicole and I glanced at each other—who was this "she"? What did that have to do with him living or dying?

The hair on the back of my neck tingled; I shivered. The need for fresh mozzarella, red sauce, ricotta, basil, and garlic tickled my throat.

I found my voice as I approached the bed. "I'll do it."

She was fracturing ribs more than bringing back the dead. Compassion flooded me. No one deserved this treatment. This wasn't CPR, it was torture. I saw Mini's tail twitch under the bed frame. I moved closer and put my hand on the man's wrist to check for a pulse. *Faint, if any.*

Mistress pushed back from the bed, wild-eyed and flustered. "You take over. I can't do any more. I have an appointment in town with Ms.—" She broke off and took a deep breath. "Do not let anything else happen." Mistress dripped sweat and her reddened face showed that five minutes of exertion pushed her limited physical stamina.

"Fine." I leaned closer and listened for Mr. Taylor's breath while Mistress waddled from the room. She was the before photo for weight-loss surgery ads. I made a show of breathing into his mouth, but my heart knew he was done. Mini leaned all of her weight against my shins and warmed my toes. The dizziness and fatigue surged up again briefly, then paled to background static behind my eyes.

"She's gone." Nicole shut the bedroom door, more to shield the too-curious kids than to protect me from further confrontation with Mistress, I was sure.

"So is he." I sighed, collapsing onto the floor. Mini rubbed against me, but even her comfort wasn't helpful.

"He arrived in bad shape. I don't even know why they transferred him. Left alone he probably would have died in the hospital today." Nicole sat down next to me, not touching me, but close enough for me to feel her presence.

"Mistress is getting worse," I said.

Nicole nodded. "I know. It's like she's coming unhinged."

"There was one time when I saw her—" I couldn't say the words out loud. The horrific helplessness I'd experienced when Mistress put that needle in the vein of my honorary grandfather was unthinkable. Too much. I pushed that memory deeper. If Kirian hadn't been here I might have run away, taken my chances on the streets. And then he'd gone too and there was nothing left to fight for.

Nicole nodded as if she already knew the story.

Tears pricked my lids. I sniffed them back as Mini leapt up onto the bed and perched. She meowed plaintively.

My heart broke for Mr. Taylor's passing this way. *I try so hard to make it okay for them. For us all.*

As if I had spoken my thoughts out loud, Nicole said, "Juliet, you do more than you know." She smoothed the hair that had escaped my braid.

The tears came in a flash flood. "It's not enough."

She leaned closer, wrapping her arms around me. "Oh, my friend, it is."

Mini jumped down to me. She marked my hands and face with her head. She acted as if she could rub the bad away.

"They have no one. We have no one." I lay curled on my side, my head in Nicole's lap. Exhaustion and self-pity rolled over me. "No one." The sobs came one, then the next, with barely a pause to breathe as my frame was racked with the release of so many built-up emotions.

Nicole let me cry it out, whispering words of reassurance.

I tried to pull myself together. I hated this place. This life. The people who came here to die in front of me, day after day. The kids I cared for, like a mother, without the resources or the knowledge to do it right. "No one. We have no one."

"We have each other. And they have their families waiting. They are not alone when they die."

"I don't believe that." Furious, I sat up. How could she say such a thing? "If they had family who cared about them, they wouldn't be here. None of us would be here. If we had one person, just one, none of us would be here. Dying alone. Living alone. We're biding time, all of us, until what? Death? What's good about that? Why wait?" I beat my fists against the linoleum tiles until I knew bruises would show tomorrow. I couldn't feel the pain.

Nicole spoke softly. "There's a world you can't quite see yet. But they can see it. Feel it." Nicole rubbed my cheeks with tissues, with an expertise that belied her young years.

I snorted.

"I'm serious. There's more to all of this than you or I know. You have to trust. You have to believe. To hope."

I shook my head.

Her voice sharpened. "What good is all the hearts and flowers and rainbows you tell the kids about, if you don't let yourself believe just a little? You owe yourself a little of that faith."

"Maybe." Inside, in my deepest and darkest places, I hoped so. I hoped there was more to this than misery and suffering and god-awful loneliness. But it was a tiny hope, a hope that barely flickered, with pale light, the longer I was here. It was fading. My spirit wilted under the strain. "I don't know how much longer I can—"

"You will until you won't have to. Until." Nicole's tone was firm, inarguable. "So what are we eating while Mistress is out?"

I snorted snotty bubbles, which made us laugh. "Stuffed ravioli. Maybe a Caprese salad, if you can rustle up fresh mozzarella?"

"I wouldn't have pegged him for liking Italian. He seemed more like a meat-loaf-and-mashed-potatoes guy."

"Fond memories of his time in the service." I knew this without being able to say how. I pictured the lives of those who died here—at least, I had a solid imagination of what I thought they might have been like. I couldn't explain how I knew the deceased's favorite foods and recipes, but maybe I was just lucky with food.

Nicole took these pronouncements with easy acceptance. All the kids did. "That makes sense. I've never tasted food as good as yours."

I shrugged off the compliment. "I'm nothing special."

"Oh, Juliet, you are so special. You have to start believing that."

Impossible.

Mini stood with her front paws on my shoulders, carefully licking my face until not a trace of tears or snot remained. No need for exfoliation, either.

When we opened the door, we hugged the kids and sent them off to play hide-and-seek. Nicole waited for the funeral home to come collect the body, while I headed to the kitchen.

I put the pasta water on to simmer and made fresh noodles before Bodie came to find me. All I really wanted was sleep and the oblivion it brought, but there were hours of chores left to do before that was possible.

"There's a man here to see you," he said.

"Me?" I put the paring knife down.

"A dolt." He shrugged.

"An adult?" I loved the way Bodie's pronunciation came and went. "I guess that's me." I hoped this would be an easy interaction. Someone who wanted a pamphlet for DG or needed directions toward town.

The tallest man I'd ever seen stood in the foyer, holding a stack of colored papers. His back was to me as he studied the portraits of the house's past residents and owners with a particularly serious, straight posture. I'd looked at the portraits so much, I'd memorized their subjects' features and given them all elaborate lives for my bedtime stories.

"May I help you?" I asked. Mistress hated us talking to outsiders, but she wasn't here and I didn't want to be rude.

"Ah, lovely." His blue eyes widened and his toothy smile bloomed when he turned his attention to me. He seemed so pleased I felt slightly unnerved.

"Have we met?" I asked. His snow-white beard was tamed into an intricate braid, not unlike the French braid in my own hair.

He lost his smile. "No, I'm sorry. You reminded me of a friend. I'm Rumi. I have a glass studio down the road, in Carmel. I hoped to invite the staff here to an open house I'm having?" His sincerity put me at ease immediately, though he squinted, as if he needed glasses, when he looked at me.

"Our headmistress isn't here right now."

"That's okay. May I leave a few of these invitations?" He held the sheaf of papers toward me.

I reached to take them, even though I knew I could never give them to Mistress. I'd be punished. "Maybe a couple."

"As many as you like. I'm sorry, I didn't catch your name."

He continued to hold the papers toward me but kept his distance.

"I'm . . . Juliet." I was too tired to make up a name; he didn't feel threatening.

"Ah, lovely name."

"I guess." I shrugged off the compliment.

"Best song by my favorite band. Come by the shop and I'll play it for you." He hummed a few lines.

"Sure." I agreed with no intention, no ability, to actually take him up on the offer.

"Well, then. Are there lots of kids here?" he asked, as he moved to the door. "Your brothers and sisters?"

"Oh, no. We're foster kids." I always felt shame when I confessed that to people. As if we'd done something wrong, something to deserve this fate.

"Ah." He seemed at a loss. "Well, then. I hope we'll meet again." He paused, hesitated, and then left.

"Goodbye." I shut the door behind him, heard him whistling his way down the walk.

"Who was that?" Sema peeked her face around the column of curtains hanging in the living room. She often hid in the curtains, for hours at a time. I'd learned to look for her toes along the bottom when I entered a room.

"No one." I quickly burned the flyers in the fireplace until the invitations were charred curls of carbon. "No one," I repeated until I started to believe it.

Oh, the music I heard in the deaths tonight
makes angels weep.

Cassie Ailey

March 1878

CHAPTER 12

I'd spread Auntie's journal and a couple of notebooks out
on the cottage's kitchen table. There were only a few blank
pages left and I'd added an entry or two. I felt like what I
wrote had to be vital to be worthy of getting added. As if
a panel of my ancestors scrutinized every stroke of my
pen. Soon, the book itself would need to be changed and
maybe I'd write more in it, when all I saw was my own writing. The thick leather binding was covered in embossed
roses, windows, candles, and silhouettes of animals and insects. The paper was thin, fragile parchment. Occasionally,

I found greasy, dirty fingerprints on the pages, and the fading ink wasn't waterproof. I was searching for an entry, a mention, even a lowly sentence that might illuminate how best to figure out if Nocti or Fenestra lived in that broken place.

A Fenestra can be accustomed to the feeling of human death from a very young age. If left unaware of her talents, she can be forced to change. If a Nocti sacrifices another Fenestra in her presence she may have little choice but to combine energies with the Nocti to survive. It is a rape of her free will, of her innocence. This is where the tradition of hiding Fenestra children, out of sight of Nocti, came from.

"Almost, almost." I was close to seeing a pattern here. *Maybe.*

"What?" Tens glanced up from the laptop. He took the more modern approach to research. Since he'd discovered technology he was in love with gadgets. He even wanted me to transcribe the journal into a Word document so we could cross-reference the information better.

"I'm close," I said, not taking my eyes from the text.

"To what?"

I growled. "I don't know. Something." Right there in the fringes, in the mist, an important piece waited for me.

Custos barked and pawed at the front door.

I jumped. "Custos!" She'd been edgy all day.

A demanding knock came a few seconds later.

"That's just creepy," I muttered, and grabbed the journal, putting it under the stack of papers and tossing a napkin at the spine. If it fell into Nocti hands . . .

Tens ambled to the door. "Ready?" I saw a bulge at his back. A weapon?

I skittered away from the table. "Sure." The visitor was probably just Joi with cookies or leftover Danish.

Tens opened the door a crack, then wider. "Rumi?"

"I come bearing word of your spirit angel." The man's voice boomed like a freight train.

How does he know? I sat down. We'd never given him details about who or what we were looking for. Just mentioned a girl, not that she was a Fenestra.

"I think you'd better come in then." Tens shut the door behind him.

The herbs drying on the ceiling hooks almost smacked Rumi on the head. "Do not worry. I said nothing. She is luminiferous like you. Glows about the edges." He pointed at me.

"What do you mean, I glow?" I asked.

"As if you stand in front of the sun. You have a lambent, lightsome quality about your outline. It's fuzzy." He asked Tens, "Do you not see it?" Without waiting for a response, he turned back to me and asked, "You must see it in the mirror when you're doing your sonsy makeup and such?"

I shook my head; so did Tens. I might be denying the obvious to Rumi, yet in all honesty I didn't see the Fenestra in me that way. More like a movement outside of my vision, a brush of something or someone other.

My expression must have read as disbelieving or appalled, because Rumi lowered himself into a carved rocking chair by the fireplace. He appealed to us. "I am not mad. Eccentric, maybe, but not howling bleezed."

I couldn't hold back my laughter. "We don't think you're crazy. Honest." He appeared so completely befuddled. "Would you like some tea?" I got him a mug and pulled down the basket of assorted tea bags.

"Sure, always a good time for a cuppa. Though I prefer coffee if you've any."

"Sorry." I shrugged. We drank the stuff, but usually only if someone else made it.

"Ah, well, then give me something black and strong."

I grabbed milk and sugar, since I knew he drowned his black in white.

I poured myself grape soda and Tens a Coke.

"Tell us more about the girl." Tens picked up his drink and settled on the couch next to me.

Rumi gestured behind him toward the propane logs. "Won't be turning that on later in the week. There's a warm front coming, something fierce."

"It's going to warm up? How do you know?" I sipped.

"How did you know what to eat for breakfast?"

"Tens put it in front of me." I smiled.

Rumi beamed at me. "Ah, a cynic. I enjoy a good and cunning logodaedalus."

"The girl?" Tens prompted. Rumi's conversations wandered on tangents. Then there was his vocabulary, which a dictionary wouldn't help with; I didn't have the first clue how to spell most of the words he used.

"Ah, well. I got to thinking, about how to get a lot of people together, you know, so you could ask questions, take their vibes, listen to the chavish. Whatever it is you do." He shrugged. "I decided to host an open house at the studio to kick off Feast Week. The best way to get numbers of people to cross my path, and perhaps find this girl of yours."

Tens twitched his lips. I squirmed, trying to keep up.

Rumi took it with good humor. "I appreciate the quest, you understand. Without being trusted with full disclosure. I made a point of visiting establishments housing us elderly types since you said the girl, and the cat, are connected to a nursing home. Correct? People like to talk, so I took invitations around to see what there was to see." His gaze meandered, as if he was lost in his own thoughts. His expression grew stormy and troubled.

"And?" I prompted, leaning closer to Tens, whose face had cleared to blank alert. I wasn't sure I wanted to hear the rest of this story.

Rumi had lost a quotient of his lightness. "She's a lacerated soul. Sad one, eyes full of sausade. To the point of breaking under the omnistrain. Full of rage." He shook himself.

"You got all that by squinting at her?" I asked.

"No, of course not. She's tall, gifted with a body built to survive hard physical labor and childbirth, broad shoulders, broad hips—perhaps with the right diet she'd bloom to zaftig. She's solid. Built to withstand, you see? Long hair, longest I've seen on a girl in some time; I'd wager she's never cut more than a little at a time. Golden hair, the kind of real blond that no chemical or salon can make. Strands were white like fresh butter, others a deep burnished wheat at harvest, still more caught the light and turned lemony. Her eyes were unexpected. Those threw me a skosh."

"Blue? Green?"

"Golden brown. Glandaceous, like ripe acorns. I don't see that color often in eyes. I look into everyone's eyes—they're like glass if you're paying attention. Clear or cloudy, bright or damp. They speak. If eyes are windows into someone's soul, hers are shuttered and battened down for the big one." Rumi shivered dramatically. "But that place—Lord help the souls in there. Or maybe I should say *you* help the souls in there. I have an idea of a friend to call, but they'll need the second coming of pick-your-savior. You'll do, I suspect."

I blanched. "I'm not God." *I am so not godlike.*

"Ah, so that's the first time you've told me anything about yourself." He appeared pleased with himself, as if he'd tricked me into revealing an important detail.

I rolled my eyes, echoing Tens's grin earlier, not able to contain myself. There was an intangible quality about Rumi that persuaded me, on a very elemental level, to confide all my secrets and truths. *As if he is a designated secret keeper. Like the Señora.*

He continued. "Her name is Juliet. She is a foster child. She took the flyers I gave her, but I have the distinct impression she threw them away. There's fear in that place, a compulsion to self-protect, an ambsace. Now, what do we do? Are we on a rescue mission? I have this friend—"

Here was my most honest impulse. "I have no idea." I didn't. I'd been so concerned with finding her, I had no idea what to do once we did.

Rumi shuddered, dismissing my response. "You must have some idea. Even if it's desipient. Why are you looking for her in the first place?"

Tens broke in and told him the story we'd made up about my adoption and the quest for my biological family. It was a lie, a huge one, but the one we both could remember. I knew who my family was and I wasn't a kidney patient needing a donor, but people believed us and so we stuck with that story. I felt bad lying, but it was a necessary evil to protect ourselves. I hoped we could learn to trust Rumi, because he might very well be the most delighted person in the world to find out the truth.

Rumi set his mug of tea on the table and first looked Tens square in the eye, then me. "Now, I understand you don't know if you can trust me. I honestly do apperceive that. It disappoints me, but I can work with that reality. I can also moil helping you—without knowing why, or what—if there's a larger picture we're bringing to light. But under no circumstances do I want lies." He pointed at me. "You were sick, yes, but it was soul sickness, not some kidney problem and you're well on your way to whole. Simply tell ol' Rumi you can't answer, but don't lie to me. Fair enough?"

Tens nodded. "Fair enough."

I stuttered, torn by the inexplicable feeling that given a chance, I could trust him. "I *want* to—"

"And someday you will trust me. Someday, I will beg

you to shut up, I'm sure, but until then we will be about getting to know each other. I brought you some of my Nain's artwork to look at. They may prove helpful. Or not. I'll leave them for you so you can react without my audience."

Thoughtful. "Thank you."

"Do not mention it, but return them to me tomorrow night at seven." He stood.

"Seven?" I asked.

"I'm having a dinner party to introduce you to several local folks who can be counted on."

I panicked. "I don't know—"

He brushed aside my reluctance. "Small. Just a few people. They may be helpful. They may not. But it is a place to inchoate, to start, while you decide if you're going to help me rescue that poor girl or if I'm going to have to act rashly and artistically."

"Don't." Tens put his hand on Rumi's massive forearm. "Give us until then to talk things through. There are many pieces to this—"

"And many things that could go wrong, a *schlimmbesserung,* if we're not careful. Fair enough." Rumi let Custos clean his hands, then he left, whistling a jaunty tune that belonged on the sea.

I blew out a breath as the door shut behind him. "Wow, um . . ."

"He's a force of nature." Tens's tone reflected my own feelings.

I paused. "Do you think really?"

"No, an expression. But he's definitely demanding and used to getting his way. He makes me feel really dumb."

"He doesn't mean to, but I think he'd make everyone feel stupid and babbling."

"A good ally, perhaps?"

"Maybe. I think so."

I started to unfold the pages in the wooden box Rumi had left. The pages were brittle and browning; most were black ink line drawings, others were colored in with watercolors or pastels.

All windows.

"Tens." My tone must have imparted warning, because he was at my side in a blink.

All the windows were the same. A large rectangle topped with a half circle. Each window was divided into four panes with cross bracing, and the half circle was filled with a sun, its rays unfurled like flower petals to fill the space.

Tens exhaled as he took one page after another from my hands.

The scenery beyond the windows was tiny. Intricate views, a few even showing people waiting on the other side. As if by viewing these pieces of parchment, we also saw a soul's personal window. They were images so similar to things I'd experienced, to ones Auntie had shared with us or that were mentioned in the family journal, my breath hitched. Dumbstruck, I stared for a moment. *Rumi knows things. His knowledge is about Fenestras. Spirit angels. Good Death. All synonyms?*

"He's right," Tens concluded, flipping through the pages once, twice, and again.

"He really is." Disbelief that we'd found someone, any-one, who could add to our knowledge of Fenestras settled into a tangible tension. Relief. Fear. Excitement.

Custos whined.

"He said there were writings, too, right?"

"Yes, but they're not in English," Tens cautioned, as he held a piece of parchment up.

"So, we have him translate it for us," I said.

"That'll mean trusting him."

"We have to." I sat staring at the art, trying to take in this revelation. "Let's go find Juliet."

"Do you have a plan?"

"No, but I can feel that we're in the right place."

"Good enough." Tens shrugged and picked up the truck keys. "Let's go."

* * *

Custos crouched behind us, every so often turning her nose to the air or the ground and puffing like a bellows.

"We should see if Bodie's out here first." I hoped he would be.

"Then what? We knock on the front door?"

"Maybe." I didn't think so. *Not yet.*

I prayed Bodie would be hiding up in his tree so we could get him to bring Juliet out to us, rather than risk knocking on the door and coming face to face with a Nocti or worse. *We tell her we're friends. She'll know it instinctively and she'll come with us. That's how it will play out. That's how it* has *to play out.*

Hours ticked by while we waited along the creek side. I think I dozed a little, until my legs cramped up from sitting still for so long. "He's not coming out." I was disappointed.

"He doesn't know we're here." Tens flexed his feet and knees.

"Should we try again in the morning?" I started to stand.

"Wait, I see movement." Tens put his hand on my arm.

Custos's tail beat an excited thump. An animal pranced from the shadows and purred while it rubbed itself along her legs. Custos sniffed it all over and licked its face.

"Is that a cat?" It looked more like walking furniture, an ottoman, or even a horse. It looked at me like it completely understood my thoughts. "Is that the cat from the news—"

"That's the cat I saw before." Tens reached out a hand to touch it. When his fingers met the cat's fur he froze.

"Tens! Tens!" I couldn't break their contact. The cat too stilled, in midstretch.

Tens didn't breathe, didn't move. *What do I do? What do I do? Break their contact. I have to break their contact.*

I tackled him. It was like running into a concrete wall, but he dropped to the ground with a *whoosh*. The cat twitched its tail, coiling and uncoiling, while it glared at me.

Tens lay there gasping for breath, coughing oxygen back into his lungs.

"What the hell was that?" I touched his face and chest, and shooed at the cat, trying to get space. Custos seemed completely unperturbed. *Bad kitty. Bad, bad kitty.*

"Wow. Give me a minute." Tens blinked, inhaling deep breaths.

"What happened?" I kept myself between him and the cat, ready to intrude before the creature did any even crazier freezing.

"What did it look like?" Tens asked, not moving his head, staring up at the sky.

"You froze like in a cartoon." *Like a scary Medusa-turning-to-stone, crazy abandon-me thing.*

His breathing evened out, but I watched his pulse flutter like a hummingbird hovering at the base of his throat. "That's what it felt like. Only more like a download."

"What?" I glanced at the cat. *Computer cat?*

"Minerva. The cat's name is Minerva. She's of the Creator. She scolded us for taking so long."

I shot the cat a dirty look. "Really."

"She says Juliet is who we're here to help. And it's getting dicey."

"Oh? Did you tell her if we'd had GPS coordinates, or a special forces team to command, maybe this wouldn't have taken so long?" I paused, getting in his face. "Are you making this up? Playing with me?" *This is a really bad time for Tens to get a sense of humor.*

Tens didn't respond, just gripped my hand.

Okay, not playing. "What else?" I asked.

"Minerva and Custos go way back." He blinked, and tears dripped from the corners of his eyes, not tears from crying, but like tears from peering at the sun too long.

"They know each other?"

"Yeah, they do."

I nodded. "Custos is more than—"

"She's a Protector's animal to call."

"And the cat is a Fenestra's? Is that why Custos found you?" Hmm, at least it was nice to know more of the truth rather than having to fill in the blanks with guesses.

"More like sought me out, maybe?"

"Interesting."

"Minerva says there's another of the Creator in there helping, keeping Juliet alive. But there's a Nocti, too, a powerful, ancient evil, coming and going."

I refused to consider the fact we were now talking to animals and taking their words at face value. What did it say about us that a cat and a wolf were our guides?

I blew out a disappointed breath. *Does there have to be a Nocti in there too?*

"She says we're to come back tomorrow. Be here in the morning, before the sun."

With that the cat gave Tens another swat with her paw, twitched her tail at me, and trotted back into the bushes. Custos rolled over on her back and wagged her tail with her tongue touching the ground. She barked, looking at us upside down, and scratched her back by wiggling in the grass.

When we looked back, Minerva was gone. I hoped she'd left to make Juliet's life a bit more bearable. "I'm going to go out on a limb and say the Creators have a sense of humor."

Tens rolled to his feet, moving slowly.

"Are you sure you're okay?" I hugged his side to steady him.

"I feel like I ran headfirst into a wall. Wow." He leaned on me as we wandered back down the path.

"So we come back in the morning?"

Come back and do what? Specifics, Minerva? Is that asking too much?

I rested at a house bearing our welcome orna-
ment. Those who can see have the kindest hearts.

Lucinda Myer

1786

CHAPTER 13

I drove us back to the cottage, snatching glances at Tens.
When we arrived, he collapsed on the bed.

"Stop staring at me, I'm fine," he mumbled against the
pillows, his eyes squeezed shut.

I turned my back and tried to noiselessly tidy up the
kitchen. The space was tight and I found it impossible to
be quiet. The more I tried, the louder I became. Finally, I
dropped a glass and it shattered. Cleaning it up was even
noisier.

Tens covered his head with a pillow and growled, "Too

much noise. Go shopping, wander—buy something to wear tonight."

"Rumi's dinner party? I don't think so. I'm canceling." I'd forgotten about it, but no way was Tens up to being social.

"No, you're not. I'll be fine once I get some sleep. Go away for a little while. Please?" He whined the last bit.

He was right in a weird way. The only clothes I had were ones we'd picked up at chain stores. Things that came in packages of three or were under five bucks a pop, items that we could grab and go. Jeans didn't quite fit; T-shirts either hung loose or were too tight. Not a skirt to see, since I'd ditched my old private-school uniform at Auntie's. "Are you sure?"

"Uh-huh. Positive. Go wild. Buy me a new shirt, too. Whatever."

"How about boots?"

"If you can find fourteens."

"Is that big?" No clue here. Sammy was just out of boys extra-small.

"Yeah, good luck. Focus on the possible. Now go." He turned his back to me. "Custos, keep an eye on her."

I wagged my finger at Custos. "Stay." If I wasn't here to protect him, she needed to be. Especially if she had a red phone line to the Powers with powers.

Thankfully, cute boutiques lined the streets of Carmel. I found a little black dress that was comfortable and classy but still leaned toward sexy. Perfect for impressing Tens embarrassing the old people at dinner.

I searched for boots for Tens, but only found ones that went up to a twelve. The shirt was easier. I bought a dressy rugby shirt in a cotton-cashmere blend that mirrored the blue of Colorado's sky. It was a selfish purchase because Tens would look amazing and be irresistible to touch wearing something so soft and cozy.

That night while he showered, I admired myself in the mirror. The black knit dress fit my blossoming curves. Thin screamed ill to me, so filling it out felt right—it felt healthy and alive. I no longer resembled a starvation victim. I guessed there'd be a time or a point when I might want to stop gaining weight, but I was nowhere near that yet.

I pinned my hair up and put on the chandelier earrings I'd bought. They made my neck look long and graceful, but quite bare. "Are you sure you feel okay?" I asked Tens, as he came out of the bathroom dressed, his hair tousled and damp against his collar.

"Yep, sleep helped."

I thought he was lying, but I let it go. "Do I look all right?"

"Hmm." Tens studied me. "You're missing something."

"A sweater?" *It might be colder than it looks. January isn't July.*

"Maybe, but open this." Tens handed me a gift bag exploding with colored tissues and ribbons. The Helios crest decorated the outside of the bag.

I reached in and immediately knew by feel that this was the stunning emerald green velvet scarf I'd coveted when we'd first arrived. The one Joi had purposefully commented on with a wink for Tens.

"I was saving it for a special occasion." Tens wrapped it around my neck and let it drape carefully across my collarbones and over my breasts.

"Thank you." I leaned up and kissed him quickly, adoring the feel of the velvet on my bare skin. It fluttered as I moved and grew warm, as if I carried a living creature twined around my neck. Hugging him, I knew I'd made the right shirt choice—he rocked the blue.

He gazed down at me. "You're beautiful. Always beautiful, Supergirl."

"Even in SpongeBob flannels?" I teased.

"I'm terribly disappointed those no longer fit." Tens's voice dropped to a gravel pitch and hinted more than a little.

"Those were sexy." I laughed until my heart seized with the memory. *Sammy gave them to me.*

"You miss him, don't you?"

I didn't pretend to misunderstand Tens. This was one of those times he knew my heart better than me. "More than words. I hope he's okay."

He rested his head on the crown of mine. "I'd know if he wasn't. I'm sure I'd know."

"You think?" I breathed in his warmth, his steady heartbeat.

His tone completely confident, he rushed to assure me. "I'm sure. I'm supposed to protect you. How can I do that if things like that sneak up on me? Maybe we should try to find them?"

"Maybe." I tensed. *Can I take that? Can I talk to my mom and not scream at her, or hate her, or say all the things I've shoved deep?*

"When you're ready, okay?" He backed off.

"Not yet." I was still blindingly angry with my mother. I wasn't as upset with my father, who'd been kept in the dark as much as me. *What did he think when the dead piled up around me? When I seemed plagued with illness and injury and ghosts?* I knew what he'd thought. The same things I'd assumed, the names I'd heard whispered at my back. *Freak. Sideshow act. Witch.*

My mother was the one who'd never told us. Not until it was too late and the Nocti had already found me. Us. Not until I'd been shipped off to Revelation and my parents took my little brother to run to points unknown. I wasn't sure I'd ever be able to forgive her blatant omissions of what could have saved us all so much pain and suffering. *If only she'd told me.*

"It might help to hear what she has to say." Tens stepped away, pulling me toward the door.

I shook my head. "We're going to be late." Changing the subject abruptly, I twined my fingers in Tens's and we hurried on foot to Meridian Street and Rumi's home. The air felt heavy with moisture, like we were standing beside the ocean.

Rumi's living quarters were in the back of his warehouse studio and gallery. The entrance was a sliding glass patio door.

We hadn't even knocked before he slid the door open. "Come in, come in." Soaring strings played in the background, and candlelight danced behind forged iron lanterns and candlesticks. Scents of grilled red meat and hot bread, along with those of hyacinths and paperwhites, drifted over us. The lively chatter of guests wasn't off-putting, but instead relaxed me immediately. The whole evening felt friendly and open.

I was unsure of what to expect because I rarely had good experiences in groups of people. I avoided crowds.

The soaring ceilings of the industrial space seemed like the only way a man of Rumi's stature wouldn't feel confined. Tibetan prayer flags hung from the rafters. I glanced around quickly, surprised to see very little glass, very little of anything. The decor was almost monastic. Few electronics, save a small stereo system, and bare walls dotted with wood mandalas and natural elements like driftwood and bird-feather wreaths that brought the outside in. The palette was browns, greens, and creams. Calming and meditative. The furniture was wood or iron, or a combination of both. It was the opposite of the candy-bright breakable clutter of the glass studio beyond the dividing wall.

I tried to hand Rumi a bag with his archives in it. "We'd like to look at these again if it's possible," I whispered.

"Just keep them for now," he answered in hushed tones, and set the bag with our coats. "Let me introduce you to my friends." Rumi circled the group and made introductions. Everyone else seemed very familiar with each other. With the exception of one woman, Nelli, who worked for the attorney general investigating abuse and neglect in the Department of Child Services, they all looked like they'd been AARP eligible for decades. Which didn't mean they appeared infirm, or diminished in any way. The opposite was true; this was the vibrancy I had seen in Auntie beyond the window, not the dying person I'd met in Colorado. I was only beginning to understand how much work, how hard it was for most people to die.

Rumi referred to all of them as Ms. or Mr. and their first name, as if he owed them a respect that couldn't be achieved on a first-name basis alone. None of them seemed to find it odd that a couple of teenagers were joining what felt like a regular gathering.

We sat down to eat almost immediately. The table was an impressive expanse of solid burl wood, topped with glass. Each place setting matched itself, but the items clearly came from different artists, working in different mediums. Even the silverware was to each its own pattern. Juicy, garlicy meat loaf, creamy scalloped potatoes, blanched greens with slivered almonds, French bread, and salads full of bright colors and textures were placed on the table and passed around family style. I sat by Tens, and Rumi and Gus took the ends, which left Faye, Sidika, and Nelli across from us.

The conversation was pleasant but not heady, until Rumi asked all of us to share a little more about ourselves.

Gus began, his full white mustache that curled at the ends bracketing his mouth. "I'm a retired history professor from Butler University. These days, I teach occasional classes. But mostly I'm a reenactor." He pushed his wire-framed glasses up his nose with every other word.

"I'm sorry?" Tens asked my question, while everyone else nodded.

"I dress up and reenact battles from Indiana's past. Jolly times. Uniforms, guns, cannons. Good fun." He rolled up his sleeves, exposing sinewy, freckled forearms.

"Like the Civil War guys?" I asked.

He beamed, flashing cigarette-stained teeth. "Exactly, only around here there are more options than blue versus gray."

Faye chuckled and shook her electric-red chin-length bob. "If you consider sleeping on the ground and eating hardtack fun . . . maybe." Her manicure was an unmarred coral and she wore multiple rings on each finger. Her olive complexion hinted at Greek or Italian roots, but her accent was one I was coming to associate with Hoosiers.

"Ah, you're just jealous of our state-of-the-art washing facilities," Gus teased her.

She spoke directly to Tens and me, gesticulating wildly. "They're making them use Porta-Potties for the environment these days, or they'd still be peeing behind trees. I'm so happy I'm not a pioneer woman with all those layers of skirts. Can you imagine trying to defecate with dignity back then?"

I snorted cider bubbles up my nose. Not what I had expected to hear from that wrinkled, good-natured mouth. I shook my head because she seemed to be waiting for my answer.

The conversation lulled while we ate. But at Rumi's urging, the introductions continued: "It's terribly hard to follow that mental image, but I write historical Indiana fiction, mostly about teenagers." Sidika's white hair reminded me of dandelion fluff. Her eyes sparkled with humor and her pastel pink chamois shirt was unbuttoned at the neck, revealing a chain with a gold wedding band hanging close to her heart.

"Fabulous novels," Rumi boomed.

"You're too kind." She blushed with an honest humility and patted his hand.

Nelli, the youngest adult, picked up the conversation. "I'm Gus's niece, and I worked for Rumi when I was in high school." She laughed. "I tried to keep him stocked in pens—"

"Now, now!" Rumi interrupted. "Don't be telling all my faults."

Nelli's dimple flashed. "I used to carry around a little dictionary to sort out his vocabulary, but while I was trying to find one word he'd throw out the next one and I'd get all confused." She leaned in conspiratorially. "Don't bother, just go with the flow and if you don't understand a word ask him for a synonym until he says a word you know."

Rumi's laughter erupted. "That's the impertinence that got you fired."

"I went to college."

"Same difference!" he called.

Gus turned his full attention to Tens. "Tell us about your name. Is Tens short for something?"

Tens wiped his mouth with his napkin and set down his fork. "Hmm, yeah, it's, um . . . Tenskawtawa."

Gus's face lit up, as did Sidika's. "Oh. For Tecumseh's brother?"

"Who?" Tens asked, his eyes widening in question.

"Are you from around here?" Sidika clucked.

"No, I grew up mostly in Seattle." His expression said that wasn't quite the whole story.

"Your parents, then, must be from the area?" Gus asked.

"Not that I'm aware of."

"Strange. Do you have Native American ancestors?"

This question helped Tens relax a minute amount. He hated being in the spotlight, but I couldn't rescue him because I didn't know the answers to give. Frankly, I was just as curious as everyone else about what he might say.

Tens nodded. "My mother's family. My grandfather was Cherokee and my grandmother was Shawnee. My grandmother named me, I think. . . ."

Gus nodded his agreement. "That's it, then. You'll see a lot of Tecumseh's name around here. On schools and roads and monuments. The brothers formed a town called Prophetstown. Up until the interests of Tecumseh's people clashed with those of the fledgling American government—this wasn't a good thing. His brother, Tenskawtawa, is much less understood and documented."

"Figures," Tens muttered.

"What else?" I asked, to keep the conversation heading in this direction.

"His name came to be synonymous with 'the Prophet,' and he had quite the band of followers. He was steadfast in his beliefs, not given to compromise, didn't see the need to change for the sake of his people. He was an all-or-nothing kind of guy. Some might say he was not quite right in the head. Others suggest he had religious visions. But that tends to be what historians conclude when they're writing from the opposite point of view of their subject."

The entire table nodded. "True. Much easier to say someone is crazy, then it is to try to understand their perspective," Sidika concurred.

"And if I may ask your last name, child?" Gus gesticulated with his fork.

"Valdes."

"With an accent mark, or no?"

Why does that matter?

"No," Tens answered.

"Cuban?"

"I think so. Maybe. It's murky. My father's parents came from there. I don't know much."

I needed to bring Tens to dinner parties more often. Who knew he'd open up when questioned by other people? Why didn't he answer my questions this easily?

"Do you know the history of your surname, then?"

"No. Is there one?"

"Of course. All names have history. That's what gives us scholars something to study." Gus smiled.

There was a collective chuckle and Rumi proposed a toast to scholarship and study. "You don't grow old when your mind is busy," he added.

"Pshaw. My knees and knuckles grandly disagree with you!" Faye said with a smile. "Now, tell us more about this Valdés history, Gus."

He swallowed and wiped his spotless mouth precisely with his napkin before saying, "Infants at a particular orphanage were placed in a turnstile door and a bell was rung. The nuns would come out to retrieve the baby; they'd take care of him and educate him until he reached adulthood. It was founded by Bishop Valdés of Cuba. Male children were taken in on the condition that boys who were raised at Casa de Beneficencia be given his surname, but without the accent on the *e*."

"Why not?" I asked.

"That way, his biological relative who kept the accent would remain recognizable. They did this until the nineteen fifties, when they started picking surnames randomly from the telephone directory. Much less romantic."

"So perhaps your paternal grandfather was an orphan?" Sidika asked.

Tens shrugged. "It's possible, I guess."

I knew he wasn't trying to be evasive.

"And Meridian, where are you from originally?" Faye seemed to deliberately direct conversation away from Tens's obvious discomfort.

"Portland."

"And are you still in school?"

"No, I'm taking some time off."

Rumi turned the conversation to the town's politics and public education. Then a heated discussion erupted about the war, the attorney general's new investigative branch into child and elder care, and an even hotter dissection of global warming legislation.

I enjoyed listening. I admired passionate people with strong opinions. They made life more interesting. I found the more I let myself be myself, the stronger I felt about almost every subject. I didn't know if that was being a Fenestra and getting pieces from other people, or if that was me alone claiming my own skin. What my father might have referred to as growing up. I wasn't sure I knew how my father or my mother felt about any of these issues. They didn't just ignore my Fenestra fallouts, they kept our interactions as shallow as possible. Fear made people do the unthinkable.

Rumi asked Nelli about her current caseload. She was slammed with reports of missing children lost in the system. Her job was more puzzle and private investigator than social worker at the moment. I started to eavesdrop, but didn't catch much before Faye turned to me and asked, "Will you be going to the Feast of the Fireflies along the Wabash?"

Tens and I shared a questioning glance. "What is that?"

The other conversations died away as everyone gave their attention to our ignorance. I think we were the entertainment for the evening in the way visitors allow residents to be tourists for an hour, or a week.

"It's a grand celebration that commemorates the French and Native American traders who met together annually at Fort Ouiatenon in the mid–seventeen hundreds."

"There's more to it than that." Rumi refilled the adults'

glasses with wine and ours with sparkling cider. "Miss Sidika, tell us the story?"

"Oh, well—"

"Please. A favor to me. Our new arrivals should know the histories we celebrate in these parts." Rumi winked at me.

She settled back in her chair, contemplated where to begin, and said, "Okay then, the lore says that a French settler child got lost in the woods along the Wabash River. It was late winter, around this time of year, and unusually snowy, quite cold."

Gus interrupted. "So cold, the Wabash itself froze over solid."

Sidika nodded and continued. "The animals all went to earth or fled. Food was not plentiful in the best of winters, but in this one, food was scarcest. Bark was boiled for teas; people even started to make mud griddle cakes, simply to put weight in their bellies.

"Now, the division of labor was rather simple in those days. Gender roles were clear when possible, but not always. The hard life on the frontier made it so everyone, all ages, carried a huge burden for survival. The children checked the traps for small animals like muskrats and beavers, while the men went out after bigger game like deer, bear, or wild turkey. These kids—who we'd consider young, probably between ages seven and ten, maybe younger—bundled up in furs and set out as usual. Hungry, cold, but determined to bring home some tiny morsel of food for their families."

"The ladies?" Faye asked.

"Stayed behind tending the youngest, but also very much in charge of security at the fort. By that time there was nothing worth stealing, except lives."

Sidika paused for a sip of wine, then picked up her story. "The men set off in the opposite direction from the kids, trying to follow deer tracks. Hours later, all the boys came home, save one. No one remembered seeing him and they'd stayed tightly together, so not one of them knew when he'd become lost.

"Now, this lost boy was the son of a lieutenant, the mayor of sorts for the fort. He was the son of an important man, a man who understood and respected the ways of the indigenous peoples. The boy, and his father, had several friends among the local tribes. At first, the settlers believed that he must have set off to visit his friends."

"A typical kid." Rumi smiled his words and sighed.

Sidika shrugged. "He was in big trouble, but no one worried too much until the men came home. With them was a warrior. He was said to be brave and strong and connected to the spirit world. He came to find the men because fireflies had appeared to him. They'd told him that the boy was injured and had an important destiny. It was too early in the seasons for fireflies to appear, but this man didn't make up stories, so the lieutenant believed him."

"What was the boy's destiny?" I asked, imagining all kinds of possibilities.

She smiled at me and waggled her eyebrows. "That's part of the story. By this time, the winds had picked up, and blown snow into chest-high drifts, which made foot-prints and tracks impossible to find. It was very danger-ous for anyone to set out in the storm, but the boy's father refused to abandon him. The rest of his family had per-ished the winter prior; his son was all he had left. So the father left the fort, knowing he might very well freeze to death before finding his son.

"The warrior knew the pain this father felt as his own; he asked the fireflies to guide them to the little boy.

"A swarm of fireflies appeared and lit up the sky. They created so much light and so much heat that the two men didn't need their lanterns; instead they followed the glow of the insects, along the banks of the Wabash. They hiked over downed trees and through thickets of brambles. The father thought they were going too far—what little boy could walk that far in chest-high snow and survive? But giving up was not an option. He kept plowing on, taking turns with his friend to break the path, trying to find his child."

I pictured Tens and me, searching for Celia, the little girl lost in the woods behind Auntie's home in Colorado. Celia had been lured into those woods and tricked into stepping into a brutal foot trap. The trap mangled her leg. By the time we found her she was dying from loss of blood and hypothermia. She tried to use me to pass into the afterlife, but we found out afterward that Perimo had sucked her through to hell—which was why she hadn't killed me in her attempt. I will never see Dora the Explorer without also seeing Celia's twisted, shredded leg. I knew what plowing through the snow hoping to find a child alive felt like. I knew what finding a child critically ill and dying felt like too. Perimo had used my grief against me in the caves. Tens and I shared a brief frown—he'd picked up on my feelings.

Sidika continued. "In the distance, the sun rose. The father began to lose all hope. For what little boy could survive all day, and all night, out there alone? The man broke down and wept. The warrior pulled him to his feet and told him that the sun didn't rise in that direction—the sun rose behind them, so whatever was glowing up ahead was not the sun. It was still night.

"The snow around them began to disappear, melting in patches. The closer they drew to the light, the less snow there was, and the more bare earth was visible. At the brightest point, where the fireflies numbered thousands their light was constant and not a pulse, fresh shoots of wild onion and greens broke the earth like on a June afternoon. Berries, already ripe, hung heavy on limbs of vines and honeycombs dripped in the hollows of trees. Persimmon and black walnut trees bent under their edible burdens. Birds sang in the trees and fat rabbits hopped under the men's feet. They heard water rushing close by; unsure what they heard, it took them a moment to realize they'd forgotten the sound of the Wabash River at its springtime peak.

"There, surrounded by fireflies, lay the young boy sound asleep. He'd pulled his furs off to make a pillow; his face was covered with berry juice, his fingers sticky with honey. He'd clearly eaten his fill of the food he could reach, but one of his legs was stuck deep in the earth, so tangled in an old, rotted stump that he'd been unable to remove it."

My stomach clenched. I knew what tangled legs looked like. But I prayed this story had a better ending than mine.

"The father and the warrior ate their fill, drank from the river until their thirst was quenched. While the child slept, they dug out the earth around his leg, the dirt gifting them with rabbits, beavers, and possums hibernating in that old tree. They piled the animals on their sledge to take back to the fort for the others to eat. Finally, they pulled the child's leg from the log. He was unhurt.

"They picked berries and persimmons, dug onions and roots, harvested honey and wild corn, and added those to their sled. The fireflies waited, keeping the earth warm and the light blazing until the men could carry no more. By then, the snowstorm outside of their bubble had stopped, the sun rose in the east, and the men easily saw their trail back toward their home and Fort Ouiatenon.

"One by one, the fireflies disappeared until it was as if they'd never existed. The Wabash froze again, and the vines and trees and earth disappeared back under the blanket of winter."

"I love this story." Faye sighed. "Such a happy one."

Sidika grinned at her. "Shall I finish?"

"Please," I said, clearing my throat to get the word out.

"The trio arrived back at the fort, where another

mother and child had starved to death in the night and the mood was desperate and somber. They unloaded the food alongside the tables. The lieutenant sent the warrior to bring his people to feast with them, because they, too, were suffering from the long, brutal winter.

"The first Americans came bringing wood and dried animal dung for bonfires. The settlers pulled out their instruments; there was singing, dancing, and rejoicing. The flow of food never ended. For three days and three nights, the stacks of food among the tables never diminished. The more they shared, the more food appeared. Word spread and more people arrived looking for their own miracle. Then, on the third day, the sun rose high in the sky and warmed the earth, clearing away the ice and snow from around the fort. The food lasted another month, slowly disappearing until spring was in full swing and the settlers didn't need it anymore.

"When questioned, the boy said he'd seen a firefly and followed it, thinking it was his mother calling to him."

Gus broke in. "So every year we Hoosiers from around the state, from all kinds of backgrounds, gather at the fort and along the banks of the Wabash to feast and rejoice at the nearing of spring. We burn big bonfires to chase away the darkness and welcome in the light. There's eating and drinking and whatnot. People dress in costume and re-enact the search for the boy, and children dress as fireflies." He shook his head with regret. "Most people don't even know why we're there. Not really."

"Don't sound bitter, honey." Faye patted his hand.

"History teaches us things about ourselves, but you have to listen for the lessons. You have to be really still to hear the whispers."

My mind was stuck back on the little boy and whatever this destiny of his was. "What was his destiny? Just to feed all the people?"

Sidika answered. "That, and he grew up to advocate in the fledging American government for the rights of the indigenous people. He purchased land so his friends had a place to live out their lives their own way. He organized and spoke about tolerance and respect. He signed the Declaration of Independence and then traveled to France to help in their revolution. He did many great things that he's very well known for, but that winter he was simply the boy who'd followed his mother's soul in the firefly."

Gus added, "So we remember him as such."

"Animals are spectacular creatures," Rumi declared.

"I like it." I saw the story play out as a movie in my mind.

Tens asked, "When is the Feast?"

"Soon, coming right up. I sell my glass there. Beads, vases, delicate butterflies and fireflies, and the Spirit Stones, of course. It's a good way to meet all kinds of people. Blacksmiths and history nuts, plus there's a big concert on the final night. *Dolce vita*."

"Sounds lovely. Of course we'll have to go." I knew Tens was thinking the same thing.

"Who'd like dessert?" Rumi stood.

"Please." Tens raised his hand and made the table laugh.

"Oh, to be young again." Gus smiled at me.

"Speak for yourself. My wisdom is ageless." With a grin, Faye lightly swatted him.

"Yes, but your metabolism isn't."

**I loved your father. He wanted you as much as
I did.**   **—R.**

CHAPTER 14

Juliet

I'll run away. Before my sixteenth birthday I could leave. Pack my stuff. Head south and sleep on the beach. Get jobs cleaning. Cooking.

And leave the kids? Leave Bodie and Nicole to suffer this alone? Leave whatever kids might show up between now and February tenth?

I focused my attention on the creek ahead of me. The water crept by, muddy brown like hot chocolate. The trees were giant stacks of chopsticks and toothpicks reaching for spring. Noses of turtles broke the surface of the icy water. In the murky water, catfish seemed as big as the Loch Ness Monster itself. Damselflies flitted along the banks with cardinals, and scampering gray squirrels were mere shapes and illusions of movement.

I curled over my stomach. *Coward.* I wouldn't leave. Couldn't leave the kids behind. Couldn't take them with me. I'd be reported for kidnapping. I'd end up in prison. Would it be worse than DG? Could it be? If I was honest with myself, odds were even that the roughest place for a juvenile had to be better than this. I was almost at the point where I was willing to try. Willing to risk and see. But then, I'd be stuck in that prison instead of this one, the kids would come right back here, and I'd never be able to help them. No kid had ever stayed at DG beyond their sixteenth birthday—why was I so set on being the first? I could barely look past this minute. The future overwhelmed and evaded me, like trying to find a particular salt molecule in the entire dark ocean.

No, I must stay. Maybe I could convince Mistress to let me work here until I was eighteen. If I worked harder, promised more of me, somehow found more hours to slave, hid my injuries better. I was too afraid, too paralyzed to do more than stay and tell myself I didn't care what happened next. Maybe if I repeated to myself that I didn't care, said it enough, I'd start to believe it.

I pulled out the postcard Ms. Asura had given me. I'd tucked it into my shoe so Mistress wouldn't find it. *Kirian.* I was thirteen when he'd left in the night, no goodbye, no kiss.

I'd thought he was my family, my friend, my boyfriend. And then he left me here. Occasionally, I got postcards like this one, passed through Ms. Asura. *Miss you. Working hard to save up for us. I love you, Kirian.*

> *In the dark of the attic, Kirian reached his hand out and touched mine. We entwined our fingers. My heart beat so hard I was sure he could hear it.*
>
> *"Where should we go first?"*
>
> *"Hollywood," he answered.*
>
> *"Why?"*
>
> *"Lots of beaches, and we can camp on the sand."*
>
> *"I'll cook."*
>
> *"We can start a restaurant. You'll do the food and I'll—"*
>
> *"Take care of our children!" I giggled.*
>
> *"Kids?" He guffawed. "How many?"*
>
> *"Lots and lots and lots. And pets. I want a potbellied pig like Miss Claudia talked about."*
>
> *"A pig?"*
>
> *"And a dog. A parrot."*
>
> *"No cat?"*
>
> *"Of course, and a horse."*
>
> *"A horse, of course!"*

Evening fell around me. I stole ten minutes out here while the kids finished eating and Mistress was still away. Nights were seasonally cold, with ice and frost, but the days were oddly warm—enough so I didn't need to be in more than shirtsleeves to sit outside. My thrift-store hand-me-downs had fewer threads than were ideal. We could scavenge anything from the belongings of those who left in body bags. By the time it was our turn, nothing of value remained. But I could at least squirrel away clothes that kids might sleep in, or play in, or layer on during the cold nights when Mistress refused to heat the attic and they all huddled in a pile. Tonight, I wore a purple wool cardigan. Mrs. Mahoney's sweater had the faintest hint of lavender soap clinging to it, no matter the number of times I washed it. There was a time when I had sat with all the guests and listened to their stories and knew their names and histories.

I chewed on my cuticles. The sting and pinch as I peeled skin back made me feel something, which I desperately needed. My fingers looked as if I'd taken a cheese shredder to them. They bled. Often and profusely. I tried not to pick at them, I really did. But the blood reminded me I lived, at least for now, and the sting of disinfectant while I cleaned helped keep me awake. Not even NoDoz kept me going like pain.

I pulled off my shoes and socks and tucked my toes into the water and mud along the creek bed. My crooked and swollen toes quickly stiffened with cold and the rest of me was racked with a chill. Numbing.

I turned my head to rest it on my knees, so I was able to stare at DG behind me. The three stories of dormers and white columns gave it a stately if neglected appearance. Up close the paint was yellowed and chipped, far away it was harder to tell. Mistress would make the kids paint the house this summer. *I won't be here to help.*

DG was the only home I'd ever really known. I didn't remember anything before arriving here. Nothing solid. Just feelings and fuzzy dreams that I was fairly certain I made up to make my reality more bearable.

There was staff employed by Mistress to help with the guests, to clean, to repair, but mostly to keep an eye on us kids. Some of them were chasing their own American dreams, illegally and in the shadows, keeping their heads down to get paid. Not seeing us. Others filled the air with the scent of unprosecuted criminals—people for whom the system failed the rest of us. Of these, I made sure they were never left alone with a kid or a guest, but there was only so much I could control.

The few times an employee seemed to notice, to actually witness what happened here and worry for us, they stopped coming to work. I didn't know what happened to them. They disappeared as quickly and mutely as they came.

But one woman, Miss Katie, asked me many questions, took photographs of bruises, told me things, things about why this wasn't the way the world should be. *That not all places were like this. That the police would help us.* With wide eyes one evening before she left, she snuck me a scrap of paper with her cell-phone number on it and told me to call her any time, that if I needed to get out, she'd help me. She stopped coming in to work and when I called that number a week later I'm fairly certain Mistress was the one who answered.

People who cared didn't care for long. This left us with people who didn't speak English, and while their eyes worked fine, they were blinded by fear, or necessity, or something else. Victims, prisoners, like the rest of us. No one was going to rescue us.

> "I don't care what they say. I'm not leaving without you."
> "They'll make you."
> "They can't make me. I'll fight them."
> "You can't fight all of them."
> "Watch me. I'm getting you out of here with me. . . ."

Kirian wasn't going to ride in on a white horse and slay the dragon for me. No matter what his postcards might imply.

Bodie ran out to find me. "Juliet, she's back. It's bad."

I grabbed my shoes and ran to the house, outdistancing Bodie. Mistress was home early. Had the kids finished eating the ravioli? Were the dishes cleaned? *Damn it, you're an idiot, Juliet.*

I heard the screeching while I wiped the mud off my feet with hurried, clumsy fingers. Tracking dirt in would definitely draw my blood.

"Nice of you to join us, Missy," Mistress accused.

"I told you she was bathing." Nicole blinked, but didn't look at me. *At least I know which lie to stick with.*

"Shut up, little girl. Bathing is a luxury she can do when her work is finished. Isn't it?"

My cue. "Yes, ma'am."

"Who brought this abomination into my home?" She pointed at a plate with a few specks of white Parmesan cheese and red marinara sauce. Even though the kitchen windows were open wide, there were still the scents of garlic, basil, and tomato clinging to the air.

Tell her? Don't tell her? My mind raced with the options and lies and stories. Try to find the least painful choice. Everything was a gamble. Some days she'd beat; some days she'd take away necessities but not lay a hand on anyone.

I was still weighing the options when Sema piped up. "It's just pasta."

"It's just pasta, you say? Nothing is just anything. This wasn't on the week's menu. This wasn't purchased by our budget, was it? Who provided the money to purchase it? Who bought it and gave it out? Who? I want to know exactly who was involved, don't I? This isn't the first time I've noticed strange foods or smells around here, is it? Was this made in this kitchen? Was it? Made in this house with my supplies and my tools and my time? I don't pay for you, or care for you, to make 'just pasta,' do I?" Her face flushed a matching tomato red and sweat dribbled down her nose, hanging for a second before dripping off. Her ire nauseated me and I threw up a little in my mouth, then swallowed it back.

I felt Bodie tremble.

Out of options. I shuffled forward a step. "I made it."

"You made it? You who lazes about like a queen bathing can make a fresh sauce? You can't warm soup or heat fish sticks. Do you really think me stupid enough to believe that?"

"It's the truth." I crossed my arms behind my back, twisting my thumbs against each other.

"Truth? Haven't you learned yet that I speak the truth, not you? None of you are hungry anymore, are you? Bodie, aren't you hungry after cleaning the bathrooms today? Oh, wait, you didn't actually do much cleaning, did you?"

It wasn't that she knew our tricks to protect the little kids from punishment; she simply assumed we hadn't done the tasks. We were guilty until proven, well, guilty.

"Are you hungry, Bodie?" This was a trick question. If we were hungry, then she'd make us eat horrid things from the trash cans, but if we weren't, then we'd go empty for a meal, or three.

"I'm full," Bodie said.

Nicole told me the law stated that patients had to be fed all meals, even when they no longer tolerated solid food. The kids knew they got whatever they wanted after fifteen minutes of food sitting in front of a guest. Mistress's theory was it kept us hungry to work and was good for the environment. No waste. Efficient. And it cut down on the food bills. Why it was one of the few laws she followed was beyond me.

Very rarely did Mistress let me feed the kids in addition to whatever food was served guests. Of course, the exception was the day Ms. Asura came to visit. This meal was planned well in advance. Which is why I cooked while Mistress was out and we hid nonperishable food for those days when there wasn't enough provided for us.

Bodie's expression hardened with a child's stubbornness. "Yes, I'm full."

"Oh, you are, are you? Are the rest of you just as full as our little prince here?"

We nodded. I knew the smaller kids took their cue from me, but I didn't know what would come next.

"Then, Juliet, bring me the grater, please."

I hesitated.

"Do you not know where it is?"

I knew exactly where it was kept. "There are several sizes, Mistress."

"The one with the handle, then, okay?" she sneered.

"The menu doesn't call for grating this week?" I tried to make it a question, but I didn't move.

"Are you questioning my request?"

"No, ma'am."

"Then, where is it?" She held out her hand.

I moved slowly, my stomach clenched. I snagged the grater out of a drawer and placed it in her hand without making eye contact.

"Bodie, would you like to be first?" She leaned down and over him.

He swallowed, but didn't answer.

"What was I thinking? Juliet, here." She handed the grater to me and I turned to put it back in the drawer. "You don't think we're finished with it, do you? No, of course you know better than that, don't you?"

As I turned to face her, I glanced at Bodie. His scared eyes were round and too large in his face.

"Shall he get ten, or twenty, spanks?" she asked the world around us.

Bodie's head shook. "I—I—I—" Panic made him wet himself.

"You turd. Now, who is going to clean up that mess?" She huffed. "Juliet, will you do the honors?"

"I'll clean it up."

"You know that's not what I meant, don't you? Of course you'll clean it up. Spank Bodie, then every child you served the 'just pasta' to. Ten spanks on bare buttocks should do it, won't it? Nicole, help them pull down their pants." Mistress scraped a chair back and settled her hefty frame into it like we were performing a play for her enjoyment. There was a gleam in her eye, a sparkle that only ever shone when one of us was hurt.

I'd been hit plenty. I'd seen older kids have to spank younger ones with belts and branches and wooden spoons. I'd shared the pain of those who hit me and those who got hit next to me. Up until this moment, I'd never been handed the tool and the mandate to hit.

"You're almost sixteen, Juliet."

Shocked that she remembered, I twisted and met her gaze.

"You're almost an adult. It's time I started treating you like one. Get to it."

Tears threatened, but I sucked them back, knowing they'd make everything worse.

Nicole peeled Bodie's wet pants down his legs, then pressed him against her stomach, holding his face and petting his hair. It was the most comforting she could do.

I stared at the grater in my hand. *If I do this, it will be over quickly and I can try to keep the hits as light as possible.*

"Do you think I have all day? Get cracking."

Nicole stared at me steadily. I knew that giving me strength and love with her eyes was the only way she could help.

I lifted the grater higher. *I can't.* This was my enough, my line. I swiftly lowered the grater before I changed my mind by thinking of the pain I would be forced to endure for holding my ground. "I won't hit him. Any of them."

Mistress glared at me. "Do you dare contradict an order?"

I nodded, watching Nicole tense further. "I will not hit a child."

"Are you saying none of you deserve discipline?"

"No, ma'am. You may hit me all you'd like." I carefully didn't meet her eyes and tried to appear smaller than my almost six feet.

"You'll let me, will you? Give it." She held out a hand and lumbered to her feet.

I handed the grater to her, deliberately placing my body in front of the other kids.

"Down to your skivvies now and on your knees," she barked at me. "You'll all watch. No tears, no sniffles. You'll watch and you'll remember the lesson today."

Nicole started to step forward and open her mouth, but I jerked my head and made a face so she'd cease. She was the type who'd stand next to me, to take her share to protect the others, but I feared that this wasn't about even distribution of pain, but something deeper and more personal. Nicole might very well make it all worse.

As I undressed as quickly as I could, I knew I should feel shame or embarrassment over my graying boy shorts and threadbare bra; but really, all I saw was the world hazy at the edges as I tried not to pass out. I wondered if I'd get away with taking all the hits for the kids, or if she'd still beat them, too.

It wasn't the thwacks that bothered me as much as the whistle in the air before the grater made contact. I knelt facing the kitchen window so I could see the creek and the birds. Mini perched on a top branch of a tree near the window, so even from the floor I saw her, but no one else was able to. She caught my gaze and held it. Her body grew still and even her tail didn't twitch. She just held my vision steady and strong and willed me through it.

Mistress avoided places on my back with any padding. She aimed for my ribs and my vertebrae, my shoulders and shoulder blades. I lost count at thirty.

Finally, the ringing phone grabbed her attention away from me.

"Juliet, I expect this grater to be cleaned and disinfected before you leave the kitchen. The rest of you, you have jobs to do. Go!" Mistress slammed through the kitchen hallway to her office and living quarters.

We heard the rumble of her voice on the phone before any of us moved. Nicole and Bodie helped me get to my feet.

Bodie's upper lip was caked with snot and his cheeks were streaked with saltwater tracks. "So sorry. So sorry." His breakdown opened the floodgates of the other ones. I knew physical abuse was part of the past for several of them. Even in my pain-filled stupor, I knew I needed to somehow make this right for them. To show them I was okay, that I would survive, that this wasn't the end of my world.

Pain made my muscles twitch and seize, but I choked that down until my clothes were all in place and I faced the kids. My back was warm and sticky; the skin stung with the contact of the fabric. It was the bone bruises I knew would echo much longer.

"I'm okay. I'll heal. You did nothing wrong."

Sema's little voice piped up. "You should have beat us."

"No, I shouldn't have." I didn't bend well, but I made sure I kept eye contact with her. "It's not okay. It's not okay to hit anyone. So, no, I shouldn't have. Mistress shouldn't have, but I'm strong. I'll live and we'll be okay."

"So sorry." Bodie attached himself to my leg like a barnacle. The pressure of his little arms squeezing on raw flesh forced the breath from my lungs, but I couldn't push him away.

"Juliet is right." Nicole passed out the hard butterscotch candy she always seemed to have in her pockets. "Hitting isn't okay. And someday Mistress will know that too. Now, let's do our chores and give Juliet a few minutes. Come on, Bodie, let's get you new pants." Nicole picked up the bloody grater and put it in the sink. "I'll take care of this," she said.

Gratefully, I let her shepherd the kids away. My knuckles turned white from holding myself up against the counter. I knew Mistress would check on the grater first thing. It would take me a while to get the bits of myself out of it, but when I leaned over the sink and picked it up, the metal was shiny and polished. *As if nothing had touched it.*

Mini leapt from the tree fluidly and trotted off toward the creek.

The rest of my evening flew by. Nicole put the kids to bed and tucked them in. I needed to bathe, for real this time, and have her disinfect my back so I would heal without infection. Doctors weren't an option.

"Juliet, I love you." Bodie found me doing laundry.

"What are you doing still awake?"

"I had to say sorry again."

Nicole appeared in the doorway behind him, shaking her head in apology.

I put down the towels and stacks of worn-out clothing for the kids and hugged him to me. "Bodie, I will be okay. I don't want you to feel bad. You did nothing wrong. Nothing."

"Nothing?"

I dropped my voice to a whisper, "No, nothing. Mistress is mean and horrible and she'd have hit me anyway."

"But I ate the pasta—"

"We all did. And we will again. I need you to promise me something, though, okay?"

"Any-ting."

"Tonight when you sleep? I want you to dream about cookies, okay?"

"Cookies?"

"Mm-hmm. A world where everything is made of chocolate-chip cookie dough and you can eat anything you want to."

"Everything?"

"Can you do that for me?" I winked conspiratorially.

"I can." He nodded his head like I'd given him a monumental, impossibly important task.

I kissed his forehead as Mini wandered in and meowed at me.

"Hi, kitty. Who needs Juliet?" Bodie bent and kissed Mini's forehead in the same manner I'd kissed him.

"Horsey Room needs you," Bodie pronounced before leaving.

Nicole watched him trudge away. "You want me to check on Mr. Daniels?"

"No, I'll go." I was too wiped to wonder how Bodie knew such a thing, or if he was guessing.

"You sure?"

Mini trotted along beside us up the stairs.

"Yes, I'm sure." I opened the Horse Room door. Mini jumped up onto his chest in two hurried strides.

Nicole ushered Bodie back off to bed.

I greeted Mr. Daniels, who opened his eyes at my voice. I began by telling him the day and time, and who I was. I assumed guests might have questions or might not recognize me. I tried to carefully answer any unasked questions or explain things easily misunderstood. I didn't want them more scared than they needed to be. Ever. I checked his breathing, dampened his lips lightly, and washed his face with a warm cloth. All things Kirian had taught me in the year before he'd left.

I settled into a chair with Mini in my lap. I pet her with both hands, one scratching beneath her chin, the other flowing down her back. Perhaps the soothing motion refocused my mind, away from my back, because the stinging burn of the wounds lessened.

I checked Mr. Daniel's pulse as his feet moved restlessly under the sheets and blankets. Fidgeting was a sign I'd learned to notice.

He grabbed my hand, startling me, and I met his very

clear blue eyes. "You are loved. You are special. You are a miracle."

I had no idea what to say. I'd never heard his voice. The elderly sometimes asked for people or water, but mostly they were either unconscious on arrival or Mistress kept them doped up and silent.

While gripping my hand almost painfully, he threw off his covers with his other hand and sat up. "It's so beautiful. She tried to protect you. Tried to keep you safe, but she's sent help. They're here, all around us. Loving. Helping." He saw beyond me. He smiled, showing dimples, and I briefly glimpsed the young man he once was.

"Juliet. Juliet!" My name came from a distance.

I opened my eyes to find myself leaning with my head against the mattress. Mr. Daniel's hand had relaxed and chilled in mine. His covers were askew.

"What happened?" I asked Nicole.

"I think you fainted." Nicole peered into my eyes. "Are you okay?" Her concern was palpable.

"I don't know. Mr. Daniels—he sat up and said things."

"He's gone. I left you about an hour ago, and he was gone when I came back in, but you wouldn't wake up."

I stood, clutching the bedclothes, vertigo rocking me. "Where's Mini?" My knees felt swollen and stiff like I'd been kneeling for hours on broken glass.

"I don't know, I didn't see her. You're frowning. What hurts besides your back?"

"My knees. I have a headache." The usual. "Who's the staff tonight?"

"Chi." Nicole placed a hand on my forehead. "Take a breath in."

I inhaled, but didn't have patience for her efforts to help me cope, so I exhaled almost as quickly. "Ask him to deal. I need sleep."

"Okay." Nicole helped me down to my closet. Each step we took seemed to loosen my joints. "How's your back?"

"Doesn't hurt." I realized as the words came out of my mouth that it was the truth.

That night, I dreamed of a woman with long blond hair like mine who smiled at me, hugged me, and kissed away my boo-boos. And a tiny girl with curly hair who beckoned me while holding out her hand.

There are those with us, and those who oppose us. It will always be that way for our kind.

Sunt qui nobis faveant, sunt qui nobis adversen-tur. Hoc semper erit generi humano usitatum.

Luca Lenci

CHAPTER 15

There wasn't a good way or a good time to tell Tens, but my gut feeling said I needed to go see Juliet alone. "I think I should go by myself."

"Where?" he asked.

"To meet Juliet."

Tens straightened. "Uh, no. Hell, no."

I closed my eyes and inhaled deeply. "Hear me out?"

"Why? It's moronic. Stupid idea."

I tried to remind myself that Tens was simply watching out for me. Trying to keep me safe. That he didn't mean to be bossy and dogmatic. "You don't need to be rude."

"Clearly I do if you're even contemplating this."

Licks of hot anger flickered at my heart. "I'm not stupid."

"No, you're very smart, but this idea, this plan, is really, really dumb."

I hate confrontation. I hate arguing. *I am right.* "Tens. We have to talk about this."

"No, we don't." He stoked my distress and frustration with his own.

I held my ground. "Yes, we do, but if you won't talk about it, then you can listen."

My expression, or my tone, shut him up.

"I need to go by myself because we'll intimidate her together—it's like ganging up on her." It's how I had felt with Auntie and Tens knowing more about me than I knew about myself. "I know what I'm talking about."

He swallowed but didn't answer, just continued whittling a chunk of wood to sawdust instead of the usual animal.

I tried again. "We tried waiting out there together and we didn't see her."

"No, we met Minerva and Bodie. You don't think that was important?" He shook his head like I'd told him I believed the sky was orange, not blue.

I pressed. "I'm not saying that. Of course they're important. I'm saying that I want to try alone."

Silence stretched.

He wouldn't give. He wasn't going to hear me. He'd shut down so completely that I wouldn't get through to him. I felt it.

"Are you finished?" he asked eventually.

I nodded, crossing my arms.

"I'm your Protector. Right?"

"Yes."

"I protect you."

"Right." I bit off my agreement.

"So, why would going anywhere by yourself be a good idea?"

"Oh, come on. You don't know what that means. You're not a ninja and I'm not incapable. You're my boyfriend, not my boss."

"Your boss?"

"That's what you're acting like. Like you know better and more, instead of working with me and figuring it out together."

"Maybe I do know more."

I rolled my eyes. "Care to share?" I wanted to throw a chunk of wood at him.

"You're being so immature right now."

"And you're being sanctimonious and arrogant."

He shrugged. "You go by yourself and I'll follow you."

"That's not going by myself."

"That's the deal."

Just because we're soul mates doesn't mean we have to be inseparable. "Minerva will be there," I said.

"Yes, the cat. What's she going to do, hiss at a Nocti?"

"As opposed to what? What is your special power? Besides sometimes knowing what I'm feeling, or where I am, or what I'm doing?"

"And why do you think I can do that, Merry? To aggravate you? Or maybe there's a bigger reason."

"Do you know what the reason is?" I parried.

He stuttered.

I pointed at him in triumph. "See, you don't know why either! Just because you can, doesn't mean you know more about me than I do."

"We're getting nowhere. I'll follow you. I'm not going to leave you alone to get killed."

"Why do you assume something bad is going to happen?"

"Why do you assume it won't? We have no evidence to suggest it won't."

"Tens, stop. Fine, come with me. But if it doesn't work, I'm going alone and you can hide in the bushes or up your own ass." I slammed into the bathroom.

"Nice!" He yelled through the door, and then I heard the front door crash. Custos howled.

He made me so mad. I scrubbed my face until it was raw and blazed irritation.

I knew I could count on him no matter what. And part of me rebelled. I was waiting for him to decide it wasn't fun, that he'd be better off walking away and pretending to be normal. I was waiting for him to hand me a bus ticket and pass me off.

Because he could. He could walk away and I couldn't.

It didn't matter where I went, I couldn't leave my

Fenestra self behind. But he could stop being my Protector. If he got tired of the death, and the threats from Nocti, and the constant state of not knowing what was happening around us, he could get far away from me. And so what if he occasionally knew I was sad, or happy, or scared? He could ignore that. My mother had managed to ignore the corpses that gathered around me—feelings should be no problem for him. Way harder to ignore the dead bodies and the souls crashing into me. Why couldn't I simply explain that to him? Why did I have to pick a fight and hope he got the point? I sank to the tiled floor. The adrenaline finally petered out and I saw myself with perspective.

When I exited the cottage, Tens sat in the truck; Custos lay in the bed of it, waiting. She wagged her tail at me, which gave me the strength to walk over and open the passenger door. I climbed in.

"Ready?" Tens asked. Tension smoldered between us.

I nodded. I opened my mouth but could force none of my truth out.

We drove the truck to the boat ramp and walked in, startling a covey of quail who ran like cartoons away from us until they could fly into a cover of brush. These woods were beginning to be very familiar to me; I felt like I could almost call out the names of the white-tailed deer we passed. The scent of sun on the plowed fields smelled like spring. Our pace was fast, since Tens's legs were twice the length of mine and his anger carried him forward briskly.

I jogged to keep up, refusing to ask him to slow down. Ground squirrels chastised us for bothering them.

Cardinals, grackles, and chickadees, still in their winter colors, occupied the canopy branches above us. Tiny yellow pansy-type flowers and purple crocus bloomed underfoot and several kinds of fern unfurled their tentacles for the sun as if they, too, were tired of winter.

As we neared Dunklebarger, my fingertips tingled and my legs felt like I had walked waist-deep into the ocean. A current of energy, and something else, rolled around me, threatening to overwhelm me and lift me spiritually out of my body. It required huge amounts of concentration to stay focused.

"Tens?" I whispered

I felt woogy. Odd. Not bad, but not pleasant.

"What? What's going on?" Tens grabbed my hand. "You're burning up." In that moment, we both forgot our fight and focused on the here and now.

"I don't know. I feel weird." I felt like I was shouting at him, but the words came out barely audible even to my own ears.

"How weird? We're coming up toward the house. Do you want to turn around? Go back?"

My arm wrapped around Tens's waist. I felt the cold bump of steel at the small of his back. *When did he add a firearm to his wardrobe?*

I felt like I was swimming in a bathtub. Like the world wasn't quite big enough.

"Turn around?" he asked. Concern and confusion had him reaching for me.

"No, keep going." But I wasn't sure.

He made encouraging sounds but seemed as if he was

battling the instinct to pick me up and take me home. "We're almost there. Someone's up ahead. You see?"

My gaze was focused on the ground in front of me, but I lifted my head to see. I nodded. Not Bodie, and not a cat.

"Hello?" Tens tucked me against his side, as we approached a girl looking out onto the creek.

She startled and poised herself to leave. Tall, a good foot of sturdy height on me. Thick blond hair escaped a braid down her back. Bronzed eyes full of panic and sadness and something I couldn't place. She stepped back, away from us. But not before I noted the bruising beneath her eyes and the welts on her forearms.

I didn't need Rumi to tell me this was our Fenestra. I knew it, felt a kinship immediately that spoke to my soul in a way only Auntie did. It felt like a piece of me was back in my heart. Like I'd woken from a really great nap, full of energy and ready for anything.

"Please don't go," Tens said. "Are you—"

"Juliet?" I asked, shaking off the fog.

She paled, with fear widening her eyes.

I stretched my open hands out in front of me. I entreated, "We're friends. We won't hurt you."

"We only want to talk." Tens helped me sit on a log. We didn't move any closer to her, afraid she'd spook.

She didn't leave, but didn't come closer either. "I—I—"

She seemed unable to pull words or form sentences. I wondered if she could talk, if it was fear that made her mute. It truly didn't matter. There were things she needed to know. To hear. Quickly, before she ran.

This is my one chance. I swallowed down urgency,

excitement. Tried to make my voice sound calm and patient. "My name is Meridian. This is Tens." *God, how the hell do you do this? Without sounding like a freak? Or a lunatic? Or a serial killer?*

My ears popped like we were climbing a mountain or descending one too fast.

She stumbled a little further away, but stayed close enough that I could still talk at a normal volume. "Please, you don't need to be afraid. We've been looking for you."

"Who?" Again, she moved steps away from us. Prepared to flee.

"We're staying at Helios, down in Carmel. We can help you. We were sent to help you. Are you okay?"

She laughed a bit maniacally but didn't answer the question. She backed up further.

"We're going to come here. We'll wait here. When you're ready to talk to us, we'll be here. Or you can find us at Helios. We'll help. We have answers." The desperation I felt was evident in my voice. I don't know what I had expected, but I thought she'd see me, know me, and we'd skip along like friends. *Moronic and dumb.*

She ran from us, her French braid bouncing between her shoulder blades—my mother called them angel wings and now I knew why.

"That went well." Tens spoke the obvious.

"What the hell do we do now?" I asked, sinking against him.

How shall I tell my beau of all these goings-on?
                                        Jocelyn Wynn
                                        1788

CHAPTER 16

"Meridian, Tens!" Joi bolted out Helios's kitchen door when we pulled up. She waved her hands and jogged over.

"What's wrong?" I asked, racing out of the truck. Were Nocti here? Had something happened to Rumi? Had the store been robbed?

Tens, on edge like me, didn't even take the keys out of the ignition before launching himself around the side of the truck. "What happened?"

She stutter-stepped, puzzlement filling her face. She

glanced from me to Tens and back again. "Nothing. Nothing. Who said anything about there being something wrong?"

"You were frantic," I accused, sharper than I intended.

She shook her head. "Excited. Are you okay? Do you need to sit down? Let's go inside." Joi tried to carefully shepherd me toward the cottage, clucking all the while.

"No, I'm okay. Sorry. It seemed like you . . . like something was wrong." I wasn't okay, but I tried to make my face calm and healthy.

"What's going on?" Tens stepped up behind me in support and comfort. My back fit snugly against his front.

"I remember hearing about your Father Anthony. He retired from the northern part of the state, where my cousin lives; her in-laws were in his parish. He was traveling in Africa. I don't know if he's still there or moved back to the States. I've put some calls out to find out where he is. I should know soon. That's all. I remembered and I wanted you to know before I left. It seemed important to you."

I sagged. I couldn't help it. Good news, yes, but so good that it was worth my anxiety attack? Not so much. "Thank you. Thank you," I repeated myself, hugging Joi, trying to push calm energy at her so she'd stop looking at me like I was going to faint or keel over right there.

"Get her inside and make her lie down. I'll let you know when I hear more. I'll walk slowly and smile." Joi spoke to Tens as if I weren't standing there. I didn't blame her. She thought I was a desperately ill patient.

"Sure thing." Tens led me back inside the cottage like I was fragile.

"Stop acting like I'm an invalid," I snapped.

Tens dropped my arm immediately. "Sorry."

I sighed. "No, I'm wrong. I'm sorry." I'd crossed the yellow bitch line too many times this week.

"Forget it." He pawed through the kitchen while I kicked my shoes off.

"What do we do now?"

He shook his head.

I crossed the room and laid my forehead on his back. I hugged his waist. "Look, I'm sorry about earlier. I hate fighting."

He turned into my arms. "You had a point."

"What?" I wasn't going to assume that he saw the point of the fight the same way I did and start a whole new one. I kept my head down, not making eye contact on purpose.

"We don't have to be codependent. Not all the time."

Is that what I was talking about? "Sometimes, I just—"

He lifted my chin, forcing my eyes up. I drowned in his.

I shook my head, trying to find the words. "I want us to be exponentially stronger together because we're solid individuals. I don't want us to be just the sum of our parts."

He nodded. "I only want you to be the best you. How cheesy is that?"

"It's not. I am, with you. I love you. You're the first person in my life to see me and love me unconditionally, but it scares me too."

"Scares you?" he questioned.

"Terrifies me." I nodded, desperate to make him understand.

"Oh." He didn't seem to know how to react to that and pulled away.

I had to get us back on track. "Tens, can I sense you, too? Does it work both ways?"

"I don't know." He shrugged.

"Well, how do you do it? I want to try it." I followed him and sat next to him on the couch.

"It's not like it's a switch I throw, or a trick or anything." He huffed and leaned back against the couch, resting his hands over his face.

"Okay, but do you feel me all the time?"

"I've told you, I can't read your mind."

"I know you've said it's the emotions, or big stuff like danger, but is it like the stock market scrolly sign on the news? As things change you get updates? An emotional RSS feed?"

"What is that?"

I sometimes forgot that Tens didn't live in the same popular culture world as most people. "Never mind, techie. Like I know when you're angry, or worried, or happy and relaxed. Is it like that?"

"Yeah, but how do you know?"

"Well, when you're angry your decibel level goes up— you get very loud and stop speaking in complete sentences, or your brow furrows between your eyes and gets all folded like the Rockies."

He shook his head in disagreement. "That's body language. You've learned mine; you've picked up on cues like anyone else. How did you know when Sammy was upset?"

"His lip quivered and he started crying."

"Right. That's not psychic."

"Good point." Disappointed, I knew he was right.

"I cue off your body and your face just like you do with mine. God, Merry, if I knew how I did the psychic thing, maybe I could do it better."

"What do you mean?"

"Am I supposed to know how to keep you from feeling bad about stuff? I'm your Protector, right? Am I supposed to protect you from everything, or only some things?"

"I hadn't thought about it that way. I can't imagine your job is to shield me from everything—that would be very unbalanced."

"Okay, then, what good am I really?"

"What are you talking about? Tens, do you think I could do this without you? I don't *want* to do this without you." I reached out and grabbed his knee. "I am incapable of holding it together without knowing you're there to pick up my pieces. I want to be that for you, too. I just don't know how to do it if I'm always leaning on you, you know?"

He nodded.

"When did you start feeling me?"

"I think I've always felt you. But I didn't know it. Not until much later."

"When?" I prodded.

"Early on I called you my imaginary friend. But it was more than that. I knew what you were thinking and doing, but only at certain times," he said.

"What's the first thing you remember?"

"The first time I thought I was crazy?" he asked.

Puzzled, I checked his eyes to see if he was joking. *No, very serious face.* "Crazy?"

"It's not normal to hear conversations other people have or see things through their eyes. Do you remember your sixth birthday party? I was nine."

I barely remembered. I couldn't imagine that I wanted to remember. "That was the last time Mom threw a party for me."

"Do you remember why?"

"No." I blanked.

"You went ice-skating." He cued my memory.

"In Portland?"

"It was an inside rink."

I nodded, details popping up into my mind's eye.

"There were seven little girls who came with their mommies. You overheard a couple of the moms talking about what a weird kid you were and that they'd only let their daughters come if they were allowed too. You hid under the table."

"I wouldn't come out." I remembered it like it had happened to someone else.

"Right."

"I had a headache. A really bad headache."

"And?"

"And one of the little girls, Becky, got in the way of a big kid who was going really fast and showing off."

"And?"

"And she got pushed out of the way and they fell, twisted together, and Becky hit her head really hard."

"So hard the ice turned red with the blood."

I nodded, seeing it like I was right there. "And she lay motionless. I threw up and stayed under the table and saw people's feet rushing around. An ambulance crew arrived."

"And all those mommies rushed to get their kids out of there. Your mom left you under the table in all the chaos, and when it was over, she came to find you. Drove you home and didn't talk to you for a week."

I rubbed my eyes. My mother could have reassured me. For God's sake, she knew my ancestry. She pretended I was a mistake that could be fixed by ignoring it.

"Do you remember what happened to Becky?" Tens traced circles on my back.

"No."

"The fall caused a traumatic brain injury. She broke her neck, too."

"Died."

"Not then, not that I know of."

"She never came back to school."

"You changed schools."

"I did?"

"Your mom decided you needed to start fresh."

"So you felt all this?"

"Saw it happening like I was there. Felt it like I was you. Wanted to fix it. I told my mom all about it. Details. She called my grandfather. And the next thing I knew I was on a plane to Seattle."

"She sent you away?"

"She thought I was turning into a girl or becoming schizophrenic or something she couldn't handle, I think."

"What did she say?" I asked, afraid of his answer.

"That she'd had enough of trying to get me to live in this world and if I wanted to be a crazy kid, then I could go live with crazy people."

"Her parents?" My heart broke for the little boy.

"Hmm-mmm." He closed his eyes.

"Seriously? She thought her own parents were insane, so she sent you to them?"

"I guess I'd been talking about you since your birth, and asking about girl toys and wanting to see places and people that she had to look up on the Internet. I think my wanting to go ice-skating so I could save the girl with the broken neck terrified her."

"But send you away?"

"Sound familiar?"

"You were *nine*."

"And that makes it worse?"

"Than me?" I huffed out a breath. "Yes, nine is different than sixteen. Plus, I went directly to Auntie, right?"

I dreamed last night that you'll be tall like
your daddy and strong. I wish he were here to
help us.   —R.

CHAPTER 17
Juliet

"Juliet? What's wrong?" Nicole tried to grab me when I ran
past her toward my space under the stairs. It didn't matter if
there were repercussions; I had to find a dark, quiet place to
breathe.

The walls folded in on me. The world spun too fast, with
colors too bright for my eyes, sounds too loud in my ears. *The
girl from my dream.* The tiny, curly-haired girl with her hands
outstretched had just showed up in real life at the creek.

Older than I had dreamed, but the same girl. Her face and eyes felt so familiar.

Maybe I'm still asleep. "Nico, pinch me. Hard."

Surprise and disbelief flashed across Nicole's face. "Uh, no?"

I jiggled from foot to foot, too anxious to stand still. "Am I awake?"

Her brow furrowed, and her voice dipped, "What are you talking about?"

"Are you real?" I knew I sounded like I'd finally lost it, but I couldn't explain in complete sentences. My brain tried to meld both my dream and the teens by the creek into my reality.

She hugged my shoulders, trying to quiet me. "You're awake, Juliet. What's going on?" Concern and pity marred her otherwise beautiful face.

"I can't talk now—" *What is happening to me? What does it all mean?*

We startled at the sound of the intercom button. I braced for Mistress's screech.

"Where are you, Juliet? Get your lazy self into my office pronto." Her tone didn't disappoint.

I was definitely wide awake. I never would have put rescue and Mistress in the same dream. More confused than defeated, I shrugged off Nicole's grip. "Never mind. I'll tell you later."

"Okay, but—" She tried to follow, but stopped when I waved her off.

I stumbled into Mistress's office, my feet not keeping up

with the rest of me. I caught my apology in midbreath. Sorrys made things worse. Instead, I snapped to straight, erect attention. I tried to keep my expression bland and empty.

She glared at me. "We have three new guests arriving. I need you to prepare their rooms. Make sure they're cleaner than last time. This is a respectable establishment. Clear?"

"Yes, ma'am." I waited. I knew never to turn to leave until I was dismissed. Joining the military, my long-imagined last resort, once again passed through my mind. I took orders well. Stood with my knees locked and head high for hours without breaks. I operated on little sleep. *But they'd turn away an almost-sixteen-year-old girl.*

Five or ten minutes passed. I kept my eyes on the window behind Mistress's desk. Waiting. There was more. There was always more.

When she'd kept me standing long enough, Mistress finally said, "Ms. Asura asked that you call her. You may use this phone."

Privacy? No. Bewildered, I wondered why Ms. Asura wanted to speak to me.

As if to answer my unasked question, Mistress smirked. "February tenth is almost here. Arrangements must be made."

My birthday. My stomach dropped and my mouth dried thinking about Bodie and Sema trying to survive this insanity. I knew Nicole would do the best she could, but would that be enough? I wanted to leave, but not without the innocents. There was no justice in moving on and leaving them behind. I wanted to curse; I bit my tongue until it bled.

"Do it!" she screamed, lunging into my face.

I flinched more for her benefit than because she startled me. *The more we grovel, the less she picks.* I grasped the phone and she punched the buttons while I held the handset. I'd sprout bruises from the pressure she inflicted.

"Juliet. I've been expecting your call." Ms. Asura sounded pleased to hear from me. As if it was my idea to call her. Mistress glared and shuffled papers.

"Yes?" I questioned, trying to sound both meek and humble at the same time.

Ms. Asura must not have picked up on any of the tension, because her effervescence didn't diminish. "I'd like to take you for coffee so we can talk about what's next for you. How does that sound?"

Coffee? All her promised outings never amount to anything but more promises. She was busy. I understood that. Eventually, I'd learned they were plans she liked to talk about but never follow through on. Who wanted to hang out with kids when your day job was supervising them?

"Sure," I said.

"Great. I'll pick you up tomorrow at eleven." She sounded so enthusiastic it was like I'd promised her my kidney.

"Um—" I glanced at Mistress, who'd given up the pretense of doing paperwork and now simply watched me with a scowl.

"It's okay, I've cleared it." Ms. Asura answered my unspoken question.

Mistress nodded, as if she read my hesitation too.

"Okay." Did I have a choice? Stay here, or go for coffee like a real teenager? Was there a choice? Even if things were ten times worse when I returned, I'd go.

I heard Ms. Asura clap her hands. "I'm delighted. This will be fun."

"Okay," I repeated. Her excitement felt genuine.

"See you in the morning." She hung up, and I quickly put the handset down.

"Every minute you're away will be two minutes I expect repaid when you return," Mistress grouched.

"Yes, ma'am." *More like ten.*

"Here's what must be completed before you leave." She handed me a list of odd tasks—inventorying the pantry and washing the curtains—as well as my usual.

I glanced at the filing cabinet behind her. Wished I were brave enough to try again to get my file.

"Scat!" she yelled, a vein in the middle of her forehead throbbing.

I scurried out of the room to where Nicole waited for me in the shadows.

"What's going on?" Speaking in low tones, she pressed against my side, matching my stride.

"Ms. Asura is taking me out for coffee tomorrow."

Nicole's face fell. "Really?"

"I'll try to bring you some." I could try, but odds weren't good I'd get it back into the house without Mistress dumping it on the floor and making us lick it up.

"No, I don't care about the coffee part. Just be careful, okay? I have a bad feeling." Nicole frowned.

I wanted her to stop worrying so much. "Nothing bad can happen at a coffee shop."

"Maybe, but watch what you say." Her voice was both careful and demanding.

"She wants to talk about plans." *What plans? What future?*

"Maybe. I don't like it. Has she ever taken you out before?"

"No." I didn't understand why Nicole was so upset.

"Then why now?" She wouldn't let it go.

"Because I'm turning sixteen?" I snapped.

"Are you sure that's it? Maybe you should check the files."

"How?" I wanted to. I really did.

"I'll help—"

"Enough. I can't think about this right now." I shrugged. "Three more arrivals today."

"Old or young?"

"Guests." *Old.*

Nicole let me change the subject completely, but her sadness and worry still seemed to take tangible form in the space around us.

I watched a child be wiped of memories as both of his Fenestra parents perished. The child wasn't one of us and didn't need the burden. I wonder if that was the right choice—with the removal of grief, we removed the love as well.

Meridian Laine
December 7, 1941

CHAPTER 18

Tens and I wandered into Rumi's studio. We wanted to talk to him about the box of papers. The artwork wasn't difficult to interpret, but the writing was another story. We had to trust he indeed was friendly and would translate for us accurately. The Spirit Stones hanging from the windows and rafters once again burst with light. The people in the studio glanced up at them in surprise. Not so subtle an entrance.

"Aren't these wondrous? The glass and the light have such a concinnity, a harmony. These are the Witch Balls of the seventeenth century," Rumi covered, shooing us toward the door that swung into his living quarters. "They throw any stray ray like they are the sun itself. Let me tell you of the magic—don't we all need a little magic in our lives?"

The door between the studio and his apartment swung shut behind us while Rumi continued on, selling his creations to the rapt customers. The stereo played in the corner, a familiar dance groove that seemed to be Rumi's favorite.

Tens and I worked in comfortable silence, unpacking the box, spreading the little paintings and drawings out on a big table. I studied them again, flipping through pages, squinting at faces. I felt like I should recognize something or someone. But other than a gut feeling that these had been painted by a Fenestra, I picked up nothing.

"Do you get any feeling from this stuff?" I asked Tens.

"I know you're confused and worried." He smiled. "But that's because you're biting your lips and sighing every three seconds."

"Ha-ha." I rolled my eyes.

Rumi pushed open the door and bounced in. "Ah, sorry for that. You're quite the sales device. Sold a dozen for upcoming birthdays, bat mitzvahs, baby presents. How may I be of assistance today?"

"We didn't mean to interrupt." I licked my lips, wondering not for the first time if I needed to apologize for taking up his time.

"Not a problem." He walked over to the table. "I see you're intrigued by Ma's keepings." He bent over them, smiling recognition at the pages as if they were long-lost friends come home. He lumbered to the kitchen. "Beverages?"

"Sure," I said, and Tens nodded.

Rumi made coffee for himself and poured us sparkling juice in brightly swirled tumblers that made drinking feel like swallowing a rainbow. "Did you find anything interesting in there?"

I picked up a small crinkled-leather sketchbook. "Can you tell us what the writing says?"

He nodded, sipping thoughtfully. "Most of it I can translate. Some . . . I don't understand well enough to give you the English equivalent."

"Do you know who did all these?"

"Not all of them. Some were my nain's." He shuffled through pages and pointed to initials in the bottom corner. "This is her. These are in my da's handwriting, but I didn't know him to be an artist, so I think maybe he wrote on the finished work. Like I said, I pieced it together."

"Whatever you tell us will be helpful," Tens assured him.

Rumi and Tens shared a moment of eye contact I didn't understand. "Give me a minute here to reread so I tell you correctly. Where'd I lay my paper?" He patted his pockets and glanced around, frazzled.

I found pad and pen between the couch cushions and handed them to him.

He jotted words down on fresh paper. Mumbled. Shook his head. Nodded.

Tens and I sat quietly and waited. The tension of not knowing strung my spine tight. I resisted the urge to tap my heels or my fingers

Finally, he said, "Let's start here." He sorted a stack out and gestured. "These papers all point to the summer solstice as the day Good Death appears. When young women step forward to take their places at the bonfires, to be anointed. This is when babies with the gift first cry. I'm guessing that means they're born on the summer solstice too. It's a big celebration, ancestors return. Bonfires and Good Death are mentioned here." He tapped the examples.

I shot a glance at Tens. *Summer? That doesn't make sense. If they're Fenestra wouldn't it be winter?*

"Are you sure it says summer?" Tens questioned.

"A different season, maybe?" I asked.

"Definitely summer. Not easy to confuse summer with autumn or spring."

"Winter?" My voice cracked.

He adamantly refuted, "Definitely not winter."

"And it says that's when babies are born with a gift?" Tens held up a page as if reading it himself would help the pieces fit together.

"Uh-huh. Why do I get the sense you were hoping for a specific answer to these questions?" Rumi rubbed his eyes and took another swallow of coffee so we could contemplate his question.

Tens gave him a small smile, a mere lift of his lips.

I puzzled to myself, "It's *December* twenty-first. It's the winter solstice." *Fenestras are always born on the winter solstice.*

"For what?" Rumi tapped my shoulder.

"For— Did I say that out loud?"

"Nah, of course not." Rumi must have seen something on my face because he decided at that moment he needed a beverage refill. Whistling, he walked over to the kitchen and turned on the faucet. I appreciated him trying to give us some semblance of privacy.

Tens leaned forward. "What if it's not just December, Supergirl? What if there are more family lines out there? Your ancestors found the winter solstice as theirs, but wouldn't it make sense that maybe others came to be on other dates?"

"What would that prove?" I asked.

"I don't know." Tens shrugged and leaned away. "Hey, Rumi?"

"Yes." Rumi turned off the water and leaned against the counter, his face open and calm.

Tens balanced his chair on its back legs, tipping himself precariously. He looked for all the world like a kid in detention for shooting spitballs. "Is there a birth date that's popular in your family's history?"

"Like do we all have birthdays around the summer solstice?" Rumi smiled. "You forget I'm a cagey old man. I've been trying to think. We're mostly June babies. But not all of us celebrated birth dates like they do now. Not necessarily on the solstice, but maybe. Let me look here." He went to a book stand and opened a massive book. "The family Bible. Generations of birth dates, marriages, and deaths in here."

The book must have weighed forty pounds, but he

lifted it as if it were a handkerchief and set it on the table between Tens and me. "Look here." He pointed.

We all leaned over the ancient parchment and tried to read the names and dates that branched around in a tree shape. If the words had been typed, the font size would have been a four. *Maybe.*

"I'm getting too antiquated to read this. Take a look without me." Rumi sat back at the head of the table. Tens studied one side while I did the other.

"I count six," he said.

"I see seven," I finished.

"Plus, lots of them are close on one side or the other. And the weddings are on the twenty-first as well."

Rumi whistled. "Interesting. Seems like a disproportionate number? Lots of harvest mating?"

I swallowed, not sure what to say, but it didn't matter. Rumi continued as if he were having a conversation with himself.

Rumi tapped another little black book. "Here's the next bit you should know. Might be something. Might be nothing. This belonged to my father's brother, at least according to the writer. But I never knew him. I never even knew he existed until after Ma died and I read through all this."

"Oh. But there could be all sorts of explanation for why they didn't tell you—"

"That's the part that's bothered me. I knew about uncles and aunts that died as babies, or who were sent to the British colonies because they were criminals in the twentieth century—"

"They did that in the twentieth century?"

"Yep, didn't really stop until mid-century or later. The poor and criminals got carted off in the Queen's name. I knew about the ones who died in barroom brawls and at war. Even a leper." He ticked off his fingers as if counting up the death stories.

"Big family?"

He agreed. "Yep, but family stories are family stories—they'd be brought up every reunion over whiskey or cake. I thought maybe I could have forgotten something, so I asked my sister, who has a head for facts and figures. She doesn't remember hearing about this boy at all. Never. So I asked the rest of my living siblings."

"And?"

"Nothing."

"Nothing?"

"No one's ever heard of him."

"Well, what does he say in the book?" I asked.

"I don't know if he was moonstruck or making up stories, mind you. It's hard to tell. He talked about dead animals. He used to cut them up and look at their insides. He was twisted, if what he wrote is true. But he looked forward to his birthday. In the last entry he was excited to be a man and take his place in the ritual."

"What ritual?"

"I don't know. But I know this, his birthday was June twenty-first and I can't find any mention of him anywhere. Just this little book."

A chill danced down my spine.

The phone rang deep in the cushions of a chair and

Rumi ambled over to answer it, upsetting the couch as he went.

Tens leaned into me. "Wouldn't it be harder to spot Fenestras if they weren't all born on the same day? What if different parts of the world or different families came into their own at different times?"

I followed his train of thought. "That way if the Nocti found them or they were wiped out by other forces, there wasn't a trail to all of them. Like a terrorist cell—you only know what you know, but not enough to hurt anyone else?"

"I don't think I'd compare Fenestras to terrorists, but yeah, that's what I meant."

"If he's right, then Rumi *is* related to Fenestra."

"Or Nocti." Tens frowned down at the little black book.

Tell me, why is this my destiny? Is there no one
else more deserving of the torture?

Dic mihi, cur fato meo haec patior? Nemone
cruciatu dignior est?

Luca Lenci

CHAPTER 19

We'd left Rumi working on translating more of the pieces;
I needed food, a hot bath, and a little peace. Two out of
three might be possible.

Tens slanted a glance at me in the truck cab. "Need a
soak?"

My shoulders were knotted into macramé. Rubbing
seemed to make them worse. "Maybe. Probably."

"You okay?" Tens shut off the engine, but neither of us
left the truck.

I shook my head. "No."

"More words, please?" His lips twisted up as his fingers found the bare skin where my neck and shoulders met.

A shiver from the contact and his tiny smile had me sliding closer. I snuggled into the curve of his side while he wrapped his arm around me. I inhaled the heady scent of him before saying, "I keep thinking we'll get to the place where we know what's going on."

"Hmm . . ."

"When are we going to know instead of guess? When will this whole thing be easy?"

"Which part?"

"The dying still mess with my energy, even though Auntie said I'd be able to control it."

"She said it would take time and practice. It's only been a month, Supergirl."

Only a month? Lifetimes filled that month. I felt like I lived in a dark box with no light, no clock, and no watch. Time lost all meaning. "And Fenestras—we thought we knew everyone's birth date. I thought we were all girls. And now we find out—"

"Maybe there are more? And men can be Fenestra too?"

"Right?" I sat up and held eye contact. I thought of Señora Portalso, who'd ridden the bus from Portland to Revelation with me. She'd seen the light in me and recognized me as Fenestra before I even knew what was going on. She'd brought help and kindness to the caves without strings. What if she was like Rumi? And knew there were more beings like us between humanity and the Divine? "And maybe there are people who keep the secrets and know this truth and help us? Like Rumi, human versions of Custos and Minerva? We had support, on the bus and then in the caves—"

"Señora wasn't a coincidence, you mean?"

"How much of this is us being puppets for the big guys"—I nodded up at the heavens—"and how much is free will?" I used to believe I controlled my destiny, but the more I lived, the more I wondered if there was no such thing as coincidence.

"I—"

I interrupted him. "And us—the Protector mantle and my needing you doesn't make this any easier."

"What 'this'?" He seemed baffled.

"This." I motioned between his body and mine. He'd decided, notably without my consent, that I wasn't ready to progress beyond kissing. In my mind, we'd long since gone past that stage—our bodies just hadn't caught up yet. Maybe he was right, but maybe he wasn't.

He echoed my gestures. "What 'this'? I still don't get it."

I knew mature people actually conversed about sex and their needs. At least that's what I thought they did, but faced with talking about sex, and naked antics, I wanted to bury my head in my hands, put my fingers in my ears, and sing "Twinkle, Twinkle, Little Star" at the top of my lungs. Okay, so I'd bathed him while he was sick. He'd helped me. But awake and surging and sexy— we hadn't tackled that. Why, I couldn't say.

Tens seemed determined to keep us chaste and me virginal, but I knew I could push him past that if I pressed.

I just didn't want to yet. It wasn't that I didn't want to make love with him, or that I had a moral objection to pre-marital sex; it was more that I knew it would complicate already insanely complicated reality. I wasn't in a rush. Was I? Because it did royally piss me off that Tens hadn't put the moves on me. He was way too upstanding to push, even if he was walking around with an eternal erection—which isn't to say I'd noticed one. But then my crazy lack of relationship experience couldn't fill a thimble, so what did I know?

Tens bracketed my face with his hands and forced eye contact. "Please?"

I fidgeted. "Are you not . . . um . . . Do you want to . . ." I broke off, my heart racing. What if he didn't want to? What if all of this was just him feeling like he was stuck with me and he wasn't attracted to me?

"Merry—"

"Sex." I forced the word from my lungs and it sounded more like "sucks."

He blinked, his hands squeezing reflexively before letting go of me. "This is about sex?"

I concentrated on picking up cracker crumbs stuck in the seams of the seat cushions. I nodded.

"What about it? Merry?" His voice deepened.

My mouth dry and my skin itchy, I couldn't look at him.

"Supergirl? Do you feel pressure? I've been careful—"

"No, no." I swallowed and sucked it up. He might laugh. He might agree with me. But that was no worse than continuing to think he found me as attractive as a tree stump. "Why haven't we had sex?"

"What?" If the door to the truck had been open he'd have fallen out trying to get away.

Custos barked and leapt from the back of the truck, making the whole vehicle shake with the force.

Feeling bolder, I pressed. "Are you not attracted to me?"

"I can't believe I'm hearing this—" Tens's expression rocked with incredulity. He rubbed his hands over his face and cracked the door. "Let's go inside."

His strides purposeful, almost robotic, he marched toward the cottage.

I took the keys out of the ignition and followed at a much slower pace.

There was a piece of paper taped to the door. Tens ripped it off.

"What's that?" I asked.

"I can't read it."

I undid the lock on the door and flipped on lights. "What's it say?"

"I don't care." He didn't even look at the paper, but stared at me instead. "Do you really think I don't want to? Really?"

I inhaled carefully. All in, I said, "Well—"

"Oh my God. You have got to be kidding me."

"What?"

"Merry, you have no idea. None."

"So tell me." Now I was getting ramped up.

"I love you."

"I know that. I'm not saying you don't. You love Custos too, but you don't want to sleep with her. All we ever do is kiss—"

"Come on. The dog?" He angrily unlaced his boots, his shoulders vibrating with energy. "You're sick."

I shook my head. "Not anymore."

"Really? Because I'm the one who sees you when you pass out. I'm the one who catches you and holds you."

"And that makes you not want to—"

"No, that's not what I'm saying. Meridian, you're a virgin."

As if I weren't aware of that. Kind of like pointing out to a fat person that they're overweight. "So?"

"I'm not," he huffed.

"What?" I knew he was older than me, and a boy, but I guess I had assumed. Honestly, I hadn't thought about it. "Who?"

"That's not going to help—" Tens broke off and stared up at the ceiling. "Sit down, please?"

I came over to the couch and sat on the opposite end.

"Meridian, I can't believe you don't know how much I want you."

"You do?" I squeaked, in a very unsexy voice.

He laughed mirthlessly. He turned toward me, pulling one leg up onto the couch. He reached out a hand along the back of the sofa, toward me, but stopped just short of contact. "Kills me. It kills me to pull away. To stop. I love the feel of your skin and the way you fit against me. I can't get enough of you."

"Then why?"

"I want it to be right."

"When is that?"

"Are you ready?"

"You are."

"Just because I've had sex doesn't mean I'm ready to make love to you."

"What's the difference?"

"Big difference, Supergirl." He grew silent.

"Explain, please?"

"I was living on the streets. I was cold and scared and felt completely alone. I thought you were a voice in my head that made me insane. She was older and I thought sex would make me feel more in control. More like a man."

In a small voice I asked, "Did it?"

He snorted. "No, not even a little."

"Was it bad?"

"I'm not going to lie. It felt good in the moment. I fell asleep next to her and it felt good. Close. Human contact is so underrated. It wasn't about sex, not all of it."

"And?"

"And when I woke up she was gone and so were my money and my sneakers."

"She stole from you?"

"I wasn't mad, Merry; I was the stupid one. To let my guard down. To trust her. But I learned fast. The loneliness was worse after that."

"But I'm not going to steal away—"

"I know that. Look, we could have sex right now and it might be great, or it might suck. It's not like in the movies; we have to figure it out as we go, together."

"You think having sex with me might suck?"

"Oh my God, are you deliberately trying to misunderstand me?" He grabbed my hand.

"No, but you just said—"

"We've only known each other a month. And most of that month we've been fighting for our lives, or yours, and sex changes everything and nothing."

"It makes things more complicated?"

He nodded. "And it's already really complicated. Meridian, I want you. I'm sorry you thought I didn't. I really am. But let's say we do make love and you're not ready, or I'm not ready, then what?"

"What do you mean?"

"We do it. Someone regrets it. We're not going to break up, right?"

"Right."

"We could, but it would make the rest of the Fenestra-slash-Protector crap really, really hard. All I'm trying to do is make sure we're in a place where neither of us regrets it."

"Okay, but I'm regretting that all we do is kiss. It's frustrating. I'm ready. I really am, and I don't like you making the choice for me."

He nodded. "That's fair."

"I like falling asleep with you. I love touching you. I don't want to stop every time our tongues touch."

"Then let's make a deal."

"I'm listening."

"I'll pull away when I reach my limit, not when I think you've reached yours, if you promise to stop too."

"And if I don't? If I really am ready?" I asked.

"I don't want to screw this up. You're too important. We're too important to screw over because of hormones." Tears flooded his eyes, but he blinked them back.

I scooted over, tracing his eyebrows and then his lips with my fingertips. "You won't. You can't." I pulled him to me and hugged him.

His embrace tightened around me, until I was sitting in his lap, my legs wrapped around his waist. I don't know how long we held each other. But I know his tears wet my neck.

"I love you," I whispered into his ear.

He brokenly answered, "Always."

We finally let go when Custos barked at us, picked up the note that had slid to the floor with her tongue, and mouthed it into my lap. We chuckled and I pretended not to see Tens wipe his face on his shirt.

"What does it say?"

"It's from Joi. *Anthony Theobald, former priest, now gives evening tours at the Eiteljorg Museum, 500 West Washington Street, Indianapolis. I told him to expect a friend of mine to contact him. Here's his cell-phone number.*"

"Former? Do you think it's the right one?"

"I don't know. Won't hurt to find out. Do we call him?"

"I don't think so. I think we go take a tour."

Tens glanced at the rooster-shaped clock above the kitchen sink. "We have time to get down there if we leave right now."

"Let's go."

I loved him, though he never really saw me un-masked. At least not until he flew away, but that is little comfort in my grief.

Melynda Laine
1918

CHAPTER 20

Tens found a parking place along the Central Canal and we walked hand in hand toward the museum. The fountain of frolicking bronze deer frozen in midflight wasn't working. I imagined water flowing through them like a stream in the height of summer. Set far back from the road, up a stone-block path, stood the museum.

Tens whistled through his teeth. "Impressive."

"Yeah, wow." Layers of apricot, beige, and red stone gave the impression that the museum had been carved out of the earth eons ago. The air seemed to still and grow warm the closer we got. Even at half past twilight the rock softly reflected the sun.

Tens held the door for me. I'm sure we seemed like wide-eyed tourists transported to the Old West. Native American and Western artifacts were artfully placed; I didn't know where to look first. Tens tugged me toward the information desk.

"You look just like your grandfather."

We turned in unison as a Robert De Niro look-alike strode toward us with his hand outstretched.

Tens's grandfather, Tyee Kemp, met Auntie and Charles during World War II and stayed in contact. I'd snooped and found letters Tyee had written to Auntie throughout the fifty-plus years they'd known each other. Tens didn't talk about him much and I still didn't know how Tens went from living in Seattle with his grandfather to showing up at Auntie's two years ago. He'd walked and worked his way across the country, but I wasn't privy to many details.

"Excuse me?" Tens asked.

"Am I wrong? You have to be related to my friend Tyee."

I smiled. This had to be our Father Anthony.

Tens's nod was snuffed out by a bear hug. I'm not sure I'd ever seen such shock on Tens's face, but he returned the embrace, albeit more conservatively. I was next. The man smelled of soap and a subtle aftershave that reminded me of my father's.

"Father Anthony?" I asked.

He nodded but didn't take his eyes off of Tens's face,

as if he was trying to memorize each feature. "Not any-more. It's so good to see you. Last picture I got was your second—no, third, maybe—birthday."

"You know me?" Tens asked.

"Tenskawtawa Kemp, grandson of Tyee and Rosie?"

"No. Yes, I'm their grandson, but my last name is Valdes."

"Ah, that's right. It's been so long. How is your grand-father? I was sorry to hear about your grandmother's passing."

"I didn't really know her. But my grandfather—" Tens broke off, linking his fingers with mine.

I finished, "He died."

Father Anthony sagged, his eyes filled with sadness. "My condolences. He was a good man. One of the best." He turned toward me. "I'm sorry, I don't mean to ignore a pretty lady."

I waved my hand at his apology. "I'm Meridian Sozu."

"Are you two the friends of Joi's looking for me, then?"

I nodded. "Yes, we need to speak with you."

"I have to give a tour in a few minutes."

The gal behind the information desk called out with more than a little curiosity, "Mr. Theobald, those are your only arrivals tonight."

"Well, then, would you like a tour of the museum, or would you like to go get coffee?"

"We came to meet you," Tens answered.

I felt like we needed to apologize for not being more in-terested in the artifacts. "But we'd love to see the museum at some point."

Father Anthony's eyes crinkled at the corners when he smiled at me. "Some other time, then. There's a coffee shop right down the street, across from the hotel. Why don't you meet me there in about ten minutes? I'll check out of the museum for the night."

I left Tens to his thoughts while we walked down the street. He clung to my hand, but seemed utterly bereft of words. I didn't think either of us expected Father Anthony to have a real connection to us. My assumption had been that he knew Juliet, not that he knew Tens. *How do we move forward with this? What are the right questions to ask? What did Auntie want us to talk to him about?*

At Sacred Grounds, I sipped a frothy hot chocolate and Tens played with the straws in his Americano. We sat in our usual positions: Tens against the wall, watching the door, and me sitting in such a way I could see the room and watch Tens. Father Anthony strolled in, zeroing in on our table.

"Ah, friends." He shrugged out of his navy wool pea-coat and hung it on the chair next to me. He ordered his drink and came back to our table. His average height, dark hair liberally salted with gray, and dark brown eyes complemented his carriage. He was the type of man I could easily walk by and not see, not because he faded away but because his serenity and assurance simply existed. He didn't shout for attention in his dress or manner or personality. His was a steady fluidity.

"What brings you to me?" Father Anthony scooted his chair around the corner of the table so he could see both Tens and me.

Tens glanced at me, his expression helpless and confused.

"Is that too big a question?" Father Anthony asked.

Tens nodded.

I couldn't handle Tens's continued self-consciousness. "Will you tell us about how you knew Tens's grandfather?"

"Sure. I'm happy to." He sipped, holding his cup as if he could soak up the warmth of the coffee through his hands. "I served with Tyee in Vietnam, as a chaplain. I was a young priest, very green. He was one of the best field commanders. He cared about his men, and came to me when he worried for them. He also watched out for me. By that time he'd served in Europe during World War II, fought in Korea, and had three tours in Nam. He knew what to look for, how to see it, and how to teach us beginners to survive. War creates relationships, friendships thick as quicksand, with lightning speed. You watch men die, bleeding, and hold them while they do. On the other end of that you're bonded. I can't articulate the enormity, the speed and the steel that war builds."

"You were friends after?" I asked.

"Sometime during that first tour and his last one, we became brothers. 'Friends' isn't a big enough word. He was hurt—shot out his knee."

"The left one?" Tens's gaze sharpened.

"Yes."

"You remember?" I asked.

"Some things you see are seared in. His knee was shattered, ground-up, turned inside out. I used a tourniquet, stopped the bleeding. Felt like hours I bent over that left leg. He was left-handed, told me he'd never dance again with a smile on his face."

Tens nodded. "He limped, felt the weather change in that leg. I used to ask him about the scars crisscrossing it like a spiderweb, but he wouldn't answer."

"I'm sure he didn't have the words. It can be hard to share things with people you love when you think telling them will hurt 'em. Protect them with secrets and silence. That's the code. That's what kills us from the inside out when the war is over." Sadness clouded Father Anthony's face. "We lost touch in the mid-eighties. By that time I had a parish in northern Indiana; he'd moved to the West Coast, I think."

"Los Angeles."

"That was the return address for a while. Then I got a letter from him, one with a postmark of Miami and a photograph of you. I've periodically Googled old friends, but I never saw anything about Tyee come up. It was like after Miami he fell off the world."

"They moved to Seattle, for a particular hospital, when my grandmother got sick."

"And your mother?"

"I—" Tens broke off. He shrugged and shook his head.

"Complicated?" Father Anthony's lips twisted with sympathy and understanding.

Tens nodded.

"She broke Tyee's heart when she ran off with your father. I remember that. He called me, distraught. Didn't know what to do."

"What did you tell him?" I asked.

"What I counsel any parent—to love without condition and be there when their children are ready to come back. That's all I ever knew happened."

"So, you're a Catholic priest?"

"No, not anymore. I came home from Vietnam and worked in a VA hospital outside of Chicago, then was finally assigned a parish in the northeast of the state, running an orphanage, group home, and school."

"An orphanage?"

"And a K-through-twelve school that taught many students from families in the surrounds, as well as our kids. You're too young to remember some of the scandals that rocked the church in the late 1990s. Allegations are still being presented about priests abusing children and their power in the communities. I wasn't the only priest working and living there; I found out and put a stop to abuse in areas around us. I helped the victims go to the police and seek justice. I was asked to retire while it was all swept neatly under the rug."

"I'm sorry, but I think you did the right thing." I shuddered at the thought.

"Absolutely. No one has the right to abuse children, animals, or the elderly, and that the church could tolerate such behavior sickened me. By that time, I wasn't the best politico either. As retribution of a sort the archdiocese closed our orphanage and school, although I can't prove it of course. But even knowing I was leaving, they insisted on wiping out the family we'd built there."

"What happened to the kids?"

"The students went to other parochial schools or to public ones, I'd imagine."

"No, I mean the orphans."

"It depended on the child. Most were sent to the Walker-Kinney group home in the southern part of the state. Others were placed with foster families. A few were adopted into parish families—that was always the goal, to match kids and place them with families. There was only so much parenting we could do. Never enough. Not like the real thing. But we did our best."

"And now?"

"Well, I left here to help build the new government in South Africa. I came back to Indianapolis almost a year ago now. I volunteer at the museum, soup kitchens, tutoring. I stay busy. I'm just not in any official capacity. I'm simply Tony Theobald."

Tens cleared his throat. "I don't think God cares about a collar."

Tony grinned. "Neither do I."

* * *

We dropped Father Anthony—Tony—back at his car with promises to meet for dinner. He had photographs of Tyee he wanted to give Tens.

Tens was thoughtful and even stonier than normal on the ride home.

I kept playing the conversation back over and over in my head trying to understand why Auntie had pushed us to find Tony. He didn't seem related at all to Juliet. The mention of the school and the orphans rang true for what we knew about Juliet, but maybe the pieces of Tens's past were enough of a reason. It was like trying to do a crossword without clues. Frustrated, I sighed and followed Tens into the cottage, turning on every light and flipping the thermostat up to seventy-five. A chill froze my feet and hands.

"I think it's time you know what's in here." Tens unloaded a duffel of firearms onto the kitchen table.

Where the hell did those come from? "Four?" I asked.

"We can't rely on Josiah to show up every time we face a Nocti, and until we know how one of us can kill or incapacitate them, guns are our best shot."

He cleaned and oiled all the guns with precision and concentration.

"What's that one?"

He blinked as if surprised to see me standing there. "The little one I picked up for you. It's the right size for your hand. You'd have to be up close, but it'll protect you and you don't have to be an expert marksman. We'll practice tomorrow."

Then, he pulled out several serious-looking knives and cleaned them until they reflected the light like glass.

I sat huddled in a blanket, fascinated. "You're scaring me."

His expression fierce and determined, he answered, "We're not going to be unprepared for the Nocti again. Ever. That's all."

When he'd finished it was late, but I was itchy. Warmer,

but not right. My skin felt wrong. "Let's go check on Juliet."

"Now?" He stretched.

I threw the blanket onto the bed, already heading for the door. "Now. I have a feeling."

"A feeling?" He grabbed his coat, tucking a knife in its pocket and a gun in the back of his belt.

"Let's just go," I insisted.

"Okay." Tens grabbed the keys and we drove through the night toward Dunklebarger and Juliet.

"Hurry." I visualized the window fully open, willing the souls to me.

I sleep in a room that shares a wall with the organ's pipes. When the music plays I feel it in my soul. You kick when the choir sings. They sound like angels. —R.

CHAPTER 21
Juliet

Mistress had played the casinos down on the river once a week for most of my time at DG. I knew this because she came home smelling like cigarette smoke, heavy perfume, and alcohol. Often she was tipsy enough to leave chips, matchbooks, or napkins in her wake. If that wasn't a clue, her behavior the day after, an *especially* cruel morning after for us, seemed proportional to how much she had won or lost. Big numbers in either direction created big aftershocks in our world. Her absences seemed to grow and run together until it felt as if she only showed up to scream at us or beat me.

A newish night nurse in faded scrubs and holey sneakers watched subtitled *Law & Order* reruns in the break room. Occasionally, the television would mute while she walked her rounds of the guests' rooms. This particular nurse pretended kids belonged in a place like this and ignored us completely.

I choked back tears as I tucked Bodie and Sema into their sleeping bags. Having only two little children at DG at the moment should have helped me relax, but a bad feeling tickled my neck and put me more on edge. Less than a week from now, I'd be gone when Mistress took her night off and someone else, Nicole probably, would tell the stories. My heart broke as I spun a bedtime tale about chocolate rivers and Gummi catfish. Finally, the kids slept and I crept down the rickety attic stairs.

I paused outside of Mistress's upstairs office. I heard snoring from the Train Room and machines beeping in the Green Room. Otherwise, I was alone with my impulse. "If it's locked, I'll leave it alone," I whispered, reaching a hand toward the knob. "Or I'll snoop."

The doorknob turned in my hand. *Unlocked.*

My palms sweated and my face flamed. So foreign to me was breaking Mistress's sacred rules that I felt completely overcome with panic. I rushed in before I changed my mind, closing the door behind me. I stood frozen in the dark, letting my eyes adjust, pleading silently with my pulse to slow down. The shadows and evil shapes of the furniture began to take form: chairs, side tables, filing cabinets, and her massive general's desk.

In the moonlight, I felt around for the key behind the picture frame. When my fingers brushed the ridged edge of the key, exactly where Nicole told me I'd find it, I felt a little less paranoid about getting caught.

Bodie's flashlight clutched in one hand and the key in the other, I wondered if I dared turn on the flashlight. *Do I risk it?*

I inhaled, trying to remember to breathe. My heart beat against my ribs like a shoe in the dryer, a knocking, loud thump. I was sure everyone in Indiana could hear it.

What am I waiting for? I needed the light. I turned it on, shielding most of the beam against my body.

I started my file hunt with the first drawer I touched. Flicking through files and files of guest records I saw they were neatly sorted by month of death, all from the last two years. I closed the drawer and opened the next one. More of the same. There had to be hundreds of names and lives, all labeled, sorted, and organized by death date.

I turned to the next cabinet and pulled open a drawer. I recognized names in here. Names of kids. Kids I knew for days, or weeks, or months. All were kids who'd rotated through DG, but none of the ones I recognized had been here for their sixteenth birthday.

I opened the next drawer and saw Kirian's file. I slid it out, flipping through his birth certificate, reports, medical tests. Across the front page, in red, in Mistress's familiar scrawl: *DLVRD. 2K.*

What does that mean? I memorized the notation to ponder

later. Quickly, I checked to see if there was an address for where he'd been transferred. Nothing. No mention past that last day, not a bit of contact information. The only odd thing was the red scribble on the first page. I replaced his file, disappointed. If I could call him, if he knew, if he could tell me what happened to him after he left. I needed information.

The next files were thicker than the others. I recognized names of kids who'd all turned sixteen since I'd arrived. Kids who we'd been told went to group homes, college, families. I dragged out a couple more of my friends' files. They didn't have contact information either, but they did have: *DLVRD. 5K.*

Every single file. Mistress's handwriting. In red on the first page.

What does that mean? Where's my file? I opened the next drawer down. These were kids who'd left DG between their sixth and tenth birthdays. These too had birth certificates and medical reports, forms detailing their dreams and psychological evaluations, information about their biological families. But the front of these files said: *NO MRKNGS. BCK.*

I heard a soft snick at the door and froze.

"It's me," Nicole whispered through the crack.

I heaved an exhale. "You scared me."

"It's getting late. Are you okay?"

"Fine."

She moved closer. "What are you looking at?"

"Files. You got me thinking."

"Your file?"

"I can't find it."

"It's got to be here," she insisted. "Maybe it's with Bodie's, Sema's, and mine. Is there a drawer with current kids?"

"I haven't looked at those yet." I pointed at a stack on the floor. "Or the desk?"

Nicole carefully lifted piles on the desk, reading them quickly, like it was high noon under an August sun.

"How can you see to read?" I asked her.

"Ambient light. Here they are."

"Mine?" I replaced the files I'd glanced through and shut the drawer.

"Not yet."

We pawed through the rest of Mistress's desk, careful to put everything back exactly as it had been. I imagined Mistress as one of those people who dusted for fingerprints each time she returned. Since we weren't allowed to clean in here or even enter without her presence, I thought she'd notice a fraction of change.

"Here it is." Nicole held my file toward me.

My hand shook. "You read it." I couldn't take it. *What if Mistress is right?* What if I really was unwanted and unloved?

"Are you sure?"

"Quick." I shooed her.

"What am I looking for?"

"Here, give it to me." I handed her the flashlight and took the file.

A car turned into the drive.

"No!" I dropped the file. Pages flew everywhere. "She's back." My hands wouldn't pick up pages fast enough. "Is it that late?" *Where has the time gone?*

I peeked out the window. Mistress parked her Cadillac sedan in her special parking place, near the front door.

"Don't panic." Nicole helped me grab pages. "Wait, what's that?"

"Just copy it."

Nicole threw the page into the little office copier while I checked the window again. This was one time I was grateful for Mistress's slothful pace.

"Paper jammed!" Now Nicole's voice reflected the tension I felt.

"Never mind, then."

"If it's printed, though, she'll see it."

"Damn it!" I couldn't tear myself from the window. Even knowing I should run, never stop running, didn't make my feet move.

Mistress dropped her keys. As she stooped to pick them up, I heard a voice call out from the driveway.

"Hello? Excuse me?"

Mistress dropped her keys again, picked them up again, and turned toward the voice.

I craned my neck to see out the window. "That's—" I recognized the boy and girl from down by the creek. *What are they doing here?*

"Who?" Nicole jimmied the copier innards. "Got it. It's half done. Want me to try again?"

"No, let's get out of here." I quickly sorted the pages and hoped I had the files in the right order, but all I could do was guess.

I listened to Mistress and the other voices rumble as we made one more pass around the room.

"What are they saying? Who are those people?" Nicole whispered.

"I don't know." I thought everything appeared to be in the right place and order.

"Come on, they're coming inside."

Nicole and I snuck down the hallway to peer over the staircase, quietly trying to see who Mistress had invited into the house.

"She's gushing. Friendly." Nicole sounded surprised.

I shrugged. Nothing new there. "She's always that way with strangers. Charming and smiling." It was one reason I assumed no one ever thought her abusive. To the rest of the world she was maternal and loving.

"Can't anyone see through it?"

"Not yet." I didn't think ever.

We crept closer.

The girl was speaking. *Meridian?* "Thank you again, for letting us use the phone."

"Reception out here is spotty. So close to the city and yet so far," Mistress replied with a giggle and a sigh. She sounded like an entirely different person.

I heard the low rumble of the boy's voice. *Tens?* "Right, yes, at the boat ramp at Wick's swimming hole. See you then."

"Are you sure I can't give you a ride back into Carmel?" Mistress asked.

"No, we're fine waiting for AAA by the car. It's very nice of you to let us bother you so late. My dad would kill me if he knew we'd stopped there."

I peeked around the corner and saw the girl glance in my

direction. The briefest of eye contact told me she knew exactly where we were hiding. She was blushing, flushed and feverish-looking, sweat dribbling down her neck under her low and stubby ponytail. She was either nervous or sick.

I ducked back behind the wall, praying they wouldn't ask for me or acknowledge we'd met before. If Mistress knew I was still awake she'd tell me to start on tomorrow's list and kiss off sleep.

"Good night." The boy and the girl spoke in unison, leaning against each other like they were in love and couldn't get enough touching.

"Good night. Come back if you need to!" Mistress shut the front door behind them as they left. "Stupid necking idiots. The world would be better off drowning teenagers."

Nicole elbowed me and we backpedaled down the hallway. "Do you know those kids?"

"No. I mean, I met them once down by the creek, but that's all."

"They seemed nice. I don't buy that they were hooking up by the boat ramp."

"Why not?"

"Check out the window now." Nicole pressed her face against the glass with me. "He's carrying her."

"Did she faint?"

"Maybe. But if she was sick you'd think they'd come back inside."

"She didn't look well."

"Plus, it's closer to walk into town than to out here, if they really broke down at the boat ramp."

"So what were they doing here?" I asked, watching a huge dog join their parade until they were out of sight.

Nicole shrugged.

"Nico?" Bodie stumbled down the attic stairs.

"Yes? I'm coming." To me she said, "I'll see you in the morning?"

"Sure, but I have coffee with Ms. Asura."

Nicole's expression closed and darkened. "Be careful." She hugged me quickly and tight.

What was the worst thing that might happen? I mean, *really*?

"Oh, here's this." Nicole handed me the piece of paper she'd pulled from the copier.

I smoothed it out. At a glance, it looked like I would be able to read every word. "I thought you said it was ruined?"

"Guess we got lucky." She herded Bodie back up the stairs and I tucked the page in my bra to look at when I got down to my space.

I realized alarms were going off in two rooms when the nurse came barreling up the stairs with Mistress hot on her heels.

Orphanages, slums, genocides and natural disasters are prime locations to hunt Nocti, for with a mere feathered brush bodies perish in alarming numbers.

Lynea Wynn
January 31, 1973

CHAPTER 22

"I'm okay, you can put me down now," I said to Tens. My breath clouded the words in a chilly bubble.

Tens grunted.

"Haven't we done this before?" I tried to smile.

He stopped and gently set me on my feet. "You're heavier now than you were then."

I couldn't be offended by the truth. Back at Auntie's I was sticks and sickly, painful flesh. *Real sexy.*

"What happened?" Tens leaned against a tree trunk. The lights of Dunklebarger were still visible through the bare branches of the trees.

"Do you remember when Auntie talked about ghosts? Spirits that didn't cross over for whatever reason?"

"Like Charles?"

Auntie's husband, Charles, waited and watched and kept up his protective vigil until the end. Of course, that meant he scared the crap out of me several times before I knew what was going on. "Yes and no." I sank to the ground and let the cold damp soak up the back of my legs. I felt like I'd gone ten rounds with a T. rex.

"There are old people dying in there, right?"

I nodded, the three-quarter moon beckoning me with its blue cool to believe in magic and in fairies. That wasn't quite right, though. This hadn't felt like older energy, not all of it.

"What don't I understand?" Tens asked.

"It wasn't old energy in there. Not elderly souls, but kids, teens too."

Mini and Bodie came running toward us.

"Wait!" Bodie called in a whisper-yell.

I waved to acknowledge him. Tens and I ducked further into the shadows in case his voice carried back to the house.

Mini yowled. Custos barked in response and greeted Bodie with a tongue lashing of the slobbery kind.

"You shouldn't be out here." I sounded like the kid's mother.

"I snuck. All the old folks are real sick, busy dying." Bodie gasped for breath. His little legs had worked so hard to catch us it took a moment for the words to be put together in such a way they made sense.

"What do you mean, all the old people are . . . ?"

"Dying." He nodded, still gasping.

"Catch your breath, then talk," Tens commanded, scooting his back against a tree. Like we had all the time in the world and a surprise rendezvous with a first-grader was perfectly normal.

Mini wrapped herself around my legs, reaching up with her claws to stretch her back, but I didn't feel any divine information headed my way. She meowed plaintively; maybe it was my imagination, but she sounded quite disgusted with me. She twitched her tail and turned to Tens.

Bodie knelt on the grass, but he stayed out of reach. I didn't know if that was because he didn't trust us, or because his instinct was to make sure he could escape any situation. "Mini said we needed to get you back."

"Back?"

"Uh-huh. To the house. The bells and stuff started dinging. You left and they went crazy." His eyes widened.

I glanced at Tens.

"So Mini says you have to come back and sneak into the house until it's safe again for Juliet."

"Oh—" Now the cat talked to Bodie, too? What was wrong with me?

"No." Tens talked over me.

"We can't—" I shook my head.

"You hafta," Bodie insisted.

Mini punctuated this with a yowl. Bodie scrambled up and headed back toward Dunklebarger with her. "Come on!" His voice held an authority that belied his tiny frame and oversized eyes. "Hurry!"

"Merry, you can't." Tens caught my arm as I started to follow.

"I'm okay. I can handle the willing souls fine."

He nodded acceptance.

Tens and I jogged along with Bodie until we got to the back of the house. Bodie dipped under a tall hedge of vines.

"Don't touch those," he said over his shoulder. What was easy for the boy to squeeze through was hard for me and almost impossible for Tens.

Bodie watched us struggle through. "Sorry, it's the fastest way to the house."

Vines wrapped around my neck and arms, creeping down my shirt like itchy fingers. I battled them like they were living opponents. I had to be more tired than I thought to hallucinate that much. They seemed to move at will, not as inert vines should. I shivered.

We waited outside the kitchen door, in the shadows, along the back of the building. Then we crept in at Bodie's frantic hand signals.

Tens mumbled under his breath, "We're insane."

Sneaking through the kitchen with appliances way predating this century, we heard yelling and trampling footsteps above our heads.

"In here." Bodie herded us toward the stairs, opened a small door, and shoved us into a cramped storage space. "Go to the back. Nico will get you when it's safe. Keep going." He thrust a flashlight into my hands, gestured for us to tunnel in, and shut the door behind us.

I couldn't help but wonder if this was a trap. A crazy Nocti plan to lock us in a closet and burn the house down around us. I flicked the switch and handed the flashlight forward to Tens. He pushed past stacks of toilet paper and paper towels. "There's a mattress back here," he whispered.

"Tens?" The hair on the back of my neck stood up. "I need to sit." I felt like I'd stuck my head out of a window of a car going sixty miles per hour—the world rushed up toward my face and I stood at a shining summer window.

"Hello, dear." Auntie stood next to me. She embraced me and I felt her against me, solid flesh and blood. I smelled her apple blossom soap and famous chocolate cake.

Shocked, I wrapped my arms around her. "I can hear you?" I asked. Lined up around us were six elderly men and women growing more vibrant with each second, like extra coats of colorful paint were added with each blink. And children—there were children lined up single file, just a few, confused, but there nonetheless. Were children dying in here or were these ghosts of children who'd passed but hadn't transitioned?

"We don't have much time, these lovely souls have agreed to take turns with your window. Slowly, so we can talk."

"How is this possible?" I asked, aghast.

Auntie's face grew serious. "There's no time for that. Look in the journal, 1943 and a girl named Prunella."

I nodded as if this made sense.

Auntie continued. "You have to be careful not to scare

Juliet. She won't believe. The key is Father Anthony, get her to him. She won't leave the others without making the choice be hers. You must be patient. There's a Nocti clan nearby. You must be ready for anything."

In no time at all, Auntie moved back toward the window as the last elderly man stepped across, holding the hand of a small boy I didn't recognize.

"Why are there kids here?"

"They sacrifice to convert—"

"But—" I called to her, watching her disappear across the ledge. I didn't want her to leave. I gasped for breath and blinked up at Tens, whose hand covered my mouth. The flashlight was pressed tightly against his chest, so only the faintest glow illuminated him.

I relaxed my grip on his hand; I knew my nails left deep crescent marks.

His expression questioned whether I was awake enough for him to release my mouth or not.

I nodded, gulping air. Even the stuffy, dusty, stagnant air of the crawl space quenched my need for oxygen.

My right leg cramped and I straightened it by contorting around Tens's waist. We must have looked like a freeze-frame during a game of Twister.

"Okay?" he asked, shifting.

"Better," I said as my cramp eased.

His breathing evened out, to the point that I might have believed he'd fallen asleep, if not for the tension holding his frame motionless.

I strained my ears to distinguish noises and voices

from the sounds rolling around us. My mind filled in the blanks, imagining all sorts of wild scenarios. Darkness did terrible things to my imagination. Anxiety ate at my rational self and I was transported back to Revelation, worrying that at any moment Perimo might storm in with henchmen and burn us like they burned Auntie's house and her remains. *He's dead. He's dead. He's dead. Josiah killed him. You were there. You saw it.*

My mantra brought little comfort, but I kept repeating it in my head, while trying to match my breath to Tens's. Josiah, a Sangre Warrior, the species of angel who battle evil with light, filled Perimo with so much light, Perimo's darkness disappeared for good. I didn't know enough about Sangre yet. To the best of my knowledge they were the only ones able to kill Nocti. It wasn't as if Josiah was on my speed dial. But there were more Nocti out there. Causing chaos. Creating havoc. Ripping souls from their families and taking them to the void. Hunting Fenestra to kill or turn. Manipulating the environment to take advantage of human frailty was against the rule of the Creators—that was where Sangre came into play. I think. I hadn't figured out how Fenestras could defeat Nocti if a Sangre wasn't available.

Tens turned off the flashlight. Not even the crack of light from under the small door made it to us back behind the cleaning supplies. "Merry, why is there a mattress tucked back here?" Tens whispered against my ear, his breath tickling, sending shivers down my spine.

"What?" I blinked.

"Someone sleeps here."

Or we will, if this is a trap. "Maybe they knew we were coming and made a holding cell?"

"There wouldn't be a kinda comfortable mattress then." He tsked.

"Good point." They'd throw us in a dungeon or the modern equivalent.

"So . . . who?" Tens wouldn't drop it and I took the bait.

Who sleeps here? Who tucked an air mattress and a single ratty old army blanket behind paper towels and rolls of TP? Someone hiding.

"It's hidden," I said.

Tens nodded against my neck.

I concentrated on being completely in the moment. Pushing all fear of the unknown out of my head. I closed my eyes, even though in the dark it was a redundant gesture.

"Juliet." I felt the truth in her name.

"Why?" He shifted his hips against me.

I don't know how, but I simply know. It was the same feeling I had when we'd come upon her at the creek. Pieces fit together. When I wasn't stuck in the past, in my fear of Nocti and what we'd experienced in Colorado, I felt stronger. "She escapes back here. Turn on the flashlight."

He clicked the switch back on. "Careful," he warned.

I glanced around and noticed three bottles of cleaners in the far back corner. They looked out of place. "Hand me the bleach."

"What are you doing?" He reached for the bottle and

lifted it. It rattled. Not like it held liquid, but like pieces of glass or metal were inside. He paused, quirking a brow in question.

"Open it," I demanded.

Tens shifted against me, our legs tangled in the small space. He accidentally elbowed me in the ribs.

"Umph."

"Sorry."

I shook my head. Nodded at the bottle.

He tried to unscrew the top, but it wouldn't come off.

"Wait." I saw a piece of duct tape on the bottom. "Turn it over."

Tens pointed the flashlight directly at the bottom of the jug. The contents shifted and rattled with each movement. We both turned toward the door hoping no one heard. Silence fell upon the activity above our heads.

"Not bleach."

I carefully lifted the tape and peered inside using the flashlight. I saw a collection of pebbles, shells, an arrowhead, and feathers.

Tens took a look. "What do you think this is?"

"Treasures?"

We opened another bottle and saw a bird's nest filled with empty blue eggshells, carefully wrapped in toilet paper to keep the bundle safe. I gently put it all back, pondering why Juliet kept a collection of outside trinkets disguised in plastic bottles.

We couldn't risk making more noise, because the quiet felt oppressive.

I heard doors slamming above our heads as what

seemed like several vehicles drove up outside. More doors slammed and a clatter of heels against the stairs descended.

A woman's voice? I think it was the woman who let us use the phone. A headmistress who seemed more interested in her next drink than running this place. I didn't think she was Nocti, but I felt like she had bad energy. Her heels clicked back up the stairs, with heavier footsteps following. Car doors?

A man spoke. Neither Tens nor I could catch his words, but we heard the response clearly.

His coworker said, "Sleeping like the dead I was. So freakin' inconsiderate dying in the middle of the night."

I wanted to bust out of the closet and scream at him until he understood the word *respect*. I just tightened my hold on Tens, whose expression said that he wanted to do the same thing. Only Tens would have used less words, more actions, to get his point across. Finally, the next wave of activity subsided. Engines started up and drove off. The heels clicked by and didn't return.

I shifted my neck to ease a new cramp and wondered if I'd make it to a bathroom before things hit critical mass. For the umpteenth time, I wished my special powers were more practical, like not experiencing hunger or thirst, or never needing potty breaks. Seriously, those would come in handy, whereas these death powers, these just got in my way.

"Can you reach my midback?" Tens whispered.

I brought a hand up. "I think so."

"Scratch between my shoulder blades."

I scratched gently through his shirt.

"Harder."

I felt his muscles ripple as he stretched against my hand.

"Thanks. Better."

I stopped, but left my hand on his back.

"That was driving me nuts." He smiled down at me, and for the first time I realized he lay on top of me, with his legs over mine. My heart sped up and even in this dangerous, crazy situation I wanted him to kiss me. We pressed together; parts of me were quite happy with the contact. He too was aroused by the proximity. Someone at school used to talk about fear and survival making for the best sex. Maybe they were right.

My desire must have changed my expression or muscle tension, because Tens began to lean down toward me. His tongue licked his lips and I mimicked him.

The door to the closet opened with a snick.

We leapt, tangling further, startled back to reality. It took a moment for me to regain my equilibrium, but Tens uncurled and moved between me and the door.

A face I'd only seen from a distance peered in. "I'm Nicole. It's safe, but we must hurry." We scooted out as quickly and quietly as possible. Transitioning those souls had left my legs rubbery and asleep.

I felt like a secret agent lurking around corners, following this girl toward our freedom.

Bodie poked his head out from under a table as we went by and gave us a thumbs-up.

I smiled in return, not sure what about this pleased him.

None of us spoke, relying solely on hand signals and head shakes. As the back door swung shut behind us, Nicole caught it and closed it without a sound breaking the night air.

She led the way toward the hedge along the side of the property. "Go around, not through." She pointed.

"Why? That's the way we came." I gestured toward where Bodie brought us. It would be so much faster.

"There's a terrible patch of poison ivy in there."

That was the second time I'd heard warnings about ivy. Didn't it just grow up old brick buildings? "What's that?"

"How do you not know about poison ivy?" she asked, a shocked, horrified expression on her face.

Father Anthony has been so kind. It is my hope
that he'll act as godfather for you and protect
you if I'm not able.   —R.

CHAPTER 23

Juliet

On two hours of sleep, I'd made oatmeal and toast for the
four of us kids. It was odd to have all the rooms unoccupied;
I couldn't remember that happening before.

I tasted ooey-gooey macaroni and cheese and rich,
velvety chocolate cake on the back of my tongue. I hoped
Mistress would leave the house again long enough for me to
sneak those out of my head and onto our plates.

Exhaustion from the night's events kept dragging at me

like wet winter clothes during a creek swim. I didn't know how much longer I'd be able to resist the pull of a current I didn't understand. What would happen if I laid down and refused to ever get up again?

"How are you feeling today?" Nicole put her hand on my forehead.

"A cold, maybe." My face was aflame and I felt like I was running a fever. My throat was stripped raw.

"Are you getting sick?"

"Of course not." Work didn't stop for illness.

"Maybe you should go back to bed?"

"I can't."

"I think we need to talk about your birthday."

"What about it?"

"What are you going to do?"

"Do?"

"Next. When she asks you about what you want?"

"I don't know."

"You have to think about it."

"I can't." I bit off the words. "Please just stop."

"I can't stop time." Nicole looked sad, then went to the pantry and pulled out a brown grocery bag. "Here are some clothes."

"For what?"

"You'll blend better in this stuff." She pushed the bag toward me when I didn't take it. "For coffee with Ms. Asura. Why don't you go shower? It might make you feel better."

I nodded, too achy to argue. "Thank you," I said.

She nodded, turning back to the dishes immediately.

However much I wished I could spend the day in hot water, I showered quickly, not wanting Mistress to notice my absence. I tugged on crisp black jeans, a black T-shirt with constellations silk-screened on it, and a red hoodie.

Since all Nicole wore was dresses, I knew these weren't her clothes. Besides, I would never fit my length and width into her stuff. My usual sneakers were falling off my feet and used to belong to Mrs. Kapowsky, who was here three weeks and taught me a French lullaby to sing to the kids. The shoes Nicole had given me were orthopedic and completely ugly, but black, so not as obvious as some others. I couldn't pay attention to fashion—as if I even had time to. I didn't ask Nicole where she'd found the clothes. They didn't come from the closet or suitcase of one of the deceased—they fit too well and were too new.

Mistress called me to her office as I stepped out of the steamy upstairs bathroom. She was in her usual double-polyester floral-nightmare blouse and plum—puke brown pants. With her hair scraped back slickly and too much orange blush, her already fat face looked even rounder, drawing attention to her third chin. She was brimming, in full form, not a hint that she'd worn a V-neck dress and non-sensible heels last night. I tuned back into her words before she noticed and punished me for not paying better attention. There were such things as pop quizzes around here; they usually ended with one of us kids getting popped.

Mistress harangued me. "I know you'll be on your best behavior. People have high expectations for kids from

Dunklebarger. So don't get any ideas." Her expression told me that the truth was one of those ideas I wasn't supposed to get.

"Yes, ma'am." I avoided eye contact, staring at the floor instead.

"Ms. Asura is one of my best friends."

"Yes, ma'am." I doubted that. But it might explain the way they always seemed to be in cahoots. I didn't think Ms. Asura would be seen with someone as obese as Mistress since appearances seemed to matter so much to her.

"I'll expect you to make up the work. No dawdling," she barked.

"Yes, ma'am." I peeked out from under my lashes. She'd turned toward the window with a softer, dreamier stance.

In a warm and fuzzy voice Mistress mused, "She's such an optimistic person. She sees the good in everyone. I bet she'll tell you about going after your dreams and ask you what you want to do with your life."

I held my tongue because there didn't seem to be a correct response. I had no idea what to say to this rumination.

With a snap, she turned back toward me. I dropped my eyes as quickly as I could. Mistress spit the next words with venom: "She's lying. She's paid to say nice things to you. It's her job. We laugh about it later on the phone. All your stupid little wishes." Mistress cackled, not requiring audience participation for her monologue. She settled into her desk chair and clicked on her computer screen. I had no idea what she spent so much time doing online; Nicole said it was something called FarmVille, and singles dating sites. But I'd also seen banking records and tables of numbers and names. The dating-sites idea made me nauseous; I couldn't imagine the man who would be desperate enough to take her to dinner.

I kept my shoulders back and my knees locked, even as a wave of wooziness washed over me. The throb in my temple grew worse with each passing day. I hadn't been dismissed yet, and so close to my outing I dreaded losing the privilege.

Mistress glanced at me over the tops of tiny gold-rimmed reading glasses. "I'm not going to be here forever, you know. I'm not the first headmistress and I won't be the last. I'm going to retire to Tampa and live on the beach and watch my shows, with Klaus, every day. You're stupid, Juliet, there's no hope for you, but I'm smart and I have a plan. I've worked my whole life in this hole with you retards and I'm almost there. I have my nest egg incubated and it's almost ready to hatch. Then, I'm out of here and you can all rot in hell if you're lucky enough to get there. You have no idea what's in store for your birthday."

We weren't the ones going to hell. But I kept my silence.

"Knock knock!" Ms. Asura opened the office door with a flourish and a cloud of scent that smelled like I imagined a faraway sultan's palace might smell. Exotic. Overpowering. Spicy. "Ready, Juliet?"

"She's ready." Mistress answered for me. "Mind your manners, Juliet." She and Ms. Asura shared a look I couldn't interpret.

I nodded and followed Ms. Asura to her Mercedes. When she came with kids she drove a big white van, but when it was just her, it was this boxy, expensive-looking sports car.

Ms. Asura turned up music full of angry yelling, loud drums, and screaming guitars. She tapped her polished nails on the steering wheel. I thought I might vomit from the pain in my head, so we didn't talk. The scent that had seemed exotic in the house felt completely overwhelming in the small confines of the car. The sun shone like French vanilla ice cream. It was cold outside; I'd draw attention if I rolled down the window. I tried breathing through my mouth instead of my nose and that helped a little.

We found a parking place near the coffee shop. Parents with strollers and toddlers chatted and giggled up and down the sidewalks. The foster-kid hazard was that all we saw were happy families those few times we were out. I heard once that pregnant ladies always saw pregnant ladies, or people with a certain car only saw those kinds of cars. It was the same for us, only opposite: we didn't have a family so we saw them everywhere.

This was the type of coffee shop I had walked by, peering from under my lashes at the people sitting at tables, laughing, talking, and sipping frothy drinks with no cares. I'd never been in one. I stuffed my hands deep into the pockets of my hoodie and shuffled my feet. Losing a shoe was not an option.

Ms. Asura kept smiling at me, her eyes twinkling, and if anything my continued discomfort only made her smile more. Maybe she was trying to reassure me with each twist of her lips?

The scent of fresh coffee, warm milk, yeasty doughnuts, and cakes reminded me that I'd skipped eating breakfast even though I'd cooked for everyone else. My stomach growled. It was so loud I clutched it in embarrassment.

Ms. Asura either didn't hear it or pretended not to. "Do you know what you'd like?"

"I—" I read the menu boards, not understanding most of the words. *Is this English?* There were moments when I knew how sheltered I'd been, when I looked up and realized months had passed by without my leaving DG. Most of the time, I was too busy and too tired to notice. This was one of the times I felt every second I hadn't been in school, or in a mall, or with a family of my own.

Ms. Asura patted my shoulder. Her face was patient, but the throats clearing behind us made me point at the larger-than-life sign standing by the counter. I didn't even read the description. I just wanted everyone to stop staring at me.

"Are you sure?" she asked me.

I nodded. I didn't have a clue what it was: a clear mug full of purple berries and chocolate swimming in coffee, smothered in whipped cream and drizzled with more chocolate. I wasn't sure if it was a drink or a dessert.

"Why don't you go sit down and I'll get the drinks?" Ms. Asura sent me toward a table for two in the back corner. She chatted with a couple of men in business suits like she'd known them forever.

I tried not to let awe blanket my face, but I'm fairly certain I looked like a hick in the big city for the first time. This was what normal looked like—so very normal. The green monster burned in me when I watched a gaggle of girls my age prance by the windows giggling. After about ten minutes Ms. Asura joined me with a expectant gleam in her eyes.

"People in this town are so nice. It's quaint enough to feel small and close enough to Indianapolis to offer anonymity if desired." Ms. Asura set down my drink and hers, glancing at the men, who smiled and winked.

"Do you know them?" I asked.

"Those men? No, that's what I mean. Friendly, friendly, friendly." She smiled and took a sip. The top of her coffee had a heart shape in the foam. She pointed it out to me. "Cute."

The table we sat at had a glass top under which people put business cards and signs and notices. Smack in the middle was the flyer the glass man had brought by DG.

I must have gasped or made a noise, because Ms. Asura straightened immediately. "What is it?"

I shook my head. "Nothing." But my pulse fluttered wildly.

She lost her smile and turned to get a better look at the signage. "An open house at a glass studio? Do you like glass art?"

"No, I d-don't really know," I stuttered, and started balling up the straw wrappers.

She narrowed her eyes at me. "It seemed like you recognized the sign. Have you met this man?"

"I—"

As if a switch had been thrown, she relaxed and went back to grinning at me like a girlfriend. "It's not a crime to talk to people, Juliet." She sipped and sat back in her chair.

"He came by Dunklebarger, but I didn't say anything to—"

Her smile grew. "Say no more. It'll be our secret! What did he want?"

I shrugged. "Just to invite people to a party."

"Did he call it a party?" Her voice sharpened.

"Uh, no. I guess not. I don't remember. I told him when to come back to speak with Mistress."

"Maybe I'll have to pay a visit to this nonparty. Sounds like loads of fun." She hummed. "Tell me more about you." Each word lost more of its patina of sincerity.

I began to doubt if she really cared. "Uh—"

"What are your dreams? Hopes? Where do you see your-self in ten years? Twenty?"

"I don't know." I didn't have time to dream. I didn't have the energy to hope. I never saw past today except to wish for a different tomorrow.

"Every girl dreams of something or someone. You can tell me. Is there a boy waiting for you, perhaps? What do you most want to become in this world?"

My face burned at her mention of a boy. I assumed she'd read the postcards she delivered and knew about Kirian, but I hated sharing that with an adult. "I guess—" I racked my mind for a plausible something. Anything. I finally blurted, "A mom."

"You want kids? I don't know what I'd do without mine."

"You have kids?"

Startled, she sloshed her coffee. "No, no. Not officially. But I've built a family much the way you will with people who value me and take care of—" She broke off. "What job will you do?"

"I think I'll be a mom full-time." I was drawing on con-versations and dreams I'd shared with Kirian to answer these questions. I wasn't connected to these answers on a personal level. Not anymore.

"You want to be a mom? That's all?" Her face fell.

"Sure." I latched onto that.

She seemed disappointed. "That sounds like your— Only a mom? I see you as so much more than a mother. An actress, or a politician, or a lawyer."

Why was being a mom, a real mom, the kind who put their children first and protected them and played with them and loved them forever—why was that less than being an actress or a lawyer? I didn't ask. Her answer might make me mad. I didn't think there was anything more impressive in this world than being a good—great—mom. Nothing. But to keep the conversation moving I caved. "A teacher?"

Her face took on a calculating expression. "Teacher. That sounds intriguing. I can see that. So, you'll need college. That's the benefit to a placement at Dunklebarger—you have a savings account."

I played with the whipped cream on top of my drink. "A what?"

Surprised, she asked, "Haven't I told you this? You're so mature for your age, but we usually don't tell kids before they're sixteen. You get paid for your work helping around the house. It goes into a savings account."

I'd never heard this. "Really?" I licked more cream off the top with a plastic stirrer.

She seemed genuinely upset with my ignorance. "Yes, absolutely. You didn't think you were doing all that work for nothing, did you? They don't tell the little kids—they want you to learn the value of hard work, have a work ethic before you find out. That sort of thing."

"Oh." Really? Were the beatings our Christmas bonuses? The more she talked, the more I felt like a player in a game with rules I didn't know.

She tapped bloodred nails on the glass tabletop. "But you'll need your GED to apply to colleges."

"Uh-huh." *Not happening soon.*

"There's two years until you can apply, so plenty of time. Have you given any thought to the next stage in your life?"

I inhaled and pretended I was brave. "I'd like to stay at Dunklebarger until I'm eighteen."

Her face fell and she appeared sorry, reaching a hand out to me. "Oh, honey, that's just not possible."

"But—but—" I stuttered as tears threatened. I had to make her understand. "Can't you make an exception? Just until I'm eighteen? Who will look after the kids?"

"Silly, I know you think your job as the eldest child there is an important one, and I'm sure the kids love you, but they'll be fine. You're not their guardian—they have one, and they have me, and there will be new kids coming in soon."

"But—"

"Juliet, I've been doing my job for years. Much longer than I look old enough to be. And every teenager I see says the same thing. Human beings don't like change. We resist it. I want you to stop resisting it. Change isn't the enemy. Go with it. You'll never know unless you take risks, Juliet. Trust me. I'm on your side."

I gulped my Grande Blackberry-Swirl Mocha Supreme and scalded my tongue, my throat, all the way down to my stomach. The coughing racked my frame and shook the table.

"Slow down." Ms. Asura handed me napkins and waited until I'd gotten my breath back. "There's something else bothering you, I can sense it."

I hesitated. *Do I trust her? I know better. One last time. Try again. For Bodie. Nicole. Sema. The nameless to come.*

"Juliet, I can't do my job unless you trust me. Please let me help." She reached out and touched my hand, gently, comfortingly.

"Mistress beats us." I rushed the words out. The overly sweet drink turned sour in my stomach. The moment I'd said the words, I wanted to take them back.

She snatched her hand back as if I'd burned her. I watched her pale beneath her makeup and narrow her eyes. "I'm disappointed, Juliet. I thought we'd had this conversation before. Discipline isn't the same as abuse."

"But—"

"In all my years working with kids placed at Dunkle-barger, I've never heard such an allegation. I'm shocked. Shocked." She crossed her legs and leaned toward me across the table. Her eyes turned beady and assessing.

"But—"

"I thought more of you. You aren't getting your way, so you're going to sabotage the whole place? You could ruin lives, saying this. Ruin your future. Poof! Your future can disappear."

"Uh—" I couldn't get more than a sound out of my mouth. My face burned with shame.

"This is serious. Very, very serious. You've gone and ruined my day with this terrible lie." She sighed. "I was going to get us cookies, too."

"I'm sorry."

She pouted. "Are you wrong? Did I mishear you?"

"Yes, I'm wrong." I shrank deep inside myself. "We were talking about my going to college to become a teacher."

Her smile broke across her face like sunrise on a cold morning. She prattled on about tests, courses, and colleges in the state with wonderful programs for teachers. I think she asked questions; I answered with one- or two-word answers. But all I felt turning over in my head was that I'd failed. All of them. Every kid after me. I'd failed to be brave. To make a case. To show her the wounds on my back and make her take me seriously.

I finished my coffee without tasting it and listened to her prattle on before dropping me back off at DG.

I thanked her and she told me she'd see me soon.

I failed.

Again.

Always.

I watched as my family burned. I am a coward.

Spectavi cum familia mea arderet. Ignavus sum.

Luca Lenci

CHAPTER 24

"Tens, turn around." I grabbed his collar and pushed it down to peer at his skin. Streaks of red bumps and fluid-filled blisters lined his neck, disappearing down below, on his back and over his shoulders. "Do they itch?"

"Yeah, they feel more like stings, though."

"I don't think so." Seeing his back made my own start to itch. I was one of those people who should never go to medical school—give me a list of symptoms and I totally start thinking I have them. When Sammy came home with lice in preschool I walked around scratching my scalp for weeks. Of course, once Mom poisoned the house the lice crawled into my hair to die.

"Not a big deal." Tens brushed me off. "I'll be fine." He rubbed his thigh.

My back and forearms burned too.

"Tens?"

"Yeah?"

"Humor me and look down my shirt, will you?" I turned, already pushing up my sleeves. I gasped.

My forearms were ugly masses of blisters.

"Oh no. Is that what my back looks like?" Tens held my hands, then quickly lifted my shirt. "Your back, too."

He dropped his jeans. The backs of both legs were mottled with red streaks.

"Poison ivy is bad, right?"

"Maybe it's not that." Tens scratched his back on the wall like a bear at a tree trunk. "I've had it and it wasn't this bad."

"I'm calling Joi." I picked up the phone and realized the palms of my hands were also affected. "Crap!" I dialed. "Joi? What does poison ivy look like?"

Tens heard her squawk from across the room.

"Joi?" No answer, just a dial tone. "I think she must be on her way over."

"It's on your forehead." Tens pointed at my face.

I was peering at my body in the bathroom mirror when Joi stomped into the cottage carrying an enormous basket of supplies.

"You need to get all your clothes off. There's no saving

them. It's in the sap. Take a cold shower. We're a bit late now, but it still might help. And if you touch it again, you'll start again. Take a shower, put on your undies, apply this cream, then put these on." She held out mittens, a pink pair with a black and white kitten knitted into it and a pair with an alligator wearing a cowboy hat.

"Why?"

"You'll itch while you sleep. These'll make sure you don't scratch so much you get secondary infections or scar those pretty faces. Take a Benadryl—it'll make you drowsy, but it may help a little."

"Really?"

"Yes. You're having an allergic reaction. I'm serious. Undergarments, cream, pill, and mittens. And here are new sheets. Wrap yourselves in them, drape the furniture—that way it won't matter what the greasy lotion touches. Here are ice packs. Put them on the worst places—it'll cool the itch a little."

"Is this a common thing?" I asked.

"Among children, yes." Joi smiled at me. "And travelers who don't know much about the woods. I would have thought you'd recognize it. These are the worst blister cases I've seen, though. Like you rolled around in the stuff." She raised her eyebrows and glanced at Tens. "You didn't roll about in the ivy, did you?"

He cracked a smile, but shook his head. "No, ma'am. We were a little too busy to, um . . ." He trailed off in embarrassment.

"Just checking." She went back to her bags and pulled

out containers for the fridge. "I'll leave you food so you can eat if you get hungry. One of you must go shower now. Tens, go." She barked like a mom.

He raced toward the bathroom.

"Put your clothes in a trash bag," she yelled at his back. "And you, how are you doing?"

I dropped my eyes. I felt like she could see too much. "I'm okay."

"Do we need to get you to a hospital? Is this going to make things worse? I really don't like the looks of your rash. Promise me you'll see a doctor if it gets worse? Even a little bit?"

For a moment I didn't know what she was talking about, then I remembered our cover story: I was recovering from an illness. "No, this won't make me worse. But, yes, I'll see a doctor if I don't start getting better quickly."

"Promise you'll tell me?"

"I promise."

"Is your family somewhere I should call?"

"No. We're on our own."

She grew more concerned. "You're young to be so alone."

"We've got each other."

"I see that. You love each other. You look out for each other. And there's no criminal activity. Any dolt can see that. But will you tell me if you need help? Or decide to go home?"

"Joi, please. Leave us be. We're not hurting anyone," I pleaded. "But, yes, we'll come to you if we need something.

My home is with Tens, though; there's no place to go back to."

She frowned. "Things can change. I just want you to have support."

I thought fast. "Rumi is helping us."

"The glass artist?"

"Yeah, he knows what's going on. He's helping us with the search."

"For your biological parents?"

I nodded.

"Okay, then. You need anything else from me, you tell me. Anything. I'm handy on a computer too."

"I will. We will."

With that she air-kissed me, careful not to touch me. She winked as she walked toward the door. "Remember, cold shower, undies, cream, pill—"

"And mittens," I finished with a smile.

After Joi left, Tens finished in the bathroom, walking out in boxer briefs that rode low. If I weren't so itchy, well, the blisters weren't my idea of sexy, but he managed to stay delicious even with them. "Shower, then if you can, help me?" He pointed at his back. "I can't reach."

"Sure." I didn't realize how bad the rash was until I pulled off all my clothes and turned every which way in the mirror. It looked like the vines had made stick-figure handprints all over my skin. It creeped me out. I could visualize the ivy vines trailing along my skin, leaving the poison behind. The itch made me want to rub against the walls like Tens had. I turned the water to icy and got in.

My teeth chattered and my fingertips started to turn blue, but my skin felt relieved—the chill cut the burn.

"Merry? You okay?" Tens knocked on the door. "You've been in there a while."

I loathed the idea of getting out. "Yeah. Fine." I turned off the spray and patted dry with a towel, resisting the urge to scrape the terry cloth against my skin.

"This sucks!" I yelled through the bathroom door.

"Yep." Tens sounded defeated in his agreement.

I tugged on boy shorts and a bra that was more like a bikini top, with ties around the back and neck. I hated the confines of bras, since for most of my life I'd had no breasts to cover up. Now that my cleavage was growing, I still wasn't sure what to do with it. I opted for camisole sport bras or things like this that weren't restricting. I wasn't a lingerie angel.

I wrapped the sheet around myself. With all we'd been through, I still wanted to look my best when Tens was around. Stupid, but true. And oozing blisters didn't peg anyone's sexy meter. He managed to look wounded and uncomfortable, yet stay sexy as hell.

I spread the cream on his rash, which spread like tree branches along his back. He too had a few oddly recognizable handprints. When I was finished I handed him the tube and pulled on my mittens, feeling like a fool.

"Thanks. But—wait—can you—right there—scratch it—please?" He broke almost every word.

I shook my head. "We're not supposed to scratch them."

"Do it!" He bit the words at me over his shoulder.

I used the back of my mitten to scratch at a red patch that wasn't blistered up yet. "There?"

"Hmm . . ."

"More?"

"Hmm . . . don't stop."

I gave up when my arm wore out.

"Don't stop."

"I have to." My own rash was begging for attention. "My turn. Goop me up?" I turned my back and listened to him sigh and rearrange himself.

The heat of his hands against my bare skin could have been the start of something more. But there wasn't more than a tug of regret with both of us sitting here half naked. I was too uncomfortable to consider seduction of any kind. Participating *or* initiating.

An hour later, the ointment had dried and cracked, new rash had spread, and the ice packs were room temp. I thought about taking another cold shower, but I'd have to start over on the cream application. The damn mittens kept getting in the way of me getting a good scratch and I wasn't the least bit drowsy. I wiggled on the sheets and huffed. I stared up at the ceiling, filled with frustration.

"Why didn't you know about this, Mr. Protector?" I was snippy and I didn't care. My neck, back, hands, and arms were on fire.

"Damn." Tens didn't move from his position on the couch.

"Shouldn't you have knowledge about this kind of

thing since you trekked across country from Seattle to Colorado? By yourself? Camping?" I couldn't let it go.

"I know poison ivy, but it was dark. I'm sorry."

"Can you sense what I'm feeling right now? The inside of my left ear is itchy and I can't get to the damn thing with this freakin' mitten on. Can you feel that? Are you in twice the agony?"

"Meridian, stop. I wouldn't have let you go into it, you know that—"

"Do I? You let me go first—"

"Please just shut up. Let me die in silence."

That ivy warning Bodie gave us? We should have paid attention.

The knock at the door had Custos wagging her tail and standing up to look out the little window with joy.

"I don't care who's there." I had a sheet lightly covering my bra and panties. The less to stick to, the better.

"I'll try to get it." Tens stood up and weaved his way over to the door in his boxer briefs.

"Oh, hex my hiney! You're flagellated!" Rumi's booming voice relaxed me. He was like a grandpa, and even though we'd known him for so short time I felt completely safe in his presence. Tens must have felt similarly because he made his way back to the sheet-covered couch and reclined.

"Look at the two of you." Rumi whistled disbelief as he bent over me to air-kiss my forehead. "When Joi called and said you had a case of the ivy I thought you'd be a little rashy, but this is brutal. You be sure it's poison ivy?"

I grunted.

Tens answered, "We think."

"Ah, you never heard 'leaves of three, let 'em be'?"

"Rumi?" I asked in a tone that warned him to step back. "If we'd known that little ditty don't you think we'd have avoided it?"

"True, true." He sighed, his expression forlorn. "So, you won't be coming tonight."

I sat up too quickly. "No, we want to come." In reality, I'd forgotten the open house in my wallowing. I rubbed my mittened hands against the comforter.

"You'll scare off the guests looking like that."

"Is it that bad?"

"Yes'm."

I lay back with a sigh, relieved he'd made the decision for me. I didn't want to be gutless, but at the moment I might even walk up to the Nocti and ask them to make it stop.

"I'll report back to you when all is said and done. I brought roast chicken and potatoes from the pub down the block for your lunch. Robust food for hearty healing. Joi will float you away with all the soup."

I smiled, even though it made the sores on my cheeks crack under the calamine. "Thanks."

Rumi left amid our promises to take it easy and rest.

* * *

After applying layers of lotion and taking several Benadryl, I lay staring up at the ceiling feeling miserable and aching for a distraction. I read more pages in Auntie's journal, searching for the entry about Prunella that Auntie had instructed me to find. I found a Prudence, but no Prunella. Tens was surfing on the laptop watching goofy videos and shopping for new boots.

The knock on the door was polite and too tentative to be either Joi's or Rumi's.

Tens waited to open the door until I'd thrown a nightshirt over myself. "Father Anthony?"

Father Anthony appeared sheepish, then shocked. "Tens. What happened to you?"

"Poison ivy. Come on in."

"Ah, then this makes more sense." He held a rolled-up piece of construction paper and a jar that seemed to glow. "Are you sure it's poison ivy? Terrible case. Oh, Meridian, you too?" He walked over to me, clearly upset. "What can I do for you two?"

I went to the fridge and got out drinks. "We're not contagious, right?"

"No, poison ivy isn't like a cold."

"Would you like a drink?"

"No, I'm fine. I'd like to talk to you. If that's okay."

Tens gestured to the couch and chairs. "Sure, Father Anthony. What's up?"

We sat on the couch across from him as he shook his head and said, "I joined the priesthood because my faith is what saved me. I don't want the title of Father, because that was bestowed on me by man, not God, not Christ. I work for God, not the church, so please just call me Tony."

"Okay." Tens nodded.

I added, "Got it."

Tony paused. "I don't know where to start. I'm so used to being on the listening end of things. I need to tell you something that I've never told another person. Tyee and I never spoke of it. Never said the words aloud. Even now I'm not sure of myself."

I threw him an opening. "Sometimes we can't second-guess everything. Some things defy our puny human logic."

Tony smiled. "Good point. Tyee felt things: he'd know when particular soldiers or marines were at their breaking point. He'd know where an enemy was. Men wanted to go into battle with him because he had a sixth sense. But it was more than instincts. It went beyond that."

"That makes perfect sense to me," Tens said.

I nodded. At Auntie's house, I'd snooped and found letters from Tyee to Auntie about Tens. Tyee talked about how his visions were fading and clouding. Maybe it ran in the family. Maybe Tyee's visions were a different kind than Tens's. Or maybe Tens would grow into his own.

"I need you to know that I owe your grandfather my life."

I sat straighter, not expecting to hear that.

Tens asked, "What?"

"Vietnam. I volunteered to go to the front, where we were taking heavy hits—I thought I'd best serve God and man among the dying and wounded. Tyee asked me to get a drink with him the night before. He started talking to me about faith and God. It was the most in-depth conversation

I'd had about religion and the afterlife. Death. Most of my time was spent in prayer or listening to confession, unpacking the contents of the burdens each man carried with him to lighten his load. Tyee probed with his questions and pushed me." He shook his head with a frown. "He asked if I was ready to die. He said it with such a serious face I knew this wasn't an idle question."

"What did you say?"

"I thought about my answer carefully and said that I was always prepared for death, but that I hoped I had more days on this earth to do the Lord's work. He asked me to check on the wounded in the hospital on our way back. There was a horribly burned soldier, in incredible pain, who grabbed my hand and made me promise not to leave him. He died three hours after the group heading out left. None of the men returned. We never even found their bodies. I could have put it down to coincidence, I did for a while, but there were too many of those events. Tyee spoke and men paid attention."

"I thought so too." Tens smiled. "He didn't say a lot; it was as if every word carried the weight of twenty."

I felt left out. I wished I'd known Tyee if only because it seemed like Tens was similar to his grandfather in so many ways.

"I tell you that story because I believe in things difficult to explain."

"Us too," I said, while Tens nodded agreement.

Tony lifted the paper and the glowing jar. "Your friend asked me to deliver this."

I froze in astonishment.

"Okay. Which friend?" Carefully taking the paper and the jar, Tens raised his eyebrows at me.

"You probably wouldn't believe me."

"Try us. Don't leave anything out, even if it feels ridiculous." Tens's face darkened with attention.

Tony fidgeted. "I was in Saints Peter and Paul Cathedral, downtown. It's on Meridian Street."

"The same Meridian Street as up here?"

He nodded. "Meridian continues downtown."

"Go on," I prompted.

"When I can, I pray in the chapel there. I knelt, prayed my usual, and when I glanced up a man walked out from the altar."

"From behind it?" I tried to clarify.

"No, there's nothing but a wall behind it."

"From the altar itself?" Tens asked.

"In light. The brightest light."

"What did he look like?"

"Very tall. Broad. Skin the color of plums and crushed obsidian."

I felt a smile tug at my lips. "Trench coat? Sunglasses?"

"That's him." Tony's eyes widened with relief.

"His name is Josiah. Did he speak to you?"

"Yes, in a lovely accent. Masai maybe? He didn't say enough for me to recognize his ancestry. Is he African?"

"Well . . . ," I hedged.

"He's an angel. A warrior angel, a Sangre," Tens said.

"So I assumed." Father Anthony nodded. "That explains the coming and going."

"What do you mean?"

Tony shrugged. "Churches, altars in particular, have long been thought to provide doorways, rips in the time continuum. It's thought that it's one of the ways God moves his earthly forms from place to place. Like an elevator to heaven. Of course, no one will corroborate this information. It's strictly off-limits to even whisper about it. But many church writings talk about the messengers from God arriving and leaving from the altars themselves. It used to be taught that priests weren't to approach the altar without a witness."

"A safety buddy?" I snorted.

"Yes, someone to report that a disappearance of a priest was God's work. It's thought that John Paul II—"

"The pope?"

He nodded. "Deceased now. One of his miracles was walking between the Vatican and a parish in Brazil that desperately needed him after mud slides."

"Wow." Learn something new every day.

"So this Josiah wanted you to have these."

The jar glowed, and as I took it from Tens I could feel the warmth through the glass. It looked like someone had poured a light stick inside.

Tony smiled as I turned it around in my hands. "I thought it was a jar of fireflies when he first handed it to me."

"Do you know what it is?" I asked.

"Josiah said to use it to combat the poison in your skin," Tony answered.

Tens nodded. "So it's for the ivy rash?"

"That would be my guess. I've never seen anything like it."

I glanced at Tens. What if we weren't dealing with just any plant? What if this was associated with the Nocti? Josiah wouldn't make an appearance and bring medicine because of a rash. Would he? "Why does everyone keep asking if we're sure it's poison ivy?"

Tens shrugged. "Don't know."

Tony glanced between Tens and me. "Do you trust Josiah?"

"Absolutely," we said in unison.

"Then have faith that whatever you're dealing with, he thinks you need this lotion."

"I guess we spread it over the sores?" I twisted off the lid and sniffed. It smelled like baking cake, spring earth in warm sun, clean sheets. I held the jar out to Tens. "What's it smell like to you?"

He sniffed, "Jasmine, roast chicken on the grill, fir forests of the Cascade mountains."

I smelled none of those. Curious, I held it out to Tony. "And you?"

He sniffed, then inhaled deeper with a smile. "The ocean, strawberries in the sun, and pumpkin pie."

"All good things?" I asked.

We nodded at each other and I poked a finger into the jar. The ointment resisted, the way marshmallow cream stuck and oozed. There was a heat, a soothing aspect to it that made me want to pour it all over my body, to bathe and dance in it. I put a little on my finger and leaned toward Tens. I smeared it on his cheek and his eyes widened.

"What?" I asked.

"It feels so good. Here." He smeared a glob on my neck.

It was like being cold and finally getting warm enough to relax. I sighed, feeling tension seep out of my muscles, my skin softening, letting the tightness of inflammation go. "What is this stuff?" I wondered.

Tony shook his head. "I don't know. He didn't say."

"It's miraculous." Tens and I took turns covering the rash and sores we could reach. As much as I wanted to strip down and find every single pustule I wasn't that comfortable with Tony yet.

We stood, contorted, stretched, and finished covering our reachable skin in glorious goo.

"Don't forget this part."

I turned to the paper Tony held out.

I unfolded it, saw the drawing, and lost my balance. I sat heavily.

"What is it?" Tens asked, craning to see.

"Sammy."

I was looking at a drawing of palm trees and ocean. Two figures stood side by side holding hands. He'd written *Sammy* above the smaller figure and *Mer-D* above the bigger person, who had bright red hair.

The last time he'd seen me I'd dyed my hair tomato red. In his life, my hair had been all sorts of colors. I put my hand up to my curls. Today they limped toward wavy, with uninteresting dark brown roots.

"I like your real hair color." Tens grabbed my hand and kissed the back of it.

On the page Sammy had also scrawled *Miss you.*

On the back was a phone number with a 305 area code. "Where is this?" I asked.

"I don't know. We can look it up," Tens answered.

I looked at Tony. "Did Josiah say anything to you?"

"He said to tell you there's power in unity, that a shared belief can move mountains. And"—he cleared his throat and looked at Tens dead-on—"and weapons of all kinds should be at the ready."

Okay, that was a bad fortune cookie. "Anything else?" I asked. *Like a map? Battle plan? The phone numbers of Sangre on speed dial?*

"Yes. He said to deliver this paper and to assist you. Might I know, is the paper important?"

"It's from my family. I think Josiah is telling me to call them." Were they in trouble? Were they injured or hurt or captured by the Nocti again? No, Josiah would have told me it was an emergency. Or something. He wouldn't just deliver a drawing.

"Don't think the worst," Tens cautioned me.

Love conquers nothing. Love provides the motivation only; the person must do the rest with
their own hands, heart, and feet.

Amor nihil vincit. Amore tantum causam
agendi supplet; cetera nobis ipsis per manus, cor
et pedes facienda sunt.

Luca Lenci

CHAPTER 25

Unity. Weapons. Nocti manipulating plants? I focused all
my attention on a daffodil and tried to make it raise up its
cup. Nothing. *Lunatic much?*

An hour after Tony left us to smear the rest of the ointment on our sores, I sat at the kitchen table with Auntie's
journal, Sammy's picture, and a phone splayed out in front
of me.

The blisters shrank and no longer itched like fire ants
at a dance club. I felt human again, but that left my newly
healed physical self trying to convince my emotional self
to work up the nerve to call the phone number.

"Are you going to call them?" Tens watched me surreptitiously from the kitchen. I knew how I must look. My emotions felt at war with each other, so aggravated I was surprised I didn't fall into two halves right there. *To call? Or not to call?*

"I don't know."

Tens stayed silent.

"What would you do?"

"I'm not telling you what to do."

"I know, but if it were you."

"It's not and there isn't a right answer."

"I just feel so helpless. All this stuff is happening to me, to us, and we aren't prepared for it. Like a rowboat in a hurricane, you know?"

"I hear you."

"What do the big guys have against explicit detailed instructions? Why all the subtle interpretive crap?" I griped.

"Some might say that's because they're not guys." Tens put the dish towel down and marched toward me.

"Touché." Neither one of us knew if the Creators had gender roles, and frankly, life hadn't stood still long enough for me to really delve into the possibility of that. Besides, it made my brain hurt.

"Come on." Tens picked up the truck keys and a duffel and tossed my hoodie at me.

"Where are we going?"

"Out. Come on."

Custos was riding shotgun in the truck when I got out

there. I felt odd about banishing her to the truck bed knowing her straight line to the top. Pissing off Tens's Protectoress creature probably wouldn't win me any points, and I needed all the points I could scrounge.

I slammed the door, but couldn't see Tens around Custos's shaggy frame. "Switch places with me." I climbed around her, careful to straddle the gearshift.

"Do I want to know?" Tens asked, waiting to start the vehicle until I was seated again.

Custos licked my face thoroughly. The seating arrangement was okay by her.

"Naw, we're fine." I patted his thigh, then leaned against him, watching his hands steady on the steering wheel. I wanted to pretend for a moment that we were two normal teenagers worried about getting into college and not breaking curfew. "Where are we headed?"

"Hmm . . ." He didn't answer me. But once he eased onto I-65 he slung his arm over my shoulder and kissed my temple.

I flipped on the radio, picking up a rock and country station that played a lot of songs I'd never heard. I tucked myself more firmly against his side and closed my eyes, inhaling the heat and scent I knew as his alone, my home. Maybe it was pheromones, maybe it was hormones, or maybe it was the soap, but it was Tens no doubt.

Suburban subdivisions and cookie-cutter developments thinned out. Empty fields surrounded us; the highway grew flat and open save for a few trucks and roadkill. Silos dotted the horizon, and the occasional farmhouse or red barn claimed that those living out here worked the land. Herds of cattle, some horses, pig farms, and dairies completed the animal census.

Eventually, Tens exited the highway. He pulled over on a dirt road that seemed to lead to the edge of the world.

I sat up and glanced around with more interest. "Why are we stopping?" *In the middle of freakin' nowhere?*

He pulled the duffel from behind his seat. Custos leapt out after him. When she jumped over me she left me with a mouthful of wolf hair and an imprint of her paw on my thigh.

"I have a feeling," he answered. "I've been keeping it to myself, but Josiah—" He broke off and let his words hang in the air.

"Okay." I paused, waiting to see if he'd share. No go. "And?"

"And no more feeling helpless." He shut the door, walking around to the back of the truck.

I popped open the passenger door and shimmied out. There was a chilly breeze in the air biting my cheeks. I'd be windburned over my healing blisters. *Goody*. Were those snow clouds?

Tens motioned toward a stand of trees. With foliage, I might have been able to tell what type they were, but for the moment they were just tall piles of kindling and spiderwebs of branches. "I promised you a shooting lesson. Now's as good a time as any. It'll get your mind off Sammy to focus on this instead. You can't do both when you're learning."

Makes sense. "Are you licensed to carry concealed weapons?" I teased.

"Nope. Arrest me now." He didn't crack a smile.

"Nah, I've got bigger fish to fry." I tried to lighten the mood.

"Catfish?"

"Yummy." My stomach pitched with nerves. I talked a good game about wanting to shoot and protect my man and myself. Not rely on the differently equipped—men—to provide my safety. But guns made me nervy and I wondered if that would ever change.

"Come on." Tens took my hand and we walked over the muddy ruts in the field toward a lone stand of weeping willows.

"Stop here." He planted me about ten yards from the biggest tree. Setting down the bag, he unzipped it while I checked out the surrounds. Custos sat next to the truck, behind the front fender. As if she didn't trust me to not shoot her, instead of the tree.

"Here?" Besides Custos and the trees, the only other potential targets were cows so far away they resembled flies.

"This'll do." He took the safety lock off a box and lifted out a gun. He checked and made sure it was unloaded, then he handed it to me butt-first.

"You think this is what Josiah meant?"

"Maybe."

I almost dropped the gun, but grabbed it with both hands. "This is way heavier than I expected." My mouth went dry. I'd heard that guns don't kill people, people kill people, but stupid and scared could be a combination deadly enough to push someone into the "accidental killer" category. I remembered holding the gun I'd shot Perimo with, but not what it felt like or how I'd managed to pull the trigger. It all blurred.

"What did you expect?" He waited patiently while I grew accustomed to the sensation.

I shrugged. "Light, like a toy gun." Plastic?

He shook his head. "Welcome to the real gun."

I was afraid to move.

"It's not loaded," he said.

I nodded. That should have helped. Knowing there were no bullets should have taken all the pressure off. It didn't. "I don't know that I want to do this."

He squatted, watching the cows in the distance. "I thought you wanted to be all GI Jane. At least, that's what you said at Auntie's."

Maybe I was wrong. "Yeah, well, it's a huge responsibility to actually point it." After Perimo I knew I would if I had to.

He moved behind me. "That's why you don't point it unless you're completely confident that you can pull the trigger. It's not for threatening. If you can't kill, don't pick it up."

I raised the gun to eye level, then lowered it. My arm shook badly.

"It doesn't make you a coward, Supergirl, if you don't want to do this. You faced Perimo just fine while I was out of it."

That night in the caves flooded back. I'd held a gun then. I'd used it. Failed. I hadn't protected us very well; it took an avenging angel to get it right.

"I'll always have your back," Tens whispered, his words carried off in the breeze.

"Who has *your* back, then?" I asked.

"You do."

"Not if you're the only one who can protect us."

"It's my job." He shrugged.

"My job isn't to be a fragile flower, you know."

"I know that. I'm trying to help," he growled. "What do you want me to say?"

He had a point. I inhaled. "I need to do this. For me."

"Okay, then let's start with how to hold the gun." Tens wrapped his arms around me, positioning my fingers, my palm.

I knew that if he stood like that and lent me his strength of spirit, I could face any opponent. I thought of Sammy out there with only our parents to protect him. Our parents, who had tried to hide my destiny from me because they were so afraid. Fear makes everyone vulnerable. I was tired of being afraid. "I can kill." *If I have to.*

"All right. Now, pull the trigger."

I did and heard the click.

"Now, here's what you need to know." Tens launched into how to load the gun, the hollow-point ammunition.

We spent the next hour with him teaching me to load and unload, how to stand, how to hold the gun, until my arms were tired. So tired they wanted to sink to my sides and stay there. So exhausted they started to shake involuntarily, not from fear but from muscle fatigue. I carefully turned the gun back over to Tens before I shot my foot.

"How did you learn this?" I asked.

"Grandpa taught me from the time I arrived. We'd hunt for our food, but in retrospect I also think he trained me like he'd trained soldiers."

"Did he want you to be in the army too?"

"I don't know. I don't think so. I think he just wanted me prepared for anything."

"Did he know about the Protector thing?"

"Maybe. He never said anything about it."

"Was he one?" I asked.

"Not that I know of. I don't think so. My grandmother died of a heart attack, so she wasn't a Fenestra." Which meant the odds were Tyee wasn't a Protector. We Fenestras live to one hundred and six years if Nocti don't interfere. I didn't know how long Protectors were supposed to live. Something else to research.

"Well, we know he served with Charles and Auntie during World War II."

"Right."

"And he was in Vietnam with Tony."

"So . . ."

Tens's expression clouded. He didn't want to jaunt down memory lane with me. "Want to shoot more? Try another size?"

"My arms are really tired. Another time?"

"Are you sure?" He seemed disappointed.

"Yeah, I'm scared I'll shoot the wrong thing."

The white sun turned the sky a dazzling menagerie of pinks and lavenders with the sunset. "Let's head back."

We grabbed burgers and Tater Tots at a drive-through. Custos stole a few bites of fried potatoes from my lap along with the entire pile of ketchup I'd squeezed out.

We pulled into the cottage's driveway and I felt an electric hum building in my gut. "I'm going to go clean some," I said, pointing at Helios. Maybe if I did a little mindless moving around I'd figure out why I was so anxious. Besides, Joi was kind enough to let us flex our schedules. I wanted to make sure I worked enough for her that she didn't regret her invitation.

Tens stretched his arms and rolled his head, loosening up from driving. "I'll tackle the weeding and edging by the dining room windows. I don't want to do that while people are in there eating."

"Oh, you know the old ladies would love seeing you sweaty with your shirt off," I teased him, and was rewarded with a belly laugh.

"Jealous?" he said, leaning down and kissing me.

I broke down boxes and vacuumed the carpets. Picked over the new sale items—many of them reminded me of Auntie or Sammy.

We ate a late dinner of salads and cheese scones. I tried to ignore my growing antsiness, but by nine p.m. my uncertainty turned to determination. Rumi's open house had started at seven.

"We have to go to Rumi's," I said, pulling on fresh

jeans and a snowflake sweater set Joi had marked down to not quite free on the sale table. It was so kitschy that I felt like it came from Auntie's eclectic closet. I loved it.

Tens put down his wood and whittling knives. "You feel like it? What will people think when they see us so improved?"

The ointment Tony brought us had sucked the sick out of us so that each blister was now only a red patch of freshly healed skin. We weren't pretty, but no one would think we were smallpox carriers either. "I need to go. I can't explain it. Rumi already knows we're different. Maybe we just tell Joi the truth if she's there?"

"Can we go in the back door?" Tens didn't argue, but his face said he wanted to.

"Of his house?"

"Yeah." Tens's expression was troubled. The kind of face he wore when he felt me or events in my life.

"What's wrong?"

"I'm not sure. A feeling."

I shrugged. I felt like we had to go; he felt like we needed to be very careful. Compromise made a healthy relationship, right? "Okay. We go in the back door."

Tens and I walked toward Rumi's. He wore the long black leather trench that once belonged to Auntie's Charles. I was in a quilted velvet coat I'd picked up on my Carmel shopping.

We heard the live music—fiddles, guitar, flute— blocks away. Even the pubs and bars on the main strip didn't outrollick the party happening at Rumi's studio and gallery loft. It sounded like an Irish wake—or at least, what I'd always thought one might sound like. Laughter floated by us like strands of spun sugar. I found myself smiling over the nerves in my belly.

From our vantage point across the street, I saw people packed together, clapping with the music, while others held glassware up to the lights and carried their purchases out of the shop. "I think the entire town of Carmel is in there," I said.

"Hmm." Tens continually scanned the streets around us. His eyes reminded me of one of those air traffic controller radar wheels. Sweeping, constantly scanning for blips of danger.

"We don't have to go." I chewed on my lip. I felt like we had to, but there was a fine line between trusting my instincts and learning to accept Tens's more powerful ones.

He nudged me to keep walking. "No, let's keep our eyes open."

"Peeled. Got it." I nodded.

Rumi had strung fairy lights from the eaves, wrapping them around the Witch Balls. No one would notice a sudden uptick in the brilliance of the Spirit Stones upon my arrival.

"Clever." Tens pointed to the strings of lights.

"Sweet." I nodded.

We made the block and approached his apartment door from the alley.

"There you are."

I jumped at the voice before I saw Gus, the history

professor we'd met at dinner, sitting in a rocking chair beside the door. He stood, the chair and his joints creaking at the movement. "Rumi asked me to come out here to wait for you."

"Why?"

"Don't know, but Faye has front-entrance duty, which I hear she's turned into a greeter and hostess position. Rumi simply told me your yin was inside and I had to wait here to tell you."

My what? "Do you know what he means?"

"No, he was shaky and pale. Seemed very upset, but he wouldn't elaborate. Just kept repeating to tell you not to come in yet, that 'yin' was in there. Is that a person's name?"

My yin is inside? What is Rumi talking about?

My Protector thinks he is the only one ever correct. Wrong.

Cassie Ailey
March 1, 1888

CHAPTER 26

Yin. Yin. Yin. I kept repeating the word in my head. Trying to puzzle out what or who Rumi might mean. His vocabulary was so overwhelmingly over my head, I didn't know if I should take him literally or make a metaphorical leap. Tens immediately went on high alert.

I noticed Tens subtly draw us deeper into the shadows with Gus; Custos appeared at the end of the alley. She sat with her back to us as if on watch.

I asked, "Gus, does 'yin' mean anything to you?"

He squinted at us, rubbing his chin in thoughtful

study. "Perhaps the Chinese yin and yang, though that's a terrible reach. That symbol can't possibly mean anything to you kids. I can go ask for clarification if you'd like. Maybe Faye knows more. Rumi enjoys his word games, but I don't think he's playing around. His expression was ferocious."

"Okay," I answered, then paused. Yin and yang. All I knew about it was that hippies and peace freaks tended to wear it on their clothing and treat it as synonymous with the slogan "Make love, not war."

Tens shrugged off his jacket, draped it over his arm, and pulled his weapon so quietly the movement was nearly invisible. I tried to pretend I was a peace-loving hippie, with no cares in the world, to stop the fear from transferring from me to Gus. I wanted to plug my ears and mutter "la-la-la-la" until the threat passed.

"Shall I stay with you?" Gus asked nervously, glancing at Tens and me in the ambient streetlight and white lights strung along the apartment's gutters.

Tens placed a sure hand on the man's shoulder. "Nah, why don't you go find Faye and buy her a drink?" He gave Gus a salacious wink and his voice was smooth and lazy, immediately breaking the tension around the three of us, popping it like a bubble.

Gus insisted, "Young man, there's no courting going on."

"Maybe there should be." Tens nudged the man politely toward the door.

It didn't take much prodding before Gus headed back

inside toward the music and, presumably, Faye. I'm not sure if his retreat was because of embarrassment or because he took Tens's comment to heart.

"What's my yin?" I whispered.

"Give me a minute." Tens leaned against the building and closed his eyes.

Careful to stay in the shadows of the alley, I toed a pebble until it peeled free from a clutch of dandelions. I concentrated on trying to sense my way to the interior of the party. I picked up nothing. Where was the damn Fenestra handbook?

Yin? Yang? Yin? Yang?

"You are yang. Someone is yin. If you're the white part of the symbol—"

"Then someone else is the black," I gasped. "Oh my God." I felt the back of my knees tremble. Nocti. "How?"

"How did he know?" Tens drew me toward him. We'd told Rumi some of the truth about us and our reality. We hadn't lied, since he'd asked us not to. But we hadn't told him there was evil out there. We hadn't mentioned the Nocti. "He must have read more in the notes."

It made sense to me that if his ancestors wrote about the Good Death, then they probably wrote about the bad one, too.

"Let's go in—odds are on our side nothing will happen."

"If it does there are a lot of innocent people in there."

"Yeah, but the Nocti knows who we are, or at least who Juliet is. We're at a disadvantage."

"Okay, but how did Rumi recognize him?" Or her? The only Nocti I'd seen was Perimo. His believers were both men and women, but I wasn't sure if any of them were actually official Nocti. They seemed more like pathetic victims of a cult.

"Um, kids?" Gus opened the back door slightly, not seeing how quickly Tens dashed in front of me and pointed the gun as the door creaked. "All clear from the man himself. I wish you'd let me in on the game—you forget that I've led our reenactor troupe for decades. I'm quite good at role-playing."

Tens resheathed the gun and took my hand as Gus babbled on about his soldiers and camp followers. Tens tugged me behind him. "Let's go in."

Gus disappeared into the studio space, but Tens and I took our time, heading from the apartment out toward the front, and the crowd. The scents of cigarette smoke, tightly crammed people, and wood smoke hung in the air.

Perimo had scared me, terrified me, made me feel like a rat trapped in a sinking box with no way out. I didn't have that gut feeling now, but had I felt that way because he was Nocti, or because he threatened everyone I loved? I wasn't picking up on anything, but I couldn't assume I'd feel something every time Nocti were around.

Tens dropped my hand, keeping me behind him, as we edged into the studio. Carefully edging the periphery, with our backs to each other or the outside walls, I marveled at the number of people, packed shoulder to shoulder, in the gallery.

Most hands clutched champagne flutes decorated with swirly rainbows or clear glasses with colored polka dots or ones shaped like calla lilies. Items for sale, including those glasses, were stacked on tables along with vases of all sizes and bowls sized for everything from baby food to bread making. There were plenty more creations meant to sit on shelves and catch the eye in fancy. Delicate winged creatures perched on grapevine wreaths and a tree was decorated with glass fireflies and ornaments of Indiana's landmarks. Lights shone through the chandeliers and glass sculptures hanging from the ceiling, refracting colors across guests and displays. More Spirit Stones, in deep purples and bloody reds, golden ambers and princess pinks, hung in the front windows with tiny white lights surrounding them. I wanted to gaze at the glass and daydream. There was something magical about seeing it all in one place and lit from within. But I didn't let myself lose focus.

The sound of laughter, chatter, and greetings competed with the live Celtic music.

I grabbed a bottle of water; Tens shook his head when I offered him one. We browsed, but no one appeared dangerous; we were people-watching more than anything else. I scanned the faces of the crowd. All ages.

Eventually, the crowd thinned. This was the kind of thing I imagined my parents going to, without me. Joi and her husband mingled and gossiped as if they knew everyone in the room. They probably did. She waved at us. Rumi's other dinner guests were here, including the social worker, Nelli. I wondered if she might know anything about Dunklebarger and Juliet. I tried to make my way toward her, but there didn't seem to be a good time to catch her in conversation.

I searched the eyes around me for the blank void of Dark. Where was the Nocti? Had he left or was it a false alarm? I caught myself looking specifically for Perimo, even though he was supposedly dead. He wasn't here, so who was? *What does this Nocti look like?*

Rumi glanced in our direction, and his okay signal assured me the danger was past. That didn't stop Tens from questioning the intentions of everyone here. His whispered comments to me told me he assessed, dismissed, and moved on to the next person without pause. Even the friendliest demeanors were not above his suspicion. I wished there was another way for us to live.

We found Sidika and spoke with her about the book she was working on. I listened and Tens glanced around the room, glowering at those around us.

Rumi hugged me and whispered in my ear, "Stick around. It's important." Then another patron demanded his attention.

Around eleven, the band gave way to a lone flutist and the crowd retired in a seemingly choreographed retreat. We continued to pick our way around the demolished food tables and admire Rumi's glasswork.

I picked up a small green turtle and thought of Sammy. He'd tuck this creature in his pocket and carry it everywhere. I watched light, every shade from lime to deep pine, bounce around the inside giving life.

Tens never left my side. By the time the last of Rumi's friends and admirers left, most of his inventory was sold. "Well, I'd best get back to moil tomorrow," he sighed, surveying how little of his work was left. He locked the front door and flicked off the lights. Immediately, the Spirit Stones lit up like a night-light. "Let's talk in the back. Away from all these windows."

Tens and I followed him. While Rumi brewed a fresh pot of coffee, I sipped leftover champagne. I loved the way the bubbles tickled my nose.

"You shouldn't drink." Tens frowned at me.

"Thanks, Dad." I gulped to prove my point and knew I'd regret it later. My head quickly felt detached and floating.

Rumi sat with us, and for the first time I saw the lines on his face, betraying his years. His skin lacked luster and verve. "There were two of them here. A woman, with old eyes and a young face, and a male teenager, maybe your age." He gestured at Tens. "They came in at the same time, and left together, but they didn't speak the whole time they were here. I might not have even noticed them, except I happened to be watching the door when they entered."

"If they didn't speak to each other, how do you know they were together?" I asked.

He knit his fingers, pressing his thumbs. "The way two people are comfortable near each other—they walked in too close to be strangers. And she brushed his arm as she came toward me and he walked the other way." He frowned. "She zeroed in on me like she knew exactly who

I was. And I might have thought she was the friendliest person in the world except—" He broke off, shook his head at some internal conversation, and sighed.

"Except what, Rumi?" I sat forward in my chair.

"The Stones, they blackened."

I gasped.

On alert, Tens straightened, leaning off the edge of the sofa. "What?"

Fear filled Rumi's eyes when they met mine. "When they entered, the trees in the balls turned black, black like light never reached them. The balls dimmed. Around you, Meridian, they gain a clarity, but here the opposite was true."

Silence fell for a moment as we digested this information.

Rumi closed his eyes in a long blink. "I thought Good Death was the opposite of a regular death, but I was wrong, wasn't I?"

I saw no reason to lie to him at this point, so I nodded.

"I should have known. I should have recognized that there is balance in all things in the universe. All things. Someday, you'll tell me what you call them."

Tens cleared his throat. "Is that all?"

"Dear child, if that were all, I wouldn't be graying before your eyes. She came at me, for all the world like a neighbor or a friend. She leaned toward me and she clutched my hand. I felt my heart stutter with cold and there was a strength in her grip that I've never experienced, even from a man. As if she could crush my bones, without even trying."

"What did she say?" I asked, afraid to know.

His gaze drifted off. "Hmm?"

I repeated, "What did she say to you? Who is she? What's her connection? How did she find out about you?"

"Easy, I'll tell you what I know. She asked me why I was interfering with her pets."

Tens snorted. "Pets?"

"She wouldn't tell me her name, and although she was friendly enough to everyone else, no one seemed to know her. She said Shakespeare wrote tragedies for a reason and to keep my distance from a certain leading lady."

"So she knows Juliet." I cringed. "What did she look like? Was she girthy?"

"She means morbidly obese." Tens quirked an eyebrow at my attempt at politeness.

Rumi didn't notice. "No, very stylish. Very thin. Too thin, I think. I may be wrong, but—"

"Tell us," I pleaded.

"I think her eyes disappeared at one point. I haven't seen anything about these demons—are they demons? If you're angels, they must be demons."

"They're called Aternocti, Nocti," I answered him. "I don't know what they are, but I think they're angels, too. Or were. Just a different sort."

He nodded. "And you're a—"

"Fenestra. A human with a dash of angel to help souls find their heaven. I'm the window."

He snapped his fingers. "From the paintings? That window?"

"That's what the dying see. What I see." I think the

alcohol loosened my tongue, but partly it was also because I hated hiding. I hated lying. If Rumi wanted to, he could have ambushed us with the Nocti. I was finished making him prove his allegiance.

Tens frowned at me and said to Rumi, "I'm her Protector, but we're still learning what that means exactly."

"I see. There's more." Rumi sipped his coffee.

Tens nodded. "There always is."

"This Nocti, she asked how I preferred to die."

I gasped. She would gain nothing by harming Rumi. Unless our strength was in numbers? Alone we were more vulnerable.

He heaved an exhale of defeat. "Unless, she never saw me again. Never heard my name around one of her kids. Never saw my shadow fall anywhere near that of Juliet's. She hinted that I might like to retire to a warmer clime."

"Her kids? What's her connection to Juliet?"

"She's not the guardian, is she?"

"Are there two?"

"Rumi, she means it. If she's Nocti she'll kill you and suck up your soul."

"What a dire way to kick off the Feast festivities." Rumi frowned. "I'm sorry."

It was too much to ask of him. I should have known he'd bail. "We understand." I stood. "Thank you for warning us. For your help."

"Where are you going, lassie?" Rumi asked.

"Leaving?" I queried.

"I didn't say I was easily cowed, now, did I?" Rumi motioned me to sit back down.

"But—"

"It shakes a fusty man to come face to face with malevolence. But it only cements something for me."

"What?" I asked.

"We must save that girl. How do we go about that?"

Good question. We bantered plans and ideas until all of us were too tired to think straight.

Hours later, staring up at the ceiling of our cottage, I wished I had a solid idea of how to proceed.

"Merry?" Tens whispered. "Are you awake?"

"Yeah."

I listened as Tens rustled off the couch. His footfalls were so quiet that I had no idea where he was in the room until the bed dipped under him. I scooted over into crisp, cold sheets, making room. I'd inadvertently started sleeping in the middle of the bed. That wasn't how I wanted this to work.

I rolled toward his warmth and tucked my legs between his. His arms wrapped around me and we settled into cuddling like we'd been doing it forever, rather than only a month. But it was all we'd been doing, so I guessed being good at it came from practice. My breath matched his.

I ran my fingertips up and down his arm. The solid smoothness of his shoulder dipped and curved around his biceps, then gave way to crisp hair along his forearms. I twirled my fingers across his skin, enjoying the play of textures. His T-shirt and sweats were ones we'd brought with us from Colorado; they were the soft material of beloved, often-washed clothing. Like warm butter they absorbed his body heat and seemed to melt between us.

When the lights were on, I knew these were clothes he'd worn while he was so sick. So close to death. There was nothing romantic about that time in the caves except the solitude we shared. But with the lights out, as we pressed against each other, the clothes were two layers too many.

I knew I should be thinking about Juliet and the Nocti and how we were going to keep Rumi safe too, but all I wanted was to lose myself in the night, get as close to Tens as I could. I wanted to explore, enjoy, and act on all this crazy electricity I felt building around us. Each exhale of his stirred my hair with warm breath, and left an intangible feeling crawling along my skin, like the tingle right before being zapped by static electricity. I didn't want to think, I wanted . . . Was sex like in the movies? Was I going to regret anything? No. Would he? I hoped to hell not. I tried to keep my breath matched to his, but his seemed to pick up speed too.

He tucked his arm more firmly along my ribs, right under my newish breasts. I wanted him to slide his palm up and cup my breast. I wanted to know what it felt like to have his fingers on my nipple. My heart galloped.

"Okay?" Tens's voice growled from his chest through mine.

Am I okay? Is your arm near my breast okay? Is

pretending I don't want to get naked with you because you're afraid to hurt me okay? "Fine."

His thumb swept a crescent shape from the side of my breast to my ribs and back. He shifted his head and kissed the side of my neck, and up beneath my ear. Lightly, so lightly, they could have been sighs instead of kisses.

I turned my head, my lips toward his.

Tentatively, as if this were the first time we'd ever kissed, our mouths met. We learned each other again in that moment.

I opened my mouth to mirror him and our tongues touched. He tasted of toothpaste and something rich, forbidden. Our legs brushed against each other's. My breathing ragged, I turned toward him; he moved up and over me.

The weight of him on top of me gave me a feeling of complete security. I'd never felt more vulnerable in my life, or more safe. Two opposites that should have been completely repellent melded seamlessly.

His erection pressed against my thigh. I felt strangely powerful, exhilarated to feel his passion and response so blatantly. I didn't need to ask if he was enjoying this. He buried his face in my neck and asked, "Are you okay?" He held his breath, waiting for my reply—his whole body tensed, strung tight.

I licked my lips and contemplated how to answer. This was right. This was perfect. And I'd been waiting for weeks to feel like he might want the same thing. I opened my mouth to answer and couldn't articulate all that I was feeling. Instead, I dragged his hand from my side, sliding it under my nightshirt until his palm cradled my breast. He dragged in a ragged breath, his penis jerked in reaction, and his fingers gently squeezed.

I hadn't realized how sensitive my nipple was until someone else's fingers touched it. My back arched toward his touch. The calluses on his fingers and palm, from all the manual labor and whittling, created delicious friction.

I wanted to return the favor and tugged on his T-shirt. "Off," I demanded.

"Yes, ma'am." He smiled, moved aside, leaving me cold while he peeled off his shirt. His sweats rode low on his hips, and a V of muscle disappeared below the drawstring. Before I could engage my brain enough to think about the bulge against the elastic, he returned to me.

When he came back, his skin was on fire, so hot I thought the temperature in the room must have climbed in response. He caught his weight on his elbows, bracketing me between his arms, my legs on either side of his hips. I ran the soles of my feet along the crisp hairs on his lower legs. They tickled.

My hands roamed his back and ribs, learning each indent, each rolling hill of lean muscle, sinew, and bone.

We kissed again, this time with more pressure, more urgency. My eyes closed while my other senses grappled for their bearings. My sense of touch set every nerve ending electrified, engorged. My nose picked up nuances of aroma clouding us: musky heat, soap, and fabric softener. I heard each hitch of his breath, the rub of our skin together and against the sheets, our heartbeats syncopating.

I ran my tongue around the sharp edges of his teeth, the warm satin of his inner lips. I'd never felt so desired, so powerful and wanted.

He leaned to his side, towing me with him so he could better reach my breast. He tugged and played, until I wanted the same treatment to the other one. I couldn't hold still, couldn't form sentences, never wanted to stop.

Pressure built inside me. An urgency I couldn't name. A want I couldn't ask for by name.

His hand left my breast bereft and roamed lower across my stomach. His fingers dancing, massaging, testing my flesh in a way I'd never been touched. *Don't stop.* He paused when he came in contact with the elastic band of my panties.

I bit his bottom lip, opened my eyes. I kept him captured until he opened his eyes and met mine. I smiled against his mouth and lifted my hips, nudging his hand in the process.

I lost myself in his midnight gaze. He didn't close his eyes; they were stormy, as if the black of his irises swirled and pooled like India ink.

His face was as open and vulnerable as I felt. And completely mine.

He let his hand rest between my legs. I wanted pressure, friction. *More.* I moved against his palm.

I reached for the drawstring on his sweats. I wanted to feel him, to know the difference between his secret places and my own. Above all, I wanted to feel him inside of me. He dragged in a breath, catching my hands.

Outside, Custos barked and growled. Tens froze and

listened. She barked rapid-fire warnings; her growl was a low rumble that broke the spell around us.

Tens pulled away, untangling our limbs, his chest heaving with the exertion.

I felt sweat cooling against my skin. "It's just a raccoon or a possum," I said.

"Maybe." He sat on the edge of the bed with his back to me. "Maybe not. I'll check."

I leaned up and kissed between his shoulder blades. "It's nothing." I wanted to beg. I wanted to curse Custos. For a moment, we were just two people in love and into each other. We weren't the cosmic destinies of Fenestra and Protector. "Please come back."

"Merry, I don't have any—"

I interrupted him. "I don't care."

"I do."

The mantle of responsibility fell hard back onto my shoulders. The stony expression on Tens's face as he picked up his T-shirt and shrugged it back on told me this night was over.

"I'm going to run." He grabbed his sneakers and didn't look back as the front door closed behind him.

Is he running from me? Or something else?

And then the truck started and he peeled out. When I got to the window I saw the taillights as he turned onto Main Street.

Baby, I am lying in the courtyard grass watching the Perseid meteor shower. You kick each time I see a shooting star, as if you too can see with my eyes.   **—R.**

CHAPTER 27
Juliet

The little alarm that used to belong to Mr. Franklin was set to buzz at four a.m. I turned it off at 3:31, deciding a day of work without sleep was better than trying to function after getting only a few minutes. As if I could fall asleep anyway. I dragged on woolly socks that had originally belonged to a guest I couldn't remember, one from months ago. A thick sweater and yesterday's jeans were the only relatively clean clothing options. Doing my own laundry took a backseat to everyone else's.

The walls of DG closed in on me and claustrophobia clawed at my gut. I needed a sliver of nature, a space of oxygen. I snuck out the back door and ran down the sloping lawn, toward the back fence. Using branches and an old stump, I climbed the fence and hopped to the other side. The cold chased wishes of sleep from my head and battled the exhaustion back to the periphery of my mind.

I shimmied out onto my favorite leaning tree, which dangled above the creek. I straddled it like I was riding a horse, lying forward with my cheek pressed against the rough bark. The stars shone brightly and a full moon spotlit the shadows and shades of vegetation. Grays, blacks, blues, and browns competed with whites and ecrus, a battle of light and dark around me.

Movement made me glance above. A great horned owl glided past using the creek as a byway, Interstate Wildcat. Her wings flapped once, silently, to guide her up and over the treetops. In the distance, I heard her mate call greeting and even the shriek of owlets.

From under my bra strap I dragged the piece of paper Nicole had copied, and pulled a flashlight from my back pocket. I needed to see what this piece of my file said. *What if Mistress is wrong and my mother didn't abandon me? What if she wanted me and loved me? More frightening still, what if Mistress is right?*

It was a handwritten note; I didn't recognize the scrawl. I held it closer to my face trying to read it. Words wrapped around each other, and smeared ink made it nearly impossible to decipher other ones.

Juliet Ambrose entrusted to
St. Jerome Emiliani's Home for Children
March 20, 1996
Date of Birth: 2-10-1993
Observation 1996–99
June 1996: Empathetic with other children
June 1997: Brings animals inside her dormitory room.
Unclear if animals are already dead or if she kills them.
June 1998: Bullied and outcast, very clingy
June 1999: Transfer to Dunklebarger. Keep eye on her
*   development.*
No photographic image. Test annually.

I didn't recognize the name of the children's home; none
of this information made even a little sense. February tenth
was my birthday, but I remembered nothing of my life before
arriving at DG.

A twig cracked in the woods behind me. I slung a look
over my shoulder at Mini, who meowed at me from the bank.
"Don't want to get wet, do you?" I asked her.

She answered with a disdainful yowl that critiqued my
sanity. I watched as she twitched her tail and wandered off
along the path. I turned back to the paper, trying to make
sense of what I read. When I next looked up for Mini, a dog—
a wolf—had its nose pressed against her head. Their exchange
was so unexpected I nearly lost my balance. I tightened my
thighs around the tree to catch myself. They seemed like
friends.

It was only then I realized a man stalked deeper in the

forest behind them. I saw his dark shape watching me. I gasped, dropping the paper and the flashlight into the creek below me. I lost my balance and fell forward onto my stomach.

The paper swirled down the stream.

"Sorry, sorry." He rushed forward and leaned out over the water toward the log and my perch. "I'm Tens, remember? I didn't mean to scare you."

"You were here before. Twice." I sat up, but didn't move toward him nor take his hand.

He dropped it. "With Meridian, my, um, girlfriend." The wolf licked his fingers and seemed pleased to have him here.

I didn't know what to say. "You came into DG; you lied about car trouble."

He nodded. Maybe his expression implied sheepishness but he was impossible for me to read. I didn't think I'd be able to decode his face even under a spotlight. "We lied, you're right. Merry, she thought you were in trouble."

"Trouble?" I asked.

He shoved his hands into his pockets. He was so tall I felt short. His broad shoulders were straight as a plank of lumber. "Could you come off there before you fall in?"

I shook my head. "No, I don't think so." At least out here I had distance between us. Though no one would hear me if I screamed, I doubted anyone up at DG would care.

He nodded, as if he had expected me to say no. I guess it might look scary, me up here dangling, but I knew this trunk as well as I knew my own body. Better, maybe.

"Trouble?" I repeated. "What do you mean?"

"It's hard to explain." He blew out a breath that was either frustration or irritation, maybe both, maybe directed at me.

"Try," I pushed.

"Merry would do this better. Why don't you come with me? She can tell you."

"No. Besides she already tried, remember?"

"Look, I know you don't have reason to trust me, us, but try, please?"

"What are you doing here?" I asked.

"I needed to think." His gaze dropped to the water.

"Here?"

He nodded. "I needed to check on you. Make sure you're okay."

"You keep saying that. Like you expect me not to be."

He stayed silent.

I blinked. "Are you saying I'm not okay?"

"I'm saying—" He sat down, rubbing his hands along his raggedy sweatpant-clad thighs. He wore sneakers without socks and a T-shirt that looked like it might fall apart with one more wash cycle. "I don't know what I'm saying." Maybe we had more in common than I thought.

I held my tongue. I knew what it was like to try to find words when there weren't any. I should have felt fear, or at least discontent, out here, alone with him in the middle of the night. But while I didn't feel safe, I didn't feel threatened.

He shook off the cobwebs and began, "There once was a girl—"

I cut him off with a snort. "In a faraway land? Does this

end with 'happily ever after'? Because, really, I can make up stories too."

His eyes flashed irritation. "Just listen, okay? This girl was really sick all the time; she had inexplicable pains and animals died around her. She'd wake up with them next to her pillow; they'd die in her hands. She thought she was a freak. She thought she killed them with her mind or was monstrously evil. She didn't know what was going on, but as she grew older the animals grew in size, and in number. Her physical symptoms got worse too. Exhaustion, malnutrition, stunted development. Until—" He broke off and looked at me.

My heartbeat stuttered. There were parts of this I recognized as my own truth. "I'm listening."

"Until she turned sixteen and found out that not only did animals seek her out as they died but so did people."

"What happened?" I asked, curious and drawn to this tale. I felt the maze of my life lose a few of its blind corners.

"She was special. A special kind of human that long ago added angel to her ancestry. She found out that she was a window for souls to pass through to the afterlife. But knowing wasn't enough. She had to learn how to let the souls through without being dragged along with them."

"Or what?" I cocked my head and played with the bark under my fingers.

He hesitated. "Or she died, too."

I snorted. "Cheery story."

"There's more. You want to hear?" he asked.

I shrugged. "Sure, why not?"

"There were evil angels after this girl. They wanted to

force her to choose between the people she loved and becoming one of them."

"Did the prince ride in and save her?"

"No, she saved him." He shook his head with a smile that seemed very personal.

Not the answer I expected. "Then what?"

"Then the girl and the boy were told they had to find more people like themselves. More people to work for good and help souls make it to the window. And they had to defeat the bad guys, no matter what."

"And?"

"And they're trying. They're really trying. They've found another girl and they want to help her."

I saw lights blink on high up in DG's attic. Nicole was awake. Time to go to work. "You need to work on your story-telling skills. That's creepy."

He nodded. "I told you Meridian would tell it better." He backed away, giving me room as I crawled toward him.

I hurried along the tree, scooting until my feet touched the ground. "You owe me a flashlight." *And a piece of my history.* But I didn't say that last part out loud.

"Okay, we'll leave one out here." He seemed like he had more to say.

I'd believe it when I saw it. "Sure, whatever."

Mini licked the wolf's muzzle. I heard her purring.

"What's the wolf's name?" I asked.

He swallowed. "Custos. It means 'guardian.'"

Weird name for a pet. I walked to the fence.

"Do you want to know what the cat's name is?" he asked.

"Her name is Mini." I hefted myself back over the fence.

"It's Minerva. She says Bodie wants pancakes for breakfast."

Nice try, crazy boy. "He doesn't like pancakes."

Tens shrugged.

I turned and ran back toward DG, Mini keeping pace with my strides. When I got to the door and looked back, Tens and Custos were gone.

"Morning." Inside the kitchen, Nicole had coffee brewing.

"Hi." I kept glancing out the window, expecting to see Tens standing there, waiting for me. I shook my head to clear my confusion. "It's too early. You should still be asleep."

"I came to help you." Nicole started gathering ingredients. "How are you feeling?"

"Fine." Confused. Near breaking. Falling apart.

She frowned but let my answer stand. "Bodie made the weirdest request last night as he was falling asleep."

"He wants to watch a Disney movie?"

"No, he wants pancakes with chocolate chips in them for breakfast."

I stopped, shocked. "He doesn't like them." He refused to eat anything but cold cereal or oatmeal for breakfast unless Mistress forced him. Even when I tried to make more interesting breakfasts and smuggle them to the kids, he stuck to his guns.

Nicole shrugged. "I guess he does now."

Coincidence? Crazy? Maybe.

We worked in silence. Dishes and laundry and cleaning waited. I turned my mind toward the paper from my file and tried to decipher what little of it I'd read before losing it in the creek.

"Have you looked at that paper?" Nicole lowered her voice. "Anything interesting?"

I glanced around, feeling as if the walls of DG leaned closer to hear our conversation. I was becoming paranoid. "Nothing really helpful. I was at a kids' home before coming here."

"Do you remember that? Any people?"

I shook my head. "No, I remember waking up in the attic here." With Kirian offering me his hand in friendship, love, and protection. Even though he was nine to my six years, he acted much older and took care of me until I learned the rules and routines.

"Oh, anything else?" She seemed disappointed.

"Can you— I need— Can you get a camera for me?"

Surprise made her freeze, then relax into a fake Southern accent. "Are you fixin' to make Southern fried Kodak?"

I laughed. "No, I need you to take my picture."

Nicole's face grew troubled and she turned away, suddenly very busy. "Why?"

"I can't explain it. Do you think you can find a camera? Soon?" I asked.

"Are you sure?"

"Yeah, I want photos to give to Bodie and Sema when I leave."

She nodded. "Give me a little time." She wiped her hands on a towel and hung her apron before disappearing up the stairs.

"Juliet!" Mistress barked on the intercom.

Coming!

I found Mistress in her office, pointedly staring at the clock. It had taken me two minutes to get to her. That wasn't fast enough.

"We have two new guests arriving today. They're sisters, so they've requested the same room." I knew this game. She'd charge for two rooms and tack on a special care fee for the privilege of a single. "Prepare the first room on the left; it's the only one large enough. With the rash of deaths, we need these ladies happy for at least a day or two. I'm taking a vacation as soon as they've recovered. You'll be on your own until your birthday."

"No nurses?"

"Are you implying you can't handle this?"

"It's fine." I nodded. Mistress taking a vacation? I'd never seen her shut DG down, never even heard that it had ever happened. Sure, she'd been more and more absent of late, but what would happen to the other kids?

"Get going."

My feet were glued to the floor. I felt like I had to ask. "Excuse me, but what about—"

She sneered at me. "Everything is taken care of. Now go! They'll be here by the hour, so I suggest you get moving!" she yelled in my direction, back to her preoccupation with her computer screen.

I had thirty minutes to clean the Green Room, change the bedding, and move in an empty hospital bed from another room. I'd need all hands on deck. The upstairs, especially the

Green Room, was a disaster from the deaths the night before. I knew cleaning was top of my list today, but this felt like insanity. We usually got twelve hours' notice before replacements arrived. For whatever god-awful reason, there seemed to be a waiting list to get in here. Why? I didn't know. I assumed if a person was conscious, they'd choose other care. Maybe that was why they rarely stayed conscious long.

"Nico, Bodie, Sema, I need you," I called up the attic stairs.

"Whas' up?" Bodie climbed down the rickety stairs. I hated them living up there, but Kirian once told me that, for a boy, it was like living in a tree house or a fort. That made me try to look at it like an adventure, rather than as unholy banishment.

"We have two oldies arriving soon. We have to get the Green Room spic'ed."

"'Kay. I'll find Sema. I think she's in the parlor."

"Hiding again?"

"Yep. Curtains." Bodie raced past.

I didn't know how to coax the girl into the real world. I'd think I was making progress and then she'd spend the day wrapped in brocade or dusty lace, face pressed against the windowpane, staring at the world outside. What would happen when I left? Would anyone make an effort? Notice?

"I found a camera." Nicole opened a bag for me when she reached the bottom of the stairs. "It's old. Instant Polaroid film. It works."

I bit my lip. We didn't have time now. "Later."

"Okay."

Nicole and I stripped beds, while Bodie battled dragons and evil sorcerers with the mop. Sema cleaned out what was left of the deceaseds' belongings—the night staff and transport team had claimed anything of value, so most of it was trash. We moved the dresser and armoire over to the side and shoved in a bed from the Train Room. Soon, it was as squeaky clean and empty as a hotel room. We checked the clock. Fifteen after.

I frowned. "They were supposed to be here by nine."

"Really?" Nicole arched a brow.

Rookie mistake. Crap. "No, she said the hour."

Nicole nodded. "Which means *any* hour in Mistress-speak."

I laid my sweaty face against the cool sheets. "Fine, we're not done yet."

"What?" Bodie looked around, clearly trying to figure out what we still had left to do.

"Close the door." I nodded at Sema, who did so quietly and then stood facing me, curiosity proving more irresistible than the curtains.

"Where's the camera?" I asked.

Nicole smiled. "Right here." She pulled it out from the bottom drawer of the dresser. "Why are we doing this again?"

I shrugged, not wanting to explain. "I need to see something, prove a theory."

"What exactly do you think this will prove?"

"I don't know. But I need you to take my photograph," I said.

"There are a few shots left. The camera was in Mr. Dailey's things. I don't know how well it will work."

I sighed. Nothing to lose. "We'll try."

"How's it go?" Bodie peered at it.

Nicole showed him. "I press this and then we wait for it to turn into a picture."

His eyes widened with delight. "That's all? It shows up like magic?"

"I guess." She ruffled his hair.

"Okay, take a couple and let's see." Antsy, I held my hands at my sides; I wasn't posing.

"Are you going to smile?" She looked at me over the camera.

I frowned. "This isn't a photo shoot."

"Okay, don't get snippy."

"Sorry. Just take it." I rubbed my gritty, burning eyes. The all-nighter had caught up with me.

"Why is this so important?" Sema edged over to Nicole and stared at me with haunted storytelling eyes. Her little braids needed redoing, especially since her hair had grown out.

I licked my lips and tried to dodge her question. "I can't explain it yet. Let's just see if it works."

Nicole clicked the first one, the minutes ticking by while the square of photo paper rested on the bed. We peered at it. Waiting. The edges started to turn and I held my breath as it showed the room around us. Finally, all but the center was left. A bright white blur was right over where I should have appeared in the photo.

"Is that long enough?" I asked.

"It's been twenty minutes." Nicole checked the clock. "Is there something wrong?"

I sighed, agitated. "Try another one. I'll move over here."

"Are you sure?"

"Yes, come on."

"It didn't work." Bodie flapped the photo in the air as if he could shake it into developing faster.

We tried with all the lights on. Then with none on, just the morning sunlight from the windows.

Bodie jumped up and down. "I wanna be in the picture too."

"Okay." I motioned him in.

Of the two of us only he showed up, slightly grainy, but evident. I was just a bright spot. Not even human in shape.

"That's crazy cuckoo! Where are you?" Bodie asked.

"It didn't work," I said.

"I'll take one of Nicole and you." Bodie held out his hand for the camera. "Please?" He was having fun. This was simply an experiment in new hobbies.

I didn't know what it meant that I was blank. If it meant anything. *Maybe it means nothing.* We had such little fun here that I had to lighten up, or I'd be just like Mistress and suck the life out of the little kids. "Sure."

Nicole hugged me; we smashed our cheeks together, smiling, and clowned for the camera.

Sema giggled, watching us, and quickly slapped her hand over her mouth when the sound came out. I didn't think it was possible for my heart to break more, but it did.

"Come on, you guys too." We took turns in different groups and different poses. I tried to be in all of them, or at least a part of me, to see if it made a difference where I stood or what showed.

Bodie's figure was always blurry, but he was there. He couldn't stand still long enough for me to know whether it was because he jittered, the taker moved, or something else.

But I showed up in none of them. Not even my elbow was more than a bright spot. Nicole seemed haloed by a spotlight from behind, but she appeared in the photographs. Soon, there was no film left. That's it. I frowned. I knew this was important but I couldn't untangle the why of it.

"It's so weird."

"We can find another camera." Nicole put her arm around me, trying to comfort me when she saw how upset I was.

I nodded. I wanted to find Meridian and ask her. If she could explain this, then maybe she could explain everything.

Two ambulances pulled up outside. I gathered up the pictures and handed them to Bodie. "Hide these upstairs?"

He nodded, and Sema followed him like a shadow.

Nicole waited until they were out of earshot. "What's going on? Talk to me."

I grow jealous of silly girls with silly lives.

Lucinda Myer

1775

CHAPTER 28

After cleaning two rooms and vacuuming Helios before anyone arrived, my muscles were tired, but my mind was still going full-speed with questions. I was sipping juice and nibbling on a muffin when Tens came back in. "Hey," I said carefully. Was there any word more asinine, more ridiculous to try and start a conversation with? I felt like I was introducing myself to a stranger.

In the bright light of day, I saw a wall between us and I had no idea how to scale it.

He nodded and drank juice out of the container, just

like he'd done in Revelation. He sat down, sweaty and stinky, at the table and grabbed a blueberry muffin. He wouldn't make eye contact.

"So?" I drew it out like an entire conversation. "Where'd you go?"

"Running," he answered.

Really. "In the truck?"

"Drove the truck, then ran." His tone was arrogant and closed off. He shoved more muffin in his mouth, shutting down the conversation.

Custos barked at the door, presumably for one of us to let her in. Tens got up to open it. She strolled in, carrying a sheet of paper in her mouth. She walked over to me and dropped it at my feet.

"What's this?" I picked it up, scanning the page. "This is about Juliet."

"Oh." Tens concentrated on his shoes. He looked as if he'd been caught sneaking cookies.

"What gives?" My tone was sharp.

He glanced up at me. "I went to see her."

"What?"

"I went to check on her." His shoulders lifted as if he were squaring up for a fight.

Jealousy pierced me. He'd left me, left a bed with a half-naked me to go see another girl. I put down the muffin next to the paper, my appetite gone. I shook my head, not even knowing what to say. Tears flooded my eyes.

"It's not like that." He moved toward me.

I stood up, taking my dishes to the sink. I dumped out

the rest of my juice and tossed the muffin to Custos to finish. "Okay." What else could I say?

"I needed to— I had this feeling— She's a Fenestra— God, Merry, I don't know what to say."

Was this how it was? Was I going to have to share him? Would he be drawn to *any* Fenestra?

"She was at the creek, and she was reading a piece of paper and she dropped it in the creek." He moved the page off the table. "I guess Custos went in after it."

"It's not wet," I pointed out. "Neither is she."

He shrugged, as if that were beside the point. "She's scared."

"Custos?"

"Juliet." He snarled like I'd deliberately misunderstood him.

"Uh-huh." *Me too.*

He picked up the page, read it. "Do you recognize any of this? I feel like I've heard of St. Jerome Emiliani's. Have you?"

I shook my head. Anger and insecurity blurred my vision. I really didn't give a crap what was on that piece of paper. I walked into the bathroom and sat down on the toilet. My face felt hot and the rest of me cold.

"Merry, come on. Don't hide in there," Tens said through the door.

I flipped on the shower. "I'm showering. I'll be out in a minute." Okay, so I'd already showered once this morning when I couldn't sleep, but another wouldn't hurt. I let the water wash over me. I let the tears of frustration mingle with the warm water until my head ached and my eyes felt sandy. I took my time drying off.

I put my clothes back on; I hadn't brought a change in with me. They were only a few hours' worn anyway.

I took a deep breath and exhaled. I came out of the bathroom ready to confront and conquer. "Are you *her* Protector, too?"

"Am I?" Tens sat on the couch holding a chunk of wood but doing nothing with it.

"Do you feel her?" I asked, losing my fighting edge.

He seemed surprised by my question. "I don't know. I haven't stopped to think about it."

"Well, think about it."

"Why are you being so cranky?"

I don't want to share you. I'm jealous. You left me alone right before we might have made love for the first time. "Sorry, I guess, but answer the question." I didn't feel like apologizing.

"Give me a second."

"It's not an essay question."

"Yeah, maybe it is." Tens closed his eyes.

I waited.

"I can't think about this while you're staring at me. That's why I left."

I shrugged. Like I cared. "We promised Rumi we'd help set up his booth for the Feast this morning."

Tens opened his eyes and stared hard at me. "Fine. Let's go."

"Unless you'd rather stay here. I can go without you."

"Meridian—I'm coming."

"Fine."

In the truck, I turned the radio up loud but didn't hear any of the lyrics. We didn't speak for the entire drive over to the remains of Fort Ouiatenon along the banks of the Wabash River.

The fort sat up on a hill overlooking acres of dormant grass, ringed with pine and deciduous sentries. The fields were dotted with canvas tents, with areas roped off with flags and twine for parking. The fort looked like two log cabins had been stacked and then sat on by a giant. The logs were chinked with mud and weathered gray. A light, misty fog blurred the edges and softened the riotous activity around us. The temp hovered just above freezing, but with sun it seemed as if spring was truly on its way.

A hatmaker passed us, seemingly without cares, wearing three feet of stacked wool caps balanced precariously on his head. A woman and her border collie herded leashed ewes and lambs between natty uniformed men practicing on their drums.

Saplings and branches were turned into canopy supports and rigging for tarps of sailcloth. Tables were covered with colorful wool blankets and items for sale: dolls, clothing, wooden toys and muskets, musical instruments, baskets, and lace. Scarves and mittens were crocheted and knitted on the spot for spectators to pick a pair.

I saw a candle-making station, still in the set-up phase, for kids who wanted to dip their own tapers, as well as places to watch sheep shearing, carding, and spinning fiber demonstrations. Naturally dyed yarns in golds, browns, pinks, and grays were draped across rope tied between two trees. Wooden-furniture makers hawked rocking chairs, bowls, spindles, and cradles. A blacksmith stoked his coals and hammered iron into hooks, horse-shoes, and tools.

Canoes, painted and polished, were lined up along the bank of the river. I saw a group of Native Americans in what I assumed to be ceremonial outfits with long fringes and intricate embroidery. The feathers on their head-dresses and tucked into beadwork caught the morning light; the breeze gave them an otherworldly movement. I wondered if Tens might have come to this feast with his family in clothing like this if he had lived in a different time. Did he identify himself as Native American? As Cuban? Or a wonderful wonky mixture of both? I had no idea. I saw him watching several men about his age with a hooded expression full of longing and an unknowable sadness. I knew so little about his history, his life before we met. There were moments when the curiosity was al-most too much for me to tamp down. We were early; if he wanted to say hello, I wanted him to feel like he could. "Do you want to go over there and—"

"No. Not right now." His tone biting, he turned in the opposite direction and ducked down yet another row of encampment.

I hurried to keep up, unsure whether he'd notice if he lost me among the crowds.

It took us several tries to find Rumi along the rows of vendors. The ground was frozen, but tire tracks and deep muddy grooves made me wonder what this common might be like if the temperatures rose.

Rumi's booth was near a massive stage in the process of being assembled. It looked like an odd combination of outdoor rock festival and Lincoln Logs. Evidently they were supposed to keep it as authentic-looking as possible. Even the speakers were covered in leaves and vines, to hide them. I bet all those people knew poison ivy on sight.

A couple of flannel-clad lumberjacks hefted huge sheets of plywood near us, and swore at the weight. "Hey, kid," they called to Tens. "Help?"

Tens shrugged at me, pointed toward Rumi towering over another group, and grabbed a side of the board to carry.

"Great. Thanks for the protection," I mumbled, trudging over to Rumi, who was quite thrilled to see me. At least somebody was happy to have me around.

Rumi tucked me against him in a one-armed embrace. "'Ello, angel. What do you think?" He swept his arms around the booth.

"Fantastic." I glanced around. "You're almost done?" I asked incredulously. "Are we late?"

"A troop of soon-to-be French soldiers, also known as Carmel's off-duty policemen, helped me carry it all over from the truck. Saved my back. But there's plenty left to do. Come."

I held corners and poles while Rumi fixed fastenings and hooks. I felt like the sorcerer's apprentice, not knowing what to do except for the parts right in front of me. I kept sneaking glances around to spot Tens.

Rumi noticed. "Your coals look dampened today, love. Having a bit of a lovers' spat, are you?"

"What?" I jerked, trying to stand straighter and clear my expression.

"You keep searching for him. He keeps staring at you. Mind you, not when the other is doing the gaping. It's all over your faces and your shoulders. Even the way you stamp your feet about. You expecting to be foudroyant? Tell me true?"

"Well, I don't know that I can—"

"Talking is dolorifugic, it'll make you feel better." He handed me a box of Spirit Stones to unpack from Bubble Wrap. Already glowing, they heated at my touch.

I sighed, wishing not for the first time for a best girl-friend. Which made me think of Juliet, and then made me mad all over again. "I guess. Yes. Okay, yes, we are having a fight." I felt better, more emphatic, more *right* with each word.

"You want to tell me about it, don't you?" He winked.

"Yes! No. He's a jerk."

"Hmm . . . I know him to be deeply in love with you. I'll take convincing to see him as a jerk." Rumi chuckled and handed me black draping to cover the tables with. Around us the grounds along the Wabash swelled with activity.

"He snuck out to see Juliet and he lied to me about it."

"Ah, I see." Rumi raised an eyebrow at me, as if that simply couldn't be everything I was upset over.

"And he won't—" I clamped my lips shut, mortified that I'd almost divulged the most personal details of our relationship. I had stopped myself right before telling Rumi that Tens didn't want to have sex with me. *Mortifying much?* Three semis pulled up nearby. Their engine noise and the chaos of off-loading made conversing impossible for a few minutes. Horse trailers were backed in and massive draft horses were unloaded by the time I gathered my composure.

Rumi's booth was rustic wrought iron, the size of a large bedroom. White gauzy layers of curtain swept over and around the frame, giving the space fanciful definition and whimsical grace. Real candles and ones with LED flames graced blown candlesticks. Stunning clear glass candelabra stood taller than my head and made me think of weddings and vampires. Vampire weddings.

To our left the camp for the French soldiers and settlers was taking shape. A man wearing a Davy Crockett ensemble—tanned hides, fringed moccasins, and a coonskin cap—ambled past. The earbuds and wires from his iPod were the only clue that the year was not 1800-something and we weren't living on the frontier.

Tens nodded at me when I looked in his direction, but he didn't make a move to leave the main stage. He'd shed his coat, and sweat on his skin glistened in the sun and dampened the hair along his temples. I didn't know if he was keeping his distance because the other men seemed old and heart-attack prone, or because he wanted to do anything he could to stay far away from me. I stoked my hurt and took it personally.

Bless Rumi for his silences. He let me be and didn't push conversation back to Tens and me. But as we worked, I began to notice that it wasn't because he was trying to be respectful of my melancholy.

I finally looked at him, studied his face. He was ashen and stooped. "Are you okay?" I asked.

"Let's get this clear plastic roof up, it's the final set-up." He cleared his throat.

"Okay, but first tell me what's bothering you? Please? I'll tell you more about the fight, if that's what it takes," I begged, trying to bribe him with gossip.

"Don't be confiding things you'll regret later just to see an old man smile and feel useful. Tens won't divagate."

I nodded. "Rumi, I know we . . . I . . . haven't been completely forthcoming." I reached out and touched his forearm so he'd make eye contact. "But you, your stories and your family history, have taught me about myself and maybe my future. I'm grateful. I really am."

His eyes watered, but he smiled at me. "I always wanted a daughter, you know? Never worked out for me, but you'll do. I'm morose. Today is the anniversary of my ma's death. It makes me sad each year around this time that I can't share the Feast with her. She loved this festival. Dressed up as a firefly annually, with wings that flapped and a hind end that glowed, thanks to modern engineering." He gave a chuckle that fell off at the end in a sniff.

"A firefly?" That was hard to picture. "I wish I could see that!"

He nodded. "You'll see around here there are swarms

of 'em in the evenings. She used to tell me that fireflies carried the souls of our loved ones back to earth to check up on us, and that the blinks were the souls winking at us. She'd sit on the porch for hours and watch them come out at dusk. She was a summer dreamer through and through."

The insects sounded magical. There was nothing in Portland that compared. "I can't wait to see them."

He finished tying the ties on the plastic cover. "It's early yet for the real ones. Not near warm enough. The only ones you'll see here are in artwork or costume. But maybe you'll be here when they come this summer."

"Maybe." I doubted it. I couldn't think past today, let alone where or when we'd head on. Assuming we managed to save Juliet and added a third person to our party. Assuming we got another message from the Creators on what to do next. Assuming a lot.

"You given any thought to how we rescue your sister in arms?"

No, lately I've been too busy being insanely jealous of her to want to help her. "Um, nothing yet."

"Can't we simply kidnap her?" Rumi tried to smile, though his seriousness was clear.

"I think that's illegal and probably wouldn't help our cause." *And if Nocti are involved it probably wouldn't work.*

"Ah, there is that. I do think we must tell Nelli, though."

"Uh—" I tried to stall. There were already too many people who knew too much. Weren't there?

He ignored my stutter and stepped back to inspect the

setup. "Well, I think that's all for today. Gus arrives soon to take over in case there are early-bird customers. We don't officially start until tomorrow, you know. I must go take my mum a bit of whiskey and hyacinths. My siblings are so far away." His face was etched with a sadness, a loneliness, I understood completely.

I glanced over at Tens still hauling and climbing scaffolding. "Can I come with you?"

He brightened. "Are you sure?"

I nodded. A cemetery might very well be peaceful and restful. Besides, it was a good bet there wouldn't be any ready souls. "Let me just go tell Tens."

"Here Gus comes now." Rumi pointed toward Gus's Volkswagen Bug. "I'll meet you at my car. Tomorrow, we'll unload more of the glassware and hang the balls. I've got itsy fireflies, too; I've been making and saving all year." He rubbed his hands together like a child; I loved seeing the sparkle back in his eyes.

I walked over to Tens and hesitated while he hoisted the last edge of huge wooden boxes onto the stage area.

"Tens?" I asked, hating the way my voice cracked with trepidation.

He turned. Sweat wet the edges of his hair. He'd stripped down to a T-shirt, which only served to accentuate his broad shoulders and the lean length of his muscles. He gave me a small smile, as if he hoped we were past this argument and didn't have to finish it.

A young girl strolled past with a herd of her friends and blatantly checked out his butt with a toss of her head and a lick of her lips. Then giggled with her friends in a way that set my teeth on edge.

"I'm going to go with Rumi. I'll see you back at home."

"But—"

I turned and walked away. I didn't want to hear all the reasons being without him was dangerous. It was a feeling I might have to get used to living with.

I have heard rumors of a guild of men who guard
and protect as their sworn duty. It is said they
are the ones who deliver the resting stones to
our graves.

Meridian Laine Fulbright

February 1994

CHAPTER 29

We got to Riverside Cemetery after a quick Arni's Pizza
lunch. Behind us lay railroad tracks, and grave markers
checkerboarded the hillsides, rising above us with only
huge old trees breaking up the expanse of lawn.

I opened the gate while Rumi drove the car through.
Stone angels, cherubim, and lambs knelt, guarded, or
prayed by headstones. Some were so worn they were missing the tops of wings or hands, smoothed like they'd
melted in the elements. There were newer, shinier markers with etchings of faces, names, or personal things like
motorcycles or horses running in pastures.

"How old is this place?" I asked as I got back into the car.

"I don't really know. Maybe it dates from the time of the Civil War? Graves date back to the mid–eighteen hundreds. Beyond, over there, you see that mound?" Rumi turned down a car path. Barely wide enough to drive on, it ran across the center of the yard, taking us farther up the hill.

"The hilly thing?"

"It's man-made, a Native American ancestral burial site. My guess is it was sacred when the settlers arrived and they began being buried here too. The remains of a small stone chapel are in that direction. Used to be you were simply buried on your land."

"How big is this place?" I asked as we parked and got out of the car.

"I don't know. Acres in three directions. My family plots are up this way."

I stopped by the bumper. "Do you want me to wait here?"

Rumi took a bottle of whiskey and a bouquet of flowers out of his trunk. "Oh no. I'll introduce you around. I'm curious to see what you make of my family's headstones. I think there might be a connection to the artwork. This place is full of peonies and wild roses in the summer. It's beautiful. And every Memorial Day it takes on a picnic atmosphere."

"Picnics?" In a cemetery?

He nodded. "Families come, all generations, and clean

the grave markers, plant flowers or bring fresh ones. If it's nice weather there are Ultimate Frisbee games and touch football."

"In a graveyard?"

"You've heard of All Saints' Day? Day of the Dead, in Mexico?"

"In social studies classes." *I think*.

"Well, take those ideas, jumble them together with immigrant wakes, sitting shivah, and the American Memorial Day, and you get generations of families who meet with their ancestors to pay respects. Also has a bit of family reunion, 'summer is here' vibe. It's nice. Very eclectic and American."

I nodded. "How'd your family end up here?"

"In the states, or Indiana?"

"Indiana."

"Grandparents made their way to Chicago. It was possible for immigrants to find work. I'm sure the stories were better than the reality."

"Probably."

"When my grandparents married they wanted to get out of the big city, away from all the commotion. My nain needed space around her, doctors said she had weak lungs. So my taid bought a farm here sight unseen. They up and moved, called it an adventure."

"That's gutsy."

"I think it was more desperate. She was very ill, and the country air was all that the doctors thought might help. But I think we know there was more to it now, don't we?"

"If she was a Fenestra?"

He nodded.

Thoughtful, I answered, "The country would have been easier—not as many people crowding toward the windows. Makes sense she would have felt better out here. Learned better how to do it."

"And my grandfather knew that, I think. Was he her Tens?"

"I don't know. He might have been a Fenestra too. At least what you've translated so far seems like they both might be." This was fast moving outside my range of knowledge. *I wish I had Auntie to ask.* "This place is gorgeous. So peaceful and almost—"

"Healing?"

I nodded. "Refreshing. What is that feeling?" Like a warm bubble bath or comfort food for the soul. It felt *nice.*

He smiled and shrugged. "I don't know. I've always thought it had something to do with it being sacred ground for so long. That there's a reason for that."

I saw a few shadows moving in the distance toward us. *Uh-oh.* "Rumi, I think I need to sit down. I'll be okay, don't freak out."

"We're almost there—" He gestured to a group of stones ahead.

"No, I mean now." I grabbed a headstone with one hand and slid to a seated position, my back braced, closing my eyes to see the window. A breeze rustled the curtains and it was my window, the one Auntie taught me. I smiled.

Spirits who hadn't moved on, who'd been blocked or

chose not to go during their actual death, now reunited with their families, one after another. Lots of freshly plowed fields filled with cheering greeters, and a raucous crowd in an old basketball field house welcomed those passing through me. I even saw a racetrack with cars speeding by. No Auntie, though.

I opened my eyes. Rumi was holding my hand and peering at me. "I'm okay." And I was. Maybe I'd begun to get the hang of it?

"W-were you—?" he stuttered, pale but very interested. "Was that—?"

" 'Ghosts' is the easiest word to describe them. Those who were ready to go are no longer late for their reunions. They can find me when they're ready. I guess maybe they've been waiting here for the Memorial Day party." I tried to smile while brushing my hair out of my eyes. It was curly, not the least bit limp.

He sat down hard. "Wow. Meridian, you glowed like the Stones."

"What?" I asked.

"Softly. Not like a beacon. But even these ancient eyes picked up on the change."

"I don't think that's ever happened." But I didn't feel exhausted or ill; I felt refreshed, renewed, whole. "Sorry," I said, while Rumi helped me to my feet. "I've got a long way to go before I can open the window and keep moving in the real world."

"A bit like walking while patting your head and rubbing your stomach?"

"Something like that." I smiled.

"Look behind you at the headstone. I'm seeing—"

I turned. "Your nain's paintings?" The headstone I'd leaned against was an exact replica of all his family's drawings and paintings. The round top of a half sun unfurling its rays like the petals of a flower sat on top of a window. I checked the name and date, curious to know if this person was a relative. "Are you related?"

"Come on." Rumi broke into a jog.

"What is it?" *Why is an old man beating me at sprints?*

He stopped and pointed. "I assumed they were the style of the time. It's more than that, isn't it?"

I followed his finger. Two window headstones. "Your grandparents?"

"Yes."

"They match perfectly."

"Exactly."

"So is that one over there—is that a relative of yours?"

"No. My family is all in this parcel. I'll be buried in that bare spot over there."

I cringed, unable to face or comment on Rumi's death. "Who put these here?"

"My parents? I don't know. They've always been here."

The gravestones curved like windows, like an orange slice on top of a rectangle. Stone carvers had cut the crosspieces like the pane separators. At the top of each half circle was a sun with rays like the petals of a daisy. Each was decorated with a first name, a last name, and a quote.

I knelt down at the little stones about six feet away, parallel to the headstones. "What are these?"

"Footstones," Rumi answered.

There was carving, weathered and smoothed, with lichen and moss growing in the crevices. "What do they say?"

"I've never been able to read it."

"Is it Gaelic?"

"Can't tell. I don't think so." Flames burned at the bottom, almost flickering in their intricacy. "Why the fire?"

"My best guess is that fire used to equate life. Without fire, without light, there was no life." I leaned closer, trying to make out the words. I guess I wanted a big "This person was also a Fenestra" flashing at me in red neon. *So not going to happen.* "Could it be Arabic, or Sanskrit, or Russian?" I desperately wanted to know the language written on the stones.

"I really don't know." Rumi frowned in concentration. "It's nothing I've ever seen elsewhere."

"Would your siblings know?"

"No, I'm the only one who comes here anymore. They don't talk about death, or life, for that matter. They dwell in the hard facts." His face was so full of regret and grief that I stood up and hugged him.

"I'm sorry," I said into his sweater.

"People either fear or accept what they can't explain. They fear it. I accept it."

The rest of the markers in the immediate vicinity were plain stones, small lambs, or kneeling angels, but farther down the line was another large window beside a smaller stone carved with a shield.

Rumi walked me down to them. "These belong to my parents, my ma and my da."

"Is that a sword?" I asked, stooping to get a closer look. "And a shield. What's on the shield?"

Rumi nudged me. "Go closer, she won't mind."

I tried to stay in the scant few inches between where I thought was safe and where the dead might lie, in a bizarre, ungainly attempt to stay respectful.

Rumi guffawed. "You can step on the graves, Meridian, you can't hurt 'em."

I edged my feet more firmly. "Isn't that bad luck or something?"

"I think it used to be because you could fall into the graves as they settled. These days they're concrete, steel; there's not a risk."

"That would count as bad luck. The shield carries the window shape at the top and the flames at the bottom, doesn't it?" I traced it with my fingers.

He nodded. "That's what I see."

"Did you put *these* here?"

"No, I picked out plain granite stones. My parents weren't fussy and would have gasped at the cost for death, so I kept it simple, thinking they'd want frugality over froufrou."

These were anything but simple gravestones.

"I don't know who did it." Rumi sat cross-legged in the grass. "I came the day they were supposed to be installed.

I was on time for the appointment, but they were already finished. They weren't the right ones, but the names and dates were right."

"Did you ask?"

"Of course. I called the stonemason and he said they'd delivered rectangular stones just like I'd ordered. He even came out here to see them because he didn't believe me."

"And?"

"And he couldn't explain it. I thought maybe my sister ordered them instead, to match the other family ones, perhaps? She wouldn't admit it, but she's not the type who would. Nothing sentimental in that one. The mason would have redone them for me, but I left 'em. I liked 'em. Like I said, I accept the inexplicable quite well."

"Is your mom's like any others?"

"No, I guess I always came out here to talk to them and saw them, not the graves themselves, you know. Over the years I've accepted the headstones as there, but now?"

"Now we have to wonder who put them there."

"And why," he said.

* * *

Rumi and I had gotten no further trying to understand the grave markers when he dropped me back at the cottage. Tens's truck was in the driveway, so I assumed he was inside. Arguments aside, I needed to tell him this new piece of the puzzle. We could argue later.

I threw open the cottage door. "Tens?"

There was no answer.

I tried again, my pulse accelerating, a million bad things going through my mind. "Tens? Where are you? Are you here?"

No Tens, no note, no Custos.

"Meridian?" Joi called from the path. "Are you okay?"

"Have you seen Tens?" I called to her.

"He and the wolf left here about an hour ago on foot. Running?"

"Oh." In the past, he'd have left me a note. He wouldn't have wanted me to worry.

Joi motioned me toward her. "Can you come inside? I'd like to introduce you to a friend of mine."

"Sure." I blew out a frustrated sigh and headed toward the tearoom.

Joi waited until I got to the kitchen to say more. "Miss Howard is turning one hundred and one today. She's a spitfire. You'll love her; she reminds me of you."

The dining area was decorated with pink and purple balloon bouquets, and streamers dangled between picture frames and wreaths. Lilies and lilacs in huge arrangements filled the room with the scent of spring. A large hand-lettered sign that said *Happy Birthday, Judith!* graced the far windows.

"Everyone, this is Meridian." Joi introduced me to the group but led me closer to a shrunken lady in a wheel-chair at the far end.

By far the youngest one in the room, I felt every set of eyes smile at me.

"Oh, isn't she pretty?" Miss Howard reached out toward me.

Joi made introductions. "Miss Howard, this is my new friend Meridian."

She squinted at me and motioned with her hand. "Come closer, dear, I can't see you with the light in my eyes."

Another woman announced it was time for cake and the singing of the birthday song.

The hair on my neck raised and my alarm system went off as I touched Miss Howard's hand. "Oh—"

We stood at the window, side by side. She no longer needed her wheelchair and her gnarled, arthritic fingers were straight and strong as her spine.

"You are pretty, aren't you?" She paused, tall and vital next to me, still holding my hand. "Do you have a beau?"

"Um, yes." *I think. Maybe. Can soul mates break up? Or is it like an arranged marriage where you're stuck regardless?*

"Oh, there are my boys." She turned from me and watched out the window. "What a lovely birthday surprise. There's my husband—he served in three wars, you know. And my sons, Teddy, Billy, and Ike, they served as infantrymen too. But they're gone now. Is this a movie, dear?"

I watched the men stride forward and begin to unroll a bright scroll of paper. "No, this isn't a movie." I didn't know how else to say it.

"Well then, oh, look at that." She giggled and pointed. "It says *Welcome home, we've missed you.* I always held up signs at the airport for them. Every time they got leave and came to visit me, a new sign. But why does it say that?"

She turned to me, puzzled. I'd never had a soul so unaware of what she was supposed to do. Maybe it wasn't always instinctive.

"Miss Howard, you're dead. I'm sorry." I swallowed.

"I am? Are you sure?" She blinked with surprise.

I nodded.

"Forty years I've waited for this. Are you sure?"

"Yes, ma'am. What do you mean you've waited?"

"I lost Teddy to Korea, Billy to Vietnam, Ike to a drunk driver, and my husband to cancer all before I was sixty. It was hard enough burying my husband, but seeing each of my children in the ground before me, that just isn't right. I kept thinking I was an old lady and I'd die soon. But that never happened. And here it's been another lifetime."

I teared up. It was impossible not to react to the emotion in her voice. Her joy, relief, and sense of release were immeasurable.

"What do I do? Do I fly?"

"You go to them. Through the window."

"I haven't walked that far in ages." She looked at me skeptically, then down at her feet.

"I don't know exactly how it works, but you'll be able to."

"This is real?"

"Yes."

She squeezed my hand and then let go. Carefully, with

mincing steps, she made her way to the window. She picked up one leg, slung it over the window frame, and then did the same with the other. She steadied herself with both hands against the frame, but she didn't need to. The more she moved, the better she got, until she was running toward the figures across the farmed land, spritely and fit as a twentysomething. The boys waved to me.

Colorful scarves caught my eye and I glanced to the side, away from the reunion.

"Meridian!" Auntie waved to get my attention. Beside her was the young woman. She was still terribly disfigured, but her appearance was less transparent, more opaque, almost solid.

She held a sign.

I felt the real world tugging at me. I had to read the sign. I gripped the curtains resisting the pull.

The sign said JULIET'S MOTHER LOVES HER. DIED & TRIED TO PROTECT.

I blinked and saw Joi staring down at me. My face was cold and wet.

"You fainted," she said.

Sirens stopped nearby and I heard the scurry of feet.

"Just lie still," Joi instructed. I heard wailing and sniffles around me.

"They're in here."

I heard voices I couldn't identify talking loudly. I sat up. "I'm fine. It just happens sometimes."

Joi tried to push me back to the floor. "You shouldn't get up."

"No, no, I'm fine." I moved out of the way as para-medics carrying a backboard walked in.

"That's her. She's not breathing." Joi moved the EMTs toward Ms. Howard's remains in the wheelchair.

I snuck out in all the chaos. Auntie had more for me. It made sense to me now. The side of the woman's face that was undamaged looked just like a thirtysomething Juliet. I didn't know why I hadn't seen it before.

Tens still wasn't back at the cottage, but the truck keys were on the kitchen table. I grabbed them before I could talk myself out of going to Dunklebarger.

Practice throwing up the sash with speed and facility. Deliberation might allow them to grab the soul from you.

Jocelyn Wynn

CHAPTER 30

With Juliet weighing heavily on my mind, I was unable to walk calmly down the path toward Dunklebarger; I kept breaking into a jog. The birds seemed to sense my urgency because they took up the call. Ahead of and behind me in the woods, there were calls and chatter, from Canada geese honking to woodpeckers knocking staccato rhythms on tree trunks. The sun sank low behind the trees and the tilted, crazy feeling crawling in my stomach thrashed my insides.

Suddenly, Minerva pounced from behind a log, into

the middle of my path, startling me to a stop. "Crap!" I leaned over, winded, to catch my breath. "Uh, sorry? I didn't mean to yell at you." Last thing I needed to do was piss off a creature connected to the Creators. The way things were going I didn't think getting struck by lightning for swearing was out of the question.

Minerva narrowed her golden eyes at me, almost willing me into a game of chicken. She twitched her tail in a dance that screamed volumes of displeasure. Then she meowed demandingly and stalked toward me.

I held my ground. Not because I felt the need to win chicken with a cat, but because I wasn't sure how best to approach the situation. She was a Fenestra creature, but I still didn't know if that meant she liked me or took exception to my oxygen consumption. I leaned toward the latter. Cats unnerved me with their lack of facial expression.

Standing at my feet, Minerva took a long, detailed look up my frame. Placed one set of front claws on my shin, then the second, inverting her spine and stretching in a yoga pose. The tug in my jeans was enough to tell me that, intended or not, she could very well shred my legs. She began purring like an engine revving and again meowed up at me, as if asking for . . . I had no idea what.

I reached down slowly, feeling as if I were about to pet a cobra. I ran my fingers lightly against the downy fluff along her cheeks. I'd once held a chinchilla that was our fifth-grade mascot. Petting Minerva's fur was like petting that animal. Only Minerva didn't fall over dead. I waited for a download like Tens had received while touching her. Nothing.

"Juliet's mom. That's who's been trying to talk to me with Auntie. She loved her. Was she a Fenestra too? Can you tell me?" I scratched under the cat's chin and the volume of her purring increased, but I didn't get the freeze like Tens did. No knowledge from on high came surging at me. "How come it worked for him and not me?" I asked.

The cat turned away from me, flicked her tail in invitation. She ran in a comical gait, a hybrid of a bunny hop and a horse's trot, before stopping and calling back to me in that overpowering meow. I swore I saw her nod in the direction of Dunklebarger as if to tell me we were late. *I am so losing my mind*.

"Lead the way." I followed, this time staying in the woods, parallel to the path.

As we neared the last bend, I tripped, sprawling into the leaves and mud behind a fallen tree. "What the—" I broke off, spitting out hair as Minerva seemed to deliberately stuff her whole tail in my mouth.

That was when I heard the voices. I quieted as the cat stood on my chest and pointedly stared at me until I nodded. We were *hiding*. The low rumble of a man speaking and the clipped tones of a woman giving orders drifted over to us. My first thought was Tens and Juliet were meeting in secret, but that was jealousy listening, not my brain.

The woman harangued, "I knew I'd find you skulking about here. What if she sees you? It's not time yet."

"I wanted to see her, how she's changed, before . . . ," a young man answered in a petulant whine.

"I didn't authorize this. It makes no difference whether you still want her, Kirian."

"Can't we just tell her the truth?" He sounded like Sammy when he was told to take a bath and go to bed. Not an attractive voice for any age.

I held my breath, listening, trying to make sense of who these two people were. My little arm-hair warning system was on high alert. Nocti, maybe?

A stinging slap echoed. "I wasn't asking for your opinion. When I want it, I'll tell you what it is. Clear?" The woman's tone was icy and completely in command.

"Yes, ma'am." He sounded defeated.

"Good. Now, you must convince her to leave with you. That you'll be together, visit Paris in April. Take her flowers. Seduce her. Be her Romeo." He must have nodded, because the woman continued. "Good boy. I knew you'd be my perfect boy."

My inner alarm shrieked at me. Fight or flight kicked into high gear. I'd only felt this once before, with Perimo. *Nocti?*

I heard the sounds of kissing. The suck and smooch, gasping breath, moans of pleasure. I angled my head to peer under a curve of the tree, between the earth and the wood. Only a slit, really, but if I found the right angle I might be able to see them. Bingo. The woman was in steep stiletto heels, a tight pencil skirt, and yellow leather jacket, with black hair twisted in an elegant, complicated updo. She was a foot shorter than the boy, but she still somehow managed to tower over him. He might have been cute, but the red lipstick smeared on his lips matched a bright handprint on his cheek. Sandy blond hair, all-American-quarterback look, like someone in an Abercrombie ad. I was too far away to get a look at his eyes, but his face was blank, crushed.

"Now, you do this little thing for me and we can run away together. Just like I promised." She smoothed his hair and petted his cheek.

He nodded.

"When I drop you back at the apartment you must stay put. It's not time yet. We have to set the stage with the Feast. So to speak. It'll be fun." She cackled. "Come." They cut through the woods in front of me. I held perfectly still and watched. She towed him with a white-knuckled clamp on his arm. While he went with her willingly enough, he dragged his feet and didn't help her maneuver in those heels over the broken, pitted path.

I lay there in the leaves, staring up at the sky and the clouds rushing past, until I was sure they wouldn't see me. Nocti? Was it her? Him? Both? I wished I'd seen their eyes. If they were Nocti, I'd see the black in the sockets where eyeballs should have been. I wondered if, when Nocti looked at mine, they saw light glowing. I hoped I was never again in such close proximity to have that question answered. "Nocti?" I asked Minerva as she hopped over the log and back toward the path.

The cat yowled.

"I'll take that as a yes. But who are they? And was the Romeo comment in regard to Juliet? Do I warn her?"

Minerva didn't answer.

I slowed my steps when the fence started, but took my cue from her. She didn't slow down, so I assumed we were safe for the moment.

"Merry, merry Christmas!" a little, excited voice called out to me.

"Bodie?" I started, looking up into the trees to locate him. He shimmied down. "I'm sorry, you're a monkey. I thought you were a boy. Have you seen a boy named Bodie?"

"It's me!" He hugged my legs.

"No!" I pretended not to believe him.

"Yes, it is." He giggled.

I tickled him until we were both laughing so hard we collapsed against the grass, huffing. My stomach hurt from using laugh muscles; they'd atrophied. "How's it going?" I asked, rolling up on my elbow.

Minerva sat on the top of the hill, facing Dunklebarger and twitching her tail, like a lookout sentry.

Bodie's face clouded. "Juliet is really tired. She's leaving. I want to go with her."

"Leaving?"

He nodded. "Everybody leaves. It's her birthday, then she leaves."

"To where?" I asked.

"I dunno."

"Do you think you could get her to talk to me?"

"I can find Nico. But Juliet is working. Mistress hates her."

"Do you think, maybe—" I broke off. I felt like an

idiot asking a six-year-old to deliver what might be the most important message ever.

"What? I can. I'm strong. Brave. Smart," he announced, puffing out his chest a little more with each word.

"Can you give Juliet a message for me? And get it perfect? It's really important."

"Don't none-deresti-ate me. It's insulting." Bodie wagged his finger in my face and I again thought of Sammy. He'd say the same thing and sound exactly like an adult doing it too.

"Okay. Tell her . . ." *What to say, exactly?* "Tell her that Meridian met her mom. Juliet's mom loves her and she's protecting her."

"Why doesn't she come, then?" he asked.

"I can't explain right now, but can you tell her that?"

"You saw her mom. Mom loves her and is protecting her."

"Yes, and I can tell her more. She has to come find me."

"Come find you. Got it."

"Bodie, be careful, okay? Don't tell her in front of any adults."

"I won't. We never talk about 'portant stuff in front of them." He smiled. "Bring me candy next time? Nicole has butterscotch, but I like grape Hubba Bubba."

I nodded. Easy request. "Okay." At least this time he wasn't asking me to adopt him.

"Promise?"

"Sure, I promise. Grape gum."

He disappeared over the berm and Minerva swatted at my head.

"I'm going. I'm going." I crept back into the woods and ran all the way back to the truck. I needed to call Sammy. And hug Tens.

* * *

Tens still wasn't back when I pulled into the parking lot. The tearoom was closed and empty.

I let myself into the cottage and turned on every light. I shivered. I looked at the phone.

"You can do this. You heard Bodie. Don't underestimate kids."

I grabbed the receiver and quickly dialed the number before I lost my nerve again.

I listened to it ring. I wanted it to go to voice mail and I wanted a real voice equally. *Torn much?*

My dad's voice said, "Hello."

"Dad?"

"Please leave a message and we'll call you back."

Voice mail.

I opened my mouth at the beep but couldn't force sound out. I hung up and stared at the phone as tears fell down my cheeks.

"Supergirl?" Tens opened the front door, crossed the room in double time, and wrapped me in his arms. "What's wrong? What happened?"

I let him hold me and chase away my fear with his warmth and his strength. I mumbled, "Nothing," into his neck.

He let me cry it out, holding me with that perfect strength, not overwhelming or overpowering.

He used the sleeve of his sweatshirt to wipe my face, but then he put it to my nose and commanded, "Blow."

I laughed. I couldn't help it. Love meant sacrificing a sleeve to the snot monster.

"What?" His expression was perplexed. "You're phlegmy. I can't reach the Kleenex."

The way he said *phlegmy* just made me laugh harder. Finally he started smiling and chuckling too. We dissolved into the kind of laughter that goes around and around with each glance and giggle.

I cradled into his body, smiling, refreshed.

He brushed his thumb across my cheek, my lips. His expression turned serious. "Why were we fighting?"

"I don't remember." I didn't. "Do you?"

He shook his head. "That's why I asked. I came in here all prepared to stay angry and then I saw you and I can't remember why."

I traced his eyebrows, slashes of raven's wing bracketing his coal-black gaze. "I saw Fenestra graves and an old lady died, so I saw Auntie again and Juliet's mom was there and then Minerva tripped me and there's a Nocti with a boy toy and Bodie came—"

"Slow down and start at the beginning." He shifted, toed his sneakers off, lifted his feet up onto the coffee table, and hugged me closer.

So I started the story back at when Rumi and I left the Feast.

I wonder how the little kids are handling my disappearance? Should I have sacrificed my child for them all? —R.

CHAPTER 31
Juliet

No staff and fewer kids meant I stayed up all night trying to make Mistress happy. The next morning I was barely able to keep on my feet. Patience and compassion were drained from my soul. I fought the urge to lock myself in my closet and refuse to come out.

Bodie tugged on my pant leg. "Juliet, I have to tell you something."

"Not now, Bodie."

"But—"

"Go tell Nicole." I finished tucking the fresh pillow beneath a lax and fragile head belonging to Enid, one of the sisters. The list today felt more daunting and undoable than usual. I wanted the mental and emotional energy to sit and think. Contemplate the photographs, my dreams, my future.

"But—"

The sisters were situated and as comfortable as I could make them. One was unconscious and never expected to wake. Apparently, she'd been at death's door for weeks, always one breath away from saying her farewells. The orderly didn't know what was keeping her alive. It defied logic. The other sister had a broken hip. The nurse told Mistress, "You know what happens to old ladies with broken hips."

We knew. That's why they came here.

I was changing out the linens, delivering the meal tray, freshening the water pitcher, and checking their feet for cold. I always added a layer whenever someone's toes felt too cold. It seemed to me an easy thing to do. My frigid feet never warmed and I wished someone would toss an extra blanket over mine.

"Oh dear, that tickles."

I leapt back from the bed, my gaze flying toward the voice at its head.

"I didn't mean to startle you, dear." She seemed contrite and apologetic, rubbing her eyes with one slightly shaky hand.

"Hi," I said. "It's okay, I thought you might need another blanket or—"

"I'm Enid Fairchild." She lifted a hand toward me and smiled. Her brilliantly white hair was pressed against her head like a skullcap. It looked like she usually styled it in tight curls.

"I'm Juliet . . . um, Ambrose." I shook her hand carefully, trying to make sure I didn't hurt her. Rarely were patients here conscious or talkative, but when they were, I learned a library's wealth of knowledge.

"Are you a candy striper, child?" She tried to raise her body higher on the pillows.

I leaned over her and added muscle to her efforts until she nodded. "No, what's a candy striper?" I asked.

"Why, a volunteer who helps in the hospital. Do you want to be a nurse or a doctor?"

"No!" I almost shouted. I'd spent entirely too much of my life nursing and doctoring to want to do those things as a career. "Sorry." I backed away from the bed, expecting her to scold me for raising my voice.

She blinked and glanced around. "We're not in the hospital anymore, are we?"

I bit my cuticles, hating to be the one to break the news. "No, ma'am, you're at Dunklebarger Rehabilitation Center."

"Well, that's a mouthful. Don't you just love that name, Glee?" She tried to reach a hand out to pat her sister. Her hand fell limply when she couldn't quite make it. Her sadness was a palpable curtain descending over her bed. "Can you move us closer? Please?" she asked.

Mistress would say no, but I didn't see what difference it made. So I unlocked the wheels of Glee's bed and pushed it gently toward Enid's.

"That is sublime." She brushed her sister's hair away from her forehead. "Hello, my darling."

I stepped back, feeling like an intruder.

"We're twins, you know. Identical twins." She smiled at me, her wrinkles like bird tracks across her face. They added a divinity to her smile that felt irresistible.

She made me think of Miss Claudia and Paddy, the first guests I met when I came here. I loved them. They were like grandparents, family that I never knew I missed until they died. Since then I'd kept my heart far away from anyone old who was alive enough to talk. Kept an emotional distance to protect myself, pretended I wasn't attached to them or wished for something I couldn't have, until I believed it.

"May I have a drink of water, Juliet?"

"Sure." I poured her a clean glass from a plastic bottle and held the straw while she drank.

There was a twinkle in her eyes that reminded me of someone. Brilliant blue eyes like pictures I'd seen of the South Pacific Ocean. I yearned to see every body of water on earth. Wildcat Creek was the closest I had come to and that's what kept me striving forward when Kirian left three years ago.

"I think I'll sleep now. Will you be here when I wake?" Enid asked with the vulnerability of a young child.

I tried to give her reassurance that I didn't feel. "Yes, ma'am. Probably."

"That's good. Very good." She closed her eyes and drifted off.

"Sema?" I whispered at the curtains. I couldn't remember if she was in here or not.

Sema peeked around the outside edge of the curtain. I envied her the smooth milk chocolate of her skin and the hazel green of her eyes. She'd be exotic and beautiful when she was grown, especially compared to the grass-fed heifer I saw looking back at me in mirrors.

"Can you stay in here? Come and get me if either of them wakes up?"

She nodded and disappeared back to her post at the window. She happily twirled herself into the heavy fabric. Part of me, the mothering part, wondered if I should be dissuading this obsession, but the other part didn't want to take away the one thing that comforted the little girl.

The rest of the day passed swiftly, with Mistress adding more demands when she thought I wasn't moving fast enough. The to-do list forever lengthened.

Finally, with two minutes to myself and an urgent need to empty my bladder, I sat on the toilet and leaned against the wall. Closing my eyes, I felt the pull of sleep, of something darker and more permanent. I was swimming in an ocean much more powerful and strong than I could ever hope to be. I didn't know why I kept fighting the currents when letting go had a certain comforting appeal.

"Juliet?" A tiny hand shook my shoulder.

I jerked, almost falling off the toilet. "Bodie?" I shrieked. "Get out!"

"No!" He crossed his arms and planted his feet.

"Yes!" There was no dignity in this with my panties at my ankles.

"You 'ave to listen to me!" He narrowed his eyes, peeved and determined.

"Fine, what?"

"It's a message. From Meri-de-an."

"From Meridian? What were you doing talking to her? Is she here?" I started fumbling with toilet paper.

"Stop!" Bodie squealed. "Listen."

I held up my hands in surrender. "Okay."

"She met your mom. Mom loves you, protects you."

"What?" I had expected an invitation to dinner or a fashion suggestion, anything but information about my mother.

"That's what she said. Now, you heard it." He backed out of the tiny servant's bathroom and shut the door behind him.

I called after him, "When? Where? Bodie!" I stood and tripped over my tangled feet. "Damn!" I pulled myself together and trotted out to find Bodie for more details.

I was blasted by Mistress as soon as she saw me.

"Juliet!" she screamed.

I closed my eyes and schooled my face back to neutral. I couldn't handle more physical abuse today. My bruises were better, but the bones of my back continued to ache. "Yes, Mistress."

"Has Ms. Asura been here?"

Huh? "Ma'am?"

Her eyes rolled white and wild. "When I wasn't here, was Ms. Asura in my office?"

"Not that I know of." Where was this coming from?

"You see everything that goes on here. Tell me." She stepped toward me, looking like she'd beat the answer out of me. The problem was I didn't know which answer she sought.

"I don't know."

She puffed up her cheeks and slapped a hand against the doorjamb. "She's been here. I know it. Does she think she can interfere? This is *my* house. She'll be at the Feast tonight. We'll see who's in charge here!"

I stood ramrod straight and silent, trying not to draw attention to myself.

She waddled past me. I thought she might have forgotten I was there, until she said over her shoulder, "I'll be out late."

"Yes, ma'am."

"Do not take advantage of my hospitality."

"Yes, ma'am."

The front door slammed and I sagged.

"Is she gone?" Nicole bounded down the steps.

I nodded. "Did you talk to Bodie?"

"Yep. Heavy message. Here." Nicole handed me a wrapped bundle.

"What's this?" I asked.

"Your costume."

"For what?"

"Go find answers at the Feast. That's where they are."

"The Feast? Mistress will kill me." Not an idle threat.

"She's not here and you'll be back before she is."

"She's going to be there and you know it."

"Maybe. Hunting trouble."

"Should I warn Ms. Asura?" I asked, my stomach clenching at the thought.

Nicole blanched. "Uh, no. Have I taught you nothing? That one can take care of herself. Go to the Feast. Find Meridian and Tens. They're probably with a glassblower named Rumi, the man you met before. Mistress won't recognize you. That's what the costume is for."

"Really? How do you know this stuff?"

"Magic." Nicole smiled. "Just a guess. Come on. Go. I'll handle here."

"But—"

"Juliet, you have to know the truth. Go."

I put on the pioneer costume and looked at myself in the bathroom mirror. I saw a different girl who lived a different life. I needed to find Meridian.

Could my mother really be out there? Does she love me?

Will you know the choice I faced, or will you grow up loved and happy and never need to know? **—R.**

CHAPTER 32

Juliet

The party was in full swing by the time I caught a ride on the back of a Chevy truck hauling hay and revelers toward the light and crowds. No one blinked at my costume; one of the guys even commented that I looked right out of *Little House on the Prairie.* I guessed that was a good thing. I waved thanks and hopped off on the fringes of the grounds. I tugged the brim of the bonnet farther over my face to shield my identity and stave off the cold.

The fort was lit up in the dark of night with what seemed like every spotlight in the world, including the fullest moon I'd ever been under. I'd never seen so many people gathered together. It's not possible to grow up here and not know about the Feast—that and the Indy 500 car race were in the blood of Hoosiers—but I'd never been. To either. Never even dreamed of attending.

I joined the stream of people herding toward the strobes and the noise of multiple bands. Some people were costumed like me, while others were in military uniforms or jeans and flannels, even yuppie slacks and sweaters. The diversity of the crowd was too much to take in. I was a foreigner in my own backyard.

The aroma of grilling meat and the crackle of fat filled the air. My stomach growled. People gnawed on enormous turkey legs and breaded pork tenderloin sandwiches. Spits of whole pig roasted over fires and long grill stands were covered with flocks of chickens splayed for cooking. Spicy apple cider warmed in huge cast-iron cauldrons. Everywhere around me people laughed, danced, and played. I felt myself relaxing, enjoying the festival atmosphere.

I wandered the food stalls, my stomach reminding me I hadn't eaten yet today. I had no money. I watched someone toss a half-eaten drumstick and roasted corncob into the trash pile and inched toward it.

Someone bumped me from behind and I lost my nerve. I twirled toward whoever had pushed me and saw a trio of black-robed priests in big floppy black hats propelling through the crowd as if they were late to a meeting with God. *Rude.*

I checked faces, especially those of tall men, searching for Tens among the people who towered over the crowd. I thought I might spot him faster than Meridian; she was shorter than me. I kept moving through the throngs and groups.

I turned down an artist alley as a band started playing a bluegrass tune that had the whole place tapping toes and dancing. I smiled, the joy contagious; it lightened my burden, my questing for truth.

Up ahead a booth with swirling glass stars twinkled, calling to me. The giant who'd brought the colored papers to DG called out to customers, joking and cajoling. Rumi? Nicole had mentioned he might know where to find Meridian. As I neared him, the light grew brighter. He quickly scanned the area; his face broke into wide delight when he saw me approaching.

I drew back, hesitating, afraid for a moment this was a mistake. A terrible, horrible mistake.

He motioned me toward the back wall of the booth, so I scooted quickly around, out of eyesight.

"You're a brave one tonight, aren't you?" Rumi peeked his head around the fabric.

I shrugged, unable to make my tongue work.

"I'm guessing you're here to see my other angel friend?"

My expression must have shown my confusion, because he took pity on me and stopped speaking in riddles.

"Meridian is taking a break from working in here with me, grabbing victuals with her beau, Tens. If you go two rows over, they're under those trees. They want to help you, so trust 'em if you can." He pointed. "You'll find 'em eating and drinking, pretending not to be worried about the evils in our world, for my sake."

I nodded and turned toward where he'd pointed.

"Wait, lassie." Rumi reached into his pockets and pulled out a twenty-dollar bill. "Buy yourself food too."

"No—I can't take—"

"You'll blend in better if you at least try to look like you're enjoying yourself."

I stepped forward, accepting the money. "Thank you. I'll pay you back." *Somehow.*

He winked, then disappeared back toward the front of the booth. I heard his voice engage customers, talking about the good luck Spirit Stones brought. And didn't they catch the light beautifully?

I bought a skewer of chicken. I was so hungry that I ate it before I'd reached the next stall. I think it tasted good.

I picked up my pace, reminding myself that I was here for answers, not to eat. I spotted Tens leaning against the trunk of a tree, his arms wrapped around Meridian as they swayed to the music.

I walked closer, lifting the edge of my bonnet until Tens made eye contact and nodded at me in recognition. Meridian's eyes were closed and I heard sirens at the edge of the music. Tens waited until her eyes opened and then he whispered in her ear. I saw her search for me and smile when she found me.

She motioned with her head and we walked away from the music toward the remains of the fort and the French soldiers camping there. Tens stayed a step behind us. It seemed as though he was playing the role of bodyguard.

"You got my message yesterday?" she finally said when we were far enough away from the crowd and the stage that conversation was possible.

I shrugged. "This morning. Bodie told me. Is it true?"

Meridian claimed an empty set of rocking chairs tucked under the umbrella of an old black walnut tree. She motioned to me to sit down.

I sat next to her and Tens stood with his back to the tree, watching the people around us, his hands shoved deep in his coat pockets.

I repeated, "Is it true?"

She nodded. "Sort of."

"What do you mean? You said when I had questions you had answers. I'm asking."

"I know, but it's complicated."

"You either met my mother or you didn't." My voice carried.

"I did." She nodded, trying to keep eye contact but failing. She bit her bottom lip.

"Where is she?" I asked.

"She's safe."

I rose out of the chair. "I don't want to play games."

"I know. I'm trying." She looked lost. "Can we start with an easier question?"

"Can you explain photographs to me? Why don't I show up in them?"

"That's easier." Tens snorted behind us.

"You're like me. We're related."

"Related?" *Like a sister? A cousin?*

"I don't show up in photographs either. I didn't. Because of what, of who, we are."

"What are you talking about?"

"We're Fenestra. We help souls get to heaven. We're the light they see as they die."

"Now you're insane, telling stories." I stood up and backed away, turning, ready to run. *This is why I snuck out of DG and risked brutal retribution for disobeying?*

"It's no story. That's why your mom is dead."

I stopped, but didn't turn.

Meridian walked over to me and lowered her voice. "She died protecting you and I met her when I helped a soul cross the window."

All my wishes evaporated, leaving me empty and helpless. I thought for a moment, just a tiny moment, that my mom was coming to get me and this would all be a nightmare. I'd wake up a little girl again.

"I'm sorry." She touched my forearm and I flinched. "You're why we're here. We want to help you. There are people, bad people who want to hurt you—"

"More?" I turned, and let my anger take the reins. "There are more bad people? Do you have any idea what my life is like? What I've had to survive for a decade? There can't be more. There aren't more bad people to hurt me. They've taken everything and now you stand there and take the rest."

"I'm trying to give you the truth, not take anything. Please. Please just listen: your birthday is not February tenth, but March twenty-first."

"Oh, so now my birthday is wrong? Is my name even

Juliet? You want to tell me I'm some other girl? This isn't my life?"

"Come with us, please—let us explain."

"Are you high? Why would I go anywhere with you?" I yelled.

"You're in danger. Your life is—"

"What? Over? When did it begin? What's left to end? All I do is take care of children and the elderly. I don't have a life." I thought of Kirian. Of the dreams I'd once had. The future that seemed so distant and unimportant now.

"We want to help you get one. You have to trust us." Tens stepped forward, his hand on Meridian's shoulder seeming to brace her.

Jealousy ripped through me. I had no one at my back. No one putting a hand on my shoulder in comfort or in strength. I was the hand for so many others. "Don't you understand I can't leave? I can't leave them all there. I can't let that horrible woman break them. Beat them. Starve them. There's no one else. Don't you understand?"

"But you're not *just* a foster kid."

"Yes, I am. I am *just* a kid who no one wanted."

"That's what we're telling you. That's not true. You're a Fenestra and—"

"Prove it."

She shrank as if I'd punched her. "I can't. Not yet. You have to believe me."

"I do?" I exhaled a pitiful laugh, "No, I don't. You're passing through town and you're going to leave and I'm going to be stuck here and then what?"

"We're not leaving town without you. People die around you, don't they? Animals? Insects?"

"I live in a place where people go to die. Of course they die around me."

"You know things about them. See things. You faint or black out and—" She inched into my space, right into my face.

"Meridian, stop." Tens tried to quiet her. "This isn't helping."

"When you turn sixteen you'll need my help. Or they'll turn you and you won't have a choice. Please—" Meridian sounded desperate.

"Just leave me alone." I walked away, flinging back over my shoulder, "I've never had a choice!" I ran blindly toward the sea of people.

"Wait!" both Tens and Meridian yelled. I felt them running after me.

They gave chase, but I didn't slow my steps. I darted behind a clothesline of a clothing vendor and grabbed a thick black wool cape. I draped it over my shoulders, twirling myself into the fabric, blending into the shadows until my heart rested and I'd evaded them.

I kept to the fringes of the crowd, losing myself among the revelers. I wasn't ready to go back to DG, but I wasn't prepared to have more crazy mumbo jumbo thrown at me. Special? Heaven? There was no heaven. No God. Nothing special about me. There couldn't be, or this, none of this life, would have happened to me.

I saw another group of black-clad people that made my feet stutter. I paused. There was something about them, something familiar, something primal I knew to keep my distance from.

In the firelight, I saw a man turn, and his profile looked achingly familiar, like Kirian's. For a moment I almost called out to him, wanting to be held and comforted. But he leaned down and the recognition was gone. The black-clad group huddled, until seven people with matching backpacks joined them. I wondered if these were missionaries like the ones that came to DG to save us. I observed them all check watches or phones, and then most dispersed like cotton candy in a strong rain. Running urgently. Those left followed the others' movements with their heads but stayed put. As if they were watching and waiting for something.

My feet wouldn't move. I saw a woman with long black hair flowing over her shoulders and swirling around her face. I'd seen that jewelry before. *Ms. Asura? Dressed as a priest?* I edged closer, thinking Ms. Asura surely wasn't here, dressed like that, acting oddly. Her long nails glinted like claws in the night. Couldn't be.

At that moment, a blast rocked the far end of the grounds, moving the earth. I saw people glance at each other in confusion. I wondered if this was some form of military display until I heard the screams. Another blast, closer this time, shook the earth upon which I stood so much that I lost my balance.

I glanced back and saw the woman smile up at Kirian's look-alike before they disappeared in the chaos. Fires caught and danced up the backs of stalls. A stampede of people headed in my direction. The screams intensified as another blast shocked the world, changing joy to terror in a blink.

The priests headed directly into the crowd, heading straight toward the fires already burning, the screams of anguish, the chaos.

What have they done?
Lucinda Myer
1807

CHAPTER 33

The first blast came from the direction of the stage. The stampede of people and screams came in the seconds after. "Oh God," I whispered as the next explosion ripped the air.

"What?" Tens said, going on full alert. He turned to step in front of me, trying to shield me from whatever the threat was.

"Noc—" I managed to get part of the word out before I was hit by a sudden clamoring of souls. As I faded toward the window, I gripped Tens. Before long I stood at the far end of the room, across from the window. Was this Nocti? Terrorists? A natural disaster? I could who-done-it later; right now I had to concentrate on the souls needing me.

This was bad, like the train disaster in Colorado. The sheer number of people could suck me through if I got too close to the edge of the window. I concentrated on stirring the breeze, watching the curtains, and keeping myself wide open, while protecting my own life's energy. I knew Tens would protect my body to the best of his ability.

All ages paraded through, and those who were confused I comforted with words and stories. A few people blinked toward the window and then disappeared. Chris wanted to play major league baseball. Janice loved her grandkids more than her children. Bob golfed to get away from his wife. There were video-game secrets, unrequited love, and those who'd never tried and regretted it. A few happy souls met their children on the other side. I saw a grocery store, a horse barn, fronts of houses in every economic bracket, a college campus. The taste of a dry martini, the heat of a family's secret recipe for red sauce that would never be passed on.

"Meridian!" Auntie called me. "You haven't checked Prunella, 1943. You must. You must unveil her past." There was an urgency to her.

Juliet's mother no longer flickered, but her disfigurement hadn't changed. I think she tried to smile at me.

Time stood still for me at that window, so when I woke it took me a moment to come back to myself.

"She's awake." Rumi's beard tickled my face as he leaned over me and patted my cheek. His face was covered with soot and he smelled of fire and burnt flesh. I flashed to the train derailment. It took a minute for everything to flood back into me.

I coughed, sitting up.

Tens immediately braced me, supporting my weight until the fit passed. He rested his face against my neck and I felt two hot drips of tears against my neck.

"Tens?" My throat was scratchy and hoarse.

"Easy, lassie, here's a bit of grape soda for you to sip on." Rumi pushed at Tens to get off the couch. "Go pull yourself together, boy." He said it gently, but his tone brooked no argument. He stared down at me. "You're at my place, angel. You're safe now."

Tens walked down the hall and I heard a door shut.

I roused myself to a sitting position. A small portable television played breaking news, the volume muted. A reporter stood among smoldering ruins as first responders and investigators scurried around. The official reporting was interspersed with what had to be camera-phone footage and other uploads from spectators. The scene was grisly and stupefying.

"Easy, there." Rumi steadied me.

"What happened?" I stretched, stiff and sore.

"The newspeople are calling it a terrorist event. A couple of fertilizer bombs at the stage, in the crowded areas. Sounds like suicide bombers. Enough power to set fires around the grounds."

"They're still burning?"

"Yes, they're bringing in tanker trucks and dipping into the Wabash for airdrops, but it's out in the middle of nowhere, really. Hard to get to for this."

"People died."

"A couple dozen or so victims, plus the bombers, and more are missing."

Those numbers didn't quite ring true for the souls I'd met. Nocti must have gotten more than a few souls too. It made sense they'd set the blasts, then be there to snatch up the energy of the dying.

"There were heroics, too. People were saved. The historical site itself was unharmed, mainly because the reenactment was still to come."

My memory was fuzzy, but I think I'd seen souls at the window who hadn't continued through. Was it possible for them to get to the window and then be pulled back into this life?

"Juliet?"

"I don't know." Rumi wiped at his swollen eyes. His face was a mass of small cuts.

"Are you okay? How long has it been?"

"Seven or so hours. Dayspring soon." Rumi limped to his feet without answering my other question.

I saw a bloody tear in his pants. "You're hurt."

"A scratch. Your boy came to find me in the debris. Helped me dig out of the shattered glass. Lucky this is all."

Very lucky.

Tens came back into the living room, his face scrubbed

and his hair wet, as if he'd dunked his head under the faucet.

I held my hand out and he laced his fingers with mine.

"I was worried," he whispered.

There was a knock on the sliding door, the shapes shadowy and hard to see with the glare of light against glass. Rumi tensed, checking with Tens, before they both realized who'd knocked. They'd clearly had a discussion while I was unconscious.

"Rumi? Are you in there? Are you okay?" Gus's voice shadowed Faye's as she argued for them to break in to check on their friend.

Rumi opened the door as Tens and I relaxed a bit. Every muscle in my body screamed at the movement. Even mere tensing was painful.

"Are you all right? Children? Were you there too?" Faye sped over to cluck at us.

Gus apologized. "I couldn't keep her home. She woke to the alarms and the smoke and we knew you'd have been there in the middle of the thing."

"I thought you were in the camp," Rumi answered.

Faye appeared sheepish but relieved. "He would have been there, but I had a headache and Gus was nursing me."

"Damn lucky headache, I say." Gus grinned at her.

"You look a mess, Rumi." Faye patted my hand while peering at Rumi.

"We're fine. We're fine." Rumi sank into a chair, going pale.

I shook my head a fraction, not liking the shock I saw starting to bleed the edges of Rumi's calm.

Faye caught my movement and attached to it like a dog with a juicy bone. "No, you're not. We're taking you to the doctor. Your leg is bleeding. Gus, bring the car around."

"No, no, the kids are here." Rumi tried to use us as his excuse.

Tens wrapped an afghan over my shoulders. "We're heading home."

Faye shook her head. "You should come too. Make sure you didn't hit your head or anything."

"No, ma'am, we're fine." Tens helped me to my feet. "I've got the truck."

"Are you sure? I don't like this." Faye frowned. "Rumi, you *will* go to the hospital with us, even if I have to drag you there. How much blood have you lost?"

"Go," I said.

Rumi nodded and stopped arguing with Faye. We loaded them into the car and Tens helped me into the truck. Custos laid her head on my shoulder.

Tens and I didn't speak until we got back to the cottage. He kept sneaking surreptitious glances at me. We stank of fire, smoke, and the tinny note of death.

"Shower?" I asked, heading straight for the bathroom.

We dropped our shoes and boots and he turned the water to scalding. We climbed under the spray together, still clothed. I wanted to wash all of the night away.

With the world shut out around us, with only the sound of water spray, the room lit only by a tiny night-light, I let the tears come. What if Juliet died? Were we supposed to thwart the Nocti's plan? Were we supposed to know they'd been planning this? How? *I failed.*

I leaned into Tens's chest. He dropped his chin onto the top of my head and mumbled against my hair, "I thought I'd lost you. I couldn't get you out of there fast enough. And Rumi, he was knocked out by a falling beam."

"Shhh." I tried to soothe him, even as he comforted me. What a mess.

"I had to put you down to get him out. Was that okay? I was afraid no one would see him under the glass and boards. I put you down for a second."

"Of course. You saved Rumi. I'm fine," I whispered.

His lips moved along my hairline, across my forehead, seeking solace, peace.

My fingers fumbled with the buttons on his shirt until he tore the buttons apart. I pressed my cheek against his chest and sighed. Alive. We were alive.

What if we'd failed Juliet? Auntie? The innocent?

I turned my face up. Water dripped down over us, washing away the stink of evil, of chaos, of malevolent destruction.

He pressed his lips against my cheeks, my chin, I kissed him back until our mouths blended. I sighed into him. His kiss chased the cold away.

His fingers found the skin between the bottom of my T-shirt and my jeans. They burned across my stomach. He tugged, and my T-shirt plopped into the tub behind us. I pushed his shirt down, off his arms, momentarily breaking contact.

I ran my palms over his chest, his stomach, each finger finding a groove to claim. We melted into each other. I unhooked my bra and he maneuvered it off my shoulders. My nipples pebbled with sensation, mirroring his.

I reveled when his hands cupped my breasts. Up until this moment I hadn't thought my body was enough; it was more than the flatness of a month ago, yet not enough to spill over or out. But the way he parted his lips and closed his eyes while touching me made me feel perfect, not just adequate.

I wanted more. I didn't know if it was only the wet clothing that made me feel pulled down, weighted toward the floor, but I wanted it gone.

I hooked my fingers under his waistband. Thumbed the button, felt his erection ridged against the zipper under my hands, against my belly. His breath raspy and shallow, he heaved in deep concentration. I wanted to touch him, see him even in the dim light of this magical moment.

As if by unspoken mutual agreement, he undid the zipper on my jeans while I undid his.

I tugged and pushed my pants down and off while he did the same with his. We stood in the shower, steam cocooning us, clad only in underwear. His was wet and plastered to his body, the deep indent of his buttocks concaved. The boxer briefs rode low, like a second skin. It felt like he was more naked than if I'd looked at him without the underwear. Fascinated by our differences, I wanted to turn the light on to get a better look. But that would mean leaving the shower, and I couldn't do that.

He returned my stare while I crossed my arms over my chest. He gazed at my body. I looked down at myself, trying to see through his eyes. My cheap white boy shorts, now utterly transparent, drew attention to my hips, my thighs. My pubic hair was black and coarse against the cotton, reminding me I hadn't shaved my legs. Or ever waxed my bikini line. There'd been no need to. I didn't know if that was only necessary in Hollywood movies or if he'd expect me to be hairless as a baby mouse.

I felt vulnerable. Open. My spine no longer jutted with each vertebra. My ribs could be felt but didn't protrude. My collarbones didn't sit up on my frame like a set of shoulder pads. My thighs were curved up to hips that had finally started to look more like a girl's than a young boy's.

I felt stronger, more muscular, healthier than I'd ever been, but what if I wasn't enough?

I dropped my eyes toward the drain and Tens stepped in front of the spray, blocking it with his shoulders. He lifted my face with a single finger under my chin. His eyes were hooded and deep in shadows. His face flushed, his cheekbones seemed to chisel even stronger angles.

"I love you. As you were. As you are. As you will be," he said.

I blinked. "I love you, too. You make me want to be better than I am. To be like you."

"You don't give yourself enough credit. Or you give

me too much." His eyes were serious, but his lips twitched. He shivered. "Don't be alarmed, but we've used up all the hot water."

"Oh my God!" I noticed the icicles my toes were fast becoming. "Why didn't you say anything?"

"We were having a moment." He sounded perplexed.

I collapsed in laughter against him, while he fumbled to turn off the water without hitting me with cold spray. "A moment?" I said.

His expression flashed hurt before he joined my laughter.

We grabbed fresh towels and wrapped each other in them, staying in the steamy bathroom until all the warmth seeped out and we needed clothes.

I stood on my tiptoes and leaned up to kiss him. "I love you."

He wrapped me tight in his arms and swung me up. "Always."

I am ripped, halved with contractions. How can I possibly survive this? —R.

CHAPTER 34

Juliet

Blinding light and fire flew through the sky, spinning the earth off her axis. My ears ringing and deafened, I stumbled over debris and my own feet. I ran from the screaming, hollering panic, following the mass exodus. Heat flared and seared my face and hands. Running, rocked and jostled by terrified people, I tried to stay upright. Coats and shoes dropped where people ran out of them and kept going.

Dizziness hit me in waves, sharp pain slashed my insides.

The chaos turned the world on its side and made placing my feet on solid ground impossible. I tried to hold on to trees or cars or other stationary objects to get my bearings. The further away from the disaster I moved, the clearer my head, the calmer my heart.

"Need a ride?" A group of teens with wide eyes and pale faces, in tatters of costumes in the back of a truck, slowed as they drove past me. "Where are you headed?"

I called out an address near DG, reluctant, but unable to think of a good reason to turn down their offer of help.

"Get up." A girl in combat boots and what might have been a flannel nightgown helped me into the back of the truck.

No one spoke. Shock echoed around us and there was simply nothing to say. The crisp night air cleared my head, but all I smelled were smoke, burning plastics, acrid chemicals, and charred flesh. "Thanks," I said. The same girl helped me down and went back to huddling with her friends as they drove away.

I coughed until I thought I'd hack up a lung. I felt dirty. Filthy. Nasty. I cut through the copse toward Wildcat Creek. My shoes already ruined, I waded straight into the heart of the running water. I sat down, letting the shakes rock me, letting the water gurgle a lullaby. I used gravel and sand to scrub the soot off my skin. I peeled off my clothes, not caring who might be watching or how I'd explain my nakedness at the house. *Bring it on, Mistress.*

I floated in the creek until the water felt warm and the air temperature balmy. My eyes kept fluttering closed and it was tempting, oh so tempting, to drift off, float away down the creek, float toward sleep and the oblivion of nothing.

"Juliet." My name was accompanied by a stinging slap. "Juliet!"

I opened my eyes. Nicole dragged me through the water toward the shore, where Bodie and Sema huddled together, their faces pure fear.

I tried to get my legs under me, but they wouldn't cooperate. "Wait, I can walk."

"Some half-assed guardian angel I am," Nicole muttered.

I was too busy trying to move my anesthetized limbs to contemplate her words, or her anger.

Bodie held out a blanket. Nicole went back into the creek and grabbed my costume, which had snagged on tree roots and flotsam. She stashed the fabric remains along with my shoes under a log, while I watched, trembling. My skin burned with pins and needles as blood and heat rushed back in.

I opened my mouth. Closed it. My throat was raw and felt swollen from the smoke.

"We have to get her inside." Nicole spoke to Bodie as if I were the youngest child; they talked above my head. I didn't even have the energy to bristle with indignity.

In the distance, helicopters circled spotlights. It seemed as if the night was alive with sounds of pain and suffering. Sirens echoed in all directions, bouncing back and around. *Or maybe the sound track from the Feast replayed, stuck on a loop in my head.*

Mini escorted us across the lawn, one labored step at a

time. We made it back into the kitchen. Nicole rubbed the blanket over my body briskly, painfully. Bodie grabbed a towel from the laundry room and worked on my hair with childish, fumbling fingers. Their expressions were serious and attentive. I would live.

We heard a car pull up in the driveway. Not just any car, but Mistress's.

"Crap," Bodie muttered.

Nicole helped me toward the stairs, not so that I could go up them, but so I could dive under and pull on clothes. The only saving grace was Mistress moved slowly; all that bulk needed momentum to maneuver.

"Hurry." Bodie closed the crawl-space door on my back. I imagined him scurrying around and behind the wall to hide.

I heard the front door.

"What are you doing standing there?" Mistress shouted.

Forcing myself to move quickly, I dragged a dirty T-shirt over my head and stepped into flannel pajama bottoms that used to belong to a man who passed through the Train Room. Then I pulled on thick socks from another departed guest. I dragged my hair up into a ponytail to hide any clinging debris. I smelled the fire, but I had the feeling that's all I might smell in the weeks to come.

Nicole answered, "I'm getting warm milk for the lady upstairs. She can't sleep."

"Don't be wasting that. The other one dead yet? I'm ready to go." Mistress sounded like she was in a particularly foul mood.

"No, ma'am."

"Have you seen that snake of a social worker tonight? She come by?"

I paused, listening attentively.

"Ma'am?" There was a tremble in Nicole's voice.

"You know who I'm talking about. That lying bitch, has she been here?"

"Ms. Asura?"

"Yes, her!" Mistress sounded as if she was fast losing the patience she never had enough of.

"No, ma'am," Nicole said clearly.

There was a long silence, but neither one of them seemed to move. No sounds on the stairway or toward Mistress's quarters. I pictured the expression on Mistress's face. I'd stood silent and frozen so many times waiting for an arbitrary punishment or the decision of one.

"The old bat can't sleep, huh?" Mistress's voice traveled as she moved.

There was a pause as Nicole seemed to try to catch up. "No, ma'am."

"I'll help 'em sleep." With that the floor echoed and shook. The stairs argued as the footsteps disappeared up above my head.

Bodie opened the little door. "Clear."

"You need to get to sleep, buddy."

"You tell us a story? About the Feast?"

"Not tonight. I need to go see what's going on." A bad feeling hovered over my gut, icy fingers of dread tightening my bowels.

I didn't have time to cuddle or comfort Bodie. I took his hand and pulled him and Sema up the backstairs, pushed them up to the attic. I headed toward the Green Room.

Mistress stood above Enid, holding out a little packet of pills. "You need to take your medication."

"But it's not time." Distressed, Enid sank deeper into the pillow.

"It's prescribed by your doctor. You will take this and I will stand here until you do." Mistress was calm. Too calm. There was a wild, whacked-out crazy in her eyes.

I watched Enid fight against her own helplessness. She wanted to argue. She wanted to, but she didn't. With a shaky hand, Enid took the pills in her mouth and Mistress motioned to Nicole to hold the water glass so she could suck down the pills.

I tiptoed into the room, trying to be present without catching attention.

"Your sister looks like she's in pain. We can't have that." Mistress unlocked a small cabinet that contained vials of medication and pulled out a little glass bottle. "Juliet, get me a syringe."

I blinked, then fumbled around in a drawer until I found the right size for the IV.

"Today!" Mistress barked at me.

I watched Nicole put the water glass down. Enid's wide eyes were mesmerized by Mistress. I knew by the quiver in her lips that she was scared. There was nothing I could do in that moment to comfort her or change what I feared might happen next.

It didn't happen often, but with that unhinged glint in Mistress's eyes, anything felt possible.

I shared a look with Nicole; her expression said her fears echoed mine.

I stepped between the beds, squeezing myself up and around the equipment, while Nicole grabbed Enid's hand. Mini appeared and wrapped herself around my legs.

As if in slow motion, Mistress prepared the injection and slid it into Glee's IV. She unlatched the oxygen monitor from Glee's finger and turned off the machine. "Wonderful. She'll feel much better now." Mistress didn't look back, just left the room like a weight had been lifted from her shoulders. Over her shoulder she said, "You girls best get to bed. Tomorrow is a big day."

Tears freely flowing, Enid spit out the pills as soon as the door closed, keening grief.

"Please, please be quiet." I threw myself over her. The last thing we needed was Mistress deciding to come back and finish Enid, too. "She'll come back. Please, please."

Nicole turned Glee's machine back on. When I glanced up, Nicole shook her head sadly, tears streaking her cheeks. The three of us hugged and held each other while sobs deflated our souls like a chilling soufflé. Mini wiggled her way into our embrace.

"Why? Oh why?" Enid's fingers tightened around my shoulders and in my hair. Pulling, smacking, as if her pain forced its way to the surface even as she nodded her understanding and tried to muffle the noise.

Mini yowled and kneaded the old woman's belly.

The helpless and hopeless sounds she tried to stifle in my

embrace reminded me of dying animals who'd crawled up onto DG's porches and steps.

"I'm sorry. I'm so sorry," I kept repeating.

Hiccups racked my stomach, so I stood.

Enid seemed like one of my littlest charges, shriveled and pitiful in a bed that looked four times too large. "Did she just kill my sister?" I clasped her free hand while tears continued to trail down her cheeks, soaking the pillow and hair on either side of her face.

"I think so. That's a lot of morphine," I whispered.

"But why? She wasn't doing anything. We can't do anything or go anywhere." Baffled and bewildered, she picked at her covers and played with the tube in her arm.

"I'm so sorry. She's still breathing a little."

Nicole picked up all the pills Enid spit out and pocketed them. Mini sat on my feet, then leapt up onto Glee's feet.

"Can you . . . ," Enid began to ask, then broke off.

"What?" I leaned down, smoothing her hair.

"Can you help me?" Enid tried to scoot closer to her sister. "Into the same bed?"

I nodded. Nicole and I helped Enid settle closer to her sister in the same bed. She held her, talked to her in hushed, whispered tones and patted her face and hair. Nicole turned the machine's volume to mute. The alarms were more jarring than the death sometimes.

In unspoken agreement, Nicole and I moved over to the beautiful window seat I had always wished for time to sit in, and waited. Mini lay on the bed and kept her own kind of vigil. Nicole and I sat twined together.

I looked out at the night around us until the fingers of

dawn began to creep up. Nicole touched my shoulder. Glee was dead, had been for a while.

When Enid was ready, we moved her back into her own bed. "I know it seems impossible, but she's here in spirit, dears. She's going to wait for me. We've always done everything together—passing over will be no exception." Enid appeared surprisingly peaceful and okay. She even smiled up at me before we left the room. I wondered if the trauma had broken her grasp on reality. Dead was dead.

I hoped to God, or whoever wasn't listening to my prayers, that Glee wasn't still stuck in this place.

She, we, deserved better.

The dead outnumber the living, who dwindle
aboard that Hades ship. I find myself near ex-
piring trying to bring Light into such Darkness.

Cassie Ailey

May 5, 1855

CHAPTER 35

The bombing of the Feast was not the work of international terrorists, no matter what the FBI might feed to the
news crews. The perpetrators were Nocti through and
through. There was not a doubt in my mind, nor Tens's.
Outside the cocoon of the bathroom the world felt a hell
of a lot less cozy and safe.

"Did you see the burn scars on her forearms?" I
couldn't get the image of Juliet's stricken expression and
the glimpses of her wounds from my mind.

"Cigarette butts," Tens confirmed.

"What?"

"Those are caused by cigarettes burned into the skin."

"How do you know that?"

Tens gave me his I-don't-want-to-talk-about-this shrug.

I let it drop, for the moment. Both of us were ravenous, so he cooked up a batch of "bachelor eggs," saying his grandfather's recipe was merely an excuse to use everything in the fridge. Onions, garlic, peppers, chopped-up bacon and breakfast sausage, all sautéed. Eggs were scrambled into the mixture and cheeses of several kinds were melted over the top. This time, I squeezed the orange juice.

"What's the connection to Kirian? And that woman?"

I told him about the conversation Minerva had made me eavesdrop on. Yes, I know how ridiculous it sounded to say a cat made me eavesdrop, but the ridiculous was our normal now.

"We should warn her." Tens served up plates.

"Because that worked so well." I'd watched the crowds for Nocti, but realized at some point I was merely looking for hooded black robes like Perimo and his believers wore. A few costumed priests mingled, but didn't come close enough for me to get a sense of them. Unless I saw his or her eyes, that blank void, lightless and empty, I didn't know if I could recognize one. "She didn't believe us."

"Would you?"

"What?" I asked.

"If your mother had sat you down and given you the 411, would you have believed her?"

We both focused on food while I considered. Anger was my knee-jerk response.

She could have tried. She *should* have tried.

Tens pushed Sammy's artwork across the table toward me. He didn't say anything more. He didn't need to.

By punishing my parents, was I also punishing my brother? He'd done nothing but love me unconditionally.

"I can't promise anything."

Tens nodded. "I get that."

"I'll call."

He placed a disposable cell phone on the table and began to clear the table.

"Can you please try to find an entry in the journal from 1943, talking about, or written by, a Prunella?"

"You sure?"

"It's something Auntie said."

"Okay." Tens shrugged and unwrapped the journal from the lap quilt of Auntie's I'd concealed it in.

I picked up the disposable phone and dialed. I felt sweat bead my forehead and my mouth dry out listening to the chimes.

"Hello?" My mother's voice shook across the line. She sounded older.

"Hi." I couldn't call her Mom, not yet. Mothers protect and defend and guard. She had done those things in her way, but rather than protect me from the Fenestra destiny, she should have stood in front of the taunts and nicknames and abuse I took from people around me. She should have guarded my heart against believing I was a freak, a girl who could cause death with a thought.

"Meridian. Honey, are you okay? Where are you? How

is Auntie?" Her words were filled with relief, concern, and questions.

"Auntie's dead." I didn't try to soften my pronouncement. I wanted her to hurt.

She gasped. "But—"

"Is Dad there?"

"Oh, Meridian, I'm sorry. You can't imagine how—"

"Is Dad around? Or Sammy?" I cut her off. I wasn't ready to listen to her guilt speak to me.

"Your brother misses you."

"You don't?" I bubbled up and over. "Why didn't you tell me? How could you let me just believe I was a freak?"

Tens came behind me; I grasped onto him. He tightened his hold to match my need.

She didn't hesitate. "I waited for you to ask. To open the conversation."

"How could I ask? You never let me think . . . you never acted like you saw." My anger burned brightly. I wanted to call her names. I wanted to tell her she was a terrible parent. I wanted to demand that Sammy come live with me because they weren't fit to care for a child. Any child.

"Meridian?" Dad's voice filled the line. I heard my mom's heaving sobs move farther away from the phone.

"Dad."

"I know you don't want to hear this, but she did her best."

"That's not an excuse." How could he forgive her so easily?

He sighed. "I would change things. But we can't. I miss you, honey."

"Can I talk to Sammy?"

"Sure. Sure." I heard a door close and Dad holler, "Sammy!"

There was a pause, like he was trying to figure out what to say. "Are you okay? Do you need money? Anything?"

"We're covered."

"We? You and Auntie?"

"No, um, my boyfriend. He's special, too."

"Oh. Does he treat you well?" Dad asked.

"Yes, Dad."

"Good. Good. Can I talk to him?"

"I don't have much time."

"Okay, maybe next time. Here's Sammy. He was in the bath. I love you."

I didn't remember ever hearing my dad say those words before. I didn't answer him. If I had tried, even to lie, I knew I'd lose what teeny bit of composure I had left.

"Mer-D!" Sammy squealed into the phone. "Miss you. Miss you."

"Hi, Sammy." My shoulders relaxed and my soul smiled. I pressed the speaker button so Tens could hear my brother too.

"When are you coming home? We get to share a room! It's got a view of the dolphins and the manatees. And we can walk to the beach every day."

"Wow, that sounds fantastic." I knew they were in Miami from the area code.

"I miss you."

"I know. I miss you too."

"Did you get my letter? Jo said he'd give it to you."

"I did." I giggled, thinking of Sangre Warrior Josiah answering to the nickname Jo.

"Are you coming soon?"

"I don't think so, kiddo."

"Daddy told me you're a superhero now. Do you have a cape and mask too?"

Tens cracked up into silent guffaws.

"Um, well," I stuttered.

" 'Cuz that's so cool. I miss you."

"I miss you too."

"We have to move soon. I hate moving. Maybe we can come to your house?"

"I know, I'm sorry."

Now I understood why Josiah let me have a contact number for my family. They were leaving this address, so no Nocti would be able to use them against me, us, again.

"I get a new name."

I glanced up at Tens. New names?

"Sammy, that's enough." Dad's voice cut in. "Say goodbye."

"Bye, Mer-D. Come home."

"I love you, champ." I blinked tears out of my eyes and let them swim down my cheeks.

Tens rubbed them clean for me.

"Meridian?"

"Yeah," I answered my dad.

"We're going into a protection program of sorts. Josiah's setting us up."

"I see."

"It's for the best. Safest for your brother to start over. Without knowing about you."

"I understand." Were they wiping me out?

"We will remember you but be unable to say your name. When Sammy is ready, Josiah has promised to unveil Sammy's memories, too. Josiah says when Sammy sees you again he'll remember everything."

"Oh."

"It's the only way to protect you and us."

To go back to being a secret? That was the only way?

"I'm sorry." He ran out of apologies.

"I know."

"Let me talk to her," Mom yelled.

"Goodbye, Dad." I hung up the phone as my mom's voice continued to plead in the background. I couldn't handle more. I didn't need her to feel better right now. I wasn't ready to absolve her.

"I'm gone?" I looked up at Tens and crumpled.

"I'm so sorry. So sorry. I didn't know—" Tears dripped down his face and mingled with mine. "I wanted you to have them back."

I nodded. Me too. "Oh my God, Tens, that's it!" All at once, I knew what Juliet needed to remember. I grabbed Auntie's journal to confirm my suspicions.

Was there ever a more beautiful baby?   —R.

CHAPTER 36

Juliet

"Nicole?" I called into the attic. I felt someone watching me, that itchy, uncomfortable feeling that I couldn't shake.

"Juliet?" Nicole's voice made me jump and turn around. She wasn't in the attic at all.

"I thought you were up there?" I asked.

"No." She shook her head. "What's up?"

"I need to talk to you."

"Let's go in here." She motioned and we ducked into the Green Room.

I saw Enid's head go slack and her breathing even out. I'd watched enough kids try to fake sleep to know what she was doing. "It's okay, it's just us," I said to her.

Her blue eyes twinkled as she cracked them, then sat up. "That terrible woman gave me more pills."

I held out my hand and she handed them to me. I glanced at them. I'd lived here long enough to know pills by the shape, the print, the color. "This one isn't for sleeping, it's for cholesterol." I picked up one and held it back out to her.

"No pills. What's the worst-case scenario?" She smiled sadly, resigned.

I respected her acceptance and took the pill back. "Then just cheek them and one of us will come flush them later."

She nodded. This room seemed so large with only one bed in it.

"What do you need?" Nicole crossed her arms and craned her neck up at me. For the first time I realized how tall I was compared to her.

"I'm really *hungry*," I said, hoping that Nicole would understand me.

"Oh." Nicole's eyes widened and she began to shake her head. "But Mistress and—"

"I have to." The drive to make eggnog, quiche lorraine, and a chocolate pots de créme was overwhelming. So much so that I couldn't concentrate on anything else. Glee's favorite foods were clamoring for attention.

"You know girls, I haven't been hungry in ages, but what I wouldn't give for my sister's secret-recipe eggnog. Oh, and her quiche lorraine was the best in the world. She never would tell me what she put in that eggnog, though."

"Bailey's," I answered without thinking.

"What, dear?" Enid perked up.

"Bailey's Irish Cream. In the eggnog. That was the secret part." I bit my lip. How did I explain the inexplicable?

"I won't ask how you know that because I can see the truth in your eyes."

Nicole reached out and touched my arm. "Do you trust me?"

"Of course."

"Really?"

"With my life. You're scaring me."

"I'll take care of it."

"What?" I asked, as we heard the familiar chug of the kid transport van turn into the drive. "Is it one of Ms. Asura's days to visit?"

"No, I don't think so." Nicole joined me at the window. Outside black clouds rolled along the horizon, breaking like whitecaps in the stormy sky. "Are we supposed to get a storm?"

"Maybe—" I started to answer her.

"Juliet, is it time?" Bodie ran into the room and threw himself at me, latching onto my waist with his tiny but manacle-strong arms.

"Time?"

"Is it your birthday? Is she here to take you away?"

"No, honey. I don't think so. Not yet." I didn't know.

"What's this? Take you where?" Enid piped up. "Why is the little boy so upset?"

"Who's in the car with her?" I leaned against the window

and peered down into the van below. "It's Kirian!" My heart raced and my feet followed.

"You won't leave?" Bodie gasped sobs, grabbing my leg.

"Bodie, let go of me. I have to go downstairs," I snapped at him.

"But—"

I peeled him off and thrust him at Nicole.

Mistress bellowed up the stairs, but I was already halfway down the back ones. I skidded out of the kitchen, into the foyer.

"There you are." Mistress glared. "Where's Nicole?"

"Right here." She came down the stairs with the blank, serene face I'd learned hid numerous talents.

Ms. Asura poked her head around the front door. "Girls, girls, how are you?"

"We need to talk," Mistress snapped at Ms. Asura. She didn't pretend to be nice, which surprised me. I thought they were best girlfriends.

"Yes, we do. Juliet, begin to pack your things, please. Your birthday is right around the corner."

"She's not sixteen yet," Mistress barked.

"We'll see." Ms. Asura smiled in a way that completely dismissed Mistress. "Be lovely and bring up coffee to the office?" She asked like she owned the place. I saw Mistress narrow her eyes, but she said nothing as she started up the steps.

Ms. Asura pointed to the side yard and mouthed to me, *Kirian.*

"He's outside in our spot," I said to Nicole. "He has to be, he was in the car."

"I'll take up the coffee, but I don't think you should—"

"Thanks!" I kissed her cheek, but didn't wait to hear her suggest caution. Nicole didn't trust anyone.

I closed the back door and leaned against it, wishing I had lip gloss, or a nice haircut, or pretty clothes.

"Hello, jewel in my crown." Kirian peeked out from between the hedges. From a boy to a man, the transformation was spectacular. He stood a head taller than me, with broad shoulders and bulging biceps. His dirty-blond hair had been shaved in a tight crew cut that drew attention to the chiseled look of his jaw and the strength of his chin. A tan kissed his skin golden. A hoop dangled from one earlobe and a thumb ring glinted in the sunlight. Sunglasses covered his eyes and mirrored my own back at me.

As he wrestled through the foliage, I wondered for a minute if he'd forgotten about the poison ivy growing in there. But then his charisma shoved all thought from my head and I didn't try to hide my smile. He'd come back to me.

"Romeo."

He swept me up in his arms and held me tight. So tight I almost couldn't breathe.

"I missed you, my sweet."

"Me too."

"You've grown up. Let me look at you." He held me at arm's length and inspected me from all angles until I felt a quiver of discomfort.

"You sound different," I said. I struggled to see the little boy who'd been everything to me and the young man who'd taken beatings to protect me. All I saw was a man who could have walked off a movie screen.

"I've grown up. Traveling the world will do that to a person. Come sit with me." He pulled me through the hedges toward the woods, where I realized he'd set up a picnic along a fallen log. A breeze ruffled my hair and reminded me it was only February. Not summer. He wrapped me in a blanket and poured hot chocolate. There were chocolate-covered strawberries and pastries.

"Marshmallows, right?" he asked, popping a couple into my mug.

I'd never liked them, but he loved them. I shrugged it off. It had been years. "I can't really stay." The trees around us billowed and clapped, like an audience at a play. While my hair struggled to untangle itself from my braid, not even the collar on his jacket seemed to move.

He shrugged me off. "We have time. All the time in the world."

"But Mistress . . ." Maybe he didn't remember how bad this place was. It had been three years.

His mouth thinned. "Trust me. The meeting will take a while."

I fell silent, sipping from my porcelain cup. The hot chocolate tasted bitter. My tongue begged for eggnog instead.

"I came back for you. Only you." He smiled, flashing perfectly white, straight teeth. I didn't remember him having straight teeth. Hadn't they been crooked?

"Where did you go?" I asked.

"All over the world. You'll love Paris. You got my cards, right?"

The three of them. "Yes." I nodded.

Clearly I hadn't shown enough enthusiasm, because

Kirian put down his cup. "I had to make money for us, didn't I?"

"You were adopted, right?" I pressed.

"No, I joined—" He broke off. "After I turned eighteen, then I traveled."

"Where is your family?"

"They're everywhere."

"Would you have stayed?"

"Here? At DG? Why would I have wanted to do that?" He seemed genuinely poleaxed that I might suggest it. "Besides, no one ever stays."

"But why do we have to leave on our sixteenth birthdays? Why not eighteen?" I pressed.

"Well . . . it's an opportunity, Jewel. Trust me, you won't have to clean another bedpan or teach a kid to use the toilet."

"But—"

"What's with all the questions? I had to take the deal. For you. For us. But I'm back now and we can be together."

I fell silent. That wasn't all he took before he left. And what deal? "Why do you still have your sunglasses on?"

"It's bright out here." He waved me off.

"But—"

"Jewel, get off my back." His tone stung, but he dove into a croissant, not noticing my reaction to his words.

I clammed up. Then tried again. "How much was in your savings account?" I asked, hoping he might shed light on what was going to happen to me on my birthday.

"What?" he grumbled, his forehead creased, but I couldn't see his eyes.

"The savings account? Ms. Asura says we get paid—" I broke off when it became clear Kirian had no idea what I was talking about.

"Oh, yeah, that," he said, trying to brush off his evident ignorance. "Look, just do what Ms. Asura tells you to do. It's not that hard to be what they want. And all of it I did so we can be together."

"What are you talking about? Be what? What did you do?" I wanted to scream in frustration. I felt like we were having two different conversations. One where I asked questions and one where he answered questions I hadn't asked.

Mini meowed and pranced out from behind a tree. She came up and wound around my back, leaning against my shins.

Kirian leaned forward. "Who is this beauty?" He started to reach a hand out as if to pet her.

Mini hissed and swiped the back of his hand with her claws. Dark blood immediately welled up in the tracks across his flesh.

"Mini!" Horrified, I swooped her up, dropping the blanket at my feet.

"What the hell? You should drown that cat." Kirian grabbed a cloth napkin and held it to his hand.

"She's never done anything like that before. I swear—"

"A stray? Really, Jewel, I thought you were better than that. If you want a pet, I can buy you a pet."

"She's—" I broke off. *She's my friend. She comforts me and loves me and keeps the dark at bay. If you'd stayed, I wouldn't need a cat to be my family.*

"Kirian?" Ms. Asura called from the front of the house. "Time to go."

"Crap."

I started to clean up the picnic, keeping Mini behind me, away from Kirian.

"Leave it. You're not a servant." Kirian stilled my hands and pulled me away from the mess. "It's just, I love you, you waited for me, and now we can be together. Trust me. I'll take care of everything."

"But—"

"Kirian!" Her tone was shrill and demanding.

"I'll come back. Trust me? We'll be together soon." He leaned into me, pulled my hips tight against his, flattened my breasts against his chest, and kissed me. My teeth felt too big for my mouth and in the way. *This is how he always kisses you. He takes, not gives.*

He bounded away. "Soon."

I peered around the corner of the house, my fingers on my bruised lips. I watched him get into the van with Ms. Asura. They seemed to argue before driving off. I picked up the remains of the picnic and stuffed them deep into the hedge. I'd be the one beaten for the mess if Mistress found it.

Nicole met me in the kitchen. "Do you want the good news? Or the bad news?"

Take my hand, dear sister, and fill the world with
your light.

Melynda Laine
December 21, 1922

CHAPTER 37

"Meridian, can't you tell me while we wait for Tony to
get here?" Tens sat on the couch with his wood chunks,
whittling a hamster-sized firefly.

I shook my head, not pausing to answer him with
words. It was right here. I tucked a Post-it note between
the pages of Auntie's journal.

Thunder boomed, closer this time. Lightning lit the
sky, making me jump.

"Are we supposed to get a storm?" I looked at Tens.

"I'll check." He flipped open the laptop and peered at
the screen.

I went back to reading the spidery script in the Fenestra journal. Veils. Memories. "Oh no." Tens's voice broke my concentration.

"What?"

"There are three big storms heading straight for Marion County. That's us."

The roof vibrated. It sounded like someone was dumping buckets of golf balls down on us.

Custos whined, and we got up and went to the window.

Huge ice pellets blanketed the ground in a layer of white. Suddenly, more thunder rocked the place. Lightning flashed almost instantaneously. The lights flickered.

Tens grabbed the laptop and kept reading. "There's a tornado warning."

"Tornadoes? What the hell do we do for a tornado?" Portland had storms, lots of wind, some ice and snow, the earthquake possibility, and tsunami warnings, but the closest I'd ever gotten to a tornado was on TV.

Headlights cut across the cottage windows and for the first time I realized how dark the world was.

"That's Tony," I said.

Tens grabbed a rhinestone-and-daisy umbrella from by the door and rushed out to meet him.

They came back in as rain poured in sheets from every direction, washing ice chunks along the gutters and melting them off the paths.

I grabbed towels. Thirty seconds out in the storm and they were drenched.

Dripping wet, with ice pellets frozen in his hair, Tony

took a towel from me. "I came as quickly as I could. You said it was important. I haven't heard more from Josiah." Tony hung his tweed suit coat on the back of a chair and sat at the table. "What's the text?"

"This is my family's journal," I said.

"It's old." He didn't try to touch it, but I held it out to him in invitation. He took it with gingerly fingers. "I should be wearing gloves."

"It's not an artifact. More like a working document."

"Still." He unfolded reading glasses to peer more closely at the writing.·

I appreciated his willingness to accept what he was told and take what was given.

"Is this about your grandfather?" Tony asked Tens.

"No," I answered. "It's about a girl named Prunella. But really it's about Juliet Ambrose."

He sat up and leaned toward me with excitement. "Juliet? You know her? How is she?"

Tens raised his eyebrows and gave me his lopsided grin of appreciation. "You figured it out."

I nodded, my whole body vibrating with excitement.

Tens asked Tony, "What was the name of your children's home?"

"Saint Emiliani's. Please tell me, do you know this girl? Where is she? Is she okay? Can I see her? Have you heard from Roshana?"

Tens put the pieces together. "That's it." He asked Tony, "Want some whiskey in your tea for this story?"

I giggled. "Seriously?"

"Auntie said whiskey made the impossible possible." Tens shrugged.

Tony slapped his thigh. "No spirits, just tell me what you know. If you had any idea how I've looked for her, you wouldn't keep me waiting."

I began to tell Tony what we knew about Juliet.

Tens made tea, and while the storm raged around us I told the story, leaving nothing out. It wasn't much.

"Prunella was my great-aunt Meridian's cousin. She was a nurse too. She wasn't a Fenestra but knew about my auntie's ability because she nearly died in 1943. She made it to the window and then turned back. Her heart restarted and she went on to live another forty years. However, because she knew too much and might endanger her family, a Sangre angel came to her and veiled her history. He took away her connections and started her over in another part of the world. He warned that if she ever saw Auntie again, she'd remember everything about her life."

"You think Juliet doesn't remember her mother or me? Or her first few years of life, because she was in danger?"

"That's exactly what I believe. And I think you are the key to unlocking her memories. It's the only way to get her to know."

"But what if she does know and she thinks we let her live in that hell without helping? I couldn't live with myself."

"I don't know. We came as soon as we were told—I hope that counts for something." I shrugged. I didn't know if she could forgive and move forward, but it was our best shot.

"Let's go to her. Now." Tony stood and started for the door. "We need to find her and tell her. I can't bear thinking she might have it all wrong."

I stayed seated. "I know." We had to plan carefully. We had to understand how to lift the veil. We couldn't risk making everything worse.

Tony paced. "Her mother loved her. She died protecting her."

I nodded as Joi burst through the cottage door and storm sirens began to vibrate the town around us. "Come on, all, we have to get into the storm cellar. There's a twister five miles away that's headed for us."

I grabbed the journal and the quilt. Tens grabbed the laptop and me.

As we ran to the store's cellar, wind tore at us and branches flew by. I heard glass cracking as parked cars took a beating from the elements. The sky was a swirling mass of grays and greens and blacks. We zigzagged around branches and airborne lawn ornaments.

My stomach dropped as we scrambled down into the cellar.

Please let Juliet be safe.

If I leave you with F.A. he'll protect you. I'll tell them you died in birth. I'll tell them whatever I have to. Maybe someday you'll know the truth.

—R.

CHAPTER 38

Juliet

"Are you sure?" I asked Nicole again.

"I heard a crash and a thump," Nicole whispered to me as we tried to stealthily creep toward the closed door of the office.

"What did she say exactly?" The good news was Nicole thought maybe something had happened to Mistress. The bad news was Nicole thought maybe something had happened to Mistress and Ms. Asura had done it.

"Under no circumstances were we to disturb Mistress. I don't know, it feels wrong. She made me repeat it back to her. And then she looked out the window at you and Kirian and swore. That's when she went outside and called him back."

Why didn't Ms. Asura like me talking to Kirian? She was the one who brought the postcards and mentioned him to me during her visits.

"So they left and then you heard the loud thump?"

"No, yelling first, thump next, leaving last."

Sure, Mistress disappeared. Often. More so than ever before. She left the house for obscure meetings and to gamble. She sequestered herself in her office or living quarters. But she always told one of us, and left a list of things to do that would take weeks to accomplish. Neither of us had been given our daily list and we knew from Ms. Asura that Mistress was still inside her office.

"Now nothing."

We tried to get close enough, an inch at a time, to press our ears to the door. After minutes of silence, I straightened. "I think I better knock."

"Let me." Nicole tried to tug me away. The knocker might very well be beaten.

"I'll do it." I rapped on the wood.

Nothing.

"Mistress?" I knocked louder this time.

Nothing.

Maybe she'd fallen. Maybe she'd knocked a glass over and was being ornery. But normally she'd take it out on the knocker, not suffer in silence.

I tried the knob. Unlocked.

"Juliet—" Nicole warned.

I opened the door, held my breath, and peeked in. "Mistress?" I called softly.

I saw her feet sticking out from behind the desk. I rushed into the room. Her desk was in a shambles, like she'd fallen against it and cleared it in panic. Files and papers covered the floor in a blanket of triplicate.

I knelt down. "Nicole, call nine-one-one."

Nicole was right behind me. "I don't think so."

"Mistress?" I leaned in by her face. Blood from a gash was already thickly congealed. Her eyes were glassy, her body painfully empty of life.

"She's dead," Nicole pronounced.

"But—" I didn't believe it. I felt for a pulse. Nothing. "Oh my God." *She's dead.* I wanted to dance and sing and whoop it up. I wanted to cry. "What do we do?"

"We back out of here and go about the rest of our day. When the night nurse comes to check in, let him find her."

"That's cold."

"No more than she deserves. Think about it. We start this now and Ms. Asura comes back and takes us all away, to heaven knows where. Let's make the meal you've been itching to cook, and have a party with Bodie and Sema. Buy ourselves a little time."

I nodded. It made sense. It felt like a reprieve, like a gift. "But—"

Nicole just waited, her expression daring me to break a rule.

"The hell with it. Let's cook." I smiled, and shut the door behind us. "Let's bring Enid downstairs with us."

Nicole smiled. "Great idea." Yet another rule broken— no inmates hanging out with the guests.

I opened the door to the Green Room and glanced out the big picture window, then gasped.

"I've been watching it roll in." Enid lifted a hand toward the window.

Nicole was two steps behind me. "What's going on?"

I pointed. "Have you looked outside lately? Those are twister clouds out there."

The sky was an ominous shade of pea green, with black clouds boiling on the horizon. "It was breezy when I was outside with Kirian, but not like this. Have you seen any weather forecasts today?" I asked Nicole.

She shook her head and turned her troubled gaze to the storm out the window. "It's way early in the season."

"Not too early. I remember the twisters in 'sixty-four. They started before Lent and didn't give up until August." Enid shuddered. "Spent more time in the cellar that year than we spent on the farmland. Do you have a cellar here, dears?"

Yes. But no. The storm cellar was used for storage and for Mistress. House legend said that long before us, a couple of teen inmates used it as a private place. The girl ended up pregnant and from then on inmates were told to huddle in the bathrooms when the sirens sounded.

"Would you like to go down to the kitchen with us, Miss Enid? Juliet is going to cook up a feast." Nicole tugged me

435

away from the window. The best place would be on the first floor, center of the house, just in case.

The old lady lit up. "That sounds lovely, but won't we get into trouble?"

I shook my head with a tiny twitch of my lips. "Not this time. She can't hurt you anymore."

"She can't hurt anyone ever again." Nicole's pronouncement dangled relief in my periphery. *Can we really be free of Mistress?*

"What are we waiting for?" Enid threw back her covers, but she couldn't move her legs across the mattress, nor stay upright for more than a few seconds at a time. She collapsed back onto the bed. "Oh dear. I'm a bit weak. I think I'll stay here if that's all right."

"Sure," I said, though really I wanted to force her to come downstairs where we might be safer.

"We'll bring the food up to you when it's finished." Nicole patted her hand.

"That sounds lovely. Then you can tell me all about the inspiration for this party."

"Sure." I started to follow Nicole from the room.

Enid called, "Why don't you send that Bodie up here; he and Sema can keep me company. They were so upset earlier."

Thunder cracked, shaking the house and the window-panes in their casings. My heart raced with each lash of the rain. I'd never been in a storm this bad. I wanted to be scared and hide until it was over, but I didn't have time to indulge myself.

I stopped. I hadn't seen either of the children since I'd come back in. I turned to Nicole. "Where are they?"

Nicole shrugged, her eyes widening and her cheeks paling. She shook her head.

Enid blanched. "I thought they went down to you. They said they were going with you. I thought they went with you." Her voice trailed off as the darkness rolled toward us. We were all thinking the same thing—this was not the time to play hide-and-seek.

"Bodie? Sema?" I called, racing down the hallway. "Where are you?" I had to yell over the hail bombarding the house like icy shrapnel.

Nicole darted up the rickety steps into the attic calling, "Bodie. Sema. Where are you?"

I tore down the stairs calling their names. Nothing but the storm screamed back at me.

Nicole met me in the kitchen. "They took their backpacks."

My feet and hands moved in a fury of desperation. "Where'd they go? The creek? They ran away? That doesn't make sense." I checked in the cabinets and under the table just in case.

"They said they were going with you. Where did they think you were going?" The pound of hail and rain made a normal voice impossible to hear.

The house protested with the creaks and moans of a thousand ghosts. I wondered if it could withstand such a ferocious onslaught.

"I'll check the spot where Kirian had the picnic ready. Maybe they went out there." I grabbed a rain jacket.

"No." Nicole wouldn't let me leave the safety of the house. "They're not out in that." The power blinked off, then came back on. "If they were, they'd come back in as soon as it started to rain."

"What about the creek? What if they climbed Bodie's tree? They can't swim. Nicole, what if they fell in?" I had to go out and find them.

"No, stay here." Nicole yanked my arm as the tornado sirens peeled. The world dimmed, as if the power had gone out, but it was the storm blocking out light and turning the air a vibrantly ill green. "I'll go. You get Enid to the cellar. Force her; you have to survive." She opened the back door and ice was driven by the rain across the kitchen, soaking both of us.

The cold sweat rolling down my neck made my back itch.

"Nicole, you'll get blown away." I reached for her hands, trying to change places.

"No! I'll go. You have to survive, then find Meridian!" she shrieked against my ear, though I barely understood her words. She wiggled out of my grasp and darted outside.

I tried to force the door closed, but the wind refused to yield. I gave up, knowing each second was precious.

The wind sounded like a railroad yard. The snap and crackle of branches, the sounds of car alarms and cows bawling in distress whipped under the cracks of the doors and through window seams.

I took the stairs two at a time, still calling for Bodie and Sema over the storm. Thinking, hoping, maybe they were simply hiding and scared.

I swung open Enid's door and found her sprawled on the floor. With a cry, I knelt by her, gathering her weak frame in my arms.

With her lips pressed against my ear she said as loud as she could, "The sirens, they scared me." She trembled in my arms. "I was trying to get to the cellar." She'd twisted her ankle and already the skin was a mottled purple and black. "It hurts." she whimpered. Her arm was bleeding where she'd pulled the IV needle and tubes out.

I shushed her, rocking her. "I know. We'll get there. I have to pick you up." I wondered if I was strong enough to make it more than a few steps carrying her.

Her cheeks wet with fright, she quaked. "I can't make it, dear. You go. My Glee will keep me wrapped in her hands."

"I'm not leaving you." I'd been helpless to save Glee; I wasn't abandoning her sister. I put my hands under Enid's arms and whispered a quick prayer that I wouldn't hurt her more than necessary. I hefted her upper body against my chest, dragging her weak legs out of the room and toward the hallway. I felt wind begin to ruffle the air around us as if the walls were growing thinner and intangible. As if the wind's fingers unlocked the windows and opened the doors of DG to get into each tiny space, each nook and abandoned corner.

Fear pumped adrenaline through my veins until my heart raced and my fingertips tingled.

Branches cracked in the forest outside the windows. Debris hit the house, ricocheted off the roof. I heard a window crack and shatter somewhere downstairs. Trees fell with a shudder that shook the earth. A deafening roar sounded above me and I looked up, amazed, to see that a massive gust had pulled off a huge chunk of the roof. Wind whipped my face and rain lashed my clothes about my body. I knew we were going to die. We would be next to be picked up and tossed into the current of the twister.

Enid shouted, feebly pushing against me. I didn't know if she was terrified or trying to tell me something. I didn't have time to think; the wind sucked the air from my lungs and made it hard to breathe past this nightmare come to life.

My ears popped, but all I could hear was a train's approach. A huge, angry train whistling right toward us on a collision course. I bracketed Enid against the wall, shielding her fragile frame as best I could. I prayed with everything I had for Bodie, Sema, and Nicole. I wished my life weren't ending like this, but how could we possibly survive an encounter with a tornado?

A crack near us forced my head up to investigate. There, out of the shadows, a man who seemed to be made of midnight and steel strode toward us. I think I screamed.

Natural disasters confuse souls, and many will wander aimlessly without transitioning. The best a Fenestra may do is settle and comfort the dead while the living pick up the pieces.

Meridian Laine Fulbright

May 18, 1980

CHAPTER 39

Tens hesitated at the top of the stairs to Joi's storm cellar.

"No!" I shouted up at him. "No! Stay!" I read the stubborn need written on his face. He intended to leave me in the shelter and go after Juliet. I felt like shouting "over my dead body," but I didn't think he'd appreciate my attempt at black humor.

"Come on, son." Tony nudged him down the rest of the stairs.

I knew Tens could have broken the man's hold on his shoulder. He was strong enough to push away and take off like he wanted to. But he didn't.

I should have thanked him, for picking me. But I didn't feel generous or lucky. Instead I felt pissed and cranky that he'd even considered leaving me in a tornado to check on another girl. Never mind her Fenestra status.

Tens pulled me aside and leaned down to my ear. "Merry, what if she needs—"

I felt his breath brush my cheek and stir my hair. My heart screamed "Mine!" Why didn't he understand? Why did he force this? I yelled, "You're my Protector, Tens. *Mine.*" It wasn't that I wanted anything to happen to Juliet—I didn't—but I'd lost too much already. I wasn't giving up Tens without a fight. I curled my fingers into fists, my nails digging into my palms.

I pretended not to see the confused glances Joi and Tony shared.

Tens tried again to whisper. "I know that. But you're here and safe. What if she's not?"

"She's been taking care of herself for this long." Why did I have to explain this to him? Okay, so we'd been sent because she wasn't doing a great job of that, but still. "I need you."

Tens nodded, but his hardened expression made me regret my words.

Even Joi's storm cellar was decorated with cheery florals, pillows, strings of funny lights shaped like sunflowers, candy canes, and cowboy boots. Like Helios but much cozier: only a dozen or so people would fit inside this outrageously decorated box.

I heard hail hit the heavy doors like a mob of crazy people beating to get in.

Tens sat down, far away from me, even in the tiny space, his arms crossed and his mouth pinched. Tony went to sit next to him.

Joi's frown was questioning and concerned as she glanced between us. The lights blinked out completely. "Don't move." Joi flicked on a flashlight and then moved about the space, switching the knobs on battery-powered LED lanterns.

All at once, I felt like we were back in the caves in Revelation. Just Tens and me. Did he think about that time too? He'd been so sick, I knew he didn't remember much of it. Would we ever get back to those caves? Rebuild Auntie's house? Have a life together that was normal?

I leaned against the cushions and tried to tune out the surging sounds of apocalypse outside.

Joi tucked a fleece blanket around me and patted my hand. For once she didn't ask probing questions.

"Thanks," I mumbled.

Tony and Tens spoke in hushed voices, Tens's full of dark sighs and harsh consonants, Tony's steady and calm.

"Have you told her that?" I heard Tony ask.

I perked up an ear, but didn't twitch an eyelid.

"No. How?"

"Start at the beginning. It might help."

"Maybe," Tens said.

Tony wouldn't take no for an answer. "Try."

Joi's cheery voice asked, "Would anyone like soup, tea, or coffee?"

"I'm fine, thank you," Tony answered. "How's your family in this storm?"

"I'm sure they're fine." Worry frayed the edges of her voice. Joi wandered the room fluffing pillows and straightening knickknacks.

I sat up, realizing that these storms affected more than just Tens and me and Juliet. *Self-centered much, Meridian?* "Are your husband and daughter at home?"

"No, she's back at college and he's at work. I talked to him earlier and they were working in the basement as the storm approached. Tornadoes are par for the course in the spring. These are early, though, and particularly fierce." She refolded the same blanket twice.

"How long do we stay down here?" I asked. The storm in *The Wizard of Oz* was the only tornado I was familiar with and that wasn't exactly a documentary.

Joi untied and then made new bows around the necks of bunnies and bears. She sorted the tea bags by kind and then picked up a deck of cards. "Until the radio in that corner squawks an all clear or we hear the all-clear siren. It's a good thing the restaurant wasn't open quite yet, or we'd have more folks down here with us." She seemed restless and caged. "Anyone up for a card game?"

"Sure, I'll play cards with you." I tried to smile, glancing at Tens and Tony's animated conversation.

Joi rummaged in the corner chests for game supplies, muttering the names of card games under her breath.

Tens scooted over next to me. "I'm sorry." His demeanor was purposeful and direct, but guarded.

"Me too." I licked my lips and swallowed, not sure where to begin with an explanation of my jealousy. *How do I put into words the fear of being abandoned?*

"I need to tell you something first."

"Okay." I waited. I'd learned he needed to generate momentum to start sharing; saying much of anything could derail the whole process.

Tony passed Joi a note and they moved to a small bistro table and chairs across the room. It was as much privacy as they could manage without leaving the cellar.

Tens touched my knee with a tentative tenderness. "Before Auntie's I lived in Seattle with Tyee. You know that?"

I nodded.

"The last time I saw my grandfather he'd taken me to his friend's house.

"The friend was a cop. He left me there with a backpack and money. Said if he wasn't back in the morning, I should open the bag. I was eleven.

"There was pounding on the door. The cop must have known more than I did because he pulled his gun and told me to grab my bag. I was to go into the bathroom, lock the door, and wedge anything I could against it to make it hard to get in. He told me not to come out until he said 'cauliflower.'"

"Cauliflower?"

"It was a way for me to know not to trust what came out of his mouth—you don't accidentally say 'cauliflower,' and no one puts a gun to your head forcing you to say it either."

I nodded. Picturing a scared young boy not knowing what was going on, or why.

"I think he opened the front door. I heard a struggle.

Shouting. The gun went off. Again and again. There was silence and then voices said, 'Two down, one to go.' Someone yelled to find the damned kid."

I reached out and gripped his hand.

He squeezed back but continued his story without stopping. "There was a big window above the tub. It didn't open, so I wrapped my arm in a towel and elbowed it like Tyee had taught me. He taught me how to survive. It shattered and I dove out. I ran all night. I ran until I collapsed." A single tear flowed down his cheek. "I hid under a bridge for two days until I got picked up and put in foster care. Group homes. Every time I ran away, I learned something else about being on the street. I was totally alone. No one, Meridian. There was no one out there except me. No one had my back. No one cared if I came home or if I lived through a tornado. I headed for the open spaces, for the mountains. Taking odd jobs to eat and sleep. Inching closer to Revelation and Auntie. Tyee had always preached to go to her: 'If anything happens to me, go to the Fulbrights in Revelation, Colorado.' That was a mantra from the time I arrived at the SeaTac airport."

"What happened to Tyee?"

"He's dead."

I knew that. I lifted my other hand to his cheek, trying to soak up some, any, of his pain. "I'm sorry." I wished we knew exactly what had happened. What did it mean?

He nodded.

"But you got to Auntie's, right?"

"I did. But it took me years. There was money in that

bag but not enough to buy a plane ticket or hop a train legally. Then it was stolen and I didn't even have that." He shook his head.

"I guess what I'm trying to tell you is that I know what it's like to have no one. No one. Not someone putting a roof over my head, or feeding me, or caring if I went to school or lived another day. I can't just leave Juliet to think she's alone. I can come back to you. I can leave you with people who will help you. I know you'll be okay in the short-term. You are so strong, so capable. I don't know that about her. Isn't that why we're here?"

He was right. I hated that he was right. "I'm jealous." I owned it. In the face of his heart-wrenching honesty, I couldn't delude either of us with pretty words. The truth was ugly, but it was truth.

He shook his head and leaned toward me. He captured my face with his palm. "Of what?" he asked in disbelief.

"Of her. Of you wanting to help her. And I'm afraid of losing you like I've lost everyone else."

"Meridian, you don't always need my help. Aren't you the one who said just because we're destined doesn't mean we have to be inseparable?"

"I was lying."

"No, you were right. Destiny can make an arranged marriage, but not a love match."

"What are you saying?" I asked.

"I love you because of you. Not because of Fenestras, or angels, or Creators, or wolves and cats. Because I love you. I don't feel her, Merry; I've tried over and over again and I can't sense her. But I know your heart." He hesitated as if searching for the words. "Still, I'm always going to want to help the underdog."

I swallowed, blinking. "I know. That's one of the things I love about you."

"I don't know if that's just me, or my experiences, or something else."

"Sum of all of it, probably." My heart lightened. I tried to let go of the fear, of the need to question his motivation. I learned to trust in us, in what we had together.

He dropped a light kiss on my lips. "But I'd rather we did it together. Side by side. Partners? I mean, we still have to work on your aim, but you can save my ass any day."

"I'd rather not have to." I leaned into his embrace, relaxing.

"That's where two heads are better than one." Tens smiled.

I grinned back, leaning into his mouth for a kiss that chased the shadows from my heart. I knew I could depend on Tens for whatever this life threw at me. And now, with his confession, I felt like he trusted me with his story, with his wounds and burdens. Some of them. Enough for the short-term.

The radio in the corner squawked and beeped.

Joi cleared her throat. "I think I'm coming into this story in the final act, but that's the all clear and we can go rescue"—she turned to Tony—"what's her name?"

"Juliet. Her name is Juliet. Shall we?" He held up his arm like a formal escort for Joi to the cellar doors.

"I do want to know the rest of the story." She dotted her eyes with a tissue. "I remember that age so well."

Tens stood and held on to my hand. "Let's go slay a dragon and rescue a damsel."

"No, let's go deliver a sword so the damsel can slay her own dragon."

"That's a better plan." Tony smiled at us. "Your truck, or my van?"

A large tree rested on the hood of the truck. My heart sank. Jasper's truck had treated us well, but there was no fixing the crumpled hunk of metal.

"My van it is." Tony led the way, picking branches up and moving them out of our path.

"You're not leaving me here. I'm coming too." Joi finagled a passenger seat. "Just tell me what to do."

Custos appeared beside the car, dry and untouched. She barked.

"Make room for the wolf?" I asked.

They've found me. I pray they'll never find you.

—R.

CHAPTER 40

Juliet

My hair, freed from its elastic and wet with icy rain, lashed my face and arms like a whip. We shivered, drenched, until he picked us up.

"Hold on." A deep, thickly accented voice blanketed Enid and me with a lullaby while strong arms lifted us from our position, braced against the wall and floor. We all but flew down the stairs. Before I even blinked we were under the stairs, in the farthest recesses of my cubbyhole. I saw no flashlights or lanterns, and yet the space brimmed full of the warmest, brightest light.

"You'll be safe now." He smelled of sugar and sun and summer nights. He turned at the little door, the light following him. "Hear them when they come bearing your story and believe in the power of purposeful unity. . . ."

These last words were broken by the sound of glass and tearing metal. Thumps like God's hammer and a rushing like the heaviest rapids filled my ears. The world blackened and I huddled there in the dark, holding Enid. We heard walls crash and metal snap. Above our heads the stairs lifted and flew off in chunks, raining bits of wood and plaster down onto my back.

The rain continued relentlessly even after the winds receded. Enid and I cried, holding each other, releasing our fear into the chaos around us. I froze, afraid to move, scared to open my eyes and find out that we had died.

I forced myself to just keep breathing.

After what felt like an eternity, the cold beat my fear and I lost feeling in my limbs. The softest fingers brushed against my cheeks and tickled my forehead.

"Child, they're calling you," Enid whispered in my ear. "Are you still in there?"

I lifted my head and realized I had my eyes squeezed shut so tight, my face hurt with the effort.

I heard voices calling, "Juliet? Juliet? Bodie? Nicole?"

After a moment of disbelief, I recognized Meridian's and Tens's voices, among several others. Trying to move was a chore as blood rushed back into my complaining knees and shoulders. I gently moved off and around Enid, trying to keep from hurting her further. "Are you okay?" I asked, my voice a croak, a whisper.

"I'm alive. Go get them. I'll wait here." Enid patted me and I nodded. Shifting toilet paper and towels off of us, I climbed out of the pile.

The stairs were gone; the tops of the walls looked surgically cut. The sky was a grayish blue. I couldn't see the horizon to know if more thunder cells were on the way. I was in a box without a ceiling.

I stumbled toward the door, which was shut tight against whatever lay on the outside. I hesitated. I'd wanted DG to disappear, but I'd never dreamed that might actually happen. The uncertainty about my future was paralyzing.

"Enid needs help." I whispered to talk myself into movement. I reached for the doorknob.

I pushed at the door and it swung outward. Nothing was left of DG. I gasped. The piles of debris made it look like a construction site. A lone chair from the sitting room sat exactly as it had before the storm, only there was nothing around it but the floor.

I glanced around at the foundation, with the tiles and the area rugs still in the right place. But no upstairs. No attic. No kitchen or nurses' lounge. No Mistress's office. No Mistress's body.

I felt my knees turn to jelly. I tried to wave or yell to the crowd walking toward the creek and the woods. I couldn't make a large sound, but I must have made enough of one, because I heard shouts.

"There she is!" Meridian spotted me and ran toward me. I think I simply stood there and waited for her to come.

She stopped inches away from embracing me. I could tell the devastation must have driven all hope from them, because her face bloomed with such exquisite relief. "Are you okay?" she asked.

I nodded, pointing behind me. "Enid needs help."

Meridian motioned toward others. Tens. A smiling woman who was talking on a cell phone with such animation I wondered who was on the other end. I'd do whatever she wanted.

A man came toward me. He shrugged out of his suit coat and wrapped it around my shoulders. "Ah, sweet-as-light Juliet Ambrose. Apple of her mother's eye and heart that beats in the breeze." He smiled and rubbed my arms, and I knew.

In that moment, I knew what I'd so long forgotten. "Father Anthony?" I asked, and then I fainted.

Our enemies are wily. We must be more so.

Jocelyn Wynn

CHAPTER 41

Tens and I exchanged worried, awestruck frowns as we drove toward Dunklebarger. Tony had the radio on and we listened to reports. "The funnel cloud just missed the downtown area of Carmel, but cut a seven-mile swath. The storm cell is headed east toward Noblesville. If you have a cellar you should be listening to us from there." Callers rang in with their eyewitness accounts, everything from "There's a live cow stuck in our oak tree" to "We don't have power in Fishers. Anyone know when it will be restored?"

I listened with one ear while trying to survey the

apocalypse around us. I could see the exact stretch of land that the tornado touched down on, but there was no rhyme or reason to what was damaged and what was left alone. Trees were ripped out of the ground and littered the roads with roots and power lines. More than once we bumped over fields to get around piles of houses and vehicles and dead farm animals. The fury of Mother Nature had spared nothing and no one in her path.

I didn't think anyone could have survived this. I thought we were too late. That we'd failed.

Only the smallest bit, a closet, of Dunklebarger continued to stand. The rest of the building had disappeared, as if it had never been there. "Where did it go?"

"A farmer ten miles away is probably looking at it. Happens all the time—there was a silo dumped at the Colts practice facility last year, still full of grain," Joi answered.

We piled out of the car shouting, searching. Tens and I headed toward the creek. Tony and Joi found a pile of debris in the woods and started trying to lift parts.

She can't be dead. She can't be dead. She can't be dead.

Then, the lone upright door swung open and Juliet appeared like an avenging angel ready for battle. Her hair hung lank and dripped down her face. Her hands were scratched and bleeding and her clothes clung to her skin. I ran to her, picking my way over branches and sheets of twisted metal.

She's okay. I shouted for the others to come. If Juliet had survived under the stairs, maybe Bodie and the others had too.

When Tony joined us, he and Juliet locked eyes. Hers

rolled back into her head and she collapsed. Tony caught her. Joi dialed 911 demanding help *now*.

"Breathe." Tens leaned down and whispered the single word in my ear.

I realized I'd been holding my breath.

Joi barreled into what was left of the closet and found an elderly lady, bruised but otherwise fine. Enid couldn't walk, and she couldn't really explain how they'd gotten from upstairs to the closet in time. I didn't know if she suffered dementia, or if the whole incident had rattled her beyond clarity. Directing us to do our thing, Joi took charge of Enid, to cluck over her.

Tony held Juliet, whispering prayers and comfort.

Tens and I knew Bodie, Sema, Nicole and the headmistress should have been somewhere in this mess too.

We yelled and called their names until we were hoarse. Tens, Custos, and I headed into what was left of the scraggly forest. Dumped car parts and a tractor trailer lay crumpled on the footpath. Even the creek had Sheetrock, stuffed animals, and a toilet deposited in the middle of it. The iron fence Bodie had climbed through so many times was dug up and impaled into the heart of a tree. I didn't want to imagine what that might have done to a person.

Tens and I couldn't find the kids by the creek or in any of the debris. I couldn't find Minerva, either. Though Custos did her best to nose around and bark at the odd squirrels poking their heads back out, we were fresh out of places they could hide. There was no birdsong; the world was strangely silent around us.

"Supergirl, check this out." Tens leaned down and

picked up a framed photograph. He used his sleeve to wipe mud from it.

I gasped, "Oh my God, that's Perimo!"

Frantic honking made us look up at a car barreling around debris toward Dunklebarger's remains. Rumi piled out of the car, hollering gibberish at the top of his lungs and waving his arms at us. He charged toward Juliet and we ran to meet him, Tens carrying the photograph.

"What's going on?" I asked.

Tony helped Juliet stand.

Rumi was red and sweaty; his eyes wildly took in the scene. "I checked the cottage. You weren't there or at the store. When I heard where the tornado touched down, I thought, I hoped, you'd be here." He gasped his words.

"Are you okay?" I asked.

He didn't answer, just stared at a piece of paper clutched in his hand. "I found this tacked to the door of my studio with a knife. With the storm, I couldn't get to you soon. I'm so sorry. So very lugubrious."

Tens reached out a hand. "What is it?"

Rumi handed the mangled paper to Tens. "The Nocti, she has Bodie and Sema. She wants your Juliet in exchange."

I gasped.

Juliet swayed to her feet. "The kids? Where are the kids? Are they okay?"

"Of a sort, lass."

"Where are they?" Juliet asked. "Let's go get them."

"Do you know a Ms. Asura?" Rumi questioned.

Juliet nodded, rubbing at her heart. "She's our social worker. Why are you all so upset?"

I blinked, exhaling a great gust of my own. *Of course.* How better to get close to Fenestras coming of age?

Rumi nodded. "She has the children."

"Then they're okay. Right?" Juliet's head swiveled as she glanced first at me, then at Tens, and finally Tony. "Right?"

"For the moment," Tens answered her. I leaned over Tens and saw the note.

DLVR J 2 CRK PRK
2 SM CHLDRN WLL B RTRND
ANSWR PHN 4 INFMTN
—Ms. Asura

"What does that mean?" Juliet asked Tony, puzzled.

Tens stuffed the paper in his pocket.

Rumi glanced at the new dark clouds heading toward us. "Perhaps we'd best get inside to talk strategy?" he asked Tony, as if the two older men were going to lead this charge into the unknown.

"Um, hello?" I called. "Fenestra here, remember? Protector?" I gestured at Tens, then pointed at the men. "You're human."

"You haven't lived long enough, lassie, or you'd know how silly you sound." Rumi smiled. "I know you're the top dog. Lead the way."

"Will someone tell me what's going on?" Juliet asked.

"Me too," Tony added.

Surely we march toward victory together.

Certe ad victoriam simul progredimur.

Luca Lenci

CHAPTER 42

After we told Joi where to find us with news about Enid, she left in the ambulance to care for the elderly woman.

At some point, Juliet had grabbed my hand and hadn't let go. There was no feeling left in my fingers—if anything, her grip seemed to tighten the longer she held on. There was only so much one person was able to handle; I worried we were pushing her past her point of no return.

I felt more complete touching her, though, so I understood her need to cling to that.

We trooped over to Rumi's quarters. The town itself was a mess, but by and large intact. The tornadoes had skirted the most populated areas this time. Rumi and Tony acted like old friends and kindred spirits. Maybe they were.

Rumi brewed coffee and tea, and made hot chocolate, pulling Tens and me into the kitchen. "How much can we talk about? I know it's caliginous, murky, for you."

I knew he was requesting permission to speak frankly, but I also understood he wouldn't if we asked him not to. Between Tyee's connection to Tony and Josiah's use of him as a messenger, I felt like we could trust him. Joi too. And Juliet—well, she had to know everything, even if she didn't want to. "The whole thing."

"You feel okay with that?" Tens brushed my hair behind my ear.

"Do you not?" I asked.

"No, I'm fine. I have a good feeling."

I nodded. "Like this is part of what we're supposed to do."

"Build a coalition?"

"So everything's on the table?" Rumi picked up the tray and waited for my nod. "Good. We're mightier that way."

"Ms. Asura is a social worker?" Tony started the conversation, his pen poised to take notes as needed.

"Yes," Juliet answered. "For all of us."

"She's Nocti," I said. "A bad guy." For simplicity.

"That's not right. You should have multiple caseworkers." Rumi shook his head.

Tony steered us back. "And she has two young children in her care right now."

"Three. Nicole must be there too," Juliet added.

Rumi shot us a look. I had seen the note. There was no mention of Nicole.

Tens held out the photograph he'd found at Dunkle-barger. I handed it to Juliet with my heart in my throat. Klaus Perimo was the Nocti determined to kill me or change me on my sixteenth birthday. "Do you know this man?"

She shook her head. "No, but Mistress had it in her office, on the wall. She hid the file-drawer keys behind it."

"Did she ever talk about him? Did he visit?"

Juliet snorted. "She didn't tell us anything about herself. I never saw him. There were rumors he was her son and others that he was her boyfriend. I don't know. I'm sorry."

"Do you recognize him?" Tony asked, taking the photo and passing it to Rumi, who shrugged.

Tens and I both nodded. "He's Nocti," I said.

"A bad guy?" Juliet asked in clarification.

"Yeah," I answered. A really bad guy.

"I've never seen him around here," Rumi added.

"Mistress was going on vacation." Juliet frowned.

"When?" Tens sharpened.

"She'd given the staff time off, wasn't taking more patients after the sisters. I don't know. I was being transferred for my birthday. It's not like she was going to tell me anything."

"Where were you being taken?"

"I don't know. Kids always leave DG on their sixteenth birthday or right before. No one ever stays longer than that."

"Do they tell you why?"

Juliet shook her head. "No. Ms. Asura sometimes says they go to boarding school. It's vague." She lifted her hands. "I'm sorry, I don't know more."

"Do you remember some names of the others kids? The . ones who've left?" Tony asked. "Maybe we can find them, check online."

"Ah, the Google." Rumi nodded. "Everyone comes up in Google."

The swinging door to the studio rocked open, making us all jump. Tens pulled the gun from his belt. We startled at the meow and bark as the two intruders entered the apartment with tails twitching and thumping. Custos seemed very proud of herself, and Minerva—I had no idea. I think she was pissed, but that might be her normal expression.

"Where'd they come from?" Rumi poked his head into the empty studio behind them.

I laughed. "Custos and Minerva. They're good guys."

"How'd they get in?" Rumi asked.

I shrugged. Tens tucked the gun away, but not before I saw Tony's eyes narrow in speculation.

Minerva leapt up into Juliet's lap, purring. Juliet let go of my hand to bury her face and hands in the cat's hair, but scooted closer on the couch so the sides of our bodies touched. The cat rubbed on my shoulder, the only bit of affection I'd received from her so far. Custos leaned against Tens with her tongue hanging out.

"Can you tell me . . . ," Juliet trailed off, then inhaled a shaky breath with her cheek pressed against Minerva's head. "My mother? Can you tell me what happened?" It was clear her newly uncovered memories were jumbled among years of horror.

Tony tapped a pen along his thigh. "I don't know where to start."

"When did you meet her? Start there." Juliet's voice was muffled but audible against Minerva's side.

I nodded agreement. Airing that story first might be the best way to ease both Juliet and Tony into this world. Ease into the fact that Ms. Asura was a Nocti, and odds weren't good she'd just hand over the kids without trying to take a Fenestra with her.

Tony cleared his throat, his expression one of remembrance. "Her name was Roshana Ambrose. She loved you. So much."

Juliet repeated her mother's name. "Roshana?"

Tony nodded. "I was Father Anthony in those days. Roshana came into the sanctuary late at night, when it was empty of humans and fullest of the Lord's spirit. I loved nighttime in a church, still do. So I often recited my own prayers, conducted my own conversations with God, and handed over my worry in the hours around midnight. That's how we met.

"One night, after the Christmas season, after Epiphany, she stumbled in. She had a demeanor, an expression, I've often seen within the walls of a church: of someone seeking something, wanting faith, wanting answers, but not sure how to act or where to go. A soul search in progress. I greeted her and let her be."

"What does she look like?" Juliet asked.

Did. What did *she look like.* I didn't correct her, because if Juliet was lucky she'd see her mother again at the window. Bringing up her mother's death again seemed cruel and unnecessary.

"You." He smiled. "She might have been an inch or two taller, but you have the same hair and the same eyes. The same shoulders that seem burdened by carrying the world's troubles all by yourself."

Juliet nodded, her eyes glued to the pattern in Minerva's fur. "Go on."

With Juliet sitting next to me, it was easy to see her resemblance to her mother. If Roshana hadn't been so disfigured when Auntie showed her to me, she and Juliet could have been mistaken for sisters.

Tony continued. "She carried a backpack with her, which wasn't unusual. I went about my business and when I turned she'd gone." He waved his hand. "The next night she was back. Same pew. Wearing the same clothes. The same expression. I greeted her as before and went back to my work. Again, she disappeared."

We held our collective breath as Tony shared. Even Custos and Minerva listened to the story in rapt attention.

"The third night, I placed a bottle of water and a sandwich in her pew. Just in case. Just a feeling, she might be hungry. She returned. And thanked me for the food. Again, we went our separate silent ways. Or so I thought. I went to shut up the sanctuary and found she'd fallen asleep in the pew. I couldn't wake her, nor was I willing to leave her alone. So I too made a bed of a pew across the aisle from her and napped while she slept. Nightmares woke her, her screams woke me. Asleep, she let me hold her, comfort her. Like a daughter, a child. She was young. As young as you. And so scared. Terrified."

Juliet found my hand again and clung. She too seemed to know nightmares intimately.

"It became routine to see her during the night. I brought her clothes and food. Soon it became clear she was pregnant. Almost overnight, she went from not showing to far along. She had a frame like yours, built to carry children easily. She started to trust me with her thoughts and questions. These became conversations, and after several weeks, she let me show her a back room in the recesses of the choir loft. It had been storage for instruments and books, but was empty now. It was a perfect place for sanctuary.

"I gave her the key and showed her where the visiting nun's quarters were, so she could bathe and launder her clothing. She cried. It was as if no one had ever been kind to her."

"What did you want?" Juliet asked.

"Excuse me?" Tony seemed taken aback by her question.

"Why did you help her?" I could tell Juliet wasn't trying to be rude—she genuinely didn't understand why he might help a stranger.

Tony sat forward, not breaking eye contact with Juliet. "I would have done the same for anyone—the homeless often slept in the pews when the shelter downstairs was full. It was part of my commitment to the Lord. That is part of my faith."

"But you did more than that."

"I prayed on it and I felt that it was part of a bigger plan. It felt right to help her. I wanted nothing but for her to find comfort and safety. Honestly, I had no hidden motive." Tony's expression was full of gravity.

His answers seemed to appease Juliet, who nodded at him.

Tony continued. "She began to come to Mass and then clean the pews, restock. She watched me work, mimicked me. We'd talk. Gradually she trusted me and I her. She loved to walk. She'd disappear for hours outside, even in winter, walking and thinking. Sometimes, she shared these musings with me, but mostly we talked of big ideas or books. She loved to read and began to make her way through the church library. She brought furniture from storage to make the room a home. She worked in the soup kitchen we ran and ate the leftovers. She didn't want charity; if I asked about her family she slammed shut like a door. I got her to see a nun who was also a midwife, to make sure you were doing well. She'd been silently suffering through contractions for hours by the time she alerted me. Stubborn and willful—it wouldn't surprise me if you'd inherited those strengths from your mother." He smiled. "But the night you were born was magical." He lifted his hands toward the ceiling in thanks. "At midnight on the vernal equinox. The day between the darkest and the lightest days of the year."

Juliet interrupted him. "No, you're wrong. My birthday is February tenth."

Tony vehemently disagreed. "No, she begged me to keep your birth date a secret, and you were a big, healthy baby. I'd never seen her so adamant about anything. It was easy to say that you were a month old when people asked. You never cried. Always smiled."

"But why lie about my birthday?" Juliet glanced at me.

Tony shook his head and held out his palms. "I don't know. She was adamant. I assumed it had to do with your father or her family, neither of which she'd talk about. I didn't question her further. What harm could that do? It was just a date and so important to her."

I interjected, "I think she lied about your birth date to protect you from the bad guys. We're only born on certain dates—in my family it's the winter solstice when it falls on the twenty-first. I think maybe in yours it's the spring equinox. If she knew who you were, if she was one of us, then maybe she was trying to keep you hidden by making it clear you were born at an altogether different time."

"Oh." Juliet blinked, then asked Tony, "What about my father?"

Tony's eyes saddened. "I don't know. I'm sorry. She would never say. You have to understand she arrived at the church shattered, traumatized. It took me weeks to learn her name, to move without her flinching. I needed her trust. I needed to build a relationship so she'd let me help her. I was afraid she'd run away and then be on the streets, pregnant. She didn't act like a street kid, more like she was hiding from someone awful."

"Didn't anyone else notice she was pregnant?" I asked.

"If they did, they didn't say anything. She wore layers and baggy clothes in the beginning; the closer it got to your arrival, the more she stayed hidden in her room. She only crept around at night when the church was mostly empty." He turned to Juliet, full on. "Your mother loved you. She adored you. I've never seen a more devoted mother, not even the women who came through the doors with a dozen precious darlings. She did everything for you. Never got frustrated, or whined that you required all her time and energy. She rarely set you down and you were completely at ease being carted around the sanctuary in a baby sling. She hung the stars on your eyes." His smile broadened, then dimmed.

"What happened?" I asked, when the silence stretched.

"She worried. I'd catch her having whispered conversations on her knees. 'Pleading with the Lord?' I asked. She wouldn't let me help her. She wouldn't tell me what was so grievous that she couldn't share the burden with me."

Juliet gulped. The tension in our group climbed.

"She left you with me for several hours, that last day." He paused, drawing in a labored breath as if what followed was too painful to give voice. "You were almost a year old. She looked entirely different when she returned. I almost didn't recognize her. Her clothes were conservative and tailored. Expensive. She wore impeccable makeup and had her hair pulled back in a bun at the base of her neck. She was even wearing high heels and had real pearls around her neck. Her eyes were flat, like someone who knows their days are numbered. She was different."

"How so?"

"Some of this is pure speculation, but she was clearly hiding in the church, hiding you from everyone. You were such a good baby that part was easy. 'Worried' doesn't express the fear I saw when she looked at you that day. She wouldn't hold you, wouldn't touch you. I think she was arming herself, trying to will herself to leave you.

"I followed her to the little room she'd made her home. She offered no explanation for the transformation, but instead asked me if I still believed in the ancient practice of giving sanctuary. She cited examples from our own church library collections. She didn't need to. I would have done almost anything to chase that expression from her face.

"She made me promise to find a family for you that would love you and raise you as their own. If I couldn't find one, then I was to raise you. Protect you. We baptized you and she asked me to be your godfather. She swore me to tell you the truth before your sixteenth birthday. To tell you of her and give you a book."

I perked up. "A diary?" Maybe Juliet's mom had left a journal too.

"No, it's a book of sonnets. At least, that's what it says on the cover. There's a CD tucked into it as well."

"You didn't read it? Listen to the disc?" Tens interjected.

"No, she asked me not to, not until I was ready to tell

you. I put both in a safe-deposit box and left instructions with my will, in case anything happened to me in the meantime."

"How?" Juliet whispered.

"She had a meeting to attend, she said. One that would determine your future. She hinted that it was with your father. She made me promise not to follow her."

"You followed, right?" I asked.

"I was conflicted, but yes, I followed. I thought she might need backup. The midwife looked after you. I trusted her."

"What happened?" Juliet whispered.

I squeezed her hand, trying to convey comfort. I knew this couldn't possibly be easy to hear.

"She met with a woman. Harsh. Manicured. Dark. The woman grabbed her arm and thrust her into a car. Roshana was crying. I wanted to react. I wanted to do something, but actions failed me. I kept thinking about you." He glanced at Juliet with tears in his eyes. "They drove past where I stood. And I met your mother's eyes. She nodded at me like she completely expected me to be there. She mouthed 'Thank you.' That was the last time I saw her."

Juliet turned to me and asked, "But you know her?"

How do I say this gently? "Like I told you at the Feast, I've seen her on the other side."

"Of what?"

"Of life. She's dead." I tried to speak softly, as if I could lessen the impact by gentling my tone.

"She's really dead?" Juliet grabbed her hand away

from mine. It was as if this last piece was asking too much of her acceptance.

Tens nodded to confirm my declaration.

"That's what I thought," Tony said.

"What happened then?" Rumi prodded Tony to continue.

"I went to the police. I reported an abduction. There was nothing they could do. They thought she'd merely run away again. Or her parents had found her. Like I said, she was young, around your age. They didn't take me seriously. Not that I blame them, there was so little to go on. Her name wasn't even right."

"What do you mean?" Juliet asked.

"I told them her name was Roshana Ambrose. There was no such person—not that they could find." He seemed to deflate. "I returned to the church, to you. And on my desk was a letter for me she'd left. It said that the truth would challenge everything I'd ever thought about my religion and would require a new faith from me. But that she couldn't tell me how it ended yet because she didn't know. She feared she would never return. She repeated her demands to care for you and protect you."

"Then how?" Juliet asked, aghast.

"How did you end up in that hellhole?" Tens clarified. She nodded.

Tony continued. "I raised you until you were just past your sixth birthday. I took dozens of photos. I tried to capture every moment for your mother, but I gave up when the photos kept not turning out."

"That's a Fenestra thing," I said.

"What?" Juliet turned to me.

"There's something about film and even digital images that makes it hard to capture a Fenestra—what gets captured is the light the dying see instead of our human form. As we gain control, we can have pictures taken of us."

"Do you?"

"I don't know. I wasn't able to before, but I haven't tried recently."

Juliet seemed overwhelmed, so overcome that she no longer questioned any of the reality we threw her way. It was as if she'd passed the point of ludicrous, so now everything was acceptable. "Please, go on?" Juliet asked Tony. "How did I end up here?"

"Not being able to adopt you is one of the reasons I left the church. But early in your life they transferred me to the orphanage and school, so I could help raise you there. With the nuns. You were like my own child, Juliet. I kept looking for the right family. We'd get close, but something always happened to derail the paperwork. Once you handed me a dead kitten you'd found and asked me if you could keep it—I was standing with prospective parents and they were spooked. You were such a serious child, always outdoors, always trying to heal animals who'd been hit by cars. You were fascinated by the saints and their stories. You had a favorite stuffed animal named Tiger."

"A cat?" I asked.

Tony nodded. I wondered if that was why Minerva was in this form. Juliet had a foundation of comfort from a feline. I could tell from Tens's speculative expression he was thinking the same thing.

Tony shrugged. "We made it work. I know my other parishioners sometimes suffered, but I felt my first obligation was to you. There were times when I felt like you were handed to me directly by God for my devotion, my trials. And then I was called to New York for the weekend. I left you with the same nun I had trusted in the past. Before I departed, the Bishop told me they were shutting down the school and dispersing us all. There was scandal with another priest. It was ugly, and I decided to leave and take you with me, after I returned from New York. I was actually planning to go find Tyee." Tony shrugged.

"But you didn't," Tens said.

"No." Tony stood and paced. "When I returned, chaos abounded. My nun friend was dead, a heart attack. You were gone. The other nuns said a woman had shown up claiming to be your grandmother. When they were skeptical, she produced a signed statement from me saying it was okay to release the baby, that'd I'd been delayed in New York. She left an address and contact information. Of course, I hadn't given her any of it."

"Was she the same woman?" I asked.

"As the one who rode off with Roshana? Based on what the nuns said, yes."

"Did you check the contact info?" Tens asked.

"Bogus?" Rumi added.

Tony nodded. "The building was empty and cleared out. I searched for you, Juliet. I've never stopped praying for you. And I prayed every day that God would send an angel, an army of angels, to guide you, protect you, help you survive until I found you again." Tears rolled down his face. He knelt at her feet. "Please forgive me for not doing more. If I'd taken you to New York with me, it wouldn't have happened. If I'd made your mother tell me, I could have helped her, too."

I shook my head. "Nocti are more powerful than you realize. If they were involved, you're lucky not to be dead."

Juliet fingered her braid. "You really kept looking for me?"

"I did. I pay a private investigator to look for you—he monitors online transactions and records. Anything that your name might appear on. I can't believe it's been a decade. To be in the same state, hours from you, and now to be so close and never see you. I am so sorry for what you've endured. Maybe if I had been here or stayed with the church? I don't know." He reached a hand out toward Juliet and let it hang there. "I hope that someday you'll forgive me."

Juliet lightly touched his fingers. "I remember you. I remember my mother. You've given me that. And you tried to find me." She nodded. "If you'd known I was at DG, would you have come to get me?"

Minerva rubbed against Tony's hands and shins.

"By all that I consider holy, I swear to you, I never

would have left you there. Or anywhere. I truly thought of you and your mother as my family. I'm not going anywhere. As long as you want me in your life, I'm here and I'm sticking. We'll fight the bad guys and rescue your friends."

"There's nothing to forgive, T." She gave him a small twist of her lips.

"You remember!" Tony laughed. "She used to call me T all the time!" he told the rest of us.

I felt as if I was watching Juliet heal, a fraction perhaps, but knitting her heart back together just the same.

Rumi slammed down the rest of his coffee. "I hate to bring us into the now, but there are two bantlings we have to find. How do we rescue them?"

The seriousness of our current situation turned all of us into frowning, furrowed worriers.

Tony stood, looking at Tens. "Your grandfather would tell us to turn and fight."

Tens nodded. "Agreed."

Rumi rubbed his hands together. "I packed quite a punch in my youth."

"I don't think it's going to be a fistfight." I couldn't resist a smile. Custos jumped with her paws against Rumi's chest and pushed him back into his chair. She licked his face with such verve it made all of us laugh.

The phone rang, reminding us all of what we were waiting for. It was closest to me. Rumi shrugged around Custos sitting in his lap. "The note said to pick it up."

I did, while Tens placed his hand on my shoulder and squeezed reassurances. "Rumi's Glass Studio. How may I help you?" This cracked up Rumi and made me smile too.

Until I heard "This is Kirian. Can I talk to Juliet?"

I leave these words in the margins of a book most people will never think to open. It is my hope you'll never need them because I will be able to tell you all of this in person. But Ms. Asura wants me back and I can't risk her knowing of you. Not when your gifts are like mine.

—R.

CHAPTER 43
Juliet

Meridian held out the phone, but Rumi quickly pressed the speakerphone button so we could all listen.

"Juliet?" Kirian's voice sounded scared and determined.

My head pounded. My stomach rolled. I wanted to curl up and try to assimilate all the information. My mother loved me. As much as I'd prayed to know that, it was hard to believe it was real. She *loved* me.

Kirian repeated, "Jewel, talk to me."

"How did you know I was here?" I asked. Meridian was holding the question up on a piece of paper. I was grateful she was able to think. I didn't have the strength to do this alone.

"I don't know where you are. Ms. Asura dialed the phone. You need to come to me. I can explain everything."

"So explain. I want to talk to Nicole. Put Bodie on the phone. Or Sema."

"Not on the phone. I can't. Please, Jewel? I love you. I've always loved you. We can be together. Live the rest of our lives. Travel the world. Just like we talked about. Don't you remember?" His words rushed together in excitement or desperation, as if he too was being told what to say.

I remembered a lot of things, and if I'd trusted myself more I would have realized the little boy who had loved me was gone. I didn't know this Kirian at all. "Where are Bodie and Sema? Nicole?"

"Who's Nicole?" he asked.

He sounded genuinely puzzled. "Where are they?" My voice cracked at the top.

"Calm down. Bodie and Sema are fine. You can see for yourself."

Meridian touched my arm. The paper said, *Where?*

"Where?" I asked.

"Follow the Wildcat from DG to where it merges with the Wabash," he said.

"Can't we meet at DG? Or the coffee shop Ms. Asura took me to?" I asked, hoping for something more public.

"Hold on." It sounded like Kirian put his hand over the

receiver and talked to someone. We all exchanged looks. Tens and Meridian whispered over the paper. I waited.

Finally, Kirian said, "No, you have to meet me along the creek where the waters meet."

"Let me talk to Bodie," I demanded.

"Juliet, trust me. I've never done anything bad to you. Meet me at midnight." Kirian clicked off.

"Why midnight?" Tens queried.

I shook my head. I didn't even know what day it was.

Meridian ran to the calendar hanging on Rumi's fridge. "They think tomorrow's your birthday."

"But it's not," Rumi said.

"They don't know that, though."

"At least we know something they don't," Tony said.

Rumi's phone rang again. This time it was Joi, saying Enid had been released from the hospital and was coming home with her.

"Where's the bathroom?" I asked. I needed to throw cold water on my face and gather my composure or cry. Whichever came first, the other was sure to follow.

Meridian said, "I'll show you."

I followed her down the hallway. I heard the men start talking about plans and strategies. I felt as if I were hovering above the whole scene as a spectator.

Meridian flipped on the light switch and moved out of my way. The light felt harsh as I leaned over the sink. Bruises ringed my eyes and a bloody scratch ran down one cheek. Meridian hesitated, then backed away.

"Wait." I turned to her. "Stay? Please?"

She nodded and sat down on the lip of the bathtub.

I had never been alone, not really. There was always someone needing something. Since Mini and Nicole had arrived, the brief moments of alone under the stairs or by the creek were golden gifts, but only because I knew they were there. "I don't know how to—what to do." I leaned against the sink, turned the water to cold, and splashed my face, hoping the chill might ease the ache in my head.

She stayed silent.

I stared at my face in the mirror. The bruises turned my eyes into hollow sockets. My hair was lank and dull. My skin looked as if I'd never seen the sun. Vanity was never something I clung to—I'd have been eaten alive by the need—but I certainly looked as bad on the outside as I felt on the inside. "What am I again?"

She blinked. "A Fenestra. You help the dying get to heaven, the afterlife."

"How?"

"We look human until someone is dying and then we are the light they see and move toward, through us, to transition."

"I'm not human?"

"Not all of you. It's like a recessive gene that only works if you're born on the solstice or equinox—I used to think only the winter solstice, but now I guess all the seasonal midpoints are possible."

Pieces of my life started to fit together. All those times I'd held the hand of a dying person and saw things, knew things I shouldn't have. "Then it wasn't my imagination, was it?"

"What?" She leaned against the wall like she was afraid I'd spook again. Couldn't really blame her for the caution.

"I've started to fall asleep and daydream when they're dying. I taste things, know recipes and foods that I shouldn't. Do you?"

"You're probably fainting from the strain of the energy trying to use you. But you're not a full window until you're sixteen. So souls probably push. Have you been standing at windows?"

"No, nothing like that. I dream of my mom, or cities. Mostly I can taste their favorite foods and know how to make them."

"Has it always been like that?"

"No. I mean, I've always cooked, but only in the past year, since Mini showed up. It got worse when Nicole came, but I thought that was because I could relax more—"

"Minerva is more than just a cat. I think she transitioned the souls with you to keep you safe."

I sat down on the toilet, my legs turning to jelly. "Is Nicole dead? Could she have died in the tornado?"

Meridian handed me a fluffy towel. "I don't know. Maybe. I don't think she's with Ms. Asura and Kirian, though."

"She believed in angels," I said, thinking about Nicole's necklace.

"You don't?"

"It's hard to believe in anything that let that place exist."

"You're part angel. And you're real. I know it's a lot to take in, but do you think maybe Nicole was your—"

I waved her off. "So Ms. Asura wants to trade me for the

little kids. Or Kirian wants me to leave with him? Why are they doing this?"

"There are Aternocti—Nocti for short—that take the dying to hell. They want to turn us into them, or kill us. They think that tomorrow is your birthday and it will open the window. They may try to convince you to join them nicely, but if that doesn't work, then they'll probably try to take you someplace and force you to transition."

"And you're saying that Ms. Asura is one of those Nocti?"

"Yes. And I think Kirian—"

I put my head between my knees, trying to breathe.

Meridian scooted over onto the floor, at my feet. "I know this is a lot to take in. I'm sorry, I wish I could make it easier for you. I really do. The good news is that your window won't open until March, so we have time. If we, you, can make it through this, then there's time."

"If we get through this?"

"Right," Meridian whispered.

"What if I go with Kirian?" I asked. "Will they let Bodie and Sema go?"

"You have that choice. We can't stop you."

"I have to protect Bodie and Sema." Thoughts and images swirled in my head, whirling me around until the dizziness was too much to bear.

"I know."

Does Kirian really love me? Or is it a trick? There was a time before he left that we lay wrapped in blankets by the creek in the wee hours of the morning and talked about our futures, the family we'd make together. Places we'd travel to and see.

He'd been the one person that made my world feel less scary. "He loves me." Until Nicole and Mini, he was the only person I could count on.

"Sure."

"No, he has to love me."

Meridian seemed to hesitate. "I heard a woman talking to a young man one day by the creek."

"When?"

"I was on my way to see you. Minerva tripped me. The woman—I think it was Ms. Asura—told the man he had to do whatever it took to be 'Romeo.'"

I gasped. I had called Kirian "Romeo" quietly, when no one else was around.

"I think Kirian was that man. I think maybe he's changed." She offered each word cautiously.

"Is Tens your boyfriend?" I asked.

"He's more than that, he's a Protector."

I nodded, as if that made sense. "Have you and Tens—?"

"What?"

I blushed, but I needed to know. "Um, you know, yeah?"

"No, not yet." She shook her head and bit her lip.

"Why not?"

"I think—" She shrugged. "I don't know. We haven't known each other long enough. I don't think we're in a rush. He goes above and beyond to not pressure me."

"Why not? It's what you do when you love someone."

"Maybe, but it needs to be right." She shredded a piece of toilet paper. "So you've—"

I swallowed. "Yeah, once."

"With Kirian?"

"Mmm." He was leaving the next day, his sixteenth birthday. His meager belongings were packed. That night, we crept into the vacant Train Room. In the dark, we groped and undressed. It wasn't the first time we'd made out. I wanted him to stay. I wanted to go with him. I wanted to give him a reason to stay with me. "It's pretty common for kids to hook up at DG. Sometimes it was the only thing that felt good. I loved him."

"I get it. How old were you?"

"Thirteen." Saying it aloud it made it sound young, too young. Kirian wasn't inexperienced, not like me. I gave him my virginity. "It felt right at the time."

"Now?"

"He still left without me."

"That hurts?"

I nodded.

Tens knocked on the door. "Ladies? We have a plan to go over, when you're ready."

I stood, knees shaky.

"Can you do this?" Meridian asked. "We can go without you."

"Kirian told me to come alone."

"Well, you're not alone and you're not going alone. We're a team and we'll get the kids and then maybe you can talk to Kirian. Maybe he does love you and he's not working with the Nocti."

I nodded. *Or maybe he used me, too.*

> Let the creatures of all that is good and light be
> with us tonight.
>
> **Cassie Ailey**

CHAPTER 44

The worry about Juliet's physical and mental health was overwhelming. I kept silently praying that Nicole really was her guardian angel and she'd appear to help. I didn't think Juliet could take one more blow. She was stronger than anyone I'd ever come across. To live in that horror and be able to nurture kids and love, without turning bitter and cold, blew my mind.

Tens hugged me tightly to him. We didn't speak. There were no words. Besides, I knew Tens didn't need them.

Rumi was fumbling with his stereo. "What's he doing?" I whispered to Tens.

"He says he has Juliet's anthem for her to hear."

Juliet sank onto the couch, clutching Minerva to her chest.

Tony brought over a plate of take-out food and urged her to eat. I watched her take a few bites to appease him. He hovered around her, like the father I thought he identified as.

Rumi pressed Play and said to Juliet, "Your mother named you well. Take a listen."

The B-52s called her name and Juliet lowered her head to her hands. The beat and lyrics flowed over us.

Juliet, I can feel your glow . . .
Juliet, you're not afraid anymore. . . .

I can't explain it completely, but the song warmed our souls. It was as if the sun came out and filled us with hope. I could almost see Auntie and Roshana clapping their hands in the corner of the room, smiling and laughing.

As the last note of the song faded, Juliet lifted her head. "Play it again?"

Rumi hit Repeat, turned the volume up high enough to rattle the windows and shake the glassware in the next room. He swung me into his arms for a twirl around the room. Tens's toes tapped and he bopped his head to the rhythm. Tony played an invisible drum set with the gusto of a rock star.

Custos wagged her tail and I swear Minerva batted a paw to the beat. Juliet picked the cat up and swayed with her. It was the first time I'd seen Juliet relax and even smile.

The third time through, Tens cut in, embracing me. Who knew Tens was such a good dancer? His feet moved and mine followed his steps. Tony escorted Juliet to the dance floor of the kitchen, while Rumi pranced back and forth with Custos on her hind legs and front paws on his shoulders.

We all let loose and boogied. Pure joy and a common love united all of us. We were going to rescue the kids and defeat the Nocti and heal Juliet. We *would*. There was no other possible outcome.

As the song faded, Juliet broke the silence. "So what exactly is the plan?"

"We're going to kick some ass," Rumi answered her with a grin.

We were ready.

> Be strong, my daughter, and know that generations of our line stand at your back and cheer you on.
>   —R.

CHAPTER 45
Juliet

Father Anthony—*No*, I mentally corrected myself, *Tony*—called on everything he knew about the military to help us formulate the plan. "We turn toward the ambush and fight. We don't run. They won't be expecting it. Let them think things are going their way until it's too late." He made sense. When he reminded Meridian and Tens about a man named Josiah who'd told them unity was their strength, I remembered to mention the words I'd heard from whoever, whatever, that had saved Enid and me from the tornado. Those too talked about standing together.

We'd mapped the spot where I was supposed to meet Kirian and Ms. Asura. That was where I headed now. Alone. At least it looked that way. We had no idea if they were watching me. A few minutes before midnight I stumbled over a tree root and swore.

I had a flashlight, but it didn't seem to make a bit of difference. My heart thumped a wicked, heavy tempo. Kirian had changed, but then, I knew I had too. I was no longer the little girl he'd left. I'd grown up in these three years; I'd taken care of the house and raised the kids he and Ms. Asura now threatened. I felt fierce and unstoppable. Maybe I didn't really understand our enemy, but that was okay. I trusted Tony, and Minerva. I knew it would take time to completely trust Meridian and Tens, but I was on my way to having a group of people I could count on. Right now, Bodie and Sema, maybe even Nicole, counted on me to come through for them.

In these woods, my new friends were prepared and positioned. The full moon hung creamy and voluptuous in the sky. It made the frost on the tree branches sparkle and bling and made crunching through the undergrowth noisy. I wore one of Rumi's enormous down coats, which swallowed me but chased the chill away.

Meridian was nearby. She had promised she would hear me and respond if I called out, but I couldn't see her. Her velvet scarf was wrapped around my neck and I wore Tony's gloves on my hands. There was comfort in wearing their belongings. I closed my eyes and whispered, "Mom, if you can hear me, I need you. Please help me do the right thing."

I stepped out into the clearing and a spotlight shone directly into my eyes, blinding me.

"Jewel, you came!" Kirian ran forward, sweeping me up in his arms, in an unusually demonstrative way. Shocked at his greeting, I froze while he hugged me tightly, his breath on my ear, his cheek pressed against mine. Into my ear, he whispered, "When I say run, you run. You can't trust her. Or me."

"Kirian, put her down! You stupid child," Ms. Asura, impeccably dressed as always, screeched. "Come here."

He backed away, leaving me confused and stranded under the bright light blinding me. I tried to shield my eyes until she lowered it out of my face.

"Hello, Juliet."

"Hi," I answered. "I'm here. Where are Bodie and Sema?" How I'd ever seen her as good and caring was beyond me. There was nothing warm about her, nothing loving in her eyes.

"They're nearby," she said, putting her hand firmly on Kirian's shoulder. His eyes begged my forgiveness.

"Where?" I shouted, losing patience. With new eyes, I saw how cowed he was, how scared, how desolate.

Ms. Asura shook her finger at me. "Such theatrics. First, you have to swear you'll come with us."

"Fine."

"And join our cause."

"Fine. Just let the kids go." I needed to hear where they were stashed. I needed her to say it. My mouth was dry and pasty; I was sure my heart would burst under the pressure. This had to work.

The leaves on the ground were caught up in a breeze. The trees swayed. Vines growing on the trees seemed to move too, like snakes, or arms with fingers.

"Kirian, get that bag, will you?" Ms. Asura pointed to Bodie's backpack lying against a tree on the edge of the clearing. He loped over to pick it up. As he straightened, one of the vines undraped from the tree and twined about his neck. She flicked another finger and I realized she was controlling them.

"Run!" Kirian screamed, clutching at the vine with frantic fingers. He clawed at the vine and it tightened, lifting him until he was on his tiptoes, trying to breathe. Other vines wrapped around his limbs and his torso, holding him captive.

I started forward to help him.

"Uh—don't move," Ms. Asura yelled at me.

I froze. Meridian had warned me that there was something about the poison ivy that wasn't natural. That I was to stay as far into the clearing as I could, to be on the safe side.

"I'm sure your new friends are filling your head with all sorts of stories about me. Most of them true. Maybe. Probably."

"Why are you doing this? I don't understand." I stalled, watching Kirian's face turn shades of red, then purple.

She checked her watch. "Happy birthday, Juliet. For a gift, I thought about getting you jewelry or a car. But how about something else?"

"Let him go. He can't breathe!" I screamed back at her.

"You're insane." I heard the woods whispering. The vines hanging on the trees seemed to move independently of the wind. They curled and unfurled from the trunks of trees and from the brambles like fingers crooked in our direction. Slithering like tongues darting out.

"Quite the opposite. We laughed about you, you know? While we were in bed together, Kirian told me all about your little crush. How silly you were. How sad. To think anyone could really love you. Enough to take you away? Your mommy abandoned you. Kirian laughed at you. You're not enough."

Anger clouded my vision. "Let them go. What do you want from me?"

Kirian thrashed around, trying to speak.

"We can tell her the truth now, darling," Ms. Asura said to him. Then to me, "Aren't you angry? He used you. And you suffered years of abuse. Aren't you ready for a little payback? Do you feel the rage?"

I did. I felt every slap and taunt and wound. But I gave no outward sign. Meridian's warning to not let Ms. Asura get me emotional helped shield my emotions. I'd had practice with Mistress. Practice hiding my anger, my rage, my despair. So I used all of that and channeled my grief into muscle tension and a glare that willed Ms. Asura the very pain she was inflicting on Kirian, on me.

"Give in to what I see in your eyes."

I let her see, perhaps giving her what she wanted might buy Kirian a breath.

She applauded. "Now all you have to do is let him die. Help me send him away forever. Then we can deal with the others, like Meridian."

At the mention of Meridian's name, cold doused the hot anger and I suddenly felt more in control. *I'm not alone. I'm not alone.* "I—I don't know," I stuttered. How did she know about Meridian?

"You don't really expect me to believe that, do you? He betrayed you. He's done everything I've asked of him and more. You're alone, you need me. You need us. Meridian can't give you what you want. I can tell you about your mother. Your father. I can give you history *and* a future. Then we'll show Meridi—"

"Lay off, bitch, I'm right here." Meridian stepped from the woods opposite us and came to stand next to me. She grabbed my hand and I felt instantly better.

"When I said come alone, you thought that meant bring a friend?" Ms. Asura cackled. "Priceless."

"Two," Nicole said as she came from the woods behind me and stepped up to take my other hand. Tears flooded my eyes. She wasn't dead.

"A party to initiate Juliet into our family. How nice. You know, Nicole, I didn't figure out where you came from until the tornado. Did you tell Juliet you'd been using her, trying to get her to join you?"

Holding hands with Meridian and Nicole, I saw the empty black holes where Ms. Asura's eyes should be. Nocti. As if I had any doubt after this performance.

"She didn't believe she deserved a guardian angel, thanks to all your treatment. You and that monster in charge of Dunklebarger." Nicole squeezed my hand, then continued to prod Ms. Asura. "You killed the headmistress, didn't you?"

"Of course I did. She was getting greedy. Always wanting

more money for her services. Thinking Klaus wanted her instead of me. When she told me she was the brains behind the whole operation I couldn't help myself. Don't tell me you're sad?" Ms. Asura demanded.

"No." Nicole and I spoke in unison.

"Good. Then this'll be easy. He used you, too, Juliet." The vines tightened around Kirian's throat. His face turned a black shade of purple and his eyes bulged.

Nicole seemed to try to loosen the vines with her eyes, but she shook her head sadly at Meridian. She couldn't win that battle. I didn't want Kirian to die. He didn't deserve death.

Tens came out of the woods behind a leashed Custos and took Meridian's free hand.

The wolf growled and showed all of her teeth. Rumi and Tony followed a similarly leashed Mini and stood next to Nicole. Mini was puffed up and spitting hisses. They were all draped in glowing glass balls. We were a line of light, of love, of strength.

Kirian gasped.

Meridian's hand tightened in mine and I stood next to her at a window.

"Where are we?" I asked.

"We're in my window room. I'm sorry, but I think this means Kirian is dying." She held my hand and didn't let go.

I nodded. The window looked across Wildcat Creek. On the other side I saw kids coming closer, waving, some running and jumping and playing. A few swung from branches into the creek to swim. It was summer there and the woods were in full bloom with birds and insects. Catfish swam in the creek. It was my favorite time of year. Mine and Kirian's.

"Jewel?" Kirian was next to me, looking beyond. "I'm sorry."

"I know." I didn't hold back the tears.

"I loved you. I did. It was real." He brushed the tears from my cheeks, but I couldn't feel him.

"You need to go on now," Meridian said to him.

We all turned and studied the figures approaching from the other bank. I recognized a bunch of kids and a few elderly patients—Miss Claudia and Paddy, the grandparents Kirian and I had adopted ourselves to years ago. And Enid's sister, Glee.

"Nicole!" I saw her wave from the crowd and felt a warmth around my neck. I looked down and realized her necklace was dangling over my heart. I smiled and waved back to her.

"That's my auntie." Meridian pointed. "She's holding your—"

Kirian jumped through the window, making a cannon-ball into the creek. "Be good!" he called to me, swimming to the bank and our crowd of friends.

A loud scream brought me right back into my body. Back into the cold, wintry woods. Back to our row of light and the battle against Ms. Asura and her darkness. I didn't have time to process anything.

I opened my eyes. The light we generated together was so bright, I squinted against the glare. Nicole's necklace also glowed around my neck.

Ms. Asura was screaming, screeching in a primal release that made goose bumps break across my skin.

"What's happening?" I yelled at Meridian.

"I think she's burning. I don't know," she replied, never taking her eyes off Ms. Asura.

Tony recited the Lord's Prayer in Latin. Rumi mumbled words in a language I didn't recognize. Tens and Meridian stared straight ahead. Custos barked and Mini hissed.

We are the light. Brighter than the sun on silver or glass. A million megawatts of good.

Ms. Asura was boiling. Her skin bubbled up as she ran from us into the woods.

"Should we follow?" I asked.

"No, we can't kill her without a Sangre and we need to find the kids. They could have been out here for hours."

"What if she's heading toward them? She could hurt them." Rumi took steps toward the singed path she had left. We dropped hands.

The light dimmed back down to a normal level.

Tens said, "We found the van. But the kids weren't inside. It's in that direction."

It was only seconds, but I glanced down and realized I was clutching Tony's hand. "Where's Nicole?"

They all shook their heads. No one had any idea. "Was she here?" I asked.

Meridian nodded. "She was here. But you saw her with Auntie and your mom. She's gone, at least for now—" She broke off and shrugged.

I'd puzzle it out later. I loped over to Kirian's body. "Kirian? Kirian? Help me!" I pleaded.

Tony checked for his pulse as I pulled his inert frame into my lap.

"I'm sorry. We couldn't save him." Tony held me while I wept.

"How are we going to find the wee ones?" Rumi asked.

Meridian looked up at the moon, at the stars sharing her sky. "We, uh, need help. Auntie? Josiah? Roshana? Nicole?" She called to the night. Waiting. She turned to Tens. "Any ideas where to start?"

I wiped my eyes. Bodie and Sema needed me. Kirian was beyond my help now; if he'd made it to summer at the creek, maybe life was okay for him.

A blinking in the woods sparked my attention.

"What's that?" Meridian saw it too.

Another tiny light blinked out of the woods toward us.

"And that?" Tens pointed to yet another.

"Those are fireflies," Rumi said, moving toward them.

"It's too early," Tony commented.

They came all around us in a swarm. The temperature rose and the night illuminated to day.

I gasped.

"Are you thinking what I'm thinking?" Rumi asked Meridian and Tens.

They nodded. I wanted in on the inside info.

"The story of the firefly feast? The little boy who followed his mother's soul?"

One firefly stopped in front of my nose, hovered, and seemed to wait for me to notice it. "What do we do?" I asked.

"We're following!" Rumi boomed loudly into the night. The bugs began to form a lighted trail along the creek, through the woods. They became both a lantern and the borders of a path we walked between like a garland.

"Bodie? Sema?" we called.

I don't know how far we walked. It felt like hours and only seconds rolled into one. Time stood still.

The path ended in a swarm of pulsing light. The temperature was balmy, almost too warm for my coat, and no frost covered the forest floor or trees. The kids were huddled together against a log. Duct tape covered their mouths and their hands were tied. Dirt was smeared across their cheeks and knees. They looked like they'd fallen into a mud pit.

I ran and slid into them, holding them tightly, then ripping at the bindings. "Are you okay? Are you hurt?"

Someone undid the tape and ropes and Bodie threw his arms around my neck.

"I just wanted to go with you. I'm sorry I got in the van. It was all my idea," he cried.

Sema let Rumi hold her. She put her head on his shoulder, stuck her thumb in her mouth, closed her eyes, and drifted off to sleep almost immediately.

"I know. It's okay now. It's okay."

I looked at the relieved faces around me and said, "They're okay. They're okay." I held Bodie and thanked everyone and anyone for helping us find them safe.

> Light the fires, dance the tunes, a new Fenestra
> has joined our family!
>
> Lucinda Myer

CHAPTER 46

I cracked open the spine of the large leather journal Rumi had given me for Valentine's Day. It was the first time in my life that I celebrated the day of love, in love. The first time I felt like I was loved unconditionally. Not just by Tens, but by Auntie and Rumi, Tony and Joi. Juliet and I knew we could count on the other for the big things. Now we needed time to learn the little things about each other, the things that sisters who grow up together take for granted. And while we weren't related, at least not in the biological sense, our connection went beyond a title.

I ran my hands over the cover of the journal. The green leather was embossed like Auntie's journal with roses and butterflies, ferns and animals. I knew part of my charge as a Fenestra was chronicling our experiences and knowledge for the next generation, but I had no idea where to start. I lay down my pen, taking a break from thinking, and launched myself over the back of the couch onto Tens, who *oomphed* his surprise.

"Supergirl!" He laughed.

I found the devilishly ticklish spot in his ribs.

He tried to evade. "No fair. No fair!" He grabbed my arms and pinned me against him.

"It's time to go to Rumi's for dinner," I said, gasping for air.

"Already?" he asked, checking the rooster clock hanging above the kitchen sink. Joi's cottage was fast becoming home and I knew we weren't leaving anytime soon. There was too much to unravel still. Too many unaccounted-for children that had been hidden at Dunklebarger for years. Too many sacrificed by Nocti.

"Juliet's cooking." I elbowed him off the couch and handed him the new boots I'd given for him Valentine's. Tony had helped me find them.

"Should we eat ahead of time, or can she cook?" Tens asked.

Juliet was cooking brunch for us for the first time. "When she saw Auntie she learned her recipes. Cooking and baking are her quilting." She planned on making Auntie's famous mac and cheese and her chocolate cake for us, and Glee's spiked eggnog and quiche lorraine for

Enid. There were so many dishes on the menu I didn't know what all we'd find. "Her food tastes better than anyone else's. There'll be plenty." I'd helped her grocery-shop yesterday and I'd never seen a person so excited to walk around a megamart.

"We should hurry," I said, tying my shoelaces and grabbing a spring jacket. The temperatures had stayed unseasonably warm since we'd last seen the fireflies. On March 1, the temps were in the sixties and holding, but no amount of warm weather would bring the fireflies out early. I could hardly wait to have them twinkle every evening.

"Everyone going to be there?" Tens asked, grabbing the car keys.

The aftermath of the tornado and the confrontation had solidified our friendships. I'd told Joi the truth, the whole story, over tea and cake. She took to the truth like a compulsive shopper to a sale. She never batted an eyelash in disbelief and she was relieved that Tens and I weren't a couple of rebellious teens running from caring parents. When Enid was released from the hospital there was no question where she'd land—Joi didn't give her a choice but to come live with her family. And Joi's empty nest was once again full with Bodie and Sema in residence as well. They often came over to the cottage to hang out and play video games with Tens or I'd babysit them after school.

It turned out that Sema didn't speak much, but she read like a maniac and loved books. They were what kept her from hiding in the curtains.

Tens worked regularly for Joi in the yard and fixing

the aging faucets and furniture around Helios. I cleaned and stocked in the off-hours—when it was less likely for me to stumble across a soul who was ready to transition. As Joi put it, "People will get the wrong idea."

Tony moved into a town house in Carmel large enough for him and Juliet. It was close enough for her to walk over to the cottage whenever she wanted to. He'd already begun the adoption proceedings, but he gave her space and the freedom she needed to ease into a more normal life. According to him, she didn't get out of bed until six in the morning and that was huge progress. I think he'd be thrilled if she slept till noon, blasted rap music, pierced her body, and was moody—all what he considered normal behavior for a sixteen-year-old girl.

Instead, she and I spent a lot of time together working on her practice. March 21 would be here in only three weeks and she needed to be ready. She was putting the pieces of her memories together. Tony knew how to help her deal with and process what he called the post-traumatic stress of the past decade.

Minerva came and went between all of us, but spent the most time with Juliet. I didn't feel slighted since I still wasn't sure Mini liked me. Custos was Tens's companion through and through, though she tolerated Bodie and Sema dressing her up in the doggie fashions Joi stocked in the shop.

Rumi's was our Sunday together place. He'd restocked and sold more of his Spirit Stones as word spread that they brought good luck to those who hung them. We planned to meet every Sunday to check in and move forward together. We were loud and boisterous and everything I imagined a family could be.

We'd voted to wait to enlighten Gus, Faye, and Sidika, but told Nelli almost immediately after rescuing Bodie and Sema. She took the news with a quiet determination and began unraveling a lot of the Nocti's illegal child-smuggling operation. Lots of kids over the last thirty years disappeared out of the system in the Midwest. She was trying to compile a list of the missing. It gave us a place to start looking for both Fenestra and Nocti.

The cellar at DG had been stuffed with files and papers documenting the four decades of procedures they'd used. Mistress was only the latest in a long list of greedy, malleable humans who ran the home for Nocti. Turned out Ms. Asura was years and years older than she appeared; in fact, she was the woman who'd hunted down Roshana and taken her away.

The creepiest information we'd found was Roshana's file. She'd been a kid who grew up at DG. When she vanished, so did a boy named Argi. We thought maybe he was Juliet's father, but we were still hunting.

We'd also found an explanation for the numbers of children's ghosts I'd helped cross over. The Nocti could use a Fenestra child's death to force the transition to Nocti. It made me wonder if we could do the reverse.

No one saw or heard of Ms. Asura again, but I knew we hadn't killed her. We assumed she'd gone into hiding to heal, but that she'd return. She didn't seem like the kind of woman who would take defeat lightly. We had no idea how many Nocti were still out there.

Before Juliet's sixteenth birthday I knew we had work to do. Hard work.

"Ready?" Tens asked.

"Ready. Remind me to talk to Rumi about getting grave markers for Auntie and Roshana." I wanted a place I could go to sit and visit with Auntie that wasn't while a person died. I wanted to try to see her at will, and with Juliet's help we were going to practice opening the window together. But first Juliet had to survive her transition.

"Sure." Tens held the door for me.

We were better than ever. The sum of us seemed infinite. "One-four-three." I kissed him. I'd been able to release some of my fear that he'd leave. I no longer waited for him to decide this was too hard. He'd also begun sharing more of his history with me and the journal he'd kept while traveling to Auntie's. I was beginning to understand why he'd been so guarded when I'd arrived at Auntie's. He'd survived a hundred lifetimes of adventure on his way to Revelation. I wished I'd met Tyee. I knew he'd be proud of Tens and the man he'd become.

"One-four-three-two." Tens smiled down at me, tucking my hair behind my ears.

The empty journal on the kitchen table called to me as I walked past it. Auntie's quilts. Juliet's food. Maybe words were my way of dealing with soul dust. It was something to think about; there was plenty of time.

Author's Note

I love Indiana. My roots there go back several generations. It's where I've spent some of my most glorious and also my most heartbreaking days. Summers in Indy included firefly hunting, catfish dinners, frozen custard, and Wildcat Creek.

I was thrilled to write about a setting so dear to my heart, but because it's fiction, I made a few tweaks for story flow and continuity. I've also played with the geography to make it work for me. I beg the forgiveness of Hoosiers who notice the changes. Landmarks like the Wabash River, Wildcat Creek, Fort Ouiatenon, Eiteljorg Museum, and Prophetstown really do exist and can be visited, though they're not quite as close together as I've made them.

My grandmother, Connie Wick, was instrumental in stopping the creation of a dam in Wildcat Creek that would have flooded farmland and been an environmental disaster for the state. So the Creek has been part of my family's history for many years, and it felt right to have Juliet find solace along its banks.

Carmel is a real town, and was home to an actual Helios Tea Room. I changed the store's layout, its merchandise, its design and decorations, and how it's operated. While Joi is its fictional owner, Kathy Kraft was Helios's actual proprietor. Unfortunately, between the writing of this story and its publication, Kathy lost her battle with cancer and Helios was closed.

Feast of the Fireflies is not real, but Feast of the Hunters' Moon happens each year in October, near West Lafayette, at the real Fort Ouiatenon. It is a full reenactment and does have food, merchandise and crafts demonstrations. As the song says, I do so love to be "Back Home Again in Indiana" when I visit.

acknowledgments

Every book has a team of people who work extremely hard to bring it to readers. I'd like to thank Stephanie Elliott for helping me shine the light of this Fenestra world so brightly, and my agent, Rosemary Stimola, who keeps track of numerous threads. Thanks to Krista Vitola for her work, Emily Pourciau for spearheading the fantastic PR, Angela Carlino for such a wonderful vision, and Chad Michael Ward for the beautiful cover art. I am grateful to Richelle Mead and Gena Showalter, who were willing to give my work a chance and then lend their words to it. I know how busy you are and it means so much to me! To Mark, Kate, Tim, Sarah and Kris LaMar, who wandered the Feast to get the flavor for me—thank you! Sarah Diers for being the best Sherpa and chauffeur these bad legs could imagine. You made many things possible.

Every author needs cheerleaders, and I have some of the best: Barney and Beth Wick, Tara Kelly, Katie Ott, Jennifer Rasmussen, Trudi and Bill Trueit, Erika and Scott Jones, Becky Breeze, Carolyn McClamroch, Bob and Amy Kraft, the Veatches, Misty and Donnie Bittinger, Greg Edson, Diana McFadden, Mark Wick, Keith Wick, Sue Wiant, Pete Kizer. To Kari Yadro, who makes Barnes & Noble look good every day with her awesome dedication and professionalism: you *are* the best! To those who made the publication of *Meridian* so memorable: Lisa Bjork and the SWSF board, Linda Racicot, Mary McCleod, the

Georges, the Kistlers, Lynn James, Robin Roberts, Pete O'Dell, Vanessa Link, the LMS Corduroy Bear Kids, the Reeds, LMS musicians with Jess Foley, Lynne Malecki, Molly and David Waterman, Susan Shira. The Lundgrens for the H1N1 rescue dinner, thank you. To GZL for every bit of inspiration I poured into Mistress. To my fantastic fans, who share their delight, their stories, and their connections with me, thank you—especially Aurora Momcilovich, Lindsay Sergi, Louisse Ang, and Maria Cabal. To the international agents, publishers, and translators who've helped bring my stories to readers around the globe: I am indebted to you for your enthusiasm. Thanks to the men and women of our military who served and protected while I wrote, especially Carl Herring, Jeff Morris, Amy Smith, Jane Miller, Demetrius Bussey, Linda Davis, Evan Davies, Naomi Lewis, Stephen Drake, Emanul Carter, Dennis Caliyo. Thanks to Brent and Joan Zefkeles, who supported the Puget Sound Area USO and shared their beloved Nicole Rachel Lehtinen with me. Eugene Ehrlich's *The Highly Selective Thesaurus for the Extraordinarily Literate* and Simon Hertnon's *Endangered Words* were both instrumental and pivotal for Rumi's vocabulary. Thanks to the B-52s and the True Colors Tour, whose "Juliet of the Spirits" seeded my Juliet. Mom, thank you for all the candle sniffing, newspaper clipping, driving, listening, and loving. I am blessed.

Amber Kizer has always found fireflies an enchanting part of the Midwestern summer. She was thrilled to write about a place and people who are so dear to her heart. For *Wildcat Fireflies*, Amber drew on years of family stories and favorite places to introduce Meridian and Tens to the bright soul-lights she's known in Indiana. She wrote this story while burning an Early Sunrise—scented candle and listening to a sound track that included the B-52s, Owl City, Within Temptation, Ophelia of the Spirits, Enya, Angels & Airwaves, and Áine Minogue.

The first book in the Meridian saga, *Meridian,* is

available in several languages and an audio version. *Wildcat Fireflies* is the second Meridian book; two more are forthcoming. Amber's series Gert Garibaldi's Rants and Raves follows an American teen's frank and funny adventures while growing up. *One Butt Cheek at a Time,* the first book in that series, was named a New York Public Library Best Book for the Teen Age; the second Gert Garibaldi book is *7 Kinds of Ordinary Catastrophes.*

Often reading from a towering stack of books that could bury her alive if it tipped the wrong way, Amber knows that life will never be long enough to read all the amazing stories in this world. Hard at work on her next novel, she lives with her family near Seattle. She takes breaks to watch reality TV; bake tasty, bad-for-you desserts; and herd chickens. Find her on Facebook, Goodreads, and her own sites, amberkizer.com, meridian sozu.com, and onebuttcheek.com. She loves to hear from readers; email her at Amber@amberkizer.com.